Praise for *The Second Mrs. Astor* by Shana Abé

"I was brought to tears by this shimmering account of the tragically brief courtship and marriage of John and Madeleine Astor. Abé is an exquisite storyteller, gracefully transporting the reader from Newport to Egypt to cold seas of the Atlantic. Rich in detail and deeply moving."
—**Fiona Davis,** *New York Times* **bestselling author of**
The Lions of Fifth Avenue

"One of the most beautifully written books I've ever had the pleasure to read, *The Second Mrs. Astor* brings to glittering life the romantic love story between John Jacob Astor and his young bride, Madeleine. You'll find yourself glued to every page, falling in love with this dazzling couple, and despite knowing better, hoping against hope that they avoid the tragedy that awaits them on the illfated *Titanic*. A gorgeous, phenomenal novel I won't soon forget."
—**Ellen Marie Wiseman,** *New York Times* **bestselling author of**
The Orphan Collector

"A touching, compelling, and haunting love story that will delight fans of historical fiction and enthrall those of us for whom the *Titanic* will always fascinate."
—**Hazel Gaynor,** *New York Times* **bestselling author of**
When We Were Young and Brave

"An engaging novel told with both heartbreaking care and vivid detail. *The Second Mrs. Astor* is historical fiction at its gripping and irresistible best."
—**Patti Callahan,** *New York Times* **bestselling author of**
Surviving Savannah **and** *Becoming Mrs. Lewis*

"An engaging tale. . . . This is more than another tale about the *Titanic*, it's a love story, a drama, and a fine historical novel."
—*Historical Novels Review*

"Historical fiction at its finest . . . with deep character perspective . . . engaging and intricate detail . . . passages [that] are brilliantly written and both gut-wrenching and heart-breaking to read."
—*The Florida Times-Union*

"An unexpectedly affecting interpretation."
—*The Toronto Star*

Also by Shana Abé

The Second Mrs. Astor

AN AMERICAN BEAUTY

SHANA ABÉ

KENSINGTON
PUBLISHING CORP.

www.kensingtonbooks.com

For Sean, still keeping my heart safe.

AN
AMERICAN
BEAUTY

PROLOGUE

The Homestead
Throggs Neck, New York
August, 1902

She wasn't going to be allowed inside the mansion itself, apparently. Lucy could glimpse it from the graveled path she walked, however: acres away, maybe miles away, the rows and rows of windows, diamond-sharp in the sunlight. The heavy Italianate towers marking either end, cutting cream and black against the cobalt sky.

She didn't want to be caught gawking, not by the army of straw-hatted servants working in the gardens around her, or by the footman—guard, more like—at her side. Lucy returned to pretending to admire the grounds.

It was sticky hot; she was already starting to perspire through her corset and shirtwaist. She'd had to park the Model A by the entrance gates (also maybe miles away), as the gatekeeper had informed her she'd only be allowed to proceed to the estate on foot. Lucy didn't mind the walk; she was spry enough and to be perfectly honest, the grounds were begging to be admired, a careful composition of towering trees and lushly dense lawns and flower beds that lent the entire setting an almost Elysian air.

Mrs. Huntington, known for her hunger for only the very best—the very, *very* best—of any earthly thing that might be imagined, had imagined this: this bucolic version of heaven surrounding her home, bursting with birdsong and color.

Lucy only wished she'd chosen better footwear for the occasion. If she'd known there was going to be a damned hike involved in this assignment, she'd have worn a lower heel.

The gravel—crushed shell? something pink and light—crunched delicately beneath her feet. She and her guard passed a greenhouse (massive and Moorish-looking, stuffed with palm trees), and then another. She was beginning to wonder if she was actually being escorted right the hell off the other end of the estate when her guard turned down a new curving path, one that led to yet another elegant glass greenhouse.

The footman approached the entrance, pulled open the door and stepped aside.

"Miss," he said, his eyes averted.

Lucy swiped a quick finger across her brow, then went through.

Good Lord, it was *not* any less sticky inside than out.

Instead of palm trees or ferns or whatnot, *this* greenhouse was stuffed with violets. Pots and pots and pots of violets, sitting on the ground, on elevated stands, hanging from the ceiling by long, silvery chains. The air practically shimmered with their fragrance—or maybe that was just the heat. Lucy had never seen so many shades of purple and mauve and blue before in her life.

Another spendy little bit of heaven, she thought, captured neatly behind glass.

A woman stood before one of the stands, a watering can in hand. She did not turn to Lucy, still lingering by the entrance, but instead lifted the can to one of the ceramic pots, raining a gentle shower along petals and leaves before moving on to the next plant.

Since Mrs. Collis Potter Huntington did not deign to look at her guest, her guest felt free to look at Mrs. Huntington.

A lady of a certain age, as it was said; tall; her hair still dark. She wore black, from neck to toe. Lucy had been told about this, about how the widow of the late Mr. C. P. Huntington refused to dress in any other color, even two years after his death. It wasn't just *any* old black, of course. It was Parisian black, House of Worth black, thousands of dollars of silk and satin black . . . but still. Lucy wondered how she dealt with the heat in such a getup. She thought for an odd moment that the hem of the other woman's dress was even lined in fur, but then the fur separated itself from her skirt and became a plump, smallish black dog that ambled toward Lucy, its tail swishing.

It seemed a good opportunity to speak. Lucy stuck out her hand.

"Good afternoon, Mrs. Huntington. Thank you for agreeing to see me. I'm Lucy Clarence, with the Town Topics Publishing Company."

"So I was informed," said Mrs. Huntington, still not bothering to look at her. Despite the fact that she had not lived in the Deep South for a very long while, Arabella Huntington's vowels still stretched soft and melodic. *So Ah was infawm'd.*

Lucy lowered her hand. The dog sniffed at her pink-dusted pumps for a moment, then returned to its mistress.

"You are familiar with our publications, ma'am?"

"I can't imagine there is a single soul in these United States unfamiliar with your scandal sheet, Mrs. Clarence."

"It's *miss*, actually," Lucy said, not losing her smile. "*Miss* Clarence, if you please."

Now Mrs. Huntington turned to face her. Arched an eyebrow.

She was striking still, Lucy had to concede, with lavender-gray eyes behind wire spectacles, deep auburn hair, her skin very pale and her mouth unlined. She wore pearl earbobs, heavy stacked drops that were not black but a smoky, gunmetal blue. Lucy expected they cost more than her entire year's salary.

"My employer, Colonel William Mann, sent me. He wanted to give you the opportunity, in person, to purchase a subscription to his upcoming folio."

"Did he indeed?"

"Yes, ma'am. It's to be called *Fads and Fancies of Representative Americans at the Beginning of the Twentieth Century: Being a Portrayal of Their Tastes, Diversions, and Achievements.*"

Mrs. Huntington returned to showering her violets. "Rather prolix."

"I told him the same myself, ma'am, but it happens that he's very fond of it."

The dog stretched out on the stone tiles between them, legs splayed, and began to pant.

"The colonel plans to include a fine profile on your late husband in the book. And perhaps another on Mr. H. E. Huntington, your nephew. Being that they are both such men of stature."

"I see," Mrs. Huntington said.

"He suggested you might wish to purchase a copy for your personal library. He suggested a price of ten thousand."

Lucy was proud of the way she said these words, without even a hint of her own incredulity staining her tone. It was a sum nearly ten times what anyone else was paying; she'd had to ask Mann to repeat it twice when he'd told her over the telephone because she was certain she'd heard him wrong.

But then, the wealthiest woman in America could probably afford the colonel's audacity.

Mrs. Huntington set down her watering can, turning once more to Lucy. For the space of what felt like at least a minute, but probably wasn't, Arabella Huntington only stared at her with those impressive clear eyes.

"Ten thousand dollars," she said at last, flat calm. "Colonel Mann seems to hold an exceptionally high opinion of his own prose."

"Well, you see, in order to write your husband's profile, he felt it necessary to do a good deal of research first. A good deal. He hired the very best investigators to discover all the salient details of your husband's extraordinary life. Eventually the colonel went down to Virginia himself to interview a few key people who knew

Mr. Huntington in the past. He mentioned the daughter of a Mrs. Worsham."

"*I* was Mrs. Worsham," Mrs. Huntington said.

"The other one. The *actual* wife of Johnny Worsham, I was told to say."

A bee had become trapped inside the greenhouse; it thumped against a ceiling pane over and over, clumsy and frantic.

"Colonel Mann asked me specifically to request that you take note of the word *Fancies* in the title of the book, ma'am. He thought you might appreciate the reference. That is exactly what he told me to say to you."

Mrs. Huntington smiled—a slight smile, thin and unamused.

"If it helps," Lucy added smoothly, "the folio's binding will be of tooled Moroccan leather and gold leaf. A first-rate presentation."

Mrs. Huntington lifted the watering can. As the cuff of her sleeve pulled back, Lucy finally spotted a dab of bright color: a cameo bracelet, wide and heavy and old-fashioned looking.

"Are you fond of violets, Miss Clarence?"

"Not especially," she admitted, wary of the turn in the conversation. "My mother likes them, though."

"I find violets as a species singularly impressive. They look so fragile, and yet, if properly tended, they're actually quite hardy. These are Russian and Parma violets, naturally. A scattering of English." She glanced up at the bee, still thumping. "I've met the colonel a few times. You don't resemble him."

"Why should I?"

"You're not related?"

"We are not. I am here on my own merits."

Mrs. Huntington gave a nod. "A woman of ambition. I can appreciate the steel in your spine."

Another pause between them; Lucy felt a trickle of sweat begin a slow path down her right temple and had to force herself to keep her hands at her sides. To simply let it happen.

"You're very young," observed Mrs. Huntington, with her un-ruffled calm.

"Twenty-six," Lucy said, nettled in spite of herself.

"And you did not live through the war, of course. You've never survived a war, have you?"

"No."

"How lucky for you, child, to enjoy such a charmed life."

"I'd hardly say *charmed*—"

"No?"

"Pardon me for saying so, Mrs. Huntington, but it seems to me that if anyone has enjoyed a charmed life, it is you."

Arabella Huntington's thin smile pressed thinner. "I wager you know next to nothing about my life, Miss Clarence. Kindly do not presume otherwise."

Lucy felt the discussion spinning beyond her control. She couldn't leave here without an answer, yes or no, from this woman, yet the bee was still frantic and the dog was still panting and it was so *hot*.

She drew in a slow, humid breath. "What shall I tell the colonel, ma'am? About the book subscription?"

"Tell your Colonel Mann that I will send him a check *after* I review a draft of this fine profile he proposes to write. Tell him that I await its receipt at his leisure."

Mrs. Huntington picked up a small, glazed container of fluorescent-blue flowers, stepping around the dog to carry it to Lucy. Their fingers overlapped as Lucy accepted it, a swift and warm touch, strangely intimate.

"And give these to your mother from me, Miss Clarence. Tell her I congratulate her on having such an ambitious daughter."

Part I

The Champagne Girl

1867

CHAPTER 1

Journal entry of Arabella Duvall Yarrington
June 1st, 1867

I just suffered the most wretched dream. I found myself in a room of gold, a room so grand and exquisite it surely belonged in a palace. The tables and chairs and settees were all gilded and scrolled, inset with precious gems and pearls. Curtains and tapestries adorned the walls, every one of them cloth of gold, and a fire burned in a great cream marble hearth. (A wood fire, mind you, not coal.)

Beyond the windows shone sky, only sky; deep blue, flat and brilliant as a slab of polished turquoise.

In the center of the room was a banquet table, all laid out. There were dishes such as I've never seen before, never even imagined. Dream dishes, I suppose, roasted meats and nuts and soft cheeses, fresh fruits and confections, everything so mouthwatering, and I could not wait to dine.

I walked toward that table, saw my own arm reaching out. The sleeve of my gown was as fine and golden as my surroundings; I wore a link bracelet inset with carved cameos, exactly like the one in the window at Monsieur Monroe's on Broad Street.

It looked so *right* around my wrist.

I reached for an iced petit four—chocolate, with little pink frosted roses—no gloves or fork, nothing so civilized, just my bare hand, and I picked it up and brought it to my lips and knew—oh, I *knew* how it was going to taste; *knew* how that delicious dark bite would melt across my tongue; *knew* how I would lick my fingers after I'd finished it all, sucking the very last hint of chocolate from my skin . . .

And that, of course, is when I awoke.

I cannot recall the last time I tasted chocolate. Or a petit four.

Today is my seventeenth birthday. And the clock is chiming downstairs, and I must hurry to work.

Arabella
Richmond, 1867

The best part about working for Johnny Worsham, aside from the fact that he paid reliably, and in cold Yankee cash, was that he insisted she never wear her spectacles while on the floor. Which meant that Belle never had to really *see* any of the men she served, not unless they came quite close, which some of them did. It was a blessing in disguise, although she could certainly smell Johnny's customers well enough, and feel their hands, and still had to laugh coyly at their drunken (and usually filthy) jokes.

Most nights she was the Champagne Girl, a position which sounded both joyful and amusing, but in fact meant a great deal of meandering around the faro parlors balancing a heavy silver platter along one arm, loaded with cut-crystal flutes. By dawn, her back and legs would be afire.

Some nights, the Tuesdays and Sundays Franny had off, Belle was the Piano Girl, playing a series of tunes carefully selected by Johnny himself. There were thirty-two in total. She had memorized them all.

She couldn't advance to the position of Dealer, the girls who received the best tips, because that would require her spectacles again. She'd tried to convince Johnny that she could read the cards well enough without them; the world was only *slightly* blurred, really, but he refused to take the risk. Johnny was flamboyant and debonair and deeply committed to one thing and one thing only, and that was his income.

She supposed she couldn't blame him. Worsham's illicit gaming saloon was the most popular in Richmond, not in the least because of the beautiful young women he hired to work in it. Currency of all sorts—cash, credit, conversation—drifted thick as cigar smoke through these ornate chambers, but it wasn't so very long ago that Richmond had been in flames, Richmond had been beaten and shamed and starving, and no one had forgotten that.

Money meant everything now. Maybe it always had.

So, yes, really, being paid was the best part of her job. Clutching those coins in her fist when Johnny first handed them over, the weight of them in her pocket. The sound they made as she walked home with them, a silvery clinking song, barely there but there if you listened.

It was the finest song she knew. It was a song that meant *today the earth spins on and still carries you with it. Today you will survive.*

The curtains inside the gaming house were uniformly velvet, although the colors varied from room to room. Crimson or cypress, saffron or peacock blue, they hung in heavy folds from floor to ceiling, every one of them, blocking any hint of the world beyond the windows (all but a strategic few of which were nailed shut, anyway). Not a sliver of light could slip past those folds, nothing of the sun or moon or stars, nothing of the common cares or woes of life beyond the walls of the saloon. Time had been removed from Johnny's place; there were no clocks to remind anyone of the ticking minutes; not so much as a corsage watch was permitted. If any of the girls needed to know the hour, they had to retreat to the kitchen and ask a steward.

Even the seasons had been erased here: the floor girls all wore the same low-cut gown of moiré silk, in the same shade of royal purple, no matter the month or the weather. Belle had surrendered a full six weeks' wages to purchase it. Last February she'd nearly caught her death of cold from the perilous neckline (another two weeks' wages gone), but Johnny still refused to let her wear a fichu, not even her mother's fine black muslin.

It was August now, but in the cool, languid spell of autumn and winter, with the fires burning so cheerfully—and dangerously, for a girl who could not see the andirons all that well—in the house's onyx hearths, Belle had learned to maintain a stately, constant pace around the rooms with her heavy silver tray. Standing motionless for too long slowed her heart, slowed her thoughts and her blood. Not unlike a mule bound to a millstone, she traveled the same path over and over, dreaming of her eventual escape.

Also like that unfortunate mule, Belle had come to anticipate with uncanny precision when her shift would end, when the sun was about to lift the sky from ink to ash to lilac, even though she couldn't see it. At *lilac* she was done, she could put away her tray and remove her ridiculous dress and wrap herself in something warmer and go home. And sleep.

Which was why, perhaps, at first she didn't notice the gentleman who had come to linger before her, standing there so quietly while the piano played and customers laughed and slapped down cards and Johnny's Fancy Girls conversed in low cooing murmurs, like doves tucked away in a cage.

It was about five minutes away from *lilac*, by Belle's internal reckoning. So her eyes were half-closed and her feet were aching and despite the fact that she had only three filled flutes on her tray, she hadn't bothered to return to the bar for more.

The man simply did not exist, until he gently cleared his throat.

She did not startle. She didn't spill a single drop of that precious champagne. Belle only opened her eyes fully again and pasted on a smile. She had to lift her chin to pretend to look him in the face; the man was extremely tall.

"Sir?"

"I beg your pardon," he said in a pleasant baritone, somewhat familiar. "Do you have something besides champagne?"

"The punch, sir. If you'll find Sadie—she's the one with the long strawberry hair—she has the punch tray."

"Punch," the man echoed. "Which I believe also contains champagne."

Was he smiling at her? Yes, probably. Yes, she thought so. He was bearded, certainly; she could make out that much, but most of the men around here were.

How deep his voice was, though. How clipped his words.

"Is there nothing else?" he asked, with no hint of smile in his tone.

"Madeira, a very good one. If you'll just look for Ellen—"

"No," he said.

"Whiskey? Amos will be pleased to serve you, sir, over at the bar. He also has sherry."

"Something without spirits."

"Well," Belle said, because she was tired and sore and surely it was time to go home now, surely it was time to plod home, "I suppose you might try a glass of water. I wouldn't, though, if I were you. I've seen the state of the cistern."

There was a pause. Belle looked down, wet her lips. Looked up again.

"Can I help you with anything else, sir?"

The man studied her a moment—she could tell that he did, even if she could not clearly see it, and made certain her smile held steady. Then he said, "We've met before, Miss Lenore."

(None of the girls at Worsham's used their true names.)

"Do you recall it?" he pressed.

"Of course," Belle replied, because suddenly she did. She lifted her free hand, her left one but it hardly mattered, and he took it in his own, a rough spot on his palm catching against the delicate lace of her mitt. "Mr. Huntington. Of course I recall. It was . . . what, two months ago?"

"Forty-one days," he said, still holding her hand.

"How kind of you to remember me."

"I'm afraid," Mr. Huntington said, "there's nothing especially kind about it. I have discovered that you are ensnared in my memory."

"Ah."

He released her hand. "It's almost dawn. Are you done for the night?"

Her smile deepened. "I am. But I'll be here again tomorrow, if you'd like to come by." She turned away, inched the tray a little higher up her arm and said over her shoulder, "No doubt Mr. Worsham would appreciate your patronage."

Belle had not always lived in Virginia. She'd been born in Alabama, in a cabin by a river that on warm nights captured tendrils of mist, sly dancing curls that her older sister Lizzie had tried to convince her was full of ghosts, although it wasn't.

Look there, Lizzie would whisper, pointing through the sultry night air, through the eerie dark. *Look there, Belle. A murdered settler woman in a bonnet, blood all down her skirts. A fur trapper starved to death, looking for meat.*

Belle only ever saw mist.

But there could be no denying that the woods by that cabin had *felt* haunted, had felt green and dense and impossible to fully penetrate . . . though, up until the day her father died, she and her brothers and sisters had certainly tried, gathering twigs and pawpaws and deer berries, digging barefoot in the mud for watercress or tadpoles.

But then Papa *had* died. She'd been barely nine when the cholera had swept through and taken him. He'd been a mechanic—*not* a tinker, as she had heard murmured among the neighbors—but he'd traveled so much, she had hardly any memory of him before his death. Black hair, kind eyes. Big hands. That was it.

She supposed he might be a ghost now, maybe trapped back on that wide river. Or perhaps he was one of the wraiths lingering here, in Richmond; God knew there had to be thousands of them haunting the rubble of this town. She thought she could sense them sometimes: a fleeting sharp scent of char and smoke; a disembodied murmuration of despair, sorrow she could feel sinking into her bones.

How she loathed it here, where everything was grimy and crumbling and broken, even the things that were supposed to be working again, like the street lanterns, or the railroads.

The walk home from Worsham's was short at least, only three blocks to the boarding house. And she didn't have to brave it during the dark, because by the time Belle would step out the saloon's back door, *lilac* would be transformed into morning. It might be rainy, or clear, or pink or blue or choked with coal vapor, but it would be morning, and it was hers, and she was, for a few precious hours, free.

When the wind chose to bless Shockoe Bottom from a certain direction, the streets and shadows smelled of freshly sawed lumber and the James River, a strong ceaseless flow near enough to hear but not, on Belle's walk at least, to see. More often than not, however, the air hung with the particular rotting stink of slops and manure. Mosquitoes lingered in clouds above the stagnant puddles that lined the curbs, whining and zinging, tormenting any living creature passing by.

This morning was more a manure-and-mosquitoes kind of morning, but it was also one scented with the dozen or so leftover deviled eggs from Johnny's that Belle carried in a wicker basket along her arm. So, manure and vinegar and warm eggs: she had to turn her face away from the basket to keep from gagging, even as her stomach rumbled.

Yarrington House (such a grand name for what was, in fact, a skinny, graceless two-story rectangle of red brick and peeling paint) sat close to the street, shutters open, the paving-stone steps swept. A solitary tulip tree had somehow managed to survive the war and the subsequent hunt for prime hardwood. It cast its shade across the lot, and it was under its branches that Belle lingered for a moment, listening to the sounds rising past the parlor windows, left ajar to catch what breeze they could.

A faint clattering of tableware. Her sister Lizzie's voice, softly chiding. Footsteps along the squeaky front stairs, too rapid to belong to any of the boarders, she'd bet. Likely Richard or John, hurrying to the kitchen to gulp down their porridge before the school day began.

A fly buzzed by, landed on the scrap of gingham covering the eggs. Two more joined it before she waved them away.

She hated deviled eggs. She hated porridge. She hated having to eat breakfast when her body told her it was time for dinner and she wondered, for what had to be about the millionth time, what would happen if she didn't walk up those steps and through that front door. If she just turned around and . . . left. Found something different for herself out there in the unknown corners of the world.

Something untethered. Something *better.*

But she was a mule, wasn't she? Her feet were too used to plodding the same path, and porridge was better than nothing.

Belle went inside.

CHAPTER 2

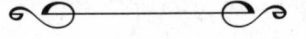

Catherine
Richmond, 1867

Much like the boarding house she had named after herself, Catherine Yarrington had been created for a different, some would say *more gracious*, time. Square-jawed and sturdy-boned, she had married for love, a decision she'd regretted nearly at once. But her beau had been so sweet, so shyly devoted . . . the well-bred Miss Catherine James Simms, who absolutely knew better, found that within weeks of meeting Mr. Richard Yarrington, apprentice mechanic (and comely, *so* comely), her thoughts and her heart were no longer her own. There was no stopping what was to come: a swift, forbidden courtship; a hasty wedding attended by none; a swelteringly hot honeymoon in the raw woods of Alabama—not even her home state—and child after child after child.

Five of her babies survived those years in the woods. Two did not.

Her hands, once so pampered and smooth, grew knobby and rough. Her hair, her golden-brown beauty, dulled into drabness. There were days she could convince herself that it was worth it, this life she had willfully chosen. That falling in love with Richard had been a gift, even when she went without supper so that her children might eat. Even when her husband was gone so often in search of work, leaving the brunt of poverty's endless, everyday miseries at her feet.

Those fine days, however, were strung few and far between, even before the war.

The soft young girl Catherine had once been melted away. The woman she became soldiered on, because really, what was the choice? Richard had died and once again Catherine adapted; she learned; and by hook or crook, she *did* manage to put food on the table for her children, nearly every day. Their small souls were her light and her reward. And weren't they such a reflection of her, these blessings of hers? Hadn't they all turned out *just* like her, sturdy and square, built to walk the earth in hard, certain steps. One damned, plodding foot forward at a time . . .

Except for Arabella, her middle child.

Arabella, who had somehow missed inheriting her mother's bony build, her mother's iron jaw. Arabella, slight and delicate as a wildwood rose, with her dark tangle of ruddy curls and those lucent eyes that must have come from Richard's line, as Catherine had never seen such a flowery, violet-gray color in any of her own kin.

Arabella, who was not her mother's light, but her mother's hope.

All of Catherine's hope in these latter days, actually, resting on Belle's lovely white shoulders. On Belle's slender, straight back.

CHAPTER 3

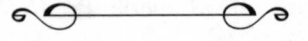

Dear Mr. Cobh,

Enclosed you will find $7 as partial payment of my balance owed to you. I beg your patience for the full amount, and also plead, most humbly, for you to reopen my tab at your butcher shop. My business has been lean of late. I have but three boarders at this time, two stevedores and a carpenter. The stevedores pay in cash but the carpenter is behind and promises me full payment for his stay within the week. When he settles his bill I assure you I shall send the money to you at once.

Most Sincerely,

Mrs. Richard M. Yarrington
Yarrington House

Arabella
Richmond, 1867

"You're late," said Lizzie.

Belle paused at the entrance to the kitchen, returning her sister's harried look with a level one of her own. Only seconds later, the wall clock in the hallway began to chime.

6:45. She wasn't late.

"What's in the basket?" Richard asked hopefully, thin and teenaged, hunched in a shepherd's crook by the sink over his bowl of boiled buckwheat.

"Deviled eggs."

Lizzie took the basket from her. "How old are they?"

"I didn't ask."

"Belle, *honestly.*"

"A little risk is good for your soul. And I can't imagine Johnny wants to poison us."

Emma shuffled into the kitchen, yawning, dressed but her hair still bound in its sleeping braid, a brownish blond snake down her spine.

"Oh," she said at last, at the end of the yawn. "What's that smell?"

"Eggs," Belle said.

"No." Emma opened her eyes fully, glancing over at the stove. "Good gracious, are those *sausages*? My heavenly days!"

"They're not for us." Mother hurried in, a platter and tongs in hand, pushing past Emma and Belle to reach the skillet. "You know better, child."

Emma and Lizzie exchanged a look. Belle was not included in it—Belle was seldom included in the private moments that transpired between her elder sisters—but she could read their expressions as clear as day.

Of course they're not for us. Nothing good is ever for us.

And oh, even excluded, Belle knew that feeling all too well.

Mother was busy transferring the links, fat and glistening, to the chipped serving platter. "Mr. Cobh has been kind enough to extend our credit a bit. Just a bit. Enough to tide us over for the week—"

"When do we get sausages, too?" demanded John, twelve years old and wildly untidy, fidgeting on his stool by the chopping block.

"—for the *week*, until I'm able to repay him more." Mother placed the tongs gently on the counter, wiped her hands on her apron. Without turning her body, only her neck, Catherine met Belle's eyes, her mouth drawn tight.

"Tomorrow," Belle said. "Tomorrow I should have some funds."

Mother nodded, picked up the platter and walked in her taut, deliberate way out of the kitchen. Just beyond the doorway she paused, still without turning.

"We'll make use of the drippings." Her voice was low, firm; the voice of a woman accustomed to bargaining. "Red beans and collards. Won't that be nice?"

All five of her children watched her walk on without waiting for an answer, the gloom of the hallway stealing her figure and any chance of meat for breakfast.

They squatted in the attic. Yarrington House had four bedrooms to let, references requested, deposit required. The main parlor was reserved for entertainment and the common dining room for meals. Richmond was rebuilding from its ashes— painfully, yes, but nonetheless—and there were nearly always men stopping by to inquire about weekly rates. But even if none of the four rooms were rented, the Yarringtons themselves did not reside in any of the bedrooms proper.

Belle would have killed to spend a single day sleeping in one of those clean horsehair beds made up by her sisters, but instead she survived in the attic: that airless, pitched space between the roof and someone else's bedroom ceiling. A place where it was impossible to ignore the snores that rattled up from the boarders below, or the conversations or smells, or the pops and snaps that bedeviled the wooden skeleton of the house, always settling.

The trip up the ladder was short and perilous. There was no natural light, of course, not even an oriel window, and the trapdoor that opened up to the floor above was a rough-sawn square without a single guardrail. But Belle made the climb quickly, the bulk of her skirts twisted up into a rope that she wrapped like a python over her left arm. The old ladder protested her weight as it always did, threatening to give. It had been borrowed before the war from a cabinetmaker sweet on Emma, a beau who'd joined up and never returned. On warm days the slats still reeked of varnish and glue.

So this, *this*, was Belle's true home:

Five camp beds (all that would fit), crammed against the eaves. One chamber pot, secreted behind a leather folding screen. One bureau, three trunks.

One oil lamp.

And shadows, so many shadows, lifting and falling, dark dancers that slipped along the canted walls.

She crossed to her cot, stripped out of her clothing, unrolled her stockings. Belle, the day dreamer, and Lizzie, the night, shared a single bed, and this morning her sister hadn't bothered to remake the covers.

Belle was too tired to care. The porridge and toast she'd eaten sat like a rock in her stomach and both her feet throbbed; her shoes were only half a year old and already too small. She was going to have to find the money for new ones soon.

But that was tomorrow's problem. All of her problems, right now, were for tomorrow.

She extinguished the lamp—she was always *extremely* certain to extinguish the lamp—crawled beneath the blankets and closed her eyes.

Mornings in Shockoe Bottom were not peaceful. Buckboards and donkey carts rattled along the cobblestones outside, mere feet beyond the house's walls. Bells rang, more distant, from the ships along the river. Men jostled by, talking or laughing or sometimes fighting; dogs barked; women gossiped in their neighborhood clusters. Children scrambled to school or to the factories, and everyone only got louder as the day brightened.

But it was the grosbeaks living in the tulip tree that Belle heard most distinctly. They'd been there since spring, two parents, three babies, then just the parents again. They trilled and trilled, enormous sweet notes lifting from such tiny bodies, unbound, lifting straight up into the open sky.

CHAPTER 4

Catherine
Richmond, 1867

The boarding house had come with a piano, a battered old upright missing five of the ivory veneers covering the keys. Catherine
supposed the previous owners of the house had left it behind because it was worthless, or at least not worth the cost of hauling it
anywhere else. But even without the five veneers, it *did* play, and
once a year she paid a tuner to tend to it. It was an unnecessary
extravagance, perhaps. Lizzie, who helped manage the books, certainly thought so. But Catherine had argued that the piano was a
lure for boarders. That they could offer an hour or so of evening
music to the men who stayed with them was a pleasant benefit of
Yarrington House, one that could only help them bring in more
paying guests.

"Oh?" Lizzie had said, caustic. "And who will be the lucky soul
who gets to entertain everyone for *an hour or so* every night after
a full day's work?"

"You will take turns," Catherine had replied, because she had
taught all five of her children to play; it was one of the few legacies

of her youth she was able to pass on. "Even the boys. And you will smile and be polite and the sky will not fall on your head, Lizzie. Arabella plays all night at Johnny's twice a week and doesn't complain."

"Arabella," Lizzie said, "enjoys better wages than I do."

"We all enjoy her wages, and *you* will enjoy a brief hour—"

"Or so!"

"—of demonstrating your skills at the keyboard and filling the air with a little beauty. Lord knows we could use more beauty these days."

After a good deal more moaning and complaining, Lizzie gave in. Four men knocked on their door during that first week, drawn by the notes drifting through the open windows, and even she had to acknowledge the cleverness of her mother's plan.

Yes, it had been a fine idea and Catherine knew it, but the heart of the matter was actually this: the piano, dilapidated as it was now, was burl walnut beneath its discolored varnish, richly grained. The legs and moldings were carved with flowers and vines; the front panel was inset with more flowers and trimmed in gilt, delicate brushstrokes of real gold, faded but there.

Just like Catherine herself, once it had surely graced a house more grand than this. And also like Catherine herself, it endured these less noble times, these less beautiful times, with a sort of solid stubbornness that defied every disaster around the bend.

Thanks to those long-ago lessons from her childhood, her own children could coax the old piano to life, could play all the old songs Catherine had taught them. And she could take a slow breath and sit back for an hour—or so—and close her eyes, remembering the years when she never starved, when her bones never ached and each new dawn promised a sparkling new adventure, a glorious new day.

CHAPTER 5

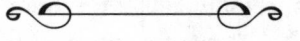

Arabella
Richmond, 1867

Citywide Saloon Raid Yields Mixed Results
—special cable to *The Daily Crier*
Richmond, Virginia
August 21, 1867

Last night at around two o-clock, in an extraordinary demonstration of both skill and stealth, the Police Force of our good city conducted a series of unexpected raids upon the illegal gambling saloons plaguing Richmond. The Mayor himself authorized the raids and subsequent detention of the Dealers, Cappers, and Proprietors. In addition, there were several arrests of Notable Citizens discovered at the tables therein. [See the List of Names, page 2]

Sources claim that all Criminal Parties were dismayed at the sudden onslaught of the law, which they had not anticipated. Games were disrupted mid-play. Fine food and wine were left abandoned in haste. Bottles were found toppled, with cards and chips left scattered along the floors.

It must be noted, however, that a good many of the parlors' Clientele avoided detention by fleeing out of windows or along the rooftops before escaping into alleyways. These Brave Personages thus eluded justice under the cloak of night.

The many new faro houses, keno parlors and houses of ill-repute in Richmond are a shameful blight upon our city. We must remain vigilant in our defense of their corrosive influence. The Respectable Citizens of our good home, and any and all Guardians of our Honor, demand nothing less.

The looking glass hanging in the dressing chamber was old and badly foxed, centered in an elaborate, tarnished frame that resembled a sunburst of knives. Johnny told everyone he'd imported it straight from Venice but that might easily have been a lie, as Johnny Worsham lied about as effortlessly as a shark sliced through the ocean. Wherever it was from, the mirror was only large enough that three of the Fancy Girls could fit before it at the same time, and even then only if one of them crouched.

As there were never fewer than eleven girls on duty at a time, in those last few minutes before the saloon opened for business, the dressing chamber was crowded. Swirls of powder hung in the air, cheaply perfumed and faintly glistening, fairy dust brushed with lamplight. Pots of cream rouge, peach and rose and coral, were passed from hand to hand, and the line of girls waiting their turn before the mirror smoothed and straightened their moiré gowns with delicate fingers.

Belle, kneeling at the base of that silvery spotted glass, was adjusting the last few hairpins in her curls when Johnny walked in.

He did not knock. He never knocked; it was, as he was fond of pointing out, his house, not theirs.

"Arabella? Are you in here? Has anyone seen—"

"Johnny," she called without rising, still concentrating on the pins.

"There you are." He crossed to her side, careful to avoid the frothy purple heap of her skirts, and stood looking down at her, frowning.

Johnny Worsham was what any sane woman would call beautiful. Black-haired and whip-lean, he had the brightest green eyes Belle had ever seen and a smile that could melt frost. He spoke like a gentleman and dressed like a dandy, always vivid brocades and silks and stickpins of solid gold. For the briefest week of her life, back when they'd first met, she'd fancied herself in love with him.

But that was what all the girls thought in the beginning. It was one of Johnny's greatest gifts, in fact: the ability not just to charm hearts but to *dazzle* them. To capture some tender young thing in that emerald gaze and tell her how *lovely* she was, how unexpectedly *lovely*, and wouldn't it be a fine world if they might have the opportunity to get to know each other a little better? An opportunity that would, indeed, enrich them both for the better?

And the tender young things nearly always agreed that *yes, it surely would be*, because these days everyone needed enrichment, didn't they?

Of course, none of them realized that they were merely bedazzled. Not at first.

"Franny's taken ill," Johnny said, still frowning at her.

Belle paused with both hands in her hair, met his eyes in the glass. "Oh? What's wrong with her?"

"Female troubles. I need you to fill in for her tonight at the piano."

"All right, I—"

"I'll need you to fill in for her for the next few weeks, actually."

"Fine, but I—"

"Good."

He turned to leave. Belle scrambled to her feet, catching up her hoops so she wouldn't trip.

"Johnny. Do you have a moment, please?"

He glanced back at her, impatient, then waved her over to the doorway. Esther, one of the Dealers, turned sideways to edge by them, headed in a staccato clip to the main parlor. Belle waited until she was out of earshot to speak.

"I wonder if I might ask a favor."

"Ask," he said.

"I need an advance," she said bluntly; there was never any use in trying to dance around the truth with Johnny. "Mother's in debt to the butcher *and* the greengrocer, but the boarders still have to eat."

My whole family still has to eat, but she left that unsaid.

Johnny sighed theatrically, scraped a manicured fingernail along the line of his jaw. She knew that sigh, that elegant long stroke of his finger, so taunting, so calculated, and made certain that her expression gave him nothing in return: not the hard lump in her throat; not her sweaty palms, hidden behind her back; not her clenched stomach. She was a doll, she was empty. She was not desperate. She was only asking.

"This is the second time in three weeks, Belle."

"I know. But I told her I'd have something by the end of the night, and if you put me at the piano I won't get the tips I would otherwise. So I don't know what else to do."

He dropped his hand, staring past her at the wall, and Belle braced herself for what would come next.

"A loan," he said at last. "Half your next wages, at five percent interest, to be paid back within the month. Deal?"

"Deal."

"Come find me at the end of your shift. And take off that pince-nez before anyone sees you."

Belle returned to the dusty glimmer of the dressing chamber, and picked up the coral rouge from the vanity. The little pot was porcelain, cool and smooth, heavy as a river stone in her palm.

"What's wrong with Franny?" she asked the rouge.

"Miscarriage," answered one of the girls, the one who'd taken her place on the floor before the mirror. "Last night."

"Bless her heart," said another, still in her chemise and corset, rubbing a halved lemon under her arms. "But no doubt for the best."

"Yes," Belle murmured, and put down the pot. "No doubt."

She remembered to remove her spectacles, tucking them into her bodice before leaving the room.

Johnny's taste in music tended toward anything romantic or bright. Schumann and Mozart were acceptable; Beethoven was not. Hymns were, of course, out of the question. Belle had been playing Johnny's selection for over a year now, so moving from piece to piece was almost relaxing. She did not have to consider it too carefully; her fingers knew the notes, the slick surface of the keys, which ones would stick if not struck with just the right force. After the first hour or so, Belle would enter a sort of a trance, a place of inner quiet to absorb the external ruckus. Without seeing anything, without having to even open her eyes, if she wished, she could read the mood of the room and adjust her list of music accordingly. Cheerful pieces for when the conversation lulled, or when someone had lost an especially deep wager. Slower, softer, for when the girls were laughing or the men toasting. Something complicated for the beginning of her shift, or the end, when she needed to remind Johnny that he had hired her for more reasons than one, for her expertise and not just her face.

She was two-thirds through Schumann's Arabeske in C Major when her ensnared gentleman approached.

"You play divinely, Miss Lenore."

Belle offered a smile, her fingers never faltering.

"Mr. Huntington, lovely to encounter you again." She worked through another measure before adding, "Are you thirsty?"

"I have been warned not to trust the cistern, I'm afraid."

"Just so. Which is why I have a pitcher of lemonade for you

right there, on the little table to your left. I made certain they boiled the water first."

There was a pause, and then he laughed, a deep laugh, not quite booming but not soft either, and not enough to break her inner quiet but it did prompt her to shift a little on the bench, to better see him. Well, to see him as best she could.

He was helping himself to the lemonade—alas, ice was impossible to procure these days, even for Johnny, so it would be lukewarm—his back to her. He wore a frock coat of dark brown and in that moment resembled nothing so much as an enormous bear. A bear in a china shop, maybe, moving with careful restraint, lifting the crystal tumbler of lemonade in his great paw of a hand, trying a swallow.

"I do apologize for the lack of ice," Belle said, facing the keyboard again. "We had two icehouses in town, but they were both destroyed during the retreat of '65. No one seems inclined to rebuild them yet."

"It's most satisfying, thank you."

"You're welcome. How is your luck tonight, Mr. Huntington?"

"Better and better."

"I'm glad to hear it."

Another pause; perhaps he was savoring the drink.

"Are you from here, Miss Lenore?"

"Oh, no. But not far. I was born in Alabama. On a tempestuous night, I'm told."

"Tempestuous?"

"We lived by a river, you see, so when the storms would come, those violent summer storms, my whole family had to retreat into the woods, away from the flooding. I was born on a bower of leaves and moss. Blessed by the rain and the wind, beneath a crown of crying birds. So I'm told."

The arabesque concluded. She shifted into "La Belle Catherine."

"To this day," she said, "birds like to follow me, singing and singing."

"I believe you are shining me on, Miss Lenore."

"Am I? I suppose you'd have to meet me in daylight to find out, Mr. Huntington."

"You do spin a pretty tale. Thank you for that."

She leaned back a little, tipped her head toward him. "That was only my beginning, sir. I have many more tales to tell."

He took a step closer. "Perhaps you might—" he began, but Belle would never learn what he would have said next, where that *might* would have led them, because in that moment four sharp clangs rang out from the brass bell positioned above the fireplace, the one connected by wire to the front door.

In a heartbeat, the room erupted. While some of the parlor's clients only stood or sat in place, confused, every single Fancy Girl and steward leapt into action.

Belle shoved back from the piano, yanked her spectacles from her bodice and snapped them in place.

"Raid!" She seized his hand, the one without the lemonade. "Come on!"

She didn't wait for him to answer; the chamber was already emptying as even the first-timers realized what was about to happen, everyone running, stampeding toward the windows or doors. She pulled her admirer firmly toward not the doorways—crammed with bodies—or the windows, which wouldn't open anyway. She pulled him instead toward the staircase that led to the second story, and after the first few steps she didn't have to pull any longer. He was springing up the carpeted stairs alongside her, surprisingly nimble, only halting when they reached the landing.

"Which way?" he asked calmly.

"Here." She found the third room to the right, darting inside. It was empty, thank goodness, all the lamps unlit, cool and silent and smothered in shadow. She left the door cracked so she could see, crossed to the iron-framed bed against the far wall and tugged it sideways, just enough to reveal the outline of the trapdoor beneath it.

Belle knelt, found the hidden crack that would open it and

jammed her fingers in. The planks lifted free of the floor, wood squeaking in protest.

She glanced at him from over her shoulder. Mr. Huntington only stood there in the middle of the room with his arms folded over his chest, his expression dubious. With his dark hair and beard and the coat, the hall light spilling in from behind him, he was more bearlike than ever.

"Do come," she whispered, urgent. There were already new voices filtering up from the story below, angry men's voices, whistles blowing. "Quickly!"

He did not budge.

Belle lifted her open palm to him, fingers stiff, more a demand than a plea. "You *will* fit. I've tested it myself. Just get in and lie flat."

He looked back at the doorway, that damningly cracked door, then went to his knees beside her, lowering himself gracefully into the hole. She padded to the door, closed it, and crept back to the bed.

It was pitch dark now, brutally dark. Good thing she was used to finding her way blind.

Her hands discovered the opening, then her feet, and she was dropping into the narrow confines of the crawlspace, pushing her skirts and hoops down to her ankles as best she could. She leaned out again to drag the bed back into place (the iron frame was hollow, deliberately light), found the handle on the underside of the trapdoor and scooted down flat to close it. The wood squealed again, horrifically loud, but then it was shut.

They *did* fit, but it was a tight space. Dusty. The stink of dank lumber and mice burned in her nose, briefly overwhelming; she began breathing through her mouth and it became more tolerable. She pushed at her hoops once more, her expensive silk dress bunched into a mess up by her knees, but the rustling and crunching of her crinoline seemed deafening. She gave it up.

Mr. Huntington said quietly, "I could have simply paid the fine."

Belle tested her fingertips against the trapdoor; it held firm. "A fine," she whispered, "imprisonment, and your name in the papers. Thirty-nine lashes for Johnny, which, I assure you, he would not appreciate."

"Ah." He released a sigh, and the mouse smell briefly mingled with that of lemons and cigar. "These quaint Southern ways. It seems you have done me more of a service than I thought, Miss Lenore."

Above them, footfalls shook the hallway beyond the room. More male voices, still angry.

"Stop talking," she breathed.

"Are you afraid?"

Mr. Huntington sounded untroubled and genuinely curious, as though their circumstances were no more unusual than taking tea after church on Sunday.

Belle removed her pince-nez, tucked it back into her dress. She rolled to her side and without asking he lifted his arm, just enough so that she could inch closer, resting her head upon his shoulder. The wool lapel of his coat felt scratchy against her cheek.

The doorknob above them gave a quick, telltale rattle. The door to the room slammed open.

As the policemen stomped above them, opening the wardrobe, wrenching apart the curtains, Belle put her lips to his ear.

"I am never afraid."

CHAPTER 6

Catherine
Richmond, 1867

Mrs. Catherine Yarrington no longer trusted banks. She no longer trusted lenders. She did not trust any financial institution that had existed before the war, because the War of Secession had proven beyond doubt that even a life of poverty, such as living in a shanty by a riverbank, could be better than whatever hungry hell came next.

Catherine's genteel family, who had abandoned her to her marriage, had since become impoverished themselves . . . and just as desperate to survive. They had contacted her, wooed her, begging for funds. But Catherine had nothing to give them besides her forgiveness. She'd long ago sold every last precious bit of her old life to finance the new: her prized but out-of-fashion debutante gowns, her grandmother's triple strand of pearls. The ruby ring her great-aunt had gifted her (and who had fortunately passed away before Richard had come into her life, so therefore could not demand it back).

Even her pony, her *pony*, Sweet Charlotte, who had been with

Catherine since she was five, who had patiently taught the child she had once been how to master a canter, a trot, a gallop through the meadows . . .

Even Sweet Charlotte was gone.

Because the world was a savage and precarious place, Catherine Yarrington kept her earnings in a strongbox in the cellar, hidden inside the coal bin. Lizzie liked to scold her for it, pointing out that the coal bin would be the first place that *anyone* nefarious would search. But it was either that or bury the box in the garden. And the garden was not large enough, or green enough, to effectively conceal a mound of fresh dirt.

Nothing in this mortal world is certain. It was a phrase that Catherine had impressed upon her children over and over.

Nothing is certain. Take what you can, when you can.

For a very long while, for most of her adult life, really, Catherine didn't realize how deeply she had absorbed this lesson into her own heart. It was merely something about her that *was*: be careful, do not trust, do not relax. Do not succumb to weakness. Do not succumb to love, because love leads to ruin.

Perhaps that was why, when the finely dressed gentleman showed up on her stoop—polite; soft-spoken; a wedding band upon his left hand and a jeweler's box in his right, asking after her fey and lovely daughter—Catherine Yarrington, née Simms, only stood back and allowed him in.

CHAPTER 7

Journal entry of Arabella Duvall Yarrington
August 22nd, 1867

I cannot pretend I understand the machinations of fate. Why are some folks born into wonder, into wealth and diamonds and food that never runs out, while others, through no fault of their own, are forced to struggle for every single bite, both bitter and sweet? Why do some of us go out and labor, by God, *labor* for our pennies and others are handed plantations and silver-bridled teams of horses, and they ride along in their landaus and show off their gems and their fine hats bobbing with feathers and think they're *better* than the rest of us?

They *are* better. That's what we all think. What we *know*, because that is what we are taught, from cradle to grave.

Three girls got caught in the raid at Johnny's. Birdie, Esther and Olivia, and I can't make sense of what they were thinking, because we all knew the escape routes. We'd memorized them, practiced them on our own, so many times. But they were too slow, or too stupid, or too ill-starred, I guess. In the crush and confusion they went the wrong way along the roof, got pinned against the chimneys with nowhere to go and the police cornered them. And now they wait in jail, those three girls, because who will trade the cash for their freedom?

Not their families, for the shame of it. Not Johnny, for his greed. Certainly none of the good gentlemen they'd spent the evening working so hard to entertain. Those men vanished like wisps in the night. I doubt we'll see them again soon.

The fact is, no one dares speak for them, not even me. Speaking out would mean scrutiny falling upon me, upon my family. Upon the boarding house too, which we cannot afford.

That's not cowardice. That's fact.

Walking to the bakery today, praying for day-old bread, I passed two splendid ladies lingering before a haberdashery window. They were not looking at the hats. They were gossiping, alight with malice, about my comrades. They tilted their heads together and cupped their hands over their mouths and the bile they spoke spilled out over their gloves, down their arms. Out into the air that I breathed.

Strumpets, they said.

Only what they deserve, they said.

Let them rot.

I tried to hurry past them, holding my breath against their poison.

I'd felt sorry for Franny before, having to abandon the piano to nurse her empty womb. But now I think about how lucky she was to be out of it all. To be tucked away back at her mama's place, unable to leave yet, unable to work.

She's safe there. For a short while longer, she'll be safe.

As soon as Johnny crooks his finger, though, all the rest of us will slink right back to him, because no one on this earth is going to just hand us plantations or landaus or feathered hats.

No one.

Arabella
Richmond, 1867

Belle seldom dreamed. It might have been that her body was too tired for dreaming, or her nature too practical. In truth, it happened so infrequently that she vigilantly recorded in her journal any dream she *did* have, because they came to her so rare and strange.

On that particular afternoon, three days after the raid, Belle was dreaming of riding a horse through a midnight thicket of cypress and oak . . . except, she realized, looking closer, it wasn't a horse. It was a hart. It had a chandelier of antlers draped with Spanish moss, ghostly tendrils of lace, and a coat that gleamed silver in the starlight. And even though Belle had never ridden a hart before—she'd never even ridden a horse—it felt perfectly natural to be sitting there astride its back in the eldritch woods. As if she had nowhere else to go. No other way to be.

Her gown was scarlet, impossibly tight, impossibly rucked up to her knees. And somehow that was normal as well.

The forest was hushed, waiting. Everything was waiting.

It was all definitely a dream and in her sleep Belle knew it, but the forest felt more like a memory than anything else. Like something she was supposed to remember.

A breeze passed over her. From the darkness a river boiled up before her and the buck, wide and black and rolling with mist.

The hart dipped its head, snorting. It raked a hoof along the ground. A single ear flicked back at her and Belle leaned forward to grab the stony prongs of its antlers, everything red and silver and shadow.

She thought, but did not say, *Yes, let's go!*

But the beast heard her anyway.

He leapt, star-bound and unstoppable, toward that vast river, where they would both surely drown.

"Belle, wake up. Get up. You have a caller."

Belle rolled over on the cot, buried her nose deeper into her pillow.

"Arabella Duvall," came Emma's voice again, sharper, accompanied by a firm shaking of Belle's left shoulder. "A *caller*! Get up, get dressed."

Belle opened her eyes. Her sister stood over her, a candlestick clutched in one hand. A dribble of tallow spilled over the top, fell into a thin yellow line down the side of the taper.

"Hurry *up*," Emma snapped, setting the candle on the bureau. "He's speaking with Mother now. You don't want her around him any longer than you can help, believe you me."

How often had she walked into this shabby little parlor and not seen what was before her eyes? The stained paper on the walls, dirty cream with faded blue pansies? The solitary rug, too small to cover even half of the room, once likely red and sage but now more the color of rust than anything else, the end near the hearth dotted with cinder marks?

The listless curtains, the chaise longue with its battered wooden legs. The Bible box beside it, not even a proper side table; just a small, prim note of polished rosewood and wrought iron amid the dullness of everything else.

When they'd first moved here, she'd made attempts to brighten it all. She'd brought home flowers pilfered from neighbors' gardens, pretty rocks she'd scavenged from parks. Once even a framed poster advertising a church jamboree that she'd found tossed in a rubbish bin, its glass uncracked, the colors still crisp and bright.

But it was never enough. There could never be enough purloined flowers or stones or prints to conceal the truth of their penury. Belle must have passed through this room thousands of times and it had become invisible to her at some point, all its flaws and sadness rendered neutral in her eyes, because what was the point of always noticing what was wrong when there was nothing she could do to fix any of it?

But oh, right now, just now, she saw with fresh eyes what she'd been ignoring, because seated upon the cushions of that chaise longue was the impressively large figure of Mr. Collis Potter Huntington, railroad tycoon and self-made multimillionaire, a man who had risen from nothing to become everything—at least everything as far as Richmond, Virginia, was concerned.

Mr. C. P. Huntington, whose name had *not* been recently printed in the local papers, thanks to her. The man who was pouring his incredible reserves of cash and experience into rebuilding the ports and trains and railroad tracks across the South in an effort to bring the world back to them, and them back to the world, one locomotive, one steamship, at a time.

Because of course she knew who he was. After their initial meeting all those weeks ago, Johnny had pulled her aside to tell her so himself.

A very important customer, he'd said. *Don't fail me.*

And it seemed that Belle had not.

"In my experience," Mother was saying in a voice Belle had not heard from her in a long while, smooth as honey, no hint of weariness, "these puritanical fevers tend to flare up every now and again, but they also quickly blow over. People around here are usually of a more practical ilk. They understand how a successful town needs to function."

"I'm most grateful to her," Mr. Huntington said. "She put herself at risk for me."

"Arabella's like that. The boldest heart, through and through. I swear I don't know where she gets it."

Collis Huntington noticed her lingering there at the doorway, rose to his feet. Mother, seated in an armchair nearby, turned in place to find her, her teacup paused halfway to her lips.

"Mr. Huntington," Belle greeted him, gliding forward, lifting her hand. Too late she remembered she still wore her wire eyeglasses, but there was nothing to be done about it now. "What a pleasant surprise."

"Miss Lenore," he said, accepting her hand, offering a short bow. "Or Miss Yarrington, I should say."

"I worry terribly for the state of your wallet. I can only imagine how much it cost to wrest my name from Mr. Worsham's lips."

Mr. Huntington smiled, a cold and fearsome smile. It was suddenly very easy to believe him the ruthless businessman they called him in the press. "I've known men like Johnny Worsham my entire life. He didn't even attempt to bargain."

"Then you were robbed."

"Happily so."

They stood a moment longer like that, facing each other, her hand cradled in his. His eyes were blue. She remembered that about him now, blue eyes, somehow both friendly and sharp. His hair was deep brown, thinning along the top and combed very sternly in place; his beard was threaded with gray. The curls around his temples were already springing free from their pomade.

He was not a handsome man. They seldom were. By Belle's reckoning he had to be nearly thirty years older than she, but honestly he didn't seem that old, even with the gray in his beard. Anyway, *handsome* was never a detail that she dwelled upon for long; *handsome* was merely a mask over a truth, like spectacles. And the truth was always more interesting than anything else.

Collis Huntington's truth struck Belle as this: power that practically radiated from him, an intensity that she might call *presence*, or even *charisma*. It felt almost like an echo of Johnny's allure, but so much stronger and more direct. More impressive.

Whatever it was, this allure of his, it certainly wasn't harmed by the fact that he was a well-groomed gentleman in an expensive suit in her mother's shabby parlor, something that Belle, in her seventeen years, had never before seen.

Conversation erupted from the hallway, muffled, quickly stifled.

Mother pushed free from the chair.

"Belle, dear, I'm afraid while we've been waiting for you the tea's gone cold. I'll go fetch us some fresh."

She set down her obviously warm cup, smiling, and exited the room. There was another brief flurry of whispering—and then footsteps and sudden silence.

Belle retreated into the chair her mother had occupied. Mr. Huntington returned to the chaise. She took a moment to smooth her palms along her skirts (apple-green muslin with thin navy stripes, Emma's Sunday best; Belle had outgrown her own church dress months past), and then lifted her lashes to take him in once more.

"I'll be frank," he began, looking back at her, but added nothing else.

She folded her hands in her lap. The muslin was thin but the air in the chamber felt thick and sluggish. Belle felt herself perspiring already, wondered if she should have taken better care to sponge herself before coming down.

"I came here to thank you, Miss Len—Miss Yarrington."

"Arabella. Belle."

"Belle." He nodded. "It suits you better, I think."

"Johnny assigned me the name Lenore when I first went to work for him. I never disliked it, but it was never me. It was never meant to be me, if that makes sense. Johnny gives all the girls their new names."

He narrowed those dark blue eyes, a vertical line between his brows. The cup of tea on the Bible box beside him sat forgotten, steam curling into the air.

Belle asked, "Are you recovered from our adventure, sir? The other night?"

His expression warmed. "Yes, thank you. And you?"

"Oh, that was nothing. Every morning I challenge pirates and henchmen along the river, sword in hand, to do battle for justice, so a little old raid is but a trifle to me."

She spoke swiftly, lightly, in a tone that had led more than one of Johnny's customers to regard her with open interest. But Mr. Huntington did not chuckle as she'd hoped, or even smile. He only bowed his head and then lifted it again, his mouth set in an expression she could not quite interpret. Maybe amusement. Maybe impatience.

"Pardon me," she said, more serious. "*I was born to speak all mirth and no matter.*"

A pause; *that* had surprised him, no question. He picked up his tea. *"Your silence most offends me, and to be merry best becomes you; for, out of question, you were born in a merry hour."*

She leaned forward slightly, lifting her chin to reveal the line of her neck. *"No, sure, my lord, my mother cried; but then there was a star danced, and under that was I born."*

He arched an eyebrow. "I've not met many women who could quote Shakespeare."

And because she hadn't lied to him before, because she truly was never afraid, Belle held his gaze and said, "Mr. Huntington, I can assure you that you've not met a woman like me before at all." She found her feet. "Would you care to walk outside with me, sir? We have a small herb garden in the back, with a bench. It's nothing special, but it seems like a fair day. It might be agreeable to sit in the sunlight."

"An excellent notion." He offered his arm.

The hallway was deserted when they passed through. Even the kitchen was deserted, the kettle empty on the stove. Belle wondered how her mother was going to eventually explain the lack of fresh tea.

But then, it was perfectly evident that Mr. Huntington had not come all this way for tea.

The garden was a postage stamp of a thing, barely five by seven feet, just enough to coax some chicory and chives and rosemary from the earth. A ragged line of lavender Belle had started years ago from a single cutting grew thick and wild against the western fence, thriving without her care.

Lavender for luck, she'd heard said, so it'd seemed like a fine idea to plant some. But Emma had given a fragrant stem to that cabinetmaker boy before he'd left, the one who was likely now buried in some battlefield, and Lizzie a handful to her husband, who'd since run off. So Belle left the lavender alone.

The bench sat in the shade of the tulip tree. She allowed him to lead her there, taking her seat first before he settled in beside her. A breeze came up, fresh with the scent of the river, just like her dream, only it was day instead of night, and the sunlight burned in lacework patterns through the branches above them, warm and cool by turns.

"Who tends the garden?" he asked.

"I do, mostly. My sisters and brothers don't have the patience and my mother doesn't have the time. I enjoy it."

"It's a good gift to have, the ability to make things thrive."

"I agree. And it's nice to add a little extra flavor to our meals."

"I enjoy gardens," Collis Huntington said softly, and it sounded almost like a confession. In the plain daylight she could see that his face was quite tanned, lined but not deeply so. "I enjoy nature, the outdoors. I was born to it. Grew up in it. Wish I got to be out in it more. Instead of . . ."

He made a frustrated sound in his throat, fell silent again.

"Well," she said carefully, "a garden is more like nature tamed, I think. But I understand, Mr. Huntington. There's solace in the greenery."

"Peace," he said.

"Yes, peace." Beyond the fence a pair of men staggered by, drunkenly arguing, and she added, wry, "As much as we may ever hope to find."

Darkened figures moved behind the glass of the kitchen window, but no one approached the open back door. A leaf spun down from the tree to land at their feet, and the lacework of light gracing them swayed gently across the ground.

One of the grosbeaks descended to the lowest branch. He tilted his head and opened his beak and released a taut, rippling ballad. Farther up the tree, his mate echoed him, a delicate counterpoint to each note.

Belle looked askance at Collis Huntington, who was looking back at her, smiling.

"I *did* tell you so," she said, and laughed.

He laughed with her, amiable and deep, and ran a hand over his hair. "Were you really born on a bed of leaves and moss?"

"To be honest, I think there might have been an old horse blanket involved as well. I don't usually mention that part."

He laughed again, quieter now. Belle had the distinct and surprising sense of something flicking into life between the two of them, something rhythmic and strong, connecting them like a heartbeat.

A romantic notion, not like her in the least. But there it was anyway.

"You came here to thank me," she prompted, in part to test that connection.

He reached into his jacket pocket and presented her with a long, flat box.

MONROE, read the black script across the red leather.

Belle accepted it with both hands, already knowing what the box contained. She was a creature knit of prudence and desire; she did not believe in premonitions, in superstition or even fate. But in this strange moment, she had a vision, bright as a spark almost, of what her life could be if she opened this box, if she accepted this gift that she had once, months ago on the morning of her birthday, longed for in a dream.

And if it *was* true, if it *was*—what then?

She opened the box.

The cameo bracelet had sat on a bed of velvet in the window of Monsieur Monroe's shop on Broad Street since May. She knew that because every time she passed by she'd stopped to admire it, the series of cunning profiles set in gold, linked with pearls, alabaster against rosy pink.

"And now," she murmured, touching a fingertip to one of those carved shell faces, "I worry for the state of your wallet even more."

"My wallet," he assured her, "has barely been touched."

"You didn't need to give me anything, but it's beautiful. Thank you."

"You're welcome. It's the least I could do."

The breeze roused once more, this time smelling of nothing but Shockoe Bottom.

"May I see you again?" Mr. Huntington asked.

The figures behind the kitchen window shifted anew; it was

Mother, it was Emma, it was Lizzie. All three of them watching while pretending not to watch, pale faces with features darkly blurred.

Belle felt a sudden need to take a deep breath, to reassess where the afternoon was heading.

"Johnny's is closed for now. I'm not sure when he'll be able to reopen. Probably not for at least two weeks, depending on whose palms he greases first."

"No," Collis Huntington said. "May I see *you?*"

She imagined cupping his face in her hands, the warmth of his cheeks and the rough silk of his beard. How his lips would feel against her own.

And this connection to him, this *heartbeat*, whatever it was, pulsed through her even stronger.

It whispered to her, *Yes, let's go!*

"You have my true name and my address, sir." Belle inclined her head. "And you have my gratitude. Please do call again whenever you wish."

CHAPTER 8

Catherine
Richmond, 1867

Arabella's gentleman *did* call again, three afternoons in a row, before he realized that Catherine's wild-rose daughter was an ensorcelled being, a fairy-tale creature who slept by day and sparkled at night. After that, he arrived after supper, usually bearing flowers or dessert or both. He would sit beside Belle in the parlor as her siblings took turns at the piano, polite as could be, just like a proper beau.

It worried her some, this rich man's politeness. His determination to follow the rules. But Belle wasn't worried; Belle was glowing, and Belle was smart. She knew just when to brush her fingers along the back of his hand as they sat side by side. When to hold his gaze, when to lean close, when to softly smile.

"Everything is fine," she told her mother, after Catherine had expressed her concerns. "Everything is proceeding exactly as it should."

One evening not long after, when a private coach rolled up to the boarding house and Arabella went into it instead of Mr. Huntington coming out, Catherine knew that Belle had been right.

She knew exactly how to proceed.

CHAPTER 9

Miss Yarrington,

 The House is opening again Monday next. I'm moving you from piano back to the floor. See Mabel P. about a new frock beforehand at yr. convenience, $23 for the silk, $7 for the labor.

—J. W.

Arabella
Richmond, 1867

September arrived, and with it a thin, sheer cooling of the sun and clouds. The temperature dropped from sweltering to tolerable, although the breeze remained as humid as ever. At night—Belle's time still, even though she had been out of work for three weeks now—the stars seemed to scatter with the wind, but that was only the clouds again, skimming and massing in pewter-black ripples, hiding heaven, revealing it again.

 Her family still slumbered at night. The whole world slumbered, except for Belle and Collis.

 She would not visit him at his hotel. She would not walk up

those public stairs and knock on his door, not even in a veil. So Collis, in that easy way that wealthy men could, arranged to rent a house down the river instead, a bijou little place fully furnished, beeches on all sides. It boasted a rooftop terrace that opened up to the sky, lovely, because they both enjoyed the night air and the clattering of leaves against the stars.

They lit no lanterns or candles on that terrace, not after eight o'clock. Light detracted from their hours together; light was the enemy of furtiveness. Even a single flame could exaggerate the shadows and interest the neighbors.

So, no flames near the open doors or windows. Only the two of them, only their sweaty skin and movements. Only their conversation, carefully modulated.

On this clement night, with a pale crescent moon pinned above them like a mark on a map, Belle lay on her back atop the mattress they'd dragged outside to the terrace. She held her arm straight up above her face and studied the darkened sky, ebony and distance between her spread fingers.

That same night sky stretched over the boarding house across town, that same pointed moon. But from this particular aspect, from this particular place, a tangle of linens beneath her and her hair unbound, it was all different. Everything around Collis was rendered different, and she honestly didn't know if it was because of his money or his body or the novelty of his mind, that ferocious intelligence that no amount of banter could disguise.

"Tell me about New York City," she said.

"Again?" Collis, cigar in hand, was seated beside her with one knee drawn up, his back against the wall behind them.

(He would not touch alcohol, but nothing she had said so far had persuaded him to abandon his tobacco at night. At least he retreated inside to strike the match.)

"Again. Can you see the constellations there?"

"No." He drew heavily on the cigar. "Not usually."

"Don't you miss them?"

He released a ring of smoke. She watched it float near her fingers, expand into nothing. "Sometimes I miss the natural world the way I'd miss a piece of my soul, I guess. I grew up on a farm, chopping wood, harvesting crops, tending stock. When I was younger, I used to take just a blanket and a pack and retreat into the wilderness for days on end. I could spend weeks alone and never yearn for civilized life. But . . . my time in Manhattan now is necessary. It's the burden I bear to be able to live as I do, to work as I do. Because of this life, I'm able to travel the world. I've admired the constellations from the Sierra Nevada to the Adirondacks. From California to Panama and back. I hope to never stop."

"Burden," she echoed, considering. "An interesting choice of word. It seems to me your *burden* involves a great many adventures. At the very least, resplendent restaurants and shops, plays and soirées and yachts. Luxurious palace cars, and meetings with congressmen. Those tiny little sandwiches served on carts with English tea."

"I don't attend soirées," he said mildly.

"I don't blame you," she said, dropping her hand back to her stomach. "They're dreadfully tedious."

"Have you been to many, Miss Lenore?"

"Hundreds. Thousands. Or maybe none at all. I notice you did not deny the sandwiches, sir."

"A man has to eat, after all."

She smiled, turning her head to see him. He was relaxed, smiling back at her. She could just make out the gleam of his teeth, the lit end of the cigar, a smoldering ruby pinched between his index finger and thumb. A train blew its horn in the distance and an owl, surely stationed in one of the trees surrounding the house, hooted a mournful response.

Belle turned back to the stars. "Now tell me about your wife."

There was a moment's silence. Then: "You *aren't* afraid, are you?"

"No."

He nursed the cigar a while longer, puffing. "Elizabeth is . . .

an estimable woman. Someone who has suffered me patiently and graciously over the years. I am in debt to her strength. To her goodness, and her devotion to me and our little girl."

"I am sure she must be estimable, if she is married to you," Belle said, and to her surprise, she meant it.

"No doubt she deserves better than me."

She rolled over, lifted herself up to an elbow, her hair falling along her chest. "I can't speak to that. But I think it's good of you to hold her in your heart. I think it must mean you're still bound in spirit, no matter what comes. That's what marriage should be, shouldn't it? A consistent union. A place to go back to."

"Miss Yarrington," Collis said, extinguishing his cigar in the saucer they'd pilfered from the kitchen, "what a surprise you continue to turn out to be. With that delightful face and devilish intellect, God has surely fashioned a formidable being in you."

"Yes, thank you, I know."

Another train whistled by. Belle closed her eyes, following its long, descending wail, the rattle of metal against metal, loud and then soft, soft, gone.

"Was that one of yours?" she asked.

"Soon to be, God willing."

"Running so late?"

"Trains run all night. Night and day, day and night. Especially now. That's how commerce moves along. That's how we improve."

She opened her eyes. "I admire your work here. I admire what you're doing for us. Helping to rebuild everything that's gone to ash. It would be worth losing a tiny part of your soul, I would think, to benefit the greater good."

"What a philosopher you are."

"A truth speaker."

"A bird charmer, at the very least."

She traced a hand along her clavicle, clearing back her hair. "I think maybe a bit of *my* soul was stolen away by them when I drew my first breath. An even exchange, I'd say, since I love so to hear them sing."

"Maybe you're secretly a changeling. A sylph who belongs to the woods."

"Maybe I am," she agreed as the eastern edge of the sky began to lift, ever so weakly, into gray. But it was still mostly dark, and in the darkness she could say anything, and anything could be true. "Maybe that's why I like you so much, Mr. Huntington. I recognize the wilderness in you."

The owl called once more, and even as Collis Huntington was reaching for her again, Belle rose to collect her belongings. There would be a carriage waiting for her downstairs, drawn by two black horses with no bells. She would head back to the boarding house before Richmond fully awoke, before the morning sun burned away the last, lingering enchantment she had so carefully constructed during the night.

"One of Johnny's flunkeys came by yesterday evening. He left this for you."

Lizzie's square, practical fingers pushed a folded sheet of paper along the kitchen countertop, where Belle stood smearing butter on a slice of brown bread.

It was not quite dawn and the house was silent; the earth was silent. Even the grosbeaks were drowsing still. The fact that Lizzie was awake and waiting for her told Belle everything she needed to know about Johnny's note.

"What does it say?" she asked anyway, not looking up from the butter.

"He wants you back. We need thirty dollars to replace the dress."

"The dress is fine," Belle said, tearing off a bite of bread with her teeth, savagely, like it was someone's head. "I didn't even rip it during the raid. It just got a little dirty, that's all."

"Then maybe he's making everyone get new dresses, I don't know. I know we don't have thirty dollars laying around."

Belle walked to the dining room with her bread. She didn't bother to sit, only stood at the window, looking out at the sky.

How many times had she stood here witnessing this moment, witnessing the fresh day rising into color and light, knowing she wouldn't be a part of it? How long had she been bound to the night? Just two years, but in her blood and bones, it already felt like eternity.

Behind her, Lizzie murmured her name.

"I'm not selling the bracelet," Belle said.

"I'm not suggesting that you do."

She turned. "Then what?"

Lizzie shook her head, her mouth a flat line. It was a look Belle knew all too well, one of both compassion and derision.

"Oh," she said. "So now I'm to wheedle cash from him? Or are you suggesting flat-out theft? Shall I just riffle through his pockets?"

"Can't he spare it?"

"*You* go. *You* go take my place at Johnny's. Why not? You stay up all night and I'll clean rooms and make beds here, and then you can lecture me about men and money."

"I haven't," said her sister, "your skills."

They stared at each other, Lizzie blond and brown-eyed and pinch-browed, Belle eight years younger and half a head taller, the bread unpleasantly dry in her mouth.

Belle faced the window again, tore off another bite.

"We're living on soup bones, Belle. We're living on charity."

"Half of Richmond is living on charity. Pardon me if I can't save us all."

"What are you doing, then," Lizzie asked softly, "if not trying to save us all?"

"Maybe I'm just enjoying myself. Maybe I'm just appreciating my leisure time with a gentleman who admires me."

"That doesn't sound like you. You're good at blending truth and lies, Arabella, but I've never known you to lie to yourself."

The bread was gone. A gleam of butter smeared her thumb; Belle licked it away.

Somewhere down the street a rooster began a loud, bragging crow. It woke an echo of dogs, barking and barking furiously.

"Do you remember the woods by the cabin?" Lizzie whispered, unexpected. "The river? How we used to splash around in it and frighten Mother into thinking we were drowning?"

"I remember how you used to try to scare me into seeing ghosts in the mists. I remember—the tadpoles. And wild strawberries."

"We're drowning here, Belle. All of us, drowning in real life. After this week, the boys won't be returning to school. Mother says it's time for John to learn a trade, and past time for Richard."

"Perhaps she's right."

Above them, the ceiling creaked. Footsteps sounded. Voices reached them, thick with sleep.

"You never saw the ghosts along the river, Belle, no matter how I tried to fool you. You could always tell the lie from the truth."

"I need to rest," Belle said, because *that* at least was true. The sky was luminous and flushed, and while everyone else was coming to, she still belonged to the night, was tied to the shadows.

Her cot, the attic, awaited.

Collis P. Huntington had risen like a blessed son from dusty, gritty destitution, the sort of destitution Belle fully comprehended. She knew this because once she had taken note of him—rather, once he had taken note of *her*—she had made it a point to discover everything about him that she could.

Johnny had actually helped in that regard. Johnny was filled with information in the same way that a penny bank was filled with coins, and for the same reason: to increase his wealth.

"Poverty Hollow," he'd told her weeks ago. "That's really the name of it, where he's from. And I'm given to understand that the name is far grander than the reality."

At thirteen, Collis had been plucked from his starving family to be raised by neighbors, until as a young man he was able to strike out on his own, his traveler's soul winging him up to New York, down south, back west, north again. He'd saved his pennies and multiplied them into dollars, multiplied the dollars by millions, and then millions more, and he began all of this as a rough, barefoot farm boy from Connecticut who had studied the dirt road leading out of town and wondered, *Why wouldn't I?*

At sixteen, he'd headed out, secured a loan to buy a horse and a wagon, and went south to peddle imported clocks and silverware to Virginians. In his twenties, he'd roamed west, offering more practical hardware to the miners drawn to the far reaches of California, those desperate fellows out hunting for gold.

As the decades unwound, he experienced firsthand how constrained his country was by a lack of reliable roads, how hobbled. So he'd blasted paths through granite mountains for his trains, adding cars, adding lines, until eventually he came up with the audacious idea of connecting railroad tracks from one end of the United States to the other, linking the Pacific to the Atlantic, a feat that many still claimed could not be done.

Collis Huntington was not only doing it, he'd had the foresight to pay his workers in genuine gold coin to ensure it would be done. And Belle (admiring his face over a midnight supper of canvasback and peas that the maid-of-all-work had left for them, pecan pralines for dessert) thought about how all of those deeds must have shaped him in some undeniable way, like a statue emerging from a rough-hewn block. No doubt he'd always had those dark eyebrows, those sturdy features, that waving hair. And perhaps he'd even been born with that unmistakable air of a general spearheading the charge. But now that she knew him—parts of him— knew the skimming of his palms against her flesh, and the taste of his mouth at the corner of hers, how his gaze would lift to find hers and he'd pause and slowly smile, blue eyes like a July sky . . .

Belle felt herself in perfect kinship with his traveler's soul. She understood that living blaze inside him, the urge to move, to think, to *change*. It was as familiar as her own blood rushing through her veins.

So she said that night, slicing her duck, "Johnny's opening the faro parlor again. In about a week, he thinks."

Mr. Huntington cocked his head. "Is that so?"

"I'm afraid it means our private time together is drawing to its conclusion."

He did not reply. Belle glanced up at him through her lashes, back down to her plate. She lifted a demure forkful of peas to her lips.

"I have to return to work," she said. "For the good of my family, you understand, I have to return."

Collis the bear, *her* bear, sat back in his cushioned chair, the India silk of his dressing gown catching the candlelight in long, golden folds.

She'd gambled much on this moment. She was its architect and its maker: planning it, polishing it, and now, rather too soon for her liking, here it was. For the rest of her years, the aroma of roasted duck and peas would fling her back to this table, sitting across from this blunt, older man gilded with light, her heart pounding and her face impassive, waiting for the mighty Collis Huntington, king of the railroads, to speak.

She placed her fork upon her plate, a muted *clink!* of metal meeting china. She lifted her water goblet and let the open fall of her own robe drape in a pink satiny scoop down her shoulder.

"Actually," Collis growled, leaning forward again, "if you'll hear me out, Miss Yarrington, I've had an idea about that."

CHAPTER 10

Catherine
Richmond, 1867

She found Arabella in the kitchen well after dawn, carefully chopping rosemary with a knife that hadn't been sharpened in years. Catherine paused at the doorway, surprised; usually Belle would be abed by now. But there she stood, silent, concentrating on her work, with Lizzie stoking the iron stove in the corner and Emma whisking the last of their eggs in a bowl for a scramble for the boarders.

The boys were just visible past the window, splitting and stacking wood, the rhythmic *thwack!* of the ax a sharp exclamation above the usual muffled clamor of men and horses and hooves.

Sunlight shafted through the room. Catherine was able to see perfectly well the slight frown that marred Belle's brow, the downward bow of her lips.

Oh no, she thought.

"Belle," she said, crossing to her, laying a hand on her arm. "I can do that. Go get some rest."

"No, I'm nearly done." She didn't look up.

Catherine hesitated, then reached up and touched an errant auburn curl nestled against Arabella's nape.

"Tell me what's happened."

Belle frowned more deeply, then said, "He's going back to New York."

Catherine let her hand fall to her side.

"He wants me to go with him." Now she looked up, found her mother's eyes, her spectacles flashing. "He wants to move me there, to Manhattan."

"What?" said Emma from across the room, her whisk frozen over the bowl.

"He'll rent me a home, he says. Something discreet, but still with servants. Something not too far from his own."

Catherine backed away a few steps, found herself up against one of the stools and pressed her hand against the seat to steady herself. Her heart filled her entire body, her entire everything, singing, *At last, hallelujah, at last . . .*

She managed, "What did you say?"

"I told him that I was flattered. That I would consider it."

"*Consider* it," Lizzie echoed, and gave a brittle laugh. "What's there to consider? Your own house, your own servants? Have you lost your mind?"

"I have not," Belle replied crisply, going back to her chopping.

"But what about his wife?" demanded Emma.

"I suppose she won't have to know."

"If you're *living* near her, this winsome young lady all alone, entertaining her *husband*—"

"Yes. He has a plan about that. He has all sorts of plans, as it happens."

"Then what about *us*?" Emma persisted, her voice rising. "Without your income from Johnny's, we won't get by. You know we won't!"

Belle wiped a finger down the flat of her blade, clearing off bits of rosemary. "Don't be foolish. I'd send you funds from New York."

"And what," asked Catherine quietly, taking note of the determined look on her daughter's face, "is *your* plan, my dear?"

Belle set down the knife. "My plan is to say yes, of course. Yes to New York, yes to the house and servants and whatever else he wants. I asked for three days to think about it."

"Too long," said Lizzie.

"No, it's just right. I won't wait three days. I'll send a note to him tonight, all tender and sweet, and tomorrow I'll go to him in person. We haven't spent a night apart in weeks, and if I manage this carefully enough . . ."

Belle paused, bit her lip. She turned to face Catherine directly, grave and brilliant and so intensely beautiful in the bold morning light that her mother had the thought, not for the first time, that it was surely impossible this child had come from her own womb.

Arabella said, "Would you be willing to move with me? Leave this place, leave Richmond, all of us together, if I can persuade him to it?"

At last, hallelujah, at last!

"Dear God," Catherine said. "Dear God, *yes.*"

CHAPTER 11

Mr. C. P. Huntington
118 East Grace Street
Chimborazo, Richmond

September 14, 1867

Dear Mr. Huntington,

I wish again to express my deep gratitude regarding your proposition to me. I understand, I think, what a tremendous undertaking it would be for us both, and I must admit that my heart soars at the notion of it.

So it is with keen regret that I must decline your generous offer. Please do not think it is because I have no desire to continue our friendship! Nothing could be further from the truth! These weeks spent with you have been the finest of my life, and I will swear to that with my hand on the Bible, if need be. The thought of continuing on with you, celebrating our adventures together in such a great city as New York, renders me almost speechless with joy.

Yet I cannot leave my family behind. My bonds of love and blood with them must supersede my own selfish desires. I am our main breadwinner, you see. My mother and siblings desperately need my support. I worry in particular about what might happen to my mother if I am gone and she remains in Shockoe Bottom. Her health has never been robust, and it has long been my belief that part of the ills that plague her stem from dwelling here, in this broken land.

If, perhaps, you would open your heart to the idea of bringing my family along? Oh, I know it is so much to ask! And I blush to ask it. But if you *could*, if you *would*—why, I would be the most grateful girl in the entire world. They needn't reside anywhere near us, in fact. Just close enough that I might visit them from time to time, to ensure their well-being.

I will close this note with my vow to you that no matter what you decide, I will always consider you a good man, a brilliant man, who has astonished me and sculpted me and *enlightened* me to a degree I never before fathomed. The thought of never seeing you again fills me with despair, but I shall be buoyed by the memories of our time together. I feel blessed indeed to have known you.

Most Sincerely,
B. D. Yarrington

Arabella
Richmond, 1867

"Mr. Worsham," greeted Collis, rising from the drawing room chair by the window. "Good of you to come."

Johnny had already handed off his hat and walking stick to the little maid who'd come with the rented house, sauntering across the rug to shake Collis's hand. He wore his usual attractive smile, warm and personable, but his eyes were cold and roving, taking in the luxury of the room, the framed oils and porcelain figurines. The costly rock-crystal chandelier, quivering with prisms.

"Mr. Huntington, sir, how could I not? Your message was so intriguing. One of the wealthiest men in America wants to discuss a business matter to my benefit? My curiosity is aflame."

Belle, who'd been lingering in the back hallway, chose that moment to step forward, her dark skirts whispering.

Johnny's smile narrowed. "Ah! And here is our Miss Lenore. An interesting twist to the situation."

"She is Miss Yarrington to you, if you please," Collis said. He lifted a hand. "Take a seat."

Johnny did so, brushing out his lapels as Belle moved to stand behind Collis's armchair, resting a hand along its back. "So this is where you've been tucked away since the raid, Miss Yarrington? I can hardly blame you. It's certainly finer lodgings than your mother's place."

"Finer than yours, as well," she retorted.

"Hmm. Definitely a sweeter-smelling neighborhood."

"Mr. Worsham," Collis said. "I understand you've owned a faro parlor in New York City?"

"Have owned," Johnny agreed, "and still do, more or less. I'm primarily a shadow partner these days. My interests have been better fulfilled here."

Collis leaned forward. "What if they may, temporarily, be better fulfilled *there*, instead?"

"Forgive my confusion. You wish to open a gaming house up north, sir?"

"No. I wish for you to return to Manhattan with Miss Yarrington at your side, and pretend to live with her as man and wife."

Johnny stared at him. Belle imagined it was the first time he'd ever been shocked beyond words.

"*Pretend*," Collis stressed. "*Temporarily*. I will provide the residence, of course. The servants, a coach and driver, and so forth. I will offer you a monthly stipend, and you will present yourself as the devoted husband of Mrs. Arabella Worsham whenever the occasion demands you do so. In addition, you will act as the happy son-in-law of Mrs. Catherine Yarrington, who will be also relocating to New York, along with the rest of her children. Beyond those two simple tasks, you'll be free to tend to your shadow interests to your heart's content."

Johnny cleared his throat. "It pains me to mention that I already have a wife."

"As do I. This transaction concerns neither of them. It is purely a matter of business between the two of us. No doubt your wife will not complain about the extra income."

Johnny looked up at Belle, still standing behind Collis, pinning her in that unholy green gaze. She could almost see his thoughts whirling, calculating his gains and losses, that sardonic lift to the corner of his mouth that she knew so well . . . too well.

Belle tilted her head and held his eyes, refusing to concede.

Collis checked his pocket watch, put it away again. "I would say you are a man of practicalities, Mr. Worsham?"

"I would say so, Mr. Huntington."

"Then let us be practical. Name your price."

It was concluded so quickly. Nary a ceremony, just two men signing a contract, and Collis handing her a simple gold band that she herself slipped onto her own ring finger, a gleaming lie. After all, one could not marry a man who was already wed.

Belle had met Johnny's wife once: Annette, thin and frazzled, the kind of woman who blinked a lot and never stopped offering pots of weak tea while her children scrambled and screamed, uncontrolled, across the furniture, taunting the pet cats.

Annette Worsham hadn't looked even once at her glamorous husband the entire time Belle was in her company. Belle heard rumors that she'd come from money over in Georgia, that Johnny had wed her just for the cash her daddy had offered him to take her off his hands. It sounded about right.

Belle suspected that Johnny's wife hated him. She suspected that thin and frazzled Annette hated him and their children and all of their cats, and couldn't blame her—at least, not regarding Johnny. It was difficult to envision a fate more unsavory than that of being the actual wife of John Archer Worsham, with his slick smile and wandering hands and effortlessly broken promises.

However, Johnny *did* know New York City, its ways and peculiarities, its respectable face and less respectable underbelly. He'd managed several gaming houses up north over the years—*arrested only once!* he liked to boast—and swore it wasn't going to be bothersome, the two of them acting as husband and wife, since it was all just for show and if there was one thing he exceled at, it was putting on a good show.

Johnny said a lot of damn things that only a damn fool would believe, though.

She gathered that Mr. Huntington comprehended that as well as she, which was why he insisted that Johnny sign his name to a contract then and there in that pretty, prismed drawing room, swearing him to silence no matter what came, upon forfeit of all monies owed and then some.

Such a dowry, and all for a false bride. But what could she do? Johnny was loathsome and he was vile, but he was the right age; he spoke with the right accent; he was wily enough to lie without effort and he knew how to distract and to flatter and to charm. Most importantly, his loyalty could be bought. Her entire plan, her entire salvation *and* that of her family, depended upon Johnny going along with it.

He left whistling a happy tune, bouncing down the front steps. Belle turned to Mr. Huntington and informed him that he'd surrendered a small fortune to a hound dog.

He had replied, "And now you hold the leash of this particular dog, Mrs. Worsham. Rejoice in this new life he has afforded us. I surely will."

CHAPTER 12

Catherine
En route from Virginia to New York, 1867

The last time she had left Virginia she was a different person entirely: younger, rounder, preposterously cloistered. Catherine had been a girl composed of piano lessons, and deportment lessons, and the cool shade of the veranda that traced a half circle around her family's old homestead. She was formed of delectable pastries that tasted of butter and sugar and cream; of box socials; of cotillions with *acceptable* young men sweeping her around and around a polished ballroom floor.

She had been, in short, the inevitable result of everything she had been raised to be, frothy and naïve, a girl with barely a notion of her own universe, its rights and its monstrous wrongs. A girl who put her faith in daydreams and who could not, for the life of her, imagine a future where everything wouldn't just continue on exactly as it always had, even when her true love had hardly a half dime in his pocket.

What did pennies or dimes matter when her new husband, that radiant young god, looked at her and smiled and kissed her knuckles and it felt like her swelling heart would hammer straight out of the cage of her chest?

How *lucky* she was, that version of Mrs. Richard Milton Yarrington had thought to herself, riding beside him on the buckboard that would eventually break down in the backwoods of Alabama.

She would gaze up at him, sunlight skimming across his raven hair, sliding languid gold along his cheekbones and his chiseled jaw and lips, and think, *How lucky I am to have him at last, all of him, all just for me.*

Yes, that buckboard was long gone, no doubt disintegrated into pulp and fungus back where they'd abandoned it, miles from the cabin she would eventually, reluctantly, and (ultimately) disbelievingly call *home*.

He'd died at night. Catherine, exhausted and struggling to keep her eyes open during it all, couldn't call it a surprise. Cholera's ravaging of her husband's formerly divine body had been inexorable, and without the funds to hire a physician, there could be no saving him.

Even with funds—a pie-in-the-sky notion—Richard likely would not have been saved. By the time he'd staggered home from his stint in Union Springs, thin and wrung-through and gasping, the disease had already sent half the neighbors around them to the graveyard.

She'd ordered the children outside to sit in the dark, to sleep if they could. There was no one to watch over them, but they tended to huddle together anyway, a pack of puppies flopped together on the porch. Lizzie, her mother knew, would hold on to the youngest even in her sleep so that he wouldn't wander off.

Catherine had done her best to remain awake to tend to her husband. She had not succeeded. Richard passed on with her hand clutched over his, and she only realized he was gone after she'd lifted her head from the side of the camp bed and noticed how cold he was, how unmoving.

His beautiful eyes were closed and his mouth was agape and all she could think was, *How dare you. How dare you strand me out here.*

It seemed unfair, almost, that such memories lingered with her, even with everything that had come after. She could never fully shake them, no matter her fortunes. Catherine could stare out the windows of the private parlor railcar that her daughter's gentleman had secured for them, the countryside rushing by at a speed she could scarcely credit, and still recall with absolute clarity the stench of her husband's death. How the bones of his hand had resisted hers, twigs frozen stiff, nothing to do with the living man who used to stroke her body into rapture.

How she'd risen from his deathbed and crossed the cabin floor to check on her children. Her legs had buckled by the time she'd reached the door, but she was able to catch herself with both hands against the frame.

Beyond the train's cinder-flecked windows, green Virginia melted away once and for all, the trees growing thinner, more golden and skeletal.

She would begin again; she was good at that. Catherine would gather up her brood in both arms and simply . . . begin again.

Arabella had ensured it.

Part II

The Mistress

1867–1870

CHAPTER 13

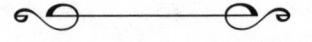

Journal entry of Arabella Duvall Worsham
October 12, 1867

It is one thing, I think, to dream of better days. To dream of a fine home one is not forced to share with strangers, or a comfortable bed one is not forced to share with a sister. To dream of remaining *awake* during the day, of stepping outside and lifting your face to the sun instead of the inconstant moon. Such gossamer wishes. They sustained me as best they could.

But now.

But today.

Gossamer has transformed into granite. Into marble. Into elegantly carved woodwork and an armoire stuffed full of gowns, all of them the latest fashion, none of them designed to lure men into placing more wagers, or indulging in another drink before the next game.

Yes, Johnny is here too, but I find myself so transported I barely mind him.

This place. This dear Manhattan home, so much more beautiful than anything I've ever seen before, ever experienced, not even Collis's rental back in Richmond.

I am Cinderella, uplifted. I am Princess Rosamond in her castle of briars, wondering what other miracles I might soon discover in the wide, exciting world now that I've been kissed awake.

Arabella
Manhattan, 1867

Mr. Huntington had secured them two separate houses only blocks apart, one on Prince Street and the other on Bleecker, both of them modish, both of them handsome. The Prince Street address was for Belle: four stories high, with Belle and Collis taking over the first two floors, Johnny on the third and the servants on the fourth. The Bleecker residence was almost as fine and slightly more spacious, enough so that every member of the Yarrington clan could have their own room.

After depositing Johnny and her luggage at her own place—a swift tour of the entranceway with its sliding mahogany-and-glass doors, the front parlor done up in shades of blue and cream, a pair of maids with downcast eyes bobbing curtsies—Belle returned to the coach to accompany her family to their new home.

"This is it?" asked Richard as they rolled near, all of them straining to get their first look at it out the window.

"Thirty-five Bleecker Street," Mother confirmed. "It says so right over the door." She looked at Belle. "You have the key?"

"I do. But there should be a footman to let us in."

"A *footman*," Emma echoed softly, and closed her eyes and gave a little laugh.

Richard was already yanking at the latch to the carriage door. "Let's go find out!"

There *was* a footman to welcome them inside, slightly older than Belle had expected, gray-haired and courteous, but also a housekeeper and a maid and a cook. The four of them stood in a line to receive the new tenants, not even turning their heads as Richard and John stampeded up a flight of buffed wooden stairs, vanishing down a hallway.

"You are gentlemen now," Mother called after them. "Do not run!"

"They'll take the best bedrooms," Lizzie fretted.

"Not if we don't let them," said Emma.

"*I*," said Catherine, "will decide the bedrooms." She turned to Belle. "Unless, my dear, you'd care to?"

Belle absorbed the startled expressions on her sisters' faces, took a step back with her palms upraised. "Absolutely not."

But even though she'd answered so quickly, so honestly, it was too late. Lizzie and Emma had already locked eyes, had already exchanged their private message of simmering dismay.

"Let's see the rest of it, shall we?" said Mother placidly, and took up her skirts to climb the stairs, following her sons.

There were vases of cut flowers adorning many of the nooks and flat surfaces, in the parlor and dining room and all of the bedrooms, white and purple lilacs, red peonies in fern. Emma dipped her nose into an arrangement in the main hall, inhaling deeply. "How are they in bloom?"

"Hothouses," Mother replied. She turned to the housekeeper, trailing silently behind them. "How often are they replaced?"

"Every four days, ma'am."

"Fresh flowers, every four days, *imagine*," Emma marveled.

With each new chamber, the marveling continued. *Someone else will make the beds. Someone else will change the sheets. Someone else will cook the meals. Someone else will shop and empty the chamber pots and dust and clean and answer the door. Someone else, someone else . . .*

And with each new step, Belle noticed how her sisters seemed to grow smaller, more tentative and awed, while the exact opposite happened to Catherine: she increased. She moved through these rooms and halls as if she had always known them, had always commanded them. She spoke to the housekeeper from over her shoulder and nodded decisively at her responses. She sailed by the stained-glass windows and tapped her fingernails against the bronze handrails, finally pausing before a set of double doors before turning around to find the housekeeper once again.

"We'll have coffee in here, thank you."

"Yes, ma'am."

It was a library, small but gleaming. Catherine crossed to a gilt-wood settee, sank gracefully upon its edge.

The Yarrington children knew something of their mother's background, how she had been born into a finer life long ago, how her father and her father's father and his father too had owned land, owned fields and cotton mills, until they hadn't. Catherine seldom spoke of any of it; she seemed embarrassed by it, ashamed, although Belle couldn't guess if she was more ashamed of the past or the present. But there had always been an echo of something *other* about her mother, something distant and aloof that even her father had never fully grasped.

Belle thought she understood it now. The debutante Catherine had once been still lived inside the woman she had grown to be—a woman who knew how to talk to servants, who knew the difference between tea service and coffee, who knew to the penny the value of her jewelry when she sold it to purchase food for her children.

Unlike their mother, not one of the Yarrington siblings had ever had a bedroom of their own, not in their whole lives. Now they all would except for Belle, who still had to share her bed with another.

But wasn't it worth it right now, seeing Catherine relax and expand in this gem of a space? Wasn't it just worth it to let her brothers and sisters all claim their own beds?

"Lizzie, Emma, would you go fetch your brothers? Tell them we can sort out the rooms after our refreshment. I'm not taking another step without coffee."

Another long look between her sisters, but maybe because they were smaller here, they were tossed upon an ocean of *unsure*, they left.

Belle took a seat opposite the settee, imitating her mother's pose, knees together, ankles crossed, hands folded across her lap.

"Perhaps you'll let me borrow some books," she said, looking around at the shelves.

"Arabella," said her mother quietly. "Surely you must understand. They are *all* your books."

The house on Prince Street was not a quiet place. As far as Belle could tell, there was no quiet place in all of the city, not even in the parks, which echoed with people and concerts and schoolboys cracking balls with wooden bats in the meadows. She had never in her life seen so many people, all of them living in such raucous close quarters. Even the giant mansions of the rich teemed with servants, with exclusive parties behind closed doors and windows, with sparkling life.

On certain days, when Collis was in town, they would take an enclosed carriage and ride slowly through Central Park, joining a parade of others. It was meant to be, he informed her, a time for the city's elite to see and be seen. It tickled them both to be a part of it, elite and *unseen*, their faces hidden behind curtains and glass.

When winter came, she tried ice skating at the park for the first time with her family and failed at it wretchedly. They all did, except for Emma, who apparently had been born to fly across frozen ponds. Within minutes of fitting the blades to her feet, she had stumbled only twice—and then was gone, arms out, skirts swishing, her paisley shawl waving *goodbye!* at them from behind. It was a half hour before she'd circled back into view, her cheeks bright and a rawboned man in a woolen coat skating at her side, speaking with loud, lively admiration.

A Mr. Warnken from Texas, bewitched by Emma's agile grace, and remaining so even as the months cycled from winter into summer. Apparently he'd become a regular caller at the Bleecker Street house. Mother seemed content with him, Emma more than content, but as far as Belle was concerned, Texas was just a shade too close to Virginia, a land that could always suck her back into memories of choking smoke and ash and desperation with just a sly, unguarded thought.

Winter or summer, she loved her home in the unquiet city. She loved it best when Johnny was gone from it—as he frequently was, minding all the unsavory corners and crevices of his little empire—because then she could believe that it truly was *her* house, hers alone.

Plus, of course, Collis.

The servants he'd hired for them were discreet to the point of invisibility. A coachman, a cook, a housekeeper and a footman and two maids: more domestic help than Belle had ever dreamed of having. It was a strange adjustment for her at first, having these polite, deferential people taking care of her, cooking and cleaning and dressing her. She knew their names and where they were from and very little else, except that they each knew to look the other way when Mr. Worsham left, and Mr. Huntington arrived. She'd never even overheard them gossiping about how Mr. and Mrs. Worsham slept in two different bedrooms, on two different stories of the house, although it had to be clear as daylight as to what was going on.

Belle supposed enough money could do that, could ensure a thin-lipped, unbroken silence. Or perhaps Mr. Huntington had made it a point to obtain their signatures on terms similar to Johnny's contract, full of legal phrases and meticulously devised legal threats. Either way, the result was the same. The house was clean; the meals were delicious; and whenever Collis tapped his silver-capped walking stick against the black-lacquered front door of 92 Prince Street, he was greeted with murmurs and curtsies and ushered at once to wherever Belle might be.

The neighbors were beginning to notice.

"So good of you both to come over," said Mrs. Jacob Harcourt (*Oh, I beg you! Call me Flossie!*), pouring tea from a pot painted with fat frolicking sheep and a simpering shepherdess. "I wasn't certain you would, honestly. After all, we've not been formally introduced, but as soon as I realized your place had been rented again—it's such a cozy home, isn't it, Mrs. Worsham?—as soon as I realized you had settled in, I told Mr. Harcourt we needed to have you over. We're right across the street, after all."

"It's good of you to have us." Johnny accepted his cup, casually crossing his legs at the knee, flicking a hand at the cuff of his trousers. It was a graceful gesture, and a studied one, a move designed to draw attention to the fine muscles of his calves and the shape of his ankles. Even here, even now, Johnny could not help but seduce.

"Yes," Belle said, taking a sip from her cup. The pot had steeped too long; all she tasted was hot cloves. "How very kind of you."

The Harcourts' receiving room was narrow and blinding with yellow. Yellow paper on the walls, yellow velvet on the chairs, yellow twill curtains. Mrs. Harcourt seemed exactly at home in its buttery pomp, an ample, older lady with a round open face and ringlets exactly like the shepherdess's on her teapot, only gray instead of blond.

She shot a look at her husband, seated beside her on a sofa the color of daffodils. "I must say, I adore your peculiar way of speaking. So sweet! So foreign! You're from the South, then, both of you?"

"Virginians, born and bred." Johnny rested a hand atop Belle's shoulder. He smiled; she smiled; she shrugged him off. "I hope you all don't mind," he went on, his brows knit in faux concern. "Considering our recent troubles."

"Oh, no! We're not like that, Mr. Worsham! The war is well past us, I say. To be honest, it hardly touched us here at all, did it, Mr. Harcourt?"

Mr. Jacob Harcourt lifted his shaggy iron brows, seeming to rouse from a stupor. "Hardly at all."

"How fortunate," Johnny commented.

"Yes," Belle agreed, her tone a shade too sleek. "How very fortunate for you."

Mrs. Harcourt leaned forward, her hands clasped. "Tell me. Was it so awfully terrible for you down there? The battles and the blockades and all? We've only heard rumors, you see, or whatever the papers chose to print. Stories impossible to credit."

Belle drew a breath. Johnny returned his hand to her shoulder, squeezed a little too hard.

"Only as much as you might expect, ma'am," he answered, solemn. "Yet here we are, friends again. What an agreeable parlor this is, Mrs. Harcourt. I do admire what you've done here. Those are Quimper-ware pieces, I believe, along the mantelpiece?"

"Oh! Yes, they are, Mr. Worsham. What a fine eye you have! Are you a collector, too?"

"Merely an appreciator, ma'am."

Mrs. Harcourt returned her gaze to Belle. "And do you collect anything, Mrs. Worsham?"

"Hearts," Johnny said, and laughed. After a moment, Belle and their hosts joined in.

"Well, I can certainly believe *that*, Mr. Worsham! Your wife is a lovely girl, just lovely! Those eyes! Those lips! You might be Proserpina from a painting, Mrs. Worsham, I swear. Don't you agree, Mr. Harcourt?"

"If you say so, Mrs. Harcourt."

"How kind," Belle said again.

"And so young! I can't imagine you're more than eighteen?"

"Yes, that's correct."

"Eighteen, and so poised. No doubt it's due to all the esteemed company you keep."

Belle went still. Beside her, Johnny stiffened and then relaxed, setting his cup of tea aside.

"Company?" he inquired, very bland.

"Oh, yes." Mrs. Harcourt's voice had gone as sleek as Belle's had been minutes ago, sleek and smug. Her round face had taken on an entirely new aspect, keener and more avid than before. Belle could not help but think of a snake's head emerging unexpectedly from the folds of a blanket. "It's thrilling for us, to be neighbors

with people who are on such close terms with Mr. Collis Huntington." She paused. "Your visitor *is* Mr. Huntington, isn't he? We
were introduced once at a benefit. It was some years ago, though,
and we're really no one at all to him. No doubt he won't remember."

Johnny's eyes met Belle's. For the first and likely last time in
her life, she knew exactly what he was thinking. Knew, and was in
concert with it.

"An old family friend," he offered to the Harcourts, resurrect-
ing his charming smile. "Just like a father to my darling Arabella."

"My father's good friend," Belle clarified. "Since well before
the war. Gracious, I can't even recall how long before, can you,
beloved?"

"Years and years. He's been taking care of a few domestic
problems for us, since we're new here, and I'm gone so often. He
and my Belle have become bosom intimates."

"We're *both* so grateful," she said. "I can't imagine what we'd
do without him."

"Yes," agreed Johnny. "I can't imagine."

Mrs. Harcourt said, "He certainly does seem to show up at all
hours."

Belle lifted her napkin, dabbed delicately at the corner of her
lips. "Well, that's how family should do, shouldn't it? They come
when we need them most."

"Of course," said Mrs. Harcourt.

Back in their own parlor, the second maid bustling away with
their gloves and hats, Belle slid the pocket doors closed and turned
to confront him.

"What did you do?"

Johnny's smile resurfaced. "What do you mean?"

"*He and Belle are bosom intimates*? Why on earth would you
say such a thing?"

"Why, Mrs. Worsham! What are you insinuating?"

"Enough," she said, and flattened both palms against the wood behind her. Her voice came low. "Enough of your games. By God, Johnny, if you don't think I'll wring your neck right here and now to keep that damned tongue in check, you should think again."

She glared at him. Johnny Worsham gazed back at her in the dim light of the parlor, the oil lamps with their opaline globes guttering.

"*Ma belle*, how changed you are up here," he said at last.

"No. I'm exactly the same as I ever was. This is just the first time you've been obliged to notice."

He walked over to the side table, reached for the decanter of whiskey that had sat practically untouched upon a tray since the day they'd first arrived. The cut-crystal stopper sparked between his fingers. "Don't worry, Arabella. Your benefactor has made it excruciatingly clear what will happen to me if I defy him. We are a secret tangled together, you and I."

"Good," she said icily. "And good evening to you."

She was angry, but she was not an idiot. When Johnny was here and Collis was not, Belle always made certain to lock her bedroom door at night.

Because even though it was technically her house, not his, Johnny still didn't bother to knock.

CHAPTER 14

Catherine
Manhattan, 1868

She'd brought the piano from the boarding house with her, that poor old battered warhorse of an instrument. Somehow in the chaos of the move from Virginia it lost another ivory veneer, but it hardly mattered. She had not wanted it for its looks, or even its functionality. To be frank, sometimes when she passed it in the parlor Catherine couldn't remember why she'd bothered with it at all, sitting there so worn and out of place in its corner.

Was it to remind herself of where she had come from, of who'd she once been? Or of the power of resiliency? Of the virtue of refusing to shatter even when all the world around you shattered?

Maybe it had something to do with the way she would catch her children looking at it: her eldest girls with wariness—as if it might leap to life and bite—the boys with open disdain. And Belle . . .

Belle was the only one who would still walk over to it, run her fingers along the keys. Occasionally she would go so far as to pull out the bench and sit down (the bench, at least, was new, with a cushion of lime velvet). She'd test the six keys missing their slick toothy tops, almost as if to ensure they still connected with wire, still obeyed the laws of sound. She'd rock back slightly, then forward, and begin to play.

Years of Catherine's lessons had honed her children's skills, whether they appreciated it or not, and each had developed their own style. Lizzie approached her playing with a brisk, almost militant attitude; Emma was more a perfectionist, making certain she never missed a note. Richard had always resented having to learn under his mother's thumb and it showed, while mischievous John liked to add flourishes to the end of every piece.

Arabella, though—

Arabella, so blessedly practical in spirit, so hard-nosed in opinion, would transform as she played. She became a dreamer, a romantic, her fingers skimming and dancing without apparent effort along the yellowed keys, cajoling music from Catherine's once-grand warhorse that would saturate the air with sweetness, with lilting drama.

She was playing just so when Catherine arrived home one rainy summer afternoon, Emma and Lizzie in tow, from a visit to a seed market downtown. Emma had a bee in her bonnet about growing their own vegetables in pots, a vision no doubt doomed to failure unless one of the maids took over, as none of the Yarringtons but Arabella had a green thumb and Belle had her own schedule to keep.

But here she was in their fine Manhattan parlor on this dreary day, done up in silk and tulle and her hat still pinned in place, just like a proper lady paying a call. She turned her head as they all came in, stopping her piece long enough to return her mother's kiss and her sisters' hellos.

"I hope you don't mind. I thought I'd drop by and the footman said you'd be back soon, so I've made myself at home."

Catherine just barely prevented herself from pointing out it actually *was* Belle's home; she hadn't missed the cold undercurrent of tension that could rise like a rogue wave between her daughters whenever matters like housing or allowances came up. There seemed no reason to invoke it.

"I thought you were lunching with Johnny today?" Emma asked, pulling at her gloves.

"I did, and had him drop me off after. He'll be by in an hour or so to pick me up."

"Why?" Lizzie asked bluntly. "Can't you just hail a cab?"

"Appearances. Today is all about public appearances, and the fuss of keeping them up. Showing the neighborhood what a happy, happy couple we are. When will the boys be back from school?"

"Around four," Catherine said.

"Oh. I'll miss them, then. A shame."

They stood there for a moment longer, all three of them, as the rain fell and Belle turned back to the piano and picked up exactly where she'd left off minutes before, the beginning of the second movement of the *Hammerklavier.*

Lizzie pivoted toward the door.

"I'm starving and my hem is all wet and I've got to get out of these shoes. But I'll ring for coffee and cake, shall I?"

"Yes," said Emma, "I'm going up to change as well."

Catherine watched them retreat into the gloss and shadows of the hall. Belle didn't look up again.

So Catherine removed her gloves, her damp hat, arranging them carefully on the credenza by the window to dry. She crossed to the settee and sat, waiting for Belle to speak.

"I've been thinking," Arabella said at last, still playing.

"Yes?"

"Thinking I might go by Johnny's faro house some evening. Just to see it."

"That seems . . . extremely unwise."

"Oh, I know. But I think I will anyway."

"Why?" Catherine asked, in the same hard tone Lizzie had used. She paused, softened her voice. "What good could come of it?"

"Knowledge. Enlightenment. Memory and wrath. Perhaps it's just the motivation I need to give Johnny his marching orders at last."

"Why?" Catherine asked again, this time alarmed. "What's happened with Johnny?"

"You'll see," Belle said.

Well, he was drunk, for one thing. That was apparent right away. Johnny Worsham stumbled out of his carriage and into the street, still handsome as sin, still smiling, but his eyes were bloodshot and his balance unsteady.

He carried no umbrella but didn't seem to mind the rain. In fact, as the footman waited by the open front door he only lingered on the steps, his hat in hand, and lifted his face to the clouds.

"*Ma belle,*" he called loudly to the doorway. "Come out and dance in the rain with me!"

Catherine picked up her skirts, descended the first step. "Mr. Worsham. Do come inside."

"Where is my lovely wife?"

"*Inside,* sir. Where you should be."

He ran a hand through his hair, flicking away drops, and clambered up to the entrance. He grabbed both of Catherine's hands in his and pressed an exuberant kiss to each, wreathed in fumes of whiskey so raw and fierce Catherine could very nearly see them steaming from his body.

She freed herself just as the footman angled behind them to close the door again.

"Mr. Worsham," she said once more, very cool. "As charming as ever."

"Mrs. Yarrington. Always an *immense* delight. I've come to fetch my—fetch my fetching bride home."

"Come into the parlor."

Arabella was already standing by the fireplace in her pelisse, her face expressionless, her gloved hands curved over her stomach. Emma and Lizzie stood nearby.

"There's still some coffee in the pot," Lizzie said, eyeing Johnny up and down. "It might help."

"Nothing helps," Belle replied, and walked past Johnny to the foyer.

Catherine watched the show from the vantage of the front window, how Belle rested her hand so gracefully on Johnny's arm, smiling up at him as he smiled down at her, the gentle rain misting them both. He tipped his head toward her as she murmured something, still smiling. He nodded but halted just before handing her up into the carriage. He turned to her, took her roughly by the shoulders and drew her in for a kiss—nothing discreet, nothing polite, but the sort of kiss a man gave a woman just before bedding her.

Belle stiffened. Perhaps no one else would notice it, how she went to stone, how her fingers clenched against the fabric of his coat and she leaned back, resisting even as Johnny tightened his embrace, then buried his face against her neck.

Catherine thought, stunned, *Good God almighty. He's fallen in love with her.*

No wonder Arabella had to get rid of him.

CHAPTER 15

Journal entry of Arabella D. Worsham
July 7th, 1869

I hardly need to be told of what happens to unmarried young women who find themselves in my condition. The disgrace of it, the scandal. Whole lives crushed up like week-old newspaper and discarded as if they'd never been. I'd wager there's not a single member of polite society, from lowly kitchen girls to the elite, who'd risk public sympathy for an unwed mother.

Fortunately, as far as society is concerned, I *am* wed—to a handsome, beguiling devil of a man, a man who can make my skin crawl with simply a look.

I am weary of living this lie. I have understood its necessity, but the sooner Johnny heads back to Virginia, the more freely I can breathe. He's growing more and more reckless, less and less convincing in his performance. The other night he actually arrived home in an unfamiliar carriage with two painted young women hanging halfway out the windows, blowing him farewell kisses. They made such a ruckus they surely woke half the block.

I hissed at him to hurry inside.

"Jealous, my beloved?" he sneered, and the girls chortled. One of them decided to toss a gin bottle out the window, a burst of wild diamonds against the cobbles. The horses snorted and kicked and when they were only just calmed she lifted her face and grinned at me: so young, so haggard, despite the paint.

Johnny stumbled directly from the front door to the drawing room sofa, and it struck me then how he wasn't nearly as dapper as he used to be. When we'd first met he'd been practically alight, electric, like dark lightning shaped into a man. But there were creases around his eyes now. Silver snaking through his hair. A bulge to his belly. His orange satin waistcoat had an oily stain down the front, a long, ugly blot.

"Perhaps I'll leave you," he mumbled.

"Perhaps you should."

"I mean it. I'll go home, back to Virginia. Back to a wife who *appreciates* me."

And I had to smile at the thought of that, of Annette Worsham *appreciating* Johnny's return.

"Go on back," I said. "I'll fix it with Mr. Huntington. You needn't worry."

He slumped forward on the sofa, dropped his head into his hands.

"Go back," I said again. "Even for a visit. See how Richmond fits you these days."

He made a sound like a groan. "You've ruined me."

"You were steeped in ruin long before we ever met. It's one of the few things we have in common."

He lifted his head, staring up at me with that terrible green stare, his hair all mussed. "Arabella. Would you miss me at all?"

"Oh, Johnny," I said, and sighed. "Tears won't do. Just go, and you'll be fine."

And thus, the whirligig of time brings in his revenges, I might have added. But I doubt Johnny Worsham knows a single word of Shakespeare.

So, matters have come to a head. Yet I admit that I'm glad that I've had a mock husband up until now, because it explains my condition without undue scrutiny.

I will not allow my life to be crushed up and tossed aside. I am not made of paper. I am made of steel, and so will be my child.

Mr. Huntington returns from his trip to Sulphur Springs this afternoon.

I'll tell him about the baby tonight. He is a man of objectivity and zeal, no drudge to anyone, or anything, conventional. God willing, he'll be pleased.

Arabella
Manhattan, 1869

She was gradually becoming accustomed to the particular, humid heat of summer in New York. Richmond had its own brand of humidity, of course, but maybe it was that she'd been more used to it, sticky on her face, under her arms, between her thighs, no matter how lightly she dressed. In her memory, the feverish air of Virginia and that of Alabama had blended into one, the same blue skies, the same winds, the same rolling clouds. In much the same way, Belle's brothers and sisters had mingled in her early memories into identical laughing faces, identical mops of unruly hair and naked legs scratched up by brambles. Sometimes she even thought she could remember Alfred and Catherine, her mother's two lost lambs, but that was likely untrue. They'd been hardly older than she when they'd died. Whatever she remembered of them was probably just stories other people had told her, anecdotes her imagination had rearranged into faces and hands and grins.

The mind was a tricky thing. It told her that the heat back in her former land had been of a more tolerable sort, had not settled so heavily in her lungs. But that was surely untrue. Humidity was humidity.

Even so, July pressed down on her like an anvil. Or maybe it only felt that way because she was no longer alone in her own body; she was breathing and surviving for two.

* * *

Collis arrived at night, as he mostly did. But tonight it was well after midnight, and unlike Johnny, Collis knew how to be discreet. So perhaps even the sharp-eyed Mrs. Harcourt might not have taken heed.

Belle was waiting for him with a meal of lamb cutlets and herbed potatoes, garnished with the rosemary and thyme she was growing herself in the little garden behind the house. Sometimes he would show up midday while she was out there on her knees, weeding and watering, and he would simply sit at the wrought iron table nearby, resting in the sunlight with his eyes closed and his fingers laced over his stomach. They would both smile at the juncos and sparrows and yellow warblers darting overhead, caroling their ardent songs.

"Tell me," she said later that night, well after their supper, "about the happiest memory from your childhood."

Beneath the cerulean canopy of the bed, Collis frowned a little, one arm crossed behind him beneath the pillows. With her head upon his chest he released a sigh, and she lifted and fell with him, both of them in concert.

"A happy memory," he mused. "You ask for more than you realize, Miss Yarrington."

"I'm sure it's there. Just try."

"My father," he began, and stopped. Started again. "My father was a good man. Stern. He could quote any passage from the Bible at the drop of a hat. He was admired near and far for his faith and his piety."

"Piety and sternness. Is that so happy?"

"While my mother," he continued, thoughtful, "was the kindest woman around. People called her an angel, and I think that was true."

"Your mother, then," Belle said. She closed her eyes, breathed in his tobacco, soapy scent. His chest was warm and solid beneath her palm. "Your mother was kind."

"Yes. And she was hopeful, I'd say. When we were merely hungry, she hoped. When we were truly hollow, she hoped more. Father prayed and prayed—as did we all; he made sure of it—but Mother was the one who had the courage to go out and ask for alms. She was not so proud as to see her children starve."

"A kind mother, wed to her proper husband. Devout and true."

"Yes."

"And . . . the memory?"

"Oh, it's not so much a memory as a feeling. Or a flavor. I remember once she baked us a blackberry pie. Blackberries grew wild out there in the country, and my brothers and sisters and I used to gather them when we could, although the bears and deer usually beat us to them as soon as they were ripe. But one year—I must have been about eleven—the heavens aligned, and we picked all the berries we could carry in our buckets and she took what was left, what we hadn't already gobbled down, and mixed them with cinnamon and sugar and—well, I don't know what. But that pie . . . that was the most glorious thing I've ever tasted, flaky and golden, scalding with juices. And she was so happy to do it." His voice fell soft, pensive. "She was thin as a thread herself, and so genuinely pleased to see us filled."

Belle tugged the satin coverlet up higher over them both. "Mr. Huntington, I promise you right here and now, in this sacred place, that I will bake you the second-most delicious pie you have ever tasted, in honor of your mother. Blackberry or blueberry or cherry, whatever you like. I will bake it for you and me and for our son."

"Son?" he said, suddenly still.

She sat up, twisted her hair into a long tail over her bare shoulder. She picked up his hand and pressed it over her womb.

"Here he is," she whispered. "Strong and thriving, just like you."

"A son," Collis said, wondering. He lay motionless on the bed, his skin burning against hers, blue eyes alight. His lips creased in a smile. "Arabella, beautiful girl. My gift, my demon. You demolish me, over and over."

"Good sir, I do know it," she said.

* * *

"And he wasn't angry?" Emma reached for another slice of pigeon pie from the tin beside the picnic basket. She placed it neatly on her plate, dusted off her fingers.

Belle's cook had packed them a luncheon of cold meats and pastries in a wicker hamper so heavy they'd had to take turns carrying it. The three sisters had clambered about Central Park before finally claiming a spot upon a mild green knoll topped by a lone elm, a slope that lifted and displayed them, like a rough grassy stage, to everyone around—something they hadn't considered before unfurling their blanket. Emma had wanted to find a different spot but Belle was already tired, and Lizzie, flopped to the ground in a pouf of petticoats and red gingham skirts, tore off her hat and flatly refused.

Your ankles are showing, Emma had scolded, and Lizzie had sent her a look of such amazed hauteur that Belle almost laughed.

"No, he wasn't angry," she said now. "I think he was delighted."

"That's lucky," Emma said.

"For all of us," Lizzie added.

The day blazed damp and hot; so far they'd gone through two jugs of tea. Belle had stretched out on her side in the grass beside the pink-striped blanket, bared ankles be damned, and ignored the stares of passersby. Because Central Park was for everyone, wasn't it? This great, egalitarian expanse of meadows and trees carved out from the heart of the city, a gift to all of New York, so that both the ordinary and the elite could remember—or at least get an idea of—what the world resembled without monoliths of brick and limestone and marble hemming the horizon.

Belle's corset was stiff but the grass was soft; she was sleepy now, slowly consuming a sandwich of pickled ginger that tingled in her mouth, a pleasant sensation that helped prick her awake.

Lizzie was balancing her tumbler of tea in the center of her palm, examining the bright beads of sweat slipping down the glass. "When are you due?"

"Next spring, I think. March or April."

"And you're certain? You're really, truly certain?"

"I am really, truly certain."

"Well, let's pray for a boy, since he's already got a daughter."

Emma murmured Lizzie's name under her breath. Lizzie set the tumbler on the blanket and picked up a chicken sandwich. Against the leaves of the elm and the airless sky, her hair gleamed sand and gold.

"Oh, are we not supposed to speak of that? I forgot, the esteemed Mr. Huntington's *legitimate* family is beyond bounds."

"What's the matter with you?" Emma asked. "You're so full of vinegar these days."

"I? I assure you, I'm the least vinegary person you know. Every morning and night I thank my lucky stars for this bountiful life. Don't you?" She went on before Emma could respond. "No, wait, I forgot—luck doesn't matter for you anymore, does it? You'll be off on your own soon, no doubt. Your Mr. Warnken is going to snatch you away to Texas. Don't deny it; I've seen all the signs. You'll be swept along on an ocean of ecstasy. You'll live on a ranch and tame broncos and lasso cattle and perhaps someday invite the rest of us to come visit."

"I won't dare tame broncos." Emma glanced down at her lap, up again. "But maybe the rest of it. Someday . . . or sooner."

Both Belle and Lizzie looked at her. A bee swung by, high and low, drunk on the honey they'd drizzled over the goat cheese tarts.

"He's asked me," Emma said. Sunlight softened the angles of her face, lit the depths of her brown eyes to caramel. She broke into a joyful smile. "He's asked me, and I've said yes."

All at once the world felt very still, very silent; everything around them, the people and the rustling leaves and the blades of grass faded away, insignificant, lost to the overwhelming weight of what her sister had just said.

Emma was getting married.

Emma was leaving.

Emma would be . . . a wife.

And then something even more peculiar happened. A sensation that Belle had never felt before, a sourness she had never before tasted, rose up strong and bitter, curling high into her throat.

Lizzie leaned back on her elbows. "Isn't *this* a day of surprises? My heartiest congratulations to you both."

"I had no idea," Belle began, then had to stop to swallow that ugly, unexpected taste. "Ahem! No idea matters between you two had grown so serious."

Emma's smile melted; she ducked her head and busied herself with waving off the bee. "How could you have? You hardly visit, do you? You've met him all of . . . what, a handful of times?"

"More than that! Why, we all just had supper together last week, didn't we?"

"It was three weeks ago," Lizzie said. "She's right. You're not around."

Belle sat up, fully awake. "Pardon me. I suppose I *have* been busy. When—when were you thinking to do it? The ceremony? And where?"

"We're planning for November. He has to go back to Austin next week, but he'll return by fall. A November wedding here, in the city, and then we'll both go back."

Lizzie had angled her face from them, gazing out at the scruffy green meadow. Lizzie, who'd been married once herself and then abandoned without a word, without an excuse, only a wife one day and then abruptly not.

Perhaps Belle was not the only one with that sour taste in her mouth.

"Do you love him?" she asked.

Emma frowned down at the blanket, plucked a small bit of debris from its folds and tossed it back to the grass.

"She does," Lizzie said. "You should see them together. It's like drowning in a vat of syrup."

Belle nodded, picked up a cracker topped with soused salmon. She knew that Emma was waiting for her to offer her own congratulations, to say *wonderful,* or *how nice,* or *what happy news.*

Yet she didn't have any of those words inside of her. What she had, surprisingly, were these, red-hot and burning against her tongue:

Why you? Why are you so chosen, and not me?

And without even giving voice to those terrible, unforgivable words, Belle knew the answer:

Because a man with a mistress, even a pregnant one, already has a wife.

"I thought you'd be happy for me," Emma said, a tremble to her voice.

"I *am* happy. Of course I am."

"You won't have to worry about me any longer. You and Mr. Huntington, you won't have to support me. I'll be married! I'll be free."

"Is *that* what being married means?" Lizzie drawled, dry as the desert.

Emma's face scrunched into a scowl. She made to stand but Belle caught her by the wrist before she could, tugged her back down.

"I *am* happy for you," she said again. "Only . . . only just be sure. Hearts can quickly cool. Marriage is a risk. It always is."

Emma yanked her arm free. She stood up, shook out her skirts and stalked off, her straw hat swinging like a weapon in her hand. People on the paths cleared out of her way. A bicyclist on a bone-shaker rang his bell.

"Oh, come back!" Belle called after her. "I didn't mean it."

Lizzie held a hand to her eyes, shielding them from the light as they watched Emma round a bend. "You did."

"If you'd been braver, you'd have said the same."

"But none of us are as brave as you, little sister. Not a damn single one of us. And if there is one thing our family has learned over these past few years, it is that irrefutable fact."

Belle tossed down her cracker, her appetite gone. "Are you an-gry about it? Are you suffering from it, my bravery? Are you not eating and sleeping in comfort, or do you really miss what you had back there in Richmond, famished all day, mopping up after strangers?"

"I miss my pride, I guess," Lizzie said, and got up and walked after their sister.

"Pride never guaranteed our bills," Belle retorted, but quietly, because the park-goers in their summer finery were turning their heads to stare at her again, a lone woman on a hillock.

Mr. Huntington was to take a journey to California at the end of August. He would be traveling with friends and congressmen and senators, and it had been planned for months, long before Belle's unexpected announcement. They would board a train in New York and plunge south, extremely south, all the way to Panama, before winding back up again through the plains and mountains of the western United States. They would linger by the mild blue Pacific for a week or so (a place Belle struggled heartily to imagine), before retracing their way back to the city.

He would be home by mid-November, Collis had informed her.

Just in time for Emma's wedding, Belle thought but did not say. She'd only gathered his hands in hers, cupped them over her growing belly and smiled. She'd kissed him and told him she would miss him dreadfully.

This was her role and she excelled at it; no one could now call the glint in her eye *desperate*.

Determined was a far better word.

But Panama! So strange and distant.

And California, the same.

"Show him what he has missed when he returns," Mother advised. "Remind him of you, and your child. Remind him of this happy world that awaits him."

And Belle would, because her world *was* happy, no matter who said otherwise. It *was*.

It was.

CHAPTER 16

Mr. J. A. Worsham
547 Bright Street
Richmond, Virginia

October 2, 1869

Mr. Worsham,

I trust you are enjoying your time in Virginia. As you are already on holiday there, it seems expedient to inform you that your services are no longer required here in New York. I thank you for your dedication to your job over the past two years. Your devotion was extremely useful.

Any remaining belongings will be shipped to you at once. A draft of your final payment to follow.

My best to your dear Annette, who is, no doubt, thrilled to have you at her side again,

B. D. W.

Mrs. B. D. Worsham
92 Prince Street
New York, New York

October 23, 1869

Ma belle,
    What a surprise to receive your missive. May I offer my sincere admiration of the scope of your machinations. It seems you were paying far closer attention to me than I ever was to you! How flattering to discover you've embraced so thoroughly the lessons I taught you. You're welcome, of course.
    I wish you success in your high-flying new life, and remain secure in the certainty that you will never forget your roots, the soil from which you came, the house that trained you and the man who first cared enough to liberate you from obscurity. Who first took you by the hand and told you who you *really* were.
    How very correct I was.

    In closing, allow me to reassure you that I am *all* the richer for our association,

J. A. W.

Arabella
Manhattan, 1869

"Mrs. Worsham! Lackaday, your attire! Has something happened?"
    Belle spun from her open front door, swift and dramatic and as dark as Hades. She wore a veil of black netting over her face, short and stiff, held in place with tortoiseshell combs; she flipped it back from her eyes. Mrs. Flossie Harcourt stood at the bottom of the porch steps, one hand pressed over her heart. The hem of her primrose skirts flounced with the breeze.

Belle lifted her own skirts—jet damask—and nodded, walking down to her.

Back inside the house, her family was moving back and forth, picking up knickknacks, putting them down again, chatting in low, solemn tones.

"It's Mr. Worsham, I'm afraid," Belle said. "He passed away last Sunday."

Mrs. Harcourt's mouth dropped open.

"Good gracious," she said. "Why, I—I could have sworn I saw him just the other day! Two days ago, or three at the most! I could have sworn!"

"Oh, no. Likely you saw my brother Richard. He's of a very similar build, and was just visiting."

Mrs. Harcourt blinked at her. Belle refolded the netting over her face.

"I'm off to live with my mother now. To find solace in the comfort of my family. That's them inside, helping to gather my belongings."

"My goodness! I simply don't know what to say." Mrs. Harcourt shook her head, peered around Belle at the open front door. "What *happened*?"

"Diphtheria," Belle whispered, leaning close. "I beg your pardon. I likely should have warned you before."

Mrs. Harcourt leapt back as if she'd been bitten. It was October, and the nights had begun to paint frost flowers along anything metal or glass, but today was lovely and mild. In the long, golden light, Flossie Harcourt's round face drained entirely of color.

"It was very swift," Belle went on, earnest. "Saturday evening he mentioned he felt a tickle in his throat, the smallest thing, and by Sunday he was just . . . gone. My poor, darling Johnny. The gentlemen from the funeral home came and took him away that very morning. So kind of them to do their business on the Sabbath, I thought." She paused. "No doubt you and Mr. Harcourt were at church, and so didn't see."

Flossie Harcourt, that secret snake of a neighbor, pressed her fingers against her throat. She made a choking sound, something between a gasp and a snort, took another step away from Belle, turned on her heel and fled.

It seemed the best solution. Collis was traveling and Johnny had finally agreed to visit Virginia—just for a month or so, he'd said. No longer. Belle hadn't bothered to inform her faux husband that she was about to pronounce him dead; despite his increasing surliness, she was sure he wouldn't have gone if he'd known. She didn't know to what degree Collis's stipend had soothed Johnny's wild moods, but she had no desire to tell him to his face that it was about to be discontinued.

He'd insisted he'd only go if she accompanied him to the train station.

"A proper adieu," he'd said. "Just as a good wife should. You can't deny me that."

And because she was so eager to be rid of him, to irrevocably pull the thorn of Johnny Worsham from her side, she'd capitulated.

Amid the hustle and scramble of the platform he'd leaned down to kiss her—*the last time*, she'd thought to herself, though he couldn't know; *the absolute last time*—and with his lips mashed to hers she'd held her breath, because he reeked of liquor and smoke and that too-familiar stink of desperation.

After a few seconds she'd pushed him back with both hands, smiling. He'd slanted her that hot emerald look, the one she'd once half drowned in, years ago, then turned and boarded the train.

Belle had gone straight home. She'd composed the letter informing Johnny of his dismissal, had the maids pack up his bags and the coachman mail off the letter and everything else.

Then she'd had the locks changed on the doors.

Then she'd realized that changing the locks wasn't enough. She needed to change her *circumstances*.

Collis had told her only as he'd been bidding her farewell that his wife and daughter would be joining him on this extended journey. He'd mentioned it casually, quietly. It was clear he knew it was significant but that he didn't want her to think that it was.

Then he'd kissed her goodbye and accepted his hat, his mind already flown from her and this moment, focused on the open skies ahead of him, on the railways yet to be built, and the mountains he would move and the oceans he would part to build them.

Belle had never feared the fact of his marriage or of his family. But she was a strategist; she excelled at chess and any other game relying upon grand designs. It occurred to her in that instant, as Collis released her hand and moved toward the door, that she had been negligent in this particular game. That it would be wise of her to take a closer look at the board.

There were two queens in chess, after all, not just one.

Without mentioning it to anyone, she'd shown up at the train station—the very same one she'd go to with Johnny, only a week later—to watch them depart. She'd borrowed her housemaid's drab felt shawl and unearthed an old hat with a veil—tan, not black—and stood at the back of the crowd milling around the platform. She'd even purchased a cheap ticket to travel uptown, in case she needed to show it to an attendant.

But no one paid attention to her. No one cared a jot about a solitary woman lingering against the back wall, ticket in hand.

Not Collis, so much taller than the men and women around him, gesturing at the shiny red-and-gold railcar behind him or the stack of trunks nearby, she presumed his own.

Not the lady at his side, much shorter, a gleam of brassy hair visible beneath her fashionable hat, a satin-corded wrap slipping sideways down one arm.

And not the little girl beside *her*, looking around the platform with wide dark eyes, a toy of some sort, a ragdoll or a stuffed animal, caught firmly in the crook of her elbow.

The train's smokestack was already belching exhaust. The air pushed by with the stink of coal and hot metal and unwashed people. The noise was truly impressive, everyone talking or even shouting to be heard. Although Collis was in conversation with a gray-bearded gentleman next to him, and Belle wasn't even thirty yards away, it was as if he were on the moon. His lips moved; she caught none of it. His eyes roved the platform; she was so diminished as to be invisible.

So, Belle focused on his wife. That good woman, that estimable woman who deserved a better husband than the one she had chosen, by Collis's own admission.

Elizabeth Huntington was also speaking, addressing her daughter as she adjusted the ties of the girl's navy-blue cape. Belle could not say if Mrs. Huntington was fair or plain from where she stood. When, once, her gaze seemed to drift over toward her, Belle turned her back and pretended to be reading an advertisement for orange-blossom soap (*Sweet & Fresh! Not a Hint of Residue Left Behind!*) tacked to the wooden wall. She counted to forty before turning back again, at first just her cheek, then her whole body.

Mrs. Huntington had tucked her arm through her husband's. She was gazing without expression at the locomotive on the next track over, a massive iron dragon that was puffing and steaming, workers smeared with oil and soot swarming all around it. Elizabeth bent down, pointed out something to her daughter with a gloved hand. The child nodded. Elizabeth patted her on the shoulder, straightened, and then looked directly back up at Belle.

It was not an accident. Mrs. Huntington did not look away again, daunted or distracted by the people scurrying past. She only stared at Belle through the unruly crowd, her head slightly cocked. The clutch of ostrich plumes curving down from the brim of her hat trembled against her chin, white and brown and rust.

It turned out that Collis's wife was neither plain nor beautiful. She was something else entirely.

She was wounded. She was angry.

And perhaps she, too, was skilled at chess.

"Excuse me, miss?"

Belle started, faced the porter who had materialized at her side.

"Are you in need of directions, miss?" he asked, with an ingratiating smile. His gaze traveled up and down her figure. His fingers fanned along the hem of his bottle-green jacket, tugging brief and hard, releasing. "Any manner of guidance at *all*, miss?"

Belle hissed a breath between her teeth, turned her shoulder to him.

"I am not."

She had tossed down the gauntlet, such as it was. She had vacated the Prince Street address, returned to her mother's home—also supplied by Collis, of course; it wasn't meant to be *that* much of a gauntlet, but still. Yet even without this trip of his taking place, this giant void of him slowly ballooning through her life, Belle had realized that her time in the other house was done.

She required something new, a respite away from her prying neighbors and their disparaging smiles and their presumptions. Also away from anything Collis thought she might simply tolerate, those whispering gossips, just because she must.

Beyond the gay façades Belle had constructed for her work, beyond the many fine stories she'd invented for anyone who'd inquired, she was still a creature of clay and earth. She truly was pregnant with his child. She was not going to be shuffled off somewhere convenient to be shushed and stifled and told to obey. She was going to stake her claim in her lover's life, and if that meant a new home, a new identity as a genteel Southern widow, so be it.

After all, it wasn't terribly implausible. The war had devoured so many and so much. There were widows scattered throughout the tragic ruins of the South, thousands of them left to rebuild their lives without husbands or sons or communities to vouch for them. To *identify* them.

Arabella Yarrington no longer resided in the Confederacy. Belle D. Worsham was *here*, asserting her right to be a part of the radiant city that was New York—because hadn't the war reunited North and South, after all?—matching her heartbeat to its own.

By God, she would not be quiet. She would not obey. She was going to take what was hers and she was going to succeed, because she *had* to succeed. Her life, her family's and her child's, depended upon it.

And she refused to be afraid.

CHAPTER 17

Monday, 7 March, 1870

Mrs. Worsham,

This note is to reaffirm our conversation regarding your antenatal examination, and to supply you with the receipt I recommend to aid in digestion (specifics enclosed, and pls. make certain the ginger is fresh, not preserved). As I mentioned to you this morning, the child is positioned quite low at this point, and no doubt will arrive at any time. Taking into consideration your prior gravidity, I feel it is imperative that you rest as much as possible. Do not consume grapes, salt, or organ meats, especially liver. Do not engage in any manner of physical exertion.

As soon as your birth pains begin, send your girl to me at once.

Dr. G. R. Fischer

Arabella
Manhattan, 1870

Time slipped by her, under her and around her, a gentle but tireless zephyr that carried her along with it into the long weeks that became autumn instead of summer, then winter instead of autumn.

Emma had her wedding with Thies Warnken, her besotted Texan. They'd held it in Belle's drawing room in her new home on Bond Street, done up for the occasion in white and silver bunting, white peonies bursting from vases, loose stems laid flat along the fireplace mantel, dark green leaves fringing soft petals: so many blooms their perfume weighted the air, turned the cool November afternoon back into sweet, heady summer.

Collis hadn't attended but all the Yarringtons were there, everyone on their best behavior, even Lizzie. John had saved the day when the groom went to first slice the wedding cake (a double-tiered fantasy of cream frosting and candied orange peel) and pushed the knife too firmly into the top. The spindled glass stand holding it tipped, began to fall, when Belle's youngest brother, fourteen and fleet, swooped in and grabbed the base with both hands, lifting it high into the air while spinning in a circle, and everyone gasped and laughed and applauded as he set it safely down again.

"I know you're in a hurry to get gone," he'd said to Thies, "but I've waited all day to taste this, so don't make me eat it off the floor!"

And everyone laughed again.

Perhaps it was the sugar in the cake. Perhaps it was the firm, beautiful swell of her baby beneath her skirts, but Belle found that the sour taste that had plagued her before at the notion of her sister's nuptials had diminished, nearly to the point of being forgotten.

More months winged by. The year changed and winter dug in, cold and clouded. Belle's body became ponderous to her, her gait as rolling as an old sailor's who'd just landed ashore. Even her dressmaker had not anticipated the eventual enormity of the Widow Worsham's breasts and belly; Belle had to return to her twice before the baby came, to either add more black panels to the somber maternity dresses she already had, or simply purchase new ones.

He was going to be titanic, her son. How could a child of C. P. Huntington be anything else?

Yet she was unused to the *awkwardness* of it all, the bulkiness, the constant pressure against her stomach and bladder and lungs. She was still pleased, so pleased, to bear his baby, but she thought if she got much bigger she'd no longer fit through the doorways.

"It could be twins," said Lizzie, matter-of-fact.

Belle sighed, rubbed her palms across the tight bulge of her middle. "Twins aren't common in his family, or ours. I asked."

It was snowing outside this dear brownstone that housed Belle and her discreet handful of servants. A little larger than her old place and far more private, it was exactly what she'd told Collis she needed. Her mother and brothers and Lizzie still kept the Bleecker Street house, but it wasn't too far, and they all dropped by when it suited everyone's schedules.

The drawing room was tall and narrow. A fire warmed approximately half the chamber from beneath the granite mantel, fed a steady diet of logs by the housemaids, or the footman, or by Belle herself, whoever happened to be nearby. It still felt like a great luxury, to have a wood fire blazing. To be able to walk into the kitchen and ask for food—for roast beef or Stilton or even hothouse strawberries, no matter the season—and be given what she asked.

From her chair by the fire, Belle stretched out her legs, rucked up her skirts to enjoy the heat against her shins and ankles. The snowfall muffled the occasional commotion of the carriages rolling by, the jingle of harnesses and the crunch of hooves against stone. It pulled the color from the sky and the earth and the row of naked sycamores standing in a line along the street, just visible from where she sat. All the world was rendered gray and white, muted.

Except for the fire, a flickering orange heart. The long, darting shadows cast by it.

Lizzie poured herself another glass of claret from the decanter on the side table. Belle kept spirits in the house for her family, for even the servants, but Collis never drank and so she didn't either, more or less. It wasn't red wine in her own glass, but the ginger-brew recipe concocted by her physician, a potion designed to soothe her stomach. She had to consume it in tiny sips; the raw ginger smarted her tongue and the lemon juice was so formidable that it made her mouth screw up, no matter how much honey she'd added to the mixture.

"When will you see Mr. Huntington again?" Lizzie asked, returning to her chair.

"Tonight. He comes by early, he leaves early."

"Does he stay for dinner?"

"No, not lately."

Lizzie made a humming sound in her throat, stared at the fire as the sky outside slowly melted into dusk.

Belle felt a surge of impatience. "Why?"

"You're due so soon. Shouldn't he be spending more time here, to see how you're faring?"

"He knows how I'm faring, it's hardly a mystery. And we see each other practically every day."

"When he's in town."

It wasn't a question, but Belle answered it anyway, her voice calm. "Yes. When he's in town."

Lizzie eased down the cushions, crossed her legs and lifted her glass to her lips. "Does he have any trips coming up?"

"I imagine so. I don't expect the earth to stop spinning because I'm about to give birth, and don't expect Mr. Huntington to interrupt his working hours just because of me."

"Not even for the birth of his own child? Maybe two of them?"

"Not even then," Belle said. "And it's just one. Just one boy."

"You're awfully sure about that."

She shrugged. "I am."

"How?"

"I can't say." She lifted her right leg parallel to the floor, turned her ankle in a circle, clockwise, counterclockwise, the black satin of her slipper gleaming. "It's just that . . . whenever I think of my baby, of holding him in my arms, it's always a boy."

She lowered her leg, lifted the left and traced another circle in the air, stretching her back at the same time. Her son shifted with her, rammed an elbow or a foot against her ribs.

Lizzie shook her head. "I suppose I wouldn't know anything about that, the prophetic dreams of impending motherhood, so I'll indulge you. Why not? It's a boy." She sat up suddenly, attentive. "What are you thinking to name him?"

Belle said nothing.

"Oh, ho!" Lizzie tossed back her head and laughed; firelight skated along her jaw and the tight coils of her hair. "You know you can't. Not ever."

"It's only one idea."

"Listen to me, little sister. There is no surer way to drive a wedge between you and your Mr. Huntington than by waving such a public flag. He cannot acknowledge you, *either* of you, not if he wishes to keep moving in the circles he does. Discover a different name."

Belle lowered her chin. Lizzie was right and she knew it, but how strange and unpleasant it was to hear it said aloud.

There could be no Collis Potter, Junior. Not by Arabella Worsham, at least.

Lizzie wet a fingertip, ran it lightly along the rim of her glass. A thin silvery hum rose and fell, a trick they'd learned in their early years, back in the untamed woods. They'd sit in a circle, all five of them, and pull music from Mother's precious punch glasses, the ones she'd carried with her all the way from her childhood home. Until one day the glasses were gone, traded to a neighbor for backstrap.

"Name him after your dearly departed husband," Lizzie suggested. "Name him Johnny."

"Not for all the bullion in the world."

"Then name him after Papa."

"Maybe." Belle tried another sip of the ginger brew, grimaced and burped.

Lizzie gestured with her glass, the claret rising into burgundy sparks. "But to return to my point. Mr. Huntington is about to gain a son, an accomplishment treasured by *all* men, of *all* ages and countries and classes. So where is he right now?"

"Running the Central Pacific Railroad?" Belle suggested, dry. "Locked away in another meeting with President Grant?"

"*Or* at home, mollifying his wife," her sister countered, sitting forward.

"What *is* your point, Lizzie?"

"Only this. This brownstone is rented in your name but not owned. Nearly everything here belongs to someone else. We eat well and we sleep well now, but the truth is, we live on a knife's edge, all of us but for Emma. Get something in writing from your gentleman, a legal document, and soon. Something to ensure his son's future, no matter what comes."

"Collis would not abandon us," she said sharply.

"Not if he has no choice." Lizzie leaned back to stare into the fire again, her eyes hooded, the glass of claret dangled idly, artfully, between two fingers.

The house on Bond Street had a nursery, a dab of a space with periwinkle walls and ivory wainscoting. The cradle had been placed against one wall and the changing table against another, an oak rocking chair positioned by the hearth. Stacks and stacks of soft flannel napkins waited in piles along the shelves beneath the table, a bowl of nappy pins next to them.

Belle would stir her fingers through the bowl sometimes, feeling the cool metal of the pins against her skin, thinking about everything they portended.

Soon her baby would need those pins, would make use of them and the napkins and sleep in the cradle, or against her chest as she rocked them both by the fire. In her mind's eye she could almost, *almost* see him; the muscles of her arms could almost test his weight. She imagined his little face, his plump hands, his scent. Anticipation simmered through her, an almost shimmering *want* for what was to come.

A son. A child of her flesh and her lover's, alive and welcome, physical proof of her connection to Collis.

Everything in her world was about to change, ready or not.

She was already different due to this child. Her bones had shifted, her pulse was wilder and her hair was longer. She looked in her dressing glass and thought her eyes burned a different hue than they had before, some brand-new color that couldn't be named.

She was transforming. She was round and taut and ready to burst, to become something new all over again.

Ready or not.

After nightfall, after the clouds had darkened to gunmetal and the snow had gathered into crescent moons along the window-panes, one after another, Mr. Huntington ducked through the nursery doorway.

"Here you are," he said, sounding surprised.

"Here I am," Belle agreed. She turned and smiled, crossing to him as gracefully as her figure would allow. She braced her hands against his forearms, stood on her toes and pressed a kiss to his lips.

Such harmony, she would marvel later—years later— considering it; how lucky they both were to truly *like* each other, to have discovered that they shared such sensibly kindred spirits. Belle savored the prickle of his mustache, the flavor of him, his particular tobacco heat. He was as familiar to her as her own self these days . . . well, the self she used to be. Before his son had claimed her body and sent her fantasies of names she could not claim for either of them.

They broke apart. She'd kept him apprised of nearly every-thing the doctor had told her, most especially about how she was supposed to remain calm and cool and unmoving.

"It's frigid in here," Collis said, frowning at the empty hearth. It was true; the nursery was in the back of the house and after sunset, quickly chilled. By the light of the solitary lamp she'd carried up with her, she could follow the smoky tendrils of his breath.

"It's not time to heat the room yet. No sense in wasting wood."

"Waste it," he said. "Waste whatever you like."

"That's a hard habit to acquire, I think, after years of lack."

"Not so hard as you might conceive, my dear. Even after a lifetime of lack."

She cupped her enormous stomach. "We'll wait for the baby. After he's here, we'll keep the fire going all night."

He pushed a finger against the cradle, sent it into a slow swaying. "You have all that you require? The supplies and whatnot? Doctor Fischer assures me he'll be here whatever the hour, whenever it's time. I was thinking to hire a midwife as well."

"Mr. Huntington," she said, her smile blossoming. "You've no call to fret. I am smart and I am sturdy. My mother will do. She managed to bring forth seven us out in the countryside, and four of the seven without even the aid of my father."

Collis looked from the cradle to the window to the hearth, almost ill at ease, and without warning her conversation with Lizzie echoed in her ears, and her sister's face flashed before her eyes: golden with firelight, both mocking and smiling, warning Belle to protect her son, protect them all, with legal papers and promises.

He won't abandon us, she thought again fiercely, even as a shaft of doubt spread through her. *He never would.*

Yet Collis looked at her aslant, still with that uneasy air.

"I'm new to this," he confessed. "This part of it all, I mean."

"Believe me, so am I."

That made him laugh, short and gruff; the doubt thickening her blood began to dissolve. "My sweet demon. Shall we go downstairs?"

He turned toward the doorway, hesitated, turned back and pulled a box from his coat pocket. He looked down at his hands, surprised again. "I nearly forgot. I found this for her."

Belle took it from him, remembering another box, another place, their first quiet moments together under the shade of that tulip tree.

"For *him*, you mean," she said.

"For him." Collis inclined his head. "Naturally, him. You *have* told me, Miss Yarrington. I apologize."

She opened the lid, pushed aside the layers of pink tissue paper.

It was a silver rattle, very bright, very clever. It had a shaped handle and a round head etched with sunflowers. When she touched it, the balls inside it released a thin, fairy cascade of song.

"It's perfect." She lifted it, shook it, the notes bouncing and fading.

"It reminded me of the trains," Collis said. "The sound of their whistles from a distance, I mean." His gaze landed on the ceramic bowl holding the pins; he picked it up, studied it, turned it around twice in his big hands. "Preposterous, I know. A steam whistle and a rattle. Point of fact, they ring nothing alike, but even so . . ."

"But even so, this reminded you," she prompted, and shook the rattle again.

"When I was a younger man, those steam trumpets used to blare from far away, a promise of something coming or going. Maybe a train that was just a homestead over, or a whole county over. Sound like that carries along for miles, you know. It always does. That's how I remember it, the sound of my hopes back then." He replaced the bowl to its shelf. "Hope and enterprise, hastening to joy. Just like now."

Belle took his hand in hers, pressed it against her middle. She stood on her toes and kissed him once more.

"Your son will adore it. How could he not?"

"That was my ambition," he said gravely.

"Mr. Huntington. Have I told you lately how much I admire your soul?"

"My *soul*, Mrs. Worsham? That's a broad design, if I do say so. I'm not sure I'm worthy of such an accolade."

"I am, though," she said. "I am sure, sir."

Collis took a long breath. He gripped her shoulders. He leaned back to meet her solemn gaze. With his palms cupping her cheeks, he brought his face to hers, closing his eyes. They melted together once more, two ungainly bodies somehow both in alignment, their beautiful alignment, even around their bellies.

The pain began in the middle of breakfast, exactly halfway through her omelet. It was a Thursday morning and she was dining alone, as was her custom. Her family was back in their own house and Collis would be with his wife, or his bankers or partners or assistants; he could have been anywhere, really. It did not pay to follow his schedule too closely.

Of all the pleasures of this fine new life Belle led, breakfast was one of the best. Her morning meal was everything she used to dream it could be: warm biscuits or toast; strawberry preserves, or apricot, or fig. Fresh coffee, fresh juice—usually orange, but sometimes something more exotic, like apple or white grape. Bacon, if she wished, or sausages, or fried slices of potatoes. Cornbread or hotcakes with syrup. And omelets. Every variety of omelet.

Thursday's omelet had been stuffed with sautéed mushrooms and a mild white cheese, she couldn't even say what kind, that hinted of garlic and chives. She was so absorbed in its flavors that when the first dull cramp clenched through her, Belle hardly noticed it. Or rather, she noticed it, but almost like an afterthought. Like a commotion happening in another room, nothing nearly as important as her next bite.

It came again, though, sharper. Belle lowered her fork. She glanced around, found the little brass bell that Collis insisted she keep nearby these days, just in case, and rang it.

Part III

The Shadow Wife

1870-1878

CHAPTER 18

March 17, 1870

My Dear Emma,

Well, it's been such a storm here. I wanted to write sooner but the streets have been impassible in too many places, and the snow just kept coming. Today is the first day of cloudless sunshine I can recall in a while. The sky blazes so cobalt it smarts my eyes, and I wish I had some of those colored-glass spectacles I've seen around lately—usually on gentlemen, but so? where do they procure them, I wonder?—just to spare my vision. I will get this posted to you today, however, even if I have to trudge for miles through this miserable wet snow New York seems to serve up in spades.

Your letters have been a lifeline to poor old lonely me. It seems marriage suits you well, and perhaps Texas even better. Mother has been enthralled with your descriptions of the hills and wildflowers and crooked creeks. The boys rather more with anything to do with cowboys. Has your Mr. Warnken a brother? I might fancy a life in the wilds of Texas myself at this rate. At least it doesn't snow there.

Belle has had her baby, a week ago now. It is a boy, a great strapping pink creature that weighed in at eleven pounds at birth. Eleven!

Can you imagine? Perhaps you can but I cannot; my body shudders to consider it. The physician declared that he had never delivered an infant so large before. I really did think it was going to be twins. Even Mother thought so. I lost a dime bet with Richard on that one.

Belle endured it all well. The entire ordeal went on for a day and a half, which seemed an eternity to me (and, I daresay, Our Friend), but in the end, she had her son and the rest of us had champagne, even the doctor.

Our Friend has visited twice to see the boy. I suppose he's very busy with his business matters, starting the new railroad company and the shipyards and such. I wasn't there when he last dropped by but Belle seemed subdued when I saw her next. She swears all is fine, though, and that she's simply tired. I hope that's the truth.

I must run if I am to make this morning's post. Enjoy your Texas heat. I think Mother is considering a visit soon and perhaps I will join her, to see those wildflowers and that creek of yours for myself.

Sincere salutations to the fine Mr. Warnken from us all,
With Love,
Your Sister Lizzie

Post Script: Belle has named him Archer Milton, after Johnny (!) and Father, just so you know. A wise combination of prudence and tradition, I thought.

CHAPTER 19

Clara
Manhattan, 1870

She would remember with stark clarity the first time she'd ever heard the word *mistress*; that is, heard it used in a hushed hiss of a conversation between adults, like it was something secret and forbidden, a word little girls were not supposed to overhear and definitely not repeat.

Before that day, Clara Elizabeth Huntington had thought that *mistress* was simply what the lady of the house was called, or the lady of any other fine house. That's what her governess had told her. But words were tricky. Words could fool you into thinking they meant one thing when they actually meant the opposite. Like *cleave*, or *dust*, or *trim*.

Mistress.

Clara was ten. They'd been strolling down the December glitter of Fifth Avenue, she and Mama, Verna the maid following behind them. Clara was excited because it was daytime and snowing and almost Christmas, and they were shopping for Papa and for Clara's best friend, Patrice. Even though Santa Claus brought gifts for all the good children in the world, Mama had explained, he relied upon *them*, the families, to find gifts for everyone else, like friends and fathers and servants.

Last year Clara had given Papa a watercolor of a dove she'd painted, and while he had thanked her and kissed her cheek and told her how wonderful it was, he did not hang it up anywhere like he did with all the other paintings in their house. It lived in the back of his desk drawer, the third one down on the left. It lived there always. Every month she checked.

So, this year she wanted to buy him something instead of making it, something marvelous and perfect that he would keep out in the open, for everyone to see. A glass paperweight, maybe. Or the little golden ram on a chain she'd seen at the jeweler's, the most cunning fob for his watch.

Even decades later, Clara could easily recall her ten-year-old delight in the afternoon itself, in the slow, serene descent of the snowflakes; in getting excused from her tedious lessons to go shopping instead.

She would remember opening and closing her hands, admiring her new crimson mittens, dotted with flaky white, and the hearty crunch of the snow beneath her boots.

She would remember her mother taking her by her hand, restraining her daughter to a more ladylike pace than the hopping skips Clara's feet kept itching to try.

But mostly, she would remember the rattle.

The silver baby's rattle, gleaming like sudden treasure atop the dirty snow of the sidewalk, bright and shiny and bold, the handle tilted up to the sky.

Clara glanced around. There were two gentlemen ambling toward them, conversing in short, frosted puffs, and a solitary lady in an amethyst hat and coat with black frogging who'd just passed by. The lady was pushing a hooded buggy.

Clara tore her hand free from her mother's, scooped up the rattle and trotted back to the woman. Her mother called her name behind her, soft and dismayed.

"Excuse me, ma'am." Clara's breath also flashed with frost, briefly clouding her vision.

The woman turned, one hand still on the buggy. Her eyes met Clara's—she was very pretty—and for a second she only stared at her with a strange, almost startled expression, her lips puckered into a rosebud and her eyebrows arched. Clara instinctively stopped in place, suddenly uncertain.

She pressed the rattle to her chest, then thrust it out with both hands.

"I think you dropped this, ma'am? Or your baby did?"

And the woman transformed. She smiled at Clara, a breathtaking smile, and even though she wore spectacles, Clara realized that she wasn't just pretty, she was *beautiful*. Like the angel in Papa's Rossetti painting was beautiful, all glowing colors and creamy skin and pastel eyes.

"Why, thank you," said the lady in a musical voice.

"You're welcome."

The rattle released a tinkling song as the lady took it from the cup of Clara's mittens.

"Merry Christmas!" Clara said.

"Merry Christmas," the lady replied, yet she was no longer looking at Clara but at Mama, and her face had changed once again, had gone cool and smooth, even as her lips still curved in a smile.

Mama grabbed Clara's hand and pulled her away. She did not wish the lady a Merry Christmas of her own, only offered a stiff nod before propelling them down the block again at a pace a tad too swift for Clara's shorter legs.

The word reached her ears later that evening. It was Verna, the maid, who uttered it, who said it twice in her secret conversation with another maid, both of them whispering at the base of the main stairs, never noticing the silent child on the landing above them.

The mistress! Right here, can you believe!

Living so close, that slut, the nerve.

(It was also the first time Clara heard the word *slut*, but for some reason that particular slur did not stick with her.)

His mistress, how could he, so cruel?

Such are men and dogs, every one of them.

The nerve of it, our poor missus, the nerve.

CHAPTER 20

Journal entry of Arabella D. Worsham
February 2, 1871

How many wishes did I waste upon stars when I was a little girl, pining for a better life? Surely thousands, enough to encompass the night sky with all of its heavenly lights and then some. On the random, dazzling occasion I caught one falling, a streak of fire against pitch, I'd think, *Maybe! Oh, maybe soon* . . .

Soon certainly did rush up to greet me. Perhaps those childish wishes weren't such a waste.

True, my *better life* isn't exactly how I once pictured it would be. I am not a wife, but I *am* a mother. I didn't meet a man who scorches my heart with true love's flames, but I have something better: a man I respect, and who, I think, respects me in turn. Even if he doesn't know all of my secrets.

About two years ago I mentioned to Mother that I might drop by Johnny's faro parlor here in New York, back when he was still around, so het up and determined to sabotage our uneasy peace. I never told her that I actually went.

I don't really even know why I did it. I suppose it was just that girl's face haunting me, that haggard painted girl inside the carriage. The one who threw the bottle at my curb in what I can only guess was a gesture of exhilaration and contempt.

It turned out that Johnny wasn't even there that night; off catting around, no doubt. I wasn't afraid to run into him. I wasn't feeling afraid of anything back then, really. I gave my name to the doorman—a bald, beefy fellow with a smashed nose—who only looked me up and down before nodding and standing back.

It was louder than the parlor in Richmond. More raucous. The floor girls all wore livid pink silk, with a neckline even more outrageous than the purple moiré I'd had to endure. The Dealers were uniformly dark-haired and heavily kohled; when they smiled, their teeth shone straw-colored against their white-dusted faces. The drink girls with their trays were all blond, and I wondered if Johnny had planned it like that or it was just coincidence.

It was probably planned. Johnny'd never left any detail of his parlors to chance.

In a small surprise, I discovered a man at the piano instead of another girl, a black-haired fellow with skin the color of copper, and he played like nothing I'd ever heard before, far better than the room deserved. As I drifted near him he shot me a quick sideways look, then faced away again, closing his eyes, never pausing.

I knew that trick too.

When I turned about, the Champagne Girl stood before me. As if I'd somehow conjured her, as if I'd known it would be, the girl of the shattered bottle and the blown kisses stared back at me, her gray eyes widened.

Poor creature. If possible, her face grew even more pale; her hands shook. The champagne flutes upon her tray seemed in peril.

"Thank you," I'd said so smoothly, lifting a glass.

"Miss," the girl said, and stopped. She swallowed heavily. "Ma'am. Missus—"

"You may call me Mrs. Worsham," I'd said.

This close to her I could discern the faint, uneven pox scars that marked her cheeks and the Roman line of her nose. The feathery cracks of rouge that bled coral along the edges of her lips. That cheap fruity scent of the powder covering her face, and oh, I knew that fragrance, didn't I? Yes, I did.

I sampled the champagne—too sweet—then set the flute back upon her tray. I took the silver dollar I'd tucked into my left palm and placed it beside the flute.

I said good evening. Then I left.

I'd wanted to remind myself of the past, to stare hard at the grit and gilt of that life I used to inhabit, and I fear my plan worked a little too well, because I felt real pain for that girl. I felt sympathy. I was her not so long ago, after all, but I will never be her again. I swear to God I won't.

I am *not* a wife now, but something else: a shadow wife, kept in my place just beyond society's golden sun, pinned at the brink of propriety at the whim and courtesy of a generous man. A shadow wife, with a shadow child.

For Archer's sake, I will find a way around all that. I will find the means to elevate us both into the hard, open light.

Arabella
Manhattan, 1871

There was no wet nurse. Belle insisted upon feeding her baby herself and only Catherine had objected, and even she not very strenuously. But Belle had argued that no one would do a better job of it than Archer's own mama, and in the end, Catherine had capitulated.

It was the first time that Belle called herself *mama*, a wild and wondrous title; saying it aloud had taken maybe both of them aback. In any event, no wet nurse, and no sleep for a good many months, but that was fine. Collis didn't seem to mind so why should she?

Yet she was no martyr. When Mr. Huntington offered to pay for a nanny, Belle accepted. She remained acutely aware of the fact that she needed to play two parts. She was a mother now, yes. But she was also still a paramour.

The nanny was Irish and circumspect and a godsend in so many ways. As Belle healed and glowed and welcomed her lover back into her arms, she had time to sit and think. To gaze down at her child's beloved face and imagine him in a different place. Thriving in a different life, free of imagined shadows.

"What is a certain guarantee of success?" Belle asked her mother and Lizzie one March afternoon, with both John and Richard back at school and Archer safe with that invaluable nanny. They were idling in an enclosed rooftop tea garden, surrounded by plum tulips and potted trees and waiters who bowed and attended and didn't remark on their accents.

The sky arched blue and bald overhead. A trio of sparrows, trapped inside the glass walls, fluttered up and down, back and forth, landing in the trees and atop empty tables, pecking for crumbs before fluttering off again.

"Family," Lizzie answered, taking a bite of scone.

Belle nodded. "Yes, all right, for some. But beyond that. More reliable than that, and more accessible. Something that anyone, born into any family or station, might achieve."

"Happiness?"

"No," Belle sighed.

"Cooperation?" her sister guessed.

"No, no! Nothing so friendly. *Financial* success. What is the one action you might take, the one thing you can do, to guarantee your *financial* success?"

"Murder for hire," Lizzie said, and Belle laughed.

"Let's not go so far as homicide. Within the bounds of law, let us say. How, for example, did the first Mr. Astor who came to these shores build his wealth?"

"I don't believe smuggling opium falls within the bounds of law."

"Land," said Mother, lowering her cup, looking at Belle directly. "If the answer isn't family, or family connections—"

"Or smuggling," cut in Lizzie.

"—then it is the acquisition of property. Less volatile than stocks, more dependable than metals or bonds."

Belle nodded. "Tenants and sharecroppers, fancy girls and servants. Folks born into nothing, and who stay stuck there. Their children too. Generations of penury, of meager rewards, all because they do not own the ground beneath their feet and therefore have no way to exploit it."

"But it can't be just any land," Mother said, thoughtful. "Location matters. Rough acreage in the South sells for pennies in some places. Who wants to live in a swamp, or in wreckage, even if in a hundred years it'd be worth something? You'd need property held in just the right location *today*, preferably something up here. Something prime."

Belle smiled, brushing the crumbs from her plate to the floor for the birds. "Exactly so."

The next evening, as she and Collis lay together on the sofa before the parlor fire, Belle nestled deeper into his arms and murmured, "Could I be more content?"

She felt his huff of laughter. "I could not say, Miss Yarrington. But I will say that I don't think that *I* could be."

They lay like that, breathing in unison as the fire muttered and hissed, until she allowed herself a small sigh.

And then another.

"My demon?" he whispered, his mouth against her temple.

"There is a vacant lot for sale," she whispered back. "Near Lexington and Sixty-Ninth. I passed by it just this morning. A foreclosure. It's going to auction early next week."

He held her with his arms crossed over her chest, their respiration as one, steady and slow.

"I was only thinking," she went on, so soft. "What a fine investment it might make."

"Do you want me to bid on it, sweet Arabella?"

"No, sir," she replied, twisting a little to turn her face up to his. She smiled at him, a slow and lingering smile that he returned at once, his eyes half-lidded and bright. "I'd like you to front me the funds to bid on it myself. And then I will improve it and resell it and pay you back, with interest."

He said, amused, "Can you do it?"

"Oh, good sir." She drew a nail down his broad, heavy arm. "Just you watch."

She bid, and lost.

She bid on a different property, not quite as glamorous but still with great potential.

And lost.

"Let my secretary handle these preliminaries for you," Collis said, nuzzling her neck in bed one early night. "He's excellent at estimating market value."

She slipped out of his arms, lifted herself up to straddle him, her hair falling in scented curls around them both.

"I can do it," she told him.

"You can do it," Collis agreed, hardly a sound, and closed his eyes as he pulled her near, both of them tangled and smothered in the French satin comforter.

"You can do it, clever demon," he gasped. "I know you can."

On her fourth attempt, she won the lot.

Then the fifth. The sixth.

Small plots, none of them nearly large enough for the future she envisioned, but even so. Prime locations, prime society addresses along blocks where the prices could only rise. She would wait for a better market and then resell at a profit, then reinvest *those* funds into something better still, one transaction at a time.

It would not happen overnight. It would probably take years, maybe decades, to realize her proceeds. But Belle was gaining ground, both literally and figuratively, advancing her planned independence and that of her son, when one day another woman stepped in: Elizabeth Huntington, that rival queen in this magnificent game Belle was playing.

And everything crumbled apart.

CHAPTER 21

June 2, 1871

Emma,

At last all of our arrangements are complete. We are scheduled to arrive in Austin on the 17th. If it's possible to adequately prepare Mr. Warnken for our chaos, I trust you will do so, however I am sure he will remember us all from New York. All except for little Archer, of course.

It will be good to see your face again. I understand you're worried about how matters have turned out for us, but Arabella assures me she has the situation in hand. We must put our faith in her.

She is quite a doting mama. I think she will be very unhappy to leave her little boy behind with us in Austin when she returns to NYC in August. It seems a harsh price to pay, but hopefully all shall end well.

Much Love,
Mother

Arabella
Outside of San Marcos, 1871

Texas, Belle thought, was best experienced either early in the morning or else closer to dusk. Not quite all the way to dusk, that slow purpling that gradually blanketed the land, falling in layers of luster . . . but about an hour or so before. Just as the sun was approaching the lower quarter of the sky, yellow as a doubloon, stretching all the shadows into slate, and the wild grasses that blew tall and green and amber along the range became saturated in that magical light, like they'd been gilded by hand. Like everything, all the blades and trees and birds and brush, had been dipped in burnished gold, one by one.

She'd never seen anything like it. Such painted sunsets, such searing skies.

Such hot, blistering days.

Her sister's home was positioned between a series of hills capped with bur oak and prickly pear, and a sweep of blackland prairie studded with Mr. Warnken's cattle. The wind would smell one moment of sweetgrass and dust, and the next of pure manure. The cows would low either way, sometimes melodic, sometimes more urgent, and Archer, hearing them, would laugh in delight.

At sixteen months, he wasn't talking yet, not really. But he would listen to the restless cows in the distance carrying on their bovine conversations, and he'd open his eyes wide and shout, *Ba ba ma ba!* or something very much like it. And Belle would reply, *Yes, my treasure, of course, you're very smart*, or something very much like that. It was a game that could last for hours, since the cows hardly ever ceased their mooing as long as there was daylight and Archer, it seemed, hardly ever rested, daylight or not.

He took after his father in that, she thought. That boundless energy, barely contained by flesh and bone.

She remembered the first time Collis had held Archer in his arms, the second morning of their son's life. He'd shown up unannounced, as he usually did, just before noon, just after Belle had finished feeding her infant, had cleaned him and swaddled him and nestled him in the slow rocking cradle. The fire was hot now in the hearth; the entire household was dedicated to keeping the nursery warm since the baby had arrived.

He'd ducked into the room—if he didn't duck, the top of the doorway would definitely get him. Belle, seated in the rocking chair, smiled up at him, her hair loose, her velvet dressing gown modestly closed. It was beryl green, a color that particularly suited her, or so Collis had said.

She'd heard him climbing the stairs. It had given her time to comb her fingers through her hair, drag the curls down her shoulders and pinch color into her cheeks.

Just past the doorway he stopped, looking at her. Looking at the cradle.

"Come in," Belle invited softly. "Come and meet him, Mr. Huntington."

But he didn't. He only stood there, frozen, so she pushed out of the rocking chair, brushed a kiss to his cheek (his hands lifted to her arms, a brief squeeze of his fingers against her sleeves), then crossed to Archer. He wasn't fussing but he wasn't yet asleep; she would eventually learn that he could spend hours like that, silent and alert.

"Here he is," she whispered to him. "Here's Papa."

Collis lifted his arms again, almost reluctant. Before he could shrink back or change his mind, Belle had deposited the snug bundle of their child in them, making certain her hands remained under the blankets until Collis gathered Archer up to his chest.

He gazed down at the infant. He shook his head, still unspeaking.

"Blue eyes," Belle pointed out. "Blue, like yours." Although the doctor had told her that might change with time.

"Only look at him," Collis muttered in a tone she'd never heard from him before, rough with happiness, or awe, or dread. He gave a hushed laugh. "Only look, Arabella, at this soul we've sparked into creation, you and I."

* * *

On her sixth night's stay at Emma's Texas ranch, after a supper of boiled tongue over green beans and rice, her sisters and mother cleaned up as Belle settled Archer into the empty dresser drawer they were using as a crib. Thies—or Mr. Warnken, as Belle still thought of him, so lean and gawky, so polite he still addressed her as *Miss Arabella*—had taken Richard and John out to the barn, where there were always more chores to be tackled, although Belle didn't know if her brothers would actually tackle them well, if at all.

Archer settled to sleep nearly at once, a pleasant change. She crept out of the guest room she shared with her son and her mother, which she suspected had been an office before their arrival, slipped by the chatter drifting from the kitchen. The screen door to the back porch opened with barely a squeak; the black heat of the evening washed over her. It had surprised her that the nights out here were nearly as hot as the days, as if the sun had only turned its face aside instead of setting, and was still burning high up in the firmament, invisible to her eyes.

She unbuttoned the top button of her collar, and then the next one. She pulled the damp muslin from her skin and fanned it up and down.

The screen door pushed open again, closed. Emma walked up, drying her hands in her apron, her hair coming loose from its pins.

"I've never seen the stars so thick," Belle offered, after a moment. "Not even back in Alabama."

"No, that's true. It's different here." Emma tucked the errant strands behind her ears.

"Beautiful," Belle said, surveying the silvered land, the shimmering sky. A coyote began a tense, climbing howl far off in the hills, and she added, "Savagely so."

Emma nodded. She was thinner than when Belle saw her last, that November wedding in Belle's drawing room, everyone bundled in wool and laughing. Thinner, her hair streaked lighter and her skin darker, lines at the corners of her eyes that hadn't been there before. Or maybe they had been. Maybe they had, and Belle had been too preoccupied with her lover and her pregnancy to notice.

"Yes," her sister said. "Texas is beautiful and savage and hungry."

Belle sent her a sideward look. Beneath the spread of stars Emma met it, then angled away. She crossed to the wooden bench placed against the house's clapboard. She sat and waited until Belle joined her before speaking again.

"We don't have enough grain for the stock. You wouldn't guess it just by looking, but it's not quite enough. It's never been quite enough. We've scrimped and purchased what extra we could up till now, Thies and I, brought it up all the way from Sonora. But we're not the only ones suffering this lack. Prices have risen." Her gaze fell to her lap. She smoothed her palms along the damp apron, down her thighs, pulling and stretching the fabric. "I was hoping . . ."

"Yes?" Belle said, feeling her stomach drop.

"That you might help us out."

Belle didn't speak. A breeze lifted; the bed of milkweed and sage hedging the porch stirred into perfume.

"You've had his baby," Emma said. "Surely that matters. Even if he's sent you away for now. That must matter."

"He was not the one," she said quietly, "who sent us away."

Emma's eyebrows climbed.

Belle studied the flower bed, lacy petals and leaves still rustling with the breeze, wishing for a whirlwind, a tornado to lift away the heat, to carry her back to New York and her own home, shuttered up now with just the coachman left as caretaker.

Collis had approached it all sideways, not quite an ambush but not quite a negotiation, either, but a clever combination of them both, a tactic he'd once told her he found useful in business discussions. He'd waited until late at night, after they'd tangled together atop her mattress, after they'd devoured the cold sliced mutton and salted almonds and cheese the maid had left out, all

while still warm and huddled beneath the covers. He'd lit a cigarillo (she refused to allow cigars in the bedroom, citing the odor
trapped in the curtains), inhaled it deeply and mentioned that it
might be time for Belle to visit her sister.

*It might be time to take our son to meet her, to take your whole
family with you, if you like, for company.*

And Belle had replied, *Company?* in the most neutral tone she
could manage.

Only for a while, he went on, as the smoke from his cigarillo
curled up to the crisp blue-and-gold jacquard draped above their
heads. *A few months at most, until matters calm.*

Matters? she'd echoed, although she knew what matters those
must be.

She knows, he'd whispered. *She knows about you and Archer.*

She's known about me for years, Belle had said, a little sharper
than she'd intended. *I've never once, never* once, *asked that you put
me before her.*

*But the boy. My son. She weeps over it when she thinks I can't
hear. We've bruised her heart, I'm afraid.*

And Belle had bit her tongue at that, because his voice was
graveled and rich with what sounded like genuine remorse. Perhaps even grief. It filled her with a combination of rage and cold
fear.

We *bruised her?* she very nearly said, but mercifully didn't.

He'd sucked at that loathsome cigarillo. *Only for a while,* he
said again, *just until Elizabeth's heart has a chance to mend,* and
Belle had said ah, or oh, some other neutral thing to cover the
unpleasant sick pounding of her own heart.

And then Mr. Huntington had lifted himself up to take her in
fully, a crease between his brows, and had added almost beneath
his breath, "Not for too long, though, by God. It won't do for
too long. Even if Archer has to wait behind without you a while
longer, you will come home to me, Miss Yarrington, won't you?"

And she had murmured *yes,* or *of course,* or something like that, while her heart kept thumping *no, no, no, I can't leave him, I can't leave here.*

But half an ambush was still an ambush, and now here she was in the wilds of Texas, miles and miles from where she wanted to be.

"Ah," Emma said tightly, "I see. One would think that a woman in her position might show a little more mercy."

Belle looked back at her. Emma's jaw was set; her eyes were shining. She went on: "I've no doubt she knew *exactly* what she was marrying long before they exchanged their vows. She knew the bargain, of course she did. Those society wives always do. I bet he's given her about everything she's ever desired in her life, everything she's ever *imagined* handed to her on a fine silver platter, but that's not enough. She needs more. She needs it all, riches *and* fidelity, as if they ever go hand in hand. So now she strikes at you because she's angry at him?"

"I am a more convenient target, I think."

"Cowardice," Emma spat. "I can't comprehend how he tolerates it."

Belle sighed, tasting that heavy dark air, the sage and flowers. "It can't be easy for her, knowing about us. Knowing that when he's gone from her, he's likely with me. That we've had a baby. She clings to the life she feels entitled to—and perhaps she is entitled to it."

Emma snorted. "It seems to me that there is enough of Mr. Collis P. Huntington to go all the way around."

Belle smiled, although nothing about her situation was particularly humorous. "I don't think she views it that way."

"You've got to get back to him. You've got to find a way back north, and then convince him to honor his son."

"I'm going back in August. You know that."

"To *honor* his *son.* Even a man devoutly devoted to his wife—and forgive me, your Mr. Huntington clearly is not—will push aside a great many obstacles for the sake of his heir."

"I hardly think Archer is—"

"Of course he is," Emma interrupted. "Who else but him?"

"A good many people! His daughter, to start—"

"A daughter isn't the same—"

"His wife. He has so many siblings and nieces and nephews I can't keep them all straight—"

"And only one son. Only one Archer, blood of his blood."

Belle removed her spectacles to her lap, rubbed a hand across her eyes. She breathed through the emotions rising through her, ire and contrition and distress, her palms pressed against the slats of the bench. "I don't know," she murmured, and to her despair, it was true. "I just don't know what to do."

Emma took hold of her hand. "Go back as you've planned. Go back and remind him of all that you have to offer, while we keep your baby safe for you here. And I promise you, we *will* keep him safe. Listen to me, Belle. You have three facts in your favor. One, you are ravishing, which isn't—hush up, I'm not done—isn't remotely your most interesting quality. Two, you're one of the shrewdest people I know, in the very best sense. And three"— she crushed Belle's fingers hard, painfully hard—"you bore him a precious child. Collis Huntington may be a rich, philandering scoundrel, but he is *your* rich, philandering scoundrel. I've seen the way he looks at you when he thinks no one else is watching. I saw it time after time whenever he came by, even all the way back in Richmond. It was as if he wanted to devour you. As if he couldn't wait for all the rest of us to go the hell away so he could just . . . *be* with you, flesh and soul, or whatever that phrase might be. Whatever this is between the two of you, it's so much more than an affair. It's so much deeper. At the minimum, your hearts are forever yoked. Archer has ensured that." Emma released her grip; Belle took back her hand, shaking off the pain. "You will always share that bond between you. You know it, and so does Mr. Huntington."

The coyote cried again, a high, sustained note that splintered into *raar! raar! raar! raar!* near the end.

Belle found her glasses, wiped the lenses along her sleeve and put them back on. Emma stood up and stretched, her spine cracking. With her hands on her hips, she stared out at the view.

"He's a tycoon, little sister. A man of the world, not a fool. Don't let either of them make *you* into a fool through their petty squabbling. Go get him back. I bet he expects you to. I bet she does, too."

A week and a half after that, Belle finally caught Thies Warnken, rancher and ice skater extraordinaire, alone. It was in the barn one sunny afternoon, the same barn her brothers were struggling mightily to master with daily muckings. A quartet of horses, three paints and a Morgan, hung their heads over their stall doors.

She had brought her son with her, balanced along one hip. As they lingered near the first stall, he reached a hand to one of the paints looking back at him, a bright white blaze down its nose. Archer let out a squeal and lunged, fingers spoked. The horse responded with a curled lip and an outstretched neck.

Belle stepped back, made certain they were both out of range of those long yellow teeth. When she pushed her son's arm down again, she got a vexed *na ba ba ma!* in return.

Mr. Warnken was bent over a bale of timothy hay, slicing at its cords with a thin curved blade, releasing clouds of dust.

"How long," she asked, "until absolute ruin?"

He straightened, turned and found her standing there. He seemed bewildered by her presence, bending his head a little to peer behind her, to the open door of the barn, then back at her again. He swiped the hand without the knife across his forehead, smearing sweat and grit into thin, finger-shaped lines.

"I beg your pardon, Miss Arabella?"

"I spoke with Emma. How long until it all goes to ruin?"

Her sister's husband sucked air between his teeth, lowering his eyes.

"Six months," he confessed. "Maybe a year."

Archer babbled something to the Morgan. It turned its massive face aside and eyeballed him and whickered. Belle looked around to make certain they were alone. All she saw were the horses and a handful of chickens and what appeared to be a lone goose sleeping against the far wall, her head under her wing.

"Mr. Warnken. I will ask you this only once, and only here, between us both. I give you my word that I will not mention any of this to my sister. Did you marry Emma thinking that I would be your savior?"

"No," he answered quickly, but the blood in his neck climbed. "No, I swear, I love her. Whatever happens next, I swear."

The chickens clucked, contented, roosting in the rafters above them.

"All right." Belle hoisted her son higher up her hip; he slapped both hands against her chest. "I cannot promise you anything, but I'll see what I can do."

CHAPTER 22

Mr. C. P. Huntington
c/o the Willard Hotel
Washington, D.C.

November 23, 1871

Mr. Huntington,

Please forgive this intrusion into your very important trip. I'm so terribly worried, and I simply don't know who else to turn to. My mother writes from Texas to inform me that Archer, my little son, is awfully ill. They're not sure what's wrong, but it's definitely a fever that has lasted nigh a week, and a cough that won't cease. Mother thinks I should come down at once. I hate to ask you this, but I am begging you to procure me a ticket to Texas, and also to help me bring my family back to New York as quickly as possible. Mother writes that with the drought and all, matters at my sister's ranch have become dire. There's no money left, I guess, for even the essentials. I truly fear if they remain down there for much longer, they'll all starve.

I understand this is a great imposition, and I am ashamed to be asking it of you. I hate to be such a bother. But you have been my good friend in the past and I hope the future as well, and I know you are the only man who would, without question, come to my aid. If you can render me any assistance at all right now, sir, I promise you will have my unending gratitude. Or if you can advise me of any other course of action, I would be happy and humbled to submit to your guidance.

Respectfully,
B. D. Worsham

Telegram to Mrs. B. D. Worsham
5 Bond Street
NYC, NY
November 27, 1871

IN RECEIPT OF YOUR LETTER. TICKETS ARRANGED. DETAILS TO FOLLOW. KINDLY SEND RANCH PARTICULARS AS SOON AS POSSIBLE FOR LINE OF EMERGENCY CREDIT IN MY NAME.
##CP HUNTINGTON

CHAPTER 23

∽⟲────⟳∽

Clara
Manhattan, 1873

Many years before she would become an actual princess, with mansions of her own, with even a castle of her own, Clara would roam the halls of her parents' Park Avenue mansion alone and in the dark, because it was nearly always dark inside, and she was nearly always alone there.

Mother needed the dark, Clara was told. Mother's nerves were famously fragile. She needed solitude, and peace.

And because this isolated, crepuscular world was all she knew as a child, Clara never really paid attention to any of it. She didn't fully realize how peculiar it was to dwell constantly in dimness, or how often she was abandoned to her own devices; it was simply how she lived. How she and her parents all lived.

Yet on the morning of her thirteenth birthday, when Mama announced over breakfast that she and Papa were taking Clara to Delmonico's for supper to celebrate, Clara understood at once that it was a tremendous gift.

Delmonico's was the most popular restaurant in town, and,

Clara knew, the most exclusive. Despite the fact that Papa was a frequent patron, she herself had only been there twice before, and both times had to remember to keep her jaw snapped closed as she gazed around at all the glorious white-and-gilt décor, and all the glorious white-and-gilt people.

Delmonico's served flavored ices between courses, creamy scoops nestled in incised crystal coupes, grapefruit and lemon and orange. Their silverware was so heavy she had a hard time keeping the many knives clenched firmly in hand; she had to be on constant guard not to relax her fingers enough to cut herself. But it was worth it.

Her friends would boast of their families' dinners there, their tables, how important their names were because no one unimport-ant, of course, was allowed through the pillared entrance, guarded by a doorman at all times.

That evening, her maid helped her into her new dress—another birthday gift, peach blossom taffeta with rows of pearled scallop-ing, like icing on a wedding cake—and pinned up her hair, leav-ing only a few long chocolate curls to bounce down her back. It wasn't until Clara was all the way downstairs, waiting for her par-ents in the drawing room, before Clara's governess creaked open the door and poked her head past the frame.

Miss Elly said Clara's name, regretful.

Papa had been called away unexpectedly on business. A shame, of course, but unavoidable.

Mother had since developed the migraine.

Also a shame. Also, Clara guessed, unavoidable.

Miss Elly eased all the way into the room. She wore a black felt hat with a long maroon feather, and her pelisse of wool and mink. She was tugging on her gloves.

"You and I," she said, and Clara nodded. She followed her gov-erness dutifully out of the room.

It was a Friday evening, well after sunset by the time their car-riage rolled up to the restaurant entrance. The marble and pillars and people seemed unchanged from her last visit, even though she'd been only nine or ten when it'd happened.

Miss Elly offered Papa's name in a quiet voice to the maître d'hôtel, who inclined his head, took them both in with shrewd eyes, then summoned a steward with a bend of his finger.

They followed him to a table set for three, a riot of lilies and roses spilling from a cut-glass vase in the center.

They sat, admiring the floral arrangement and the gold chargers and plates and beautifully polished silver. Clara felt smaller than she ever had before, dwarfed by those flowers in their towering vase and the conspicuously empty chair across from her own.

Without a word, an attendant in a white jacket and gloves removed the extra setting. Somewhere across the chamber, a group of people toasted and laughed, crystal chiming.

Clara glanced around the room. It was full of customers, of course, every table filled—why wouldn't they be? She thought she recognized some of the people from church, Mr. and Mrs. Vanderbilt, for instance, the Roosevelts. Mr. Astor, talking boisterously with a circle of friends.

And there, over there at the table right next to them, stationed by a banana tree in a pot, was her friend Patrice. Her former friend actually, since Patrice had stopped scheduling visits with her, or even responding to Clara's handwritten invitations, approximately six months ago, for reasons Clara had yet to understand.

Patrice Montgomery, seated with her parents and Mae Shaw—another girl who would not deign to speak to her—and, *and*, Freddie Payne, the only boy Clara had ever liked, because he had ginger-bright hair and long eyelashes, and he'd actually kissed her knuckles when they'd been first introduced, kissed them like he *meant* it, not simply for show.

And oh, Patrice knew. She *knew*, because before she'd snipped their friendship apart like shears through a strand of yarn, Clara had confided in her about him. Had trusted Patrice with a description of this beautifully bruised new feeling in her heart.

Freddie, looking bored, finally noticed her stare. He smiled, lifted a hand and gave a tiny wave.

Patrice and Mae turned in place to see her. Neither of them smiled.

Clara dropped her gaze to her lap. When the waiter placed the first course in front of her, split pea purée, she looked at the bowl and felt her throat close.

She didn't know what she ate. She didn't even order any of it; the food simply appeared before her like magic, course after course of mush in her mouth.

"Are you enjoying the aspic?" Miss Elly asked, and Clara nodded, slicing off another jellied bite with her spoon.

"Golly, Freddie, I don't know why you'd care," said Patrice in a clear, piping voice. "She's not even who she says she is."

Patrice's mother made a shushing sound.

"Well, she *isn't*, is she, Mama? Everyone knows it. Freddie should know too."

"Patrice," her mother snapped.

Mae gave an almost soundless laugh, like a horse snorting through its nose.

Clara lifted her eyes. Patrice was reaching for her water glass, looking straight at her.

"She's nobody. She's nothing."

"Patrice Montgomery, lower your voice this instant—"

"You said it yourself, Mama. She's only adopted. She's not a *real* Huntington. They just took her in out of pity. Just a dirty little baby they found, taken in out of pity."

Miss Elly gasped aloud. Clara's head filled with an odd, remote buzzing noise. Bees swarmed in her ears, tingled and jumped along her body.

"What?" she said loudly, scraping back her chair. "What?"

Mrs. Montgomery's face was cherry red; her husband was scowling. Freddie appeared confused, glancing from Patrice to

Clara and back again, and Patrice, so flaxen-haired, so pretty, held Clara's stricken gaze and grinned.

She ended up in the ladies' washroom. It was strange, because she had no memory of how she had gotten here. She was at the table and then she was here, seated before the vanity mirror, her eyes wide and her cheeks blanched, her hands clenched into fists against her thighs.

She was not crying. She was hardly even breathing; if her heart was still pumping, she could not feel it. She only stared at herself in the looking glass, that spectral reflection of herself covered in shadows, and thought, *You are not real. None of this is real.*

A woman in a dove-gray gown and diamond earbobs strolled over, took a seat on the bench next to Clara. She reached into her reticule, took out a compact and opened it.

"You," Clara said. Her voice sounded high and squeaky, a stranger's voice, not her own. "I don't want to see you."

Her father's mistress lifted a feathery round puff from the compact, pursed her lips and blew upon it gently. Pale motes lifted with her breath; Clara smelled jasmine and spice.

"Then don't see me," the mistress said, serene. "I'm only here to powder my nose."

Clara blinked, watching the powder sift and descend to the soapstone counter, dusting it like faint sugary snow.

"You wear face powder?" she asked, distracted in spite of herself. "Like a stage actress?"

The mistress did not respond. She only tilted her head, examining herself in the mirror, and drew the puff in a slow, curving line down her throat.

"Is that why you're so beautiful?" Clara asked.

"Am I? How nice of you to say so."

"Is that it?" Clara demanded, suddenly angry, suddenly *enraged.* "Is that how to get attention? Is it all just tricks?"

"No, Miss Huntington. It's much more than that."

Papa's mistress opened her reticule again, withdrew a folded handkerchief edged in lace. She handed it to Clara, who crushed it into a ball in her hand.

"I'm not crying," she said fiercely.

"Someone is," said the woman. "Perhaps it's your poor companion out there, stuck back at the table. I suspect she's afraid to leave. She was looking rather confounded, the last I saw of her."

Clara swiped quickly at her eyes with her left hand, remembered the handkerchief in her right, and smeared away the last of her tears.

"Is it because of you? Are you the reason Papa couldn't come tonight?"

"No. My understanding is that your father had to dash off to Philadelphia at the last moment for a meeting with a banker. I'm sure he missed seeing you."

"Then," she asked, confused, "why are you here? Did you come to spy on me?"

"Heavens, what a dramatic life you must imagine I lead! No, I did not, Miss Huntington. To tell the truth, with your papa out of town, I didn't think you'd venture out tonight at all."

"My mother might have brought me!" Clara argued, even though she knew how unlikely *that* was.

"Had your mother brought you," the mistress said gently, "I would have left at once. I know what it's like to be shamed in public. I would never deliberately do that to Mrs. Huntington."

"Oh," Clara said.

"As it happens, I only came here this evening to enjoy a nice meal with my own mother."

And of all the terrible things Clara had heard so far tonight, somehow this was the worst of all: that her father's mistress actually had a *mother*. That they went out in public together. They dined together, in *public*.

She wrung the kerchief in her hands. "Do you think it's true, what Patrice said? Do you think I'm not really Mama and Papa's daughter?"

"I do not. You *are* their daughter, no matter the circumstances of your birth."

"That's not the same thing!"

The lady lowered her dark lashes, her earbobs glittering. "Isn't it?"

"It's my birthday," Clara admitted, and to her shame, felt more tears threaten to fall.

"I know. Happy birthday to you, Miss Huntington. Here, let me have a look at you."

She shifted on the bench to face Clara, lifted her chin with one cool finger.

"Not too bad," the mistress said, narrowing her eyes. "Nothing beyond repair."

She lifted the puff, touched it lightly to the end of Clara's nose. Before Clara could sneeze or think or shrink away, the mistress had stroked the puff along both of Clara's cheeks, then leaned back.

"There," she said.

Clara turned back to the mirror. She looked the same, exactly the same, just as whey-faced and red-eyed.

"It's the same," she said, despairing.

"No, you're different now," replied the mistress. "You feel it inside, don't you? You're more now than what you were before you came in here. You're stronger. You're more resilient. And nothing those little wretches can say or do can truly wound you. You remember that. No matter what comes, you think back to this moment, and you remember the truth."

Clara shook her head, her lips quivering. "You don't even know me."

"I know that you're clever. Your father told me so. I know you're unflinching, because he told me that too."

"He did?" she whispered.

"He did. And I'll tell you something else. Never once has he ever spoken of you and called you *anything* but his daughter. So that's who you are. Regardless of your original name, or that of your parents, you're a Huntington. Your papa is one of the most powerful men in the country. That power extends to his family, and those girls out there know it." She snapped the compact closed. "They're insignificant. That's why they want to hurt you."

She was the daughter of a penniless greengrocer. That's how the newspapers would portray her for the rest of her life, the heiress who had advanced from nothing to everything, a little girl born the last of five, daughter of a man who'd died in a flood in Sacramento before even her first birthday.

Clara, of course, had no memory of that father. She had no memory of any life before the one she currently occupied. She wondered sometimes if Patrice Montgomery had not delighted in tormenting her, hadn't brayed the truth about her adoption so loudly that night at Delmonico's, if Clara would have ever learned of it. Mama and Papa had certainly seemed angry enough when they'd heard what had happened.

Clara always thought that she had been named after her mother's sister, Aunt Clara. And so she had been, although it turned out that *Aunt* Clara was actually her own mother, her *other* mother. Her first mother.

It took a very long while, weeks and weeks, for Clara to come to peace with the fact that her aunt was also her mother, that her cousins were also her siblings.

After Clara Prentice's husband had drowned in that terrible flood, Elizabeth Huntington (*Mama*, Clara had to remind herself) told her that her sister, Aunt Clara, had been desperate. She had five children to support and no ready means to do so, and since Elizabeth and Collis (*Mama and Papa!*) hadn't been blessed with children of their own, they had taken in little Clara, had taken her in and admired her and loved her, and that was the story in its entirety, they swore.

She was fortunate, she knew. She was surely the luckiest young lady in the world to be who she was now, to have the adoptive parents she had.

Never mind that on Christmas Eve, she'd sat off to the side in the drawing room, where both families had gathered, and watched her cousins laugh and tear into the tinsel and paper decorating their gifts. The youngest, the smallest, Clara had claimed a chair by the evergreen tree, caught in its keen dying scent and its merry, candlelit glow, and just . . . watched.

She'd studied her secret sister, Mary Alice, seven years older and so composed; the gray of her eyes; the butter-yellow of her hair. She'd listened to her brothers' teasing, their huge donkey guffaws. Such comfortable, unrestrained laughter. Such a loving, close family.

She'd tried not to stare at the woman who had given birth to her and then given her away, like her fifth baby was a leftover favor at a party. Or at the two people she'd believed were her real parents, who had lied to her nearly her entire life.

Clara had sat there with her unopened gift on her lap and thought, *Who are all of you? I don't know any of you.*

And she had tried very hard not to hate them all.

That night after dinner, after the celebration with her brothers and sister, Clara was tucked into bed by Miss Elly. Not too long after that, Mama bustled in to give her a kiss on the forehead and bid her goodnight.

Papa had already come by and left again. He'd had an important meeting to attend and had to hurry on his way.

"Tonight?" Clara had asked, unable to help herself. "A meeting on Christmas Eve?"

Papa had nodded and said something about how railroad matters knew no holidays, and she had nodded in return, hearing the lie beneath his tone, seeing it in his eyes.

So when Mama opened the bedroom door and walked over to the bed, Clara searched her face extra hard for any signs of distress. But she didn't see any. Mama looked the same as she had all evening. Tired. Lines around her mouth when she smiled. A dry, glittering gaze, and a sprig of holly pinned in her hair, green silk leaves and wax berries, not real.

She smelled of camphor and mint.

"She wears face powder," Clara said.

Mama frowned, adjusting the bedcovers around Clara's shoulders. "Who does, darling?"

"Papa's mistress."

Elizabeth Huntington stared down at her in shock, her hands still.

"Maybe you should too," Clara said coldly. "Maybe that would help."

She rolled away, pulled the sheet up to her chin, and closed her eyes.

CHAPTER 24

⟡────────⟡

Arabella
Manhattan, 1874

REAL ESTATE NOTIFICATIONS, INCLUDING PURCHASES, SALES,
LEASES, FORECLOSURES, AND ALL VARIANCES THEREIN, FOR THE
MONTH OF OCTOBER, 1874
—*New York Legal Land Listings, Inc.*

SOLD to Mrs. Catherine S. Yarrington, the house
and bounded property at 68 East 54th Street [refer-
ence Park and Madison], for the amount of $43,000.
10/04/74. Cash paid in full, no mortgage.

CONVEYED to Mrs. Belle D. Worsham, the house
and bounded property at 68 East 54th Street [ref-
erence Park and Madison], for the amount of $1.
10/05/74. Cash paid in full, no mortgage.

Mother finished signing her name with an elaborate flourish,
Mrs. Catherine S. Yarrington, with the tail of the "n" at the end of

the line winging boldly up, then curving down below the rest of the letters, crisscrossing itself three times over in an inky stack of curves. It was a work of art, really, a relic of her languid antebellum schooling, something that might have been affixed to Papers of Great Importance, instead of a humble real estate contract.

> I, Mrs. Catherine Simms Yarrington, do hereby convey my property at 68 East 54th Street, New York City, New York, to Mrs. Belle Duvall Worsham, for the price of $1 (one dollar, U.S.), for now and in perpetuity, pursuant to all laws and statutes of the State of New York . . .

Belle dashed off a signature below her mother's that was not nearly so elaborate. Although she had faithfully practiced her penmanship during her own schooldays, her personality betrayed her. No easy flourishes, no infinity curves winging beneath. No matter how prettily she'd tried, her writing remained the same: bold and quick, heavy and dark against the page. *Belle D. Worsham.* Not a flourish to be found.

She added the date and relinquished the pen.

"Is that it?" she inquired of Collis's attorney, and the gentleman smiled and nodded. "It's done?"

"It is, Mrs. Worsham. Most of the paperwork has already been notarized and submitted, and what remains shall be filed soon, but the property is now officially yours. Congratulations on your new home."

"Thank you."

The attorney was named Mr. Martin. He had a large gray walrus mustache and sharp black eyes. His office smelled of old leather and paper, likely from all the legal books arranged in rows on the shelves behind his desk, elaborate titles with gold lettering that were almost, but not quite, legible in the afternoon light.

Mother began to pull on her gloves. Mr. Martin reached across his desk to shake Belle's hand.

"I've known Mr. Huntington for several years. His is a most

generous nature, despite the fact he does little to advertise it. It does not surprise me in the least that he has provided a home for the widow and little son of one of his close associates."

"Yes," Belle said. "Mr. Huntington has been terribly kind. I don't know what we would have done without him."

"Your husband has passed away recently? Oh, forgive me," he said, searching her face. "I did not mean to pry."

Based on his arch half-smile, on the manner in which his eyes had roved her face and figure the entire duration of their meeting, Belle rather thought he did.

"That's quite all right. It's been two years, in fact, since Mr. Worsham was waylaid by ruffians one night, on his way home to me. Poor man, he'd spent the day ministering to unfortunates. He was a preacher, you see, and he cared so *very* much for the common folk."

"Ah," said Mr. Martin.

"He gladly handed them his wallet but they stabbed him anyway, straight through his heart."

The attorney blinked. "Good heavens! How barbaric! I would think I would have heard of such an incident!"

Mother shot Belle a look. "It was in Virginia."

"Yes," she agreed. "Virginia. Back where we're from."

"Most shocking. My deepest condolences, madam."

"Thank you. May I have the key to the house, sir?"

"Of course! I have it right here." Mr. Martin opened a drawer in his desk, produced a large brass key with a red ribbon knotted to its bow. "If you will give me one moment, good ladies, I shall see you out."

"That's quite all right," Belle said again. She placed the key inside her reticule, turning to go. "We're well used to finding our own way."

Mother sat back against the squabs on the hansom cab ride to Belle's new home, both of them rocking in place with the passage of the carriage over the rough streets, and said mildly, "You do have a flair for sensational fiction."

Belle smiled out the carriage window at the trees and people passing by. "Let the lecherous Mr. Martin lie awake tonight contemplating his presumptions about Collis and the preacher's wife."

"You cannot change the ways of the world, Belle."

"No. But I can push back against them, maybe. One impudence at a time."

Her house. *Her* house, freely given to her by Collis, freely in her own name. Belle walked through it slowly, the key to the front door still clutched like a prize in her fist, the red ribbon dangling. Mother and Lizzie followed behind or sometimes went ahead, their footsteps echoing through the rooms and halls, along carpet or stairs or polished wood.

It had been sold fully furnished. Belle trailed her fingers along the tops of divans and chairs, along the square walnut table dominating the dining room, lifting her hand periodically to inspect for dust, finding none. There was that, at least, but there was also the fact that the furniture left behind by the previous owners looked well over a generation out of date. The mustard velveteen on the wing chairs in the parlor was worn thin along the arms and seats. The highboy in the main bedroom had cracked panels of mother-of-pearl, and the runner in the drawing room was worn to the nub. Scorch marks pocked the end of it nearest the hearth; she was reminded, suddenly and brutally, of the rug in the boarding house, gradually moldering away to tatters because they never had the means to replace it.

"Are you positive you want to sleep here tonight?" Lizzie asked, approaching the mantelpiece Belle was examining, mottled gray marble, heavily veined in white. Her sister pushed the toe of her boot against the fender guarding the hearth. It was shaped like a griffin, one paw raised, snarling.

"Yes, I am."

"What about Archer?"

"No, let's let him have one more night in his familiar nursery. Tomorrow the whole move can be a grand adventure for him."

"You don't want to wait for the household? Everything should be ready by two in the afternoon, three at the latest."

"No, tonight. Today. I don't want to wait a moment longer to live in this house."

Mother joined them. "You'll need fresh linens brought over. A hamper for supper, a maid—Janey, not Elise. Janey's got better sense. Someone to procure firewood, and a lot of it, I suspect."

Belle turned around to take in the drawing room, cool and gloomy without illumination, empty and expectant without the family who had dwelled here before her. All the rest of the world wheeled by the bay windows facing the street, alive with noise and the colors of autumn.

"I'll need fresh everything, I think," she said, decisive. "Yes. Why not? This home is in want of a new beginning."

"But for tonight," advised Lizzie, leaning against the wall with her arms crossed, "just start with the linens."

There was a garden attached to her new house, neglected as the furniture was, overgrown and shabby with weeds. Rose bushes twisted, unpruned, from all four corners. Abandoned pots of snapdragons and delphinium had dropped piles of petals that drifted and rolled in pale dun snakes along the dirt.

Perhaps there had once been an official gardener here. The little shed tucked against the far wall seemed to suggest so, stuffed with old rakes and shovels and sacks of potash. But everything was crusty, rusty, gummy with spiderwebs. The watering pots were so severely riddled with holes none of them could possibly hold anything but air.

No one had bothered with this small city garden for some while, not for years at least. Yet just like the house, it brimmed with potential. From the moment Belle had first glimpsed it, she knew.

Beneath the weeds was rich brown soil. Beneath the drifts of papery petals, vegetable beds were still framed in oak—plots for turnips and squash, for lettuce and radishes and cucumbers—tin markers declaring what had once thrived in each. A patch of green beans, their stakes sadly tilted like tiny abandoned lances, had been left to dissolve into the dirt.

Belle stood in the middle of it all, her hands on her hips. She squinted up at the sky, marking the path of the sun along this forgotten rectangle of earth. She took note of the direct light, of the shade. How the roses reached for the sun like they'd just erupted from some dark, bewitched forest.

All right, then. She would replant the beds, buy fresh pots of flowers. She would tame the roses and bring the rest of it back into luscious life, because she was the Yarrington who cared about shoots, who could coax them to thrive. She was the one who could make everything flourish, just like she'd told Collis all those years ago, beneath the tulip tree.

She was the one.

CHAPTER 25

⟋⟍⟋⟍

Catherine
Manhattan, 1874

Back in Richmond, in those smoky and broken-glass days near the end of the war, it had become harder and harder to barter for food. To even *find* food.

Catherine and her children had grown used to the slightly rancid flavor of salt pork mixed with chitterlings or rice or grits; a discreet slab of fatback was easy to store in the cellar of the boarding house, easy to hide. It might last for weeks, if sliced sparingly enough.

Sugar and butter and eggs were gone; fresh meat had vanished as if it'd never been. Even the stray cats and dogs had disappeared from the streets. Occasionally illicit shipments of cornmeal or flour might make their way to a certain greengrocer. Sometimes sacks of black-eyed peas. She'd done what she could to procure them.

In her darker moments, she found herself missing her life in that wretched cabin in the Alabama woods, because at least the woods had offered oyster mushrooms and berries and wild game.

Johnny Worsham, of course, could be counted upon to offer a number of delicacies that regular folks had not seen in years. But the price of dealing with Johnny Worsham meant closing your eyes and asking no questions, especially not about the Union officers who all knew him by name. Who flocked to his saloon, night after night.

She could not forget their first meeting. How Johnny had invited her into his office to discuss the terms of her daughter's employment, *like the civilized folks we are*, he'd said, so smooth-tongued. How, right in the middle of everything, one of his kitchen workers showed up with a white china plate heaped with food and placed it on the desk right in front of her: cornbread dripping with melted butter, collard greens, banana pudding, sweet potato pie. Fried chicken still so piping hot the aroma seemed to fill the room, fill her entire being, and it was all she could do not to snatch it up with her bare hands and devour it, wolflike, in front of him.

"Mrs. Yarrington," Johnny had said, smiling his terrible sweet smile at her. "Won't you have a bite? I find business negotiations nearly always more pleasant when conducted over a meal."

And that, in fact, had been her darkest moment. Because even though she'd left her children at home with nothing but that fat-back and a handful of rice, even though she thought for one second about refusing the meal for the sake of her pride, or asking somehow—begging, really—to wrap it up and take it home for her brood, Catherine had eaten every morsel. Slowly, yes. Lady-like. Yet by the time she was finished, there was hardly a crumb on the plate, and Arabella's fate had been sealed.

But only look at how it's all turned out, she told herself, watching Belle tour her new Manhattan mansion, watching her march through the ruins of its garden with the glint of a general in her eye, taking stock of all that was now hers, planning her plans. *Look at how beautifully it's all turned out. I only did what I had to do.*

To this day, Catherine couldn't bear to eat off of plain white china.

CHAPTER 26

Arabella
Manhattan, 1874

An interesting fact about shopping for furniture (or clothing or jewels or anything else) in Manhattan's most exclusive establishments was that none of the merchants seemed to care who she was or where she was from. Perhaps she'd been naïve to think it might be otherwise, that the good gentlemen offering her Egyptian cottons or antique French commodes might recognize her name, recall a whisper of the scandal attached. That they'd see through her refined Widow-from-the-South performance and close their doors in her face.

It never happened. These marvelous stores served the upper echelon of society, they liked to boast, but it seemed any echelon would do as long as their credit was good enough. And Belle's was very good, thanks to Collis. Very, very good.

No shop doors were closed to her. Frequently, in fact, as soon as the shopkeeper or salesgirl or doorman took in her stylish garments, her silks and satins and velvets, her plumed hats, she found herself offered a seat at some low, elegant table near the back, where she was served tea or coffee or sometimes wine, and quizzed gently and expertly on what type of cupboard she might be seeking, a Pennsylvania Chippendale or a New England barrel-back? Beaded doors, or glazed? Certainly, madam, they could accommodate anything she wished.

What a peculiar and heady power it was, to have money. It was as good as lightning at her fingertips, a secret magical wand from a folktale. She could wave her hand and anything she desired materialized.

Almost anything.

There were places still in this vast city that she avoided, fashionable streets that made her uncomfortable. The back of her neck would prickle; the center spot between her shoulder blades would itch, as if she were being always watched. Perhaps she was yet trailed by those old, desperate ghosts from the war, the lost wraiths from the river along her childhood home.

Some evenings her carriage would pass by Knickerbocker mansions with their windows alight, gay balls taking place inside, the crème de la crème of society celebrating within their walls, and Belle knew there would never be an inch of space spared in there for a woman like her. Not a hundredth of an inch, no matter how good she was now, no matter how many staid and proper pasts she invented. Those doors would never open.

Even Collis didn't bother with the balls. *A series of great boring events*, he would tell her, *stuffed with a great many boring people. When I need to engage in serious conversation with any of them, which is seldom, I do it in my office or at the clubs.*

And oh yes, the clubs. There were several superior ladies' clubs sprinkled about town, unfathomable places where the most influential women of New York would meet and take tea and rip reputations to shreds, all smiles all the while. Belle had noticed her first one by chance one day not six months past. It had been May, bright and pretty, and she was walking hand in hand with Archer on a mission to find ice cream or pastries after an impromptu excursion to the playground. He'd been especially enthusiastic about the idea of a cream puff. Belle had been attempting to remember exactly which confectionary shop she'd passed by before on Park Avenue that sold them—red brick front with a striped awning? limestone with no awning? why did all the storefronts here look so alike?—when they were forced abruptly to halt. A trio of matrons had surged directly in front of them from their carriage to the curb without looking, without offering a *Pardon us!* or even pausing their discussion.

". . . couldn't possibly include her," the tallest one was saying in a low, untroubled tone. "Her mother returned from the Continent in disgrace. You heard about Mrs. Atherton and the count, did you not?"

One of the other women was straightening the line of her skirts. "Surely, Lina, the affair is not the daughter's fault."

"The stain of the mother stains the child. I am sorry to state it so candidly, but it is so. Also, the girl's face is covered in spots."

"Mrs. Astor is correct," asserted the third, as they began to climb the steps to an unassuming building Belle had never noticed before, a rectangular brass tablet with the words GOLD SALON READING ROOM, MEMBERS ONLY affixed discreetly by the left door. "We simply cannot afford her entrance to the masque. Not when we have so many other *good* girls in line, hoping for recognition . . ."

Here is what Belle would always remember about this moment, her first brush with the infamous Mrs. Caroline Astor and her cohorts: the stiff taffeta of their wraps, whishing and rustling. Their pale, grim faces, riders of the apocalypse with hair severely combed, their mouths squashed; the clicking of their pearls, heavy ropes swinging against their bosoms and waists. Belle's invisibility, hers and her son's both, as they stood barely three feet away on the sidewalk, awkwardly but willingly halted in place.

She and Archer remained a moment longer, watching together as the matrons vanished into the mysterious interior of the building, still talking.

The club's doors had clicked open without fanfare, closed again. Belle never even glimpsed the doorman.

The carriage driver in blue livery at the curb snapped his reins, called out *Hep! Hep!* and the team trotted off in a fuss of snorts and clattering hooves.

Archer was gazing up at her. "Were they rude, Mama?"

"Yes, my love." She smiled at him. "Very rude. But, remind me, didn't you want a cream puff? Or did I forget? Was it broccoli instead? A broccoli puff?"

"No! Cream!"

"Cod liver oil puff?"

"Cream!"

"Dirt flavored, I assume."

"Cream!"

"En français, s'il vous plaît."

"Chou à la crème," Archer said carefully.

"Très bien! ¿Y ahora en español?"

Archer hesitated. Belle laughed and bent down to hug him. "That's all right, darling, I'm not sure, either. We'll look it up in one of our great big books when we return home, all right?"

He nodded; Belle straightened.

"I remember now. We want cream puffs, of course."

"Yes!"

They walked on, his hand so steadfast and small, so tight around hers.

About a month after she'd moved into her new home, in the midst of a brisk, windswept November, Collis had arrived for their thrice-weekly dinner. She'd seated him opposite her at her new dining room table (delivered that very morning; kingwood, not walnut, inlaid with scrolling vines), the position a husband would occupy across from his wife, though neither of them mentioned it.

He said, "I see the house is coming along nicely. The nursery is an improvement over the last one, at least. Does Archer enjoy it?"

"Archer," she replied, "is so besotted with the new rocking horse you've given him that I think he would not notice if he were housed at Buckingham Palace."

Collis chuckled, spooning up the soup. It was terrapin, normally too greasy for her taste, but tonight's version was surprisingly light. "I'm pleased to hear it. And the new chef seems to be working out? Senator Dennis was not at all pleased I lured him away from his household, I may mention. I'll have some mending to do there, I fear."

"I don't think your mending will be in vain. We're to have peaches in chartreuse jelly for dessert tonight. Monsieur claims it's his specialty. No doubt he means to impress you mightily."

"I am well prepared to be impressed." He scraped up the last of the soup, leaned back in his chair. The fire in the hearth guttered sullen orange and gold, in want of a fresh log, but neither of them stood to attend to it.

He had taken to wearing a skullcap, an affectation she was prepared to dislike, but to Belle's surprise, it suited him. It made him look wise and confident instead of just silly, the way it did other men. But perhaps that was simply Collis Huntington overall, the very element of him. So substantial, so imposing. Whatever he wore, it was difficult to imagine him as anything less than what he was.

How different it was for women, she mused. As comfortable as she was around him, as satisfied as she might be, she would never relax enough to let him see anything but her best self, whether in haute couture or a negligée spun from cobwebs of lace, her hair pinned up in a strict knot or tumbling down her back. Every color in her home, every hand-carved stick of new furniture, was devised to flatter her; she'd be a fool to design it otherwise. Belle knew her lover's desire for her ran deeper than the mere union of their bodies, but she would never be so careless as to forget there were a great many—oh, Lord, a *great* many—young and beautiful women sparkling through the veins of Manhattan.

She concentrated on her soup a moment longer—silent, dainty sips—before murmuring, "There is an estate sale coming up next week. The Robinson place."

Collis looked away from the dying fire, attentive.

"A venerable old family collection," she said. "Furnishings, paintings, figurines. The entire lot of it will be up for auction."

"Is that so? I hadn't heard."

She tilted her head, sent him a smile. "I think this chamber is in want of some fine art, don't you?"

"A potentially astute investment," he agreed, returning her smile. "Sam Avery, my art man, could accompany you. He has a discerning eye."

"Actually," she began, replacing her spoon to her bowl, "I was wondering if *you* would do me the honor of accompanying me to the auction, so that we might peruse the collection together? I trust your judgment above all things."

Another gamble, another risk. She knew the enormity of what she was asking of him, this glorious, extraordinary leap she hoped he would take. To be seen together in public, even platonically. To openly have their names and faces linked—and, by extension, their son's. And so Belle made certain that her eyes never left his, that her smile did not falter. She reminded herself for the thousandth time that the fresh aubergine paint on the wall behind her lifted the dark red in her hair into cherry, emphasized the cream of her skin and the paleness of her irises. That the gown she wore was deep green and clinging.

Even the cheerful vases of sunflowers decorating the table were meant to remind him of open skies and light.

Every moment, every little thing, her whole world, so exquisitely planned. Now all she needed was for him to comply with her next, crucial step.

Mr. Huntington rapped his knuckles against the arm of his chair, looking at the fire, back at her, his blue gaze somber.

"Shall I beg you?" she asked softly.

"Never," he replied, very serious. "What is the date of the auction?"

"Next Thursday."

He gave a nod. "I shall look forward to it, Mrs. Worsham."

She felt an electricity along her spine, a pressure in her chest she hadn't even been aware of until this instant, begin to recede. "Truly?"

"Indeed."

"Then . . . oh, I can't wait!"

"Ah," he said, sitting up as Janey brought in the second course, baked ham and apples in orange sauce. "My favorite."

Which, of course, Belle already knew. Because she was the flatterer, the designer of this small, exquisite world.

CHAPTER 27

Clara
Philadelphia, 1876

By the Fourth of July, America's first World's Fair was in full swing, and Americans were turning out by the millions to enjoy it. The Centennial International Exposition of Arts, Manufactures and Products of the Soil and Mine, as it was officially called, had over 30,000 exhibits from thirty-seven countries—Clara had memorized that much at least, from the newspaper articles—and hundreds of buildings within its compound, more than she could easily count. She and Miss Elly had already paid fifty cents apiece to ascend a ladder positioned against an enormous copper arm and hand holding a torch; they'd been able to clamber over the top and stand upon the torch's base itself, waving down to the people below, many of whom waved back. The arm and hand and torch were going to be part of an even more enormous statue of Libertas that would eventually end up in New York Harbor, standing on her own little island. The fee Clara and her governess had paid would help fund its pedestal.

"When your children one day see the finished statue," Miss

Elly said, "you may boast to them that you've been atop it, and that surely it would not stand there at all but for your fifty cents."

They had ridden the steam-driven monorail, and sampled exotic new foods like dried kernels of corn fried in oil until they exploded—a salty, crunchy hot treat that dissolved in her mouth—and a tangy sweet tomato sauce called *catsup* spread on slices of bread, which she cared for rather less.

In their five days there so far, Clara and Papa and Miss Elly had admired the sunken gardens and fountains fanning through the Moorish extravagance of the Horticultural Hall, and the paintings and statues and objets d'art from around the world in the stately Memorial Hall. Papa had been especially interested in the Machinery Hall, full of engines and guns and cannons and tools—and mostly men. The racket there had given Clara a headache.

For four blissful hours she had gotten lost in the Main Exhibition Building (*The Largest Building in the World!* exclaimed the papers), free of her governess, simply wandering around seeing whatever she liked, talking to whomever she wished. But there were policemen on patrol specifically to reunite lost children with their parents, and as Clara was sixteen—no longer a child, thank you—she had managed to avoid the embarrassment of being hauled back to her place at Miss Elly's side by walking back to their hotel and having a bellman there send a note to her father (in a meeting with the mayor of Philadelphia) informing him that she was safe.

On the evening of their sixth and final day, Miss Elly wanted to revisit the Women's Pavilion, but Clara had seen enough of its domestic virtues. She wasn't especially interested in the newest inventions for washing dishes or stretching lace. She made a persuasive argument to go back to *her* favorite exhibit, the Japanese Dwelling and Bazaar, by reminding Miss Elly that Papa had had a hand in it by ensuring the many goods on display there made it to the Fair aboard his trains, for free, at the request of the Bureau of Transportation commission.

There was not time to visit both. Miss Elly finally agreed that they might go their separate ways, with certain provisos. Clara swore with her hand over her heart that she would not wander off to unknown places, that she would not speak to strangers, especially strange men, most especially strange Frenchmen. And that she would not dine on anything *too* foreign, for risk of upsetting her digestion.

So, for only the second time since her arrival, Clara walked alone down the broad avenues that led one to the very best of what Germany had to offer, or Sweden, or Africa's Gold Coast. She reached the Japanese Dwelling, erected in the early days of the Fair by native Japanese men using native Japanese materials, she'd read, and dutifully toured its inside, admiring room after room of spare elegance, of sliding paper doors and softly gleaming lacquer and woven reed mats.

But her real goal was the bazaar. She'd seen the most cunning little ivory carving of a dragon for sale a few days ago, and if it was still being offered, she would purchase it. Papa had given her pin money for such things, but the only thing Clara had bought so far was a set of silver souvenir teaspoons for her mother.

Yet when she searched the stalls, she couldn't find the vendor selling the dragon. It had been displayed on a table with many other tiny figurines, but where she thought she'd seen it last was now a man selling miniature pine trees in dull glazed pots. She asked him about the table with the carvings, using her hands to indicate how small they'd been, most of them no larger than a melon ball, really. He nodded and said something about *nets-kay*, and then he shook his head.

"Sold out," he said, smiling. With a slight bow, he lifted one of the baby trees in its pot, offering it to her from across the table with both hands. Clara, nonplussed, took it from him. It looked as if it had struggled to grow in a constant, sideways wind.

"It is a bonsai tree," said a woman coming to stand at her side, holding a saucer of pastel-colored dots of dough, a paper napkin caught in her fingers underneath. She glanced down at Clara. "It will outlive you if you care for it well, with proper light and water."

Clara felt herself flush, although she didn't know if it was with shock or anger or indignation. She tightened her grip around the container and the twisty stems of the little pine quavered.

"Of course," she said, and laughed, a thin, splintery sound. "Of course you're here too. Why wouldn't you be?"

"Why wouldn't I be?" Papa's mistress agreed. "It is a magnificent event, a once-in-a-lifetime event. Everyone should be here. Besides, I've enjoyed gathering ideas for new décor. The bedroom sets in the Japanese house are particularly inspiring."

"Are you where he steals off to at night?"

The mistress lifted one shoulder in a shrug.

Clara's stomach churned. She tried to hand the tree back to the vendor so she could leave, but he simply kept smiling at her, his arms at his sides.

"It would be a unique memento," the mistress said, lifting a pale green dot the size of a silver dollar with her bare fingers, severing off a delicate bite. "A reminder of your happy times here."

"They *were* happy."

"Oh, don't be churlish. I'm only trying to be amiable."

Clara glared down at the tree. She exhaled, very slowly.

"There isn't a lot of light in my house," she said at last.

"Surely there must be sunlight in your own bedroom? All it wants is a windowsill, and you will have a companion for life."

"I don't need a tree growing in my room. How big will it get?"

"Why, likely not much bigger than it is right now. It might require a bit of pruning, but that's all. Isn't that so, sir?"

The vendor nodded vigorously. "Full grown already. Beautifully grown."

The mistress smiled. "There, you see? Beautifully grown, just like you."

The little pine looked forlorn to Clara, all twisted sideways, its branches oddly bent. She supposed it *did* possess a *kind* of beauty, a sad sort of beauty, trapped by itself in its small container.

"Very well," she said.

"Do you need money for it?" the mistress asked.

Clara replied, very dignified, "I do not."

When Clara had finished her transaction, accepting her new bonsai tree in a bamboo basket, she turned around and found that the mistress had retreated to a stone bench not far down the path, still holding her saucer of doughy dots. She was watching Clara with an expression of interest but did not lift a hand to invite her over, or wave farewell, or anything else.

Clara stood there, undecided, as people passed by and the other vendors in their stalls talked about their wares and the sun sank, reminding her that she hadn't much time left to be alone.

She went to the bench, sat down. She set her tree on her lap, then moved it to the seat beside her.

"Where's your baby?" she asked, the first question that popped into her mind.

"With my mother, thank you."

There it was again, *mother*; the mistress had a mother; the mistress had a child. She wasn't just some odd, alien creature who had sprung from nothing, who would, someday, return to nothing. There was a family attached to her, as strange as it was to consider.

"And he's not a baby any longer," she went on conversationally. "He's already six. Lively as a lamb."

"Oh."

Clara looked down at her tree. She stroked her index finger along the top of it, following its sideways curve. Papa's mistress offered her the saucer.

"What is it?" Clara asked, suspicious. The flattened dots resembled French macarons, only without the filling.

"Mochi, so I'm told. A special treat made of sticky rice mashed into paste, mixed with sweet flavorings."

Clara remembered her promise to her governess. "Oh, I see. Um . . ."

"No? I assure you, it's delicious."

"I can't. I said I wouldn't."

"You said you wouldn't try anything new?" Papa's mistress looked at her askance, her lavender eyes sparkling behind her glass lenses. "You promised to be good and obedient forevermore?"

"Certainly not!"

"Certainly not. So you might try this. The green ones are tea flavored—"

"Tea? Why are they green?"

"I don't know. I suppose the tea itself must be green. It has a very unusual taste, but quite pleasing. And the pink ones are cherry, I believe."

Still Clara hesitated, thinking of Miss Elly, of her own mother, trapped back at home in her bed, glazed and silent.

The mistress said, "Come, Miss Huntington. I was informed you are unflinching."

"How do you—is there no fork?"

"The gentleman selling them offered me a pair of chopsticks to eat them with, but I have yet to master the art of eating with sticks. He assured me that fingers are equally acceptable."

Clara removed her gloves, placed them by the bamboo basket. She took the saucer, pinched a pink dot between two fingers. It was soft and giving, not firm as she'd thought it would be.

"It's very chewy," the mistress warned. "Take small bites."

It *was* chewy and gluey, slightly difficult to swallow. The cherry flavoring was subtle, almost like an aftertaste, but when she was done with it, she found she wanted more.

She chose another pink one, squeezing it between her fingers. "Why do you always look so . . . respectable?"

The mistress appeared amused. She was dressed in blue ruched silk from head to toe; she ran a hand down the stiff ruffle edging her throat. "How should I look? Wicked? Wanton?"

It was Clara's turn to shrug.

"You're in for a great deal of disappointment in life if you always expect people's exteriors to reflect their dispositions."

"So, you *are* wanton?"

"I would say I am pragmatic, Miss Huntington. Exactly like your father."

"You're not in love with Papa?" The possibility that she wasn't took Clara aback. She thought she might have forgiven a fallen woman in love with her father, rather than one who wasn't.

The mistress frowned. She retrieved the saucer, lifted a sticky green mochi and examined it thoughtfully.

"I'm not sure it's seemly we should be having this conversation. But here we are anyway, are we not? Fair enough. Shall I tell you plainly that your father and I hold each other in great mutual esteem?"

"Esteem," Clara repeated.

"Yes."

"Because," Clara said, facing her, "my mother *loves* him."

"She is a good woman, I've heard."

"Entirely."

"Alas." Papa's mistress returned the mochi to its saucer, wiped her fingers on the napkin. "It turns out that I'm only good when I try to be."

A year later, after a lavish, long-planned redecoration of the Park Avenue mansion had been completed (the entire Huntington family had removed to the Windsor Hotel for the duration of it, just over a month), Clara was utterly unsurprised to discover the new bedroom suite installed in her parents' chamber was of ebonized Japanese lacquerware, extravagant and gilded and evocatively familiar.

CHAPTER 28

Journal entry of Belle D. Worsham
August 14, 1877

I face now an unforgivable choice. The loss of my life here in my beloved New York, of everything I have worked for, my house and hearth and dreams—not to mention those of my mother and sisters and brothers. The loss of Collis Huntington.

Or, the loss of my son.

Mrs. Elizabeth Huntington, with her whining, puling ways, has yanked at his heartstrings once again. Elizabeth, who I imagine never speaks to him without great shimmery tears spilling down her cheeks; whose voice likely quivers with passion and pain like a screechy violin; who probably falls to her knees and clasps her hands to her heaving bosom as she pretends and pretends that her marriage can be salvaged, that time can be reversed, her heart can be uncleaved; her lips spitting and her hair frazzled, drowning them both in her wild demands—

He will never leave her. I know that. He may still actually love her. Whatever affection for her lingers in his heart, it anchors them together, a deadweight. I've never asked that he abandon her for me, not even for me and Archer; like a fool, I assumed the world was wide enough for us all. But to tear my own dear little family apart simply because she *can* . . .

For *him* to surrender to such outrageous terms without even *consulting* me . . .

Elizabeth.

God curse her. I loathe the very syllables of her name.

Arabella
Manhattan, 1877

In her waking dreams, Belle did not live in Manhattan. Or at least, she did not live in Manhattan by the grace of anyone but herself. She *thrived* in Manhattan, and in Paris, and London, and Budapest. She had homes in the most fashionable cities in the world. Not just homes, but mansions. Palaces. Castles of clouds.

She built nests of gold and rubies and pearls for Archer and herself. She built terraces of freedom, ready to climb to heaven, ready to entertain whom she pleased, when she pleased. She ran an empire; she *was* the empire, dependent upon no one but herself.

Sometimes these dreams pressed so close to her, loomed so present, that she had to shut her eyes and seize something solid— the back of a chair, the brass latch of a door—to stifle them. Even so, Belle could taste the flaky strudel she'd order at a café by the Danube. She could feel the ocean breeze pulsing through her hair as she stood on the balcony of her pied-à-terre in Villefranche, her skin tacky with salt. She could see Archer laughing and splashing in the cobalt waves, the two of them living their lives unbound, beholden to none.

But . . .

Those were only dreams. Imprudent idylls, really, dangerous idylls, thin as a final breath.

In her true life, Belle was not an empress. She was not free, and neither was her son.

She had her small investments, yes. She had her prime plots of land—she had her own house!—and if she wished, she could sell them all now. She'd reap a modest profit on the vacant lots, more on the house. Certainly enough to repay Mr. Huntington, as she'd promised. But it would not be near enough to turn those daydreams into reality.

In her worst moments, she lived in dread at having to move back to Richmond, to slink home with her tail between her legs, her shadow child in tow. To have to see Johnny again. To return to that life she'd hated. Infinitely worse, to subject Archer to it as well.

It would never happen. Of course it would never happen. She had enough funds to ensure that much, at least. They would not be homeless, they would not starve; she would never let them starve.

Yet whenever she found herself mired in those particularly vivid dark fantasies of Virginia, Belle realized with utter clarity that she would rather they both die than go back.

Mr. Huntington said, "She says she will leave me."

The sun was shining very brightly overhead, leaking through the loosely woven straw hat Belle wore whenever she was out working in her garden, scattering speckles of fire across her face and hands and the fine linen of her sleeves. It was a beautiful day, a cloudless day, one of those rare August delights that was not too hot but only blessed with slightly muggy air and that perfect, un-blemished light. People and wildlife were out enjoying it in force. So perhaps it was the birdsong in her ears, or the cheerful clamor of New York City thrumming beyond her garden walls, but Belle didn't really hear Collis Huntington's words, not quite at first.

But she felt them, maybe. The weight of them, falling from his lips like iron shavings.

She looked up at him from where she knelt on the ground, holding a dandelion weed she'd just pried from the earth. He had settled upon his favorite bench, the one bracketed by a feathery pair of cinnamon ferns. He wasn't looking at her but up at that flawless sky, his hands folded over his stomach and his hat back. He must've come directly from some important meeting; his suit was crisp and new; he wore a crystal tie clip carved as a horse's head that she'd never seen before. The silver in his beard and mustache glistened.

"Excuse me?" Belle said.

"She will leave me, leave our marriage. Elizabeth plans to go back to her family in Connecticut, and she will take Clara with her. She informed me of her intentions last night."

Belle was not so reckless as to say the word *divorce* out loud, but her heart leapt with it: her imprudent heart, her determined heart.

Without turning his head, Collis angled his eyes to hers, and her leaping pulse cooled.

She dropped the dandelion and sat back on her heels, concentrating on removing her clumsy leather gloves.

"What will you do?" she asked quietly.

He sighed, not answering. She came to her feet, feeling at once both light-headed and calm.

"Is this our ending, then? Are we to be banished from your life, sir?"

His eyes held hers. "No, my demon. Not both of you."

She understood him at once. "I will not be separated from Archer again," she said sharply.

Collis leaned forward on the bench, bowed his head and steepled his fingers together, almost like he was praying.

"I am a weak and selfish man. I know that. Elizabeth's been by my side for over thirty years, right there with me from almost the beginning of my journey. As a bride she traveled the continent with me, for me, without complaint, by foot and ship and mule. She helped me build our hardware store in Sacramento, the one that seeded all of my fortunes, and when it burned to the ground in the Great Fire of '52—when there was *no chance* of saving it— she still fought back the flames with nothing but her bare hands and a horse blanket she'd soaked in a trough."

With his head still bowed, Collis began to rub his palms together, up and down. His voice fell soft and fretful. "She never wavered, she never faltered, she never left me to save herself. When I lost my sight in the days that followed from those damned blinding flames, it was she who nursed me back to health. And she has *never* asked anything of me in return. Nothing like this."

"Asked of *you*," Belle said.

"I would be a worse man than I already am if I didn't acknowledge how much I owe her." He lifted his face; she had the traitorous thought that he looked so suddenly old, caught in the sunshine. "I respect her, I do. But surely you know, my darling—surely you know that you're the one who fills my heart. Who kindles my blood. You could refuse her terms, I know. You could tell us both to go to the devil and leave me well behind, and I would understand. I do not wish to lose my wife and daughter. I do not wish to lose my son. But, Miss Lenore . . . I am ensnared by you, remember? I *need* you."

She stood motionless above him, breathing through her nose, her fists clenched and her feet rooted to the ground. She felt like she was falling; she felt like she was still; she felt as though moving again would shatter her body into shards.

"Will you do this for me?" he whispered. "Will you grant me this terrible boon, even for a while? Just long enough for me to make Elizabeth see reason."

Only for a while, he'd told her once upon a nighttime, in the dark, with that stinking cigarillo and Archer not yet two. *Just until Elizabeth's heart has a chance to mend.*

"The boy can return to your sister in Texas, surely. You told me he enjoyed it there. I'll make certain he lacks for nothing, that none of your family lacks for anything ever again. More money for the ranch, university for your brothers, employment. A trust for your mother, a dowry for your sister, whatever they need. I swear it."

And when she didn't say anything, when she didn't move even her lips for fear of shattering, for fear of what words would spill out, he took the hat from his head and stood.

"Shall I beg you?"

The words spilled anyway. "Why would she do this?" Her voice sounded too high; she tried and failed to lower it. "Why does she want to take away my son?"

"Because she's in pain. Because she doesn't think either of us is strong enough to endure it as she has done. And because . . . I have told her that I cannot conceive giving you up."

Belle stared at him. She laughed a little, nodded. She slapped her gloves against her open palm, turned around and stalked back into the iron-gray shadows of the house.

Collis did not move to follow.

It was raining the afternoon she sent her child away. Not a gentle, mournful rain but a ferocious downpour, drops so vicious and hard they stabbed and sprayed the train station, the platform, the steaming iron horses and the unhappy people milling about them, needling any unfortunately exposed skin.

Belle was glad for that rain, for its hissing ferocity. It better matched her rage than a misty drizzle would have done.

A porter had already gathered up their trunks and bags—darkened and soaked like everything else under the relentlessly weeping clouds—and rolled them away, off to the gilded bowels of the private car Mr. Huntington had reserved.

Archer's fingers formed a tight curl around her own. He kept close to her side, pressing up against her pelisse and skirts. Belle tried to angle her umbrella so that it covered him completely, but rivulets of rain streamed from the spokes no matter how she adjusted it, splashing them both.

She looked down at the crown of his head, soft brown curls a little wilder than usual from the humidity. She knew those curls, each and every one, had combed them and kissed them and brushed them from his brow as he slept, so sweet and trusting in his bed, in their home. She knew his fragrance, little boy and soap and always a hint of their city life, chimney smoke and horses.

Archer lifted his face to hers; Belle made herself smile. He didn't return it, only stared up at her with grave, worried eyes.

"They're ready for us to board," Mother said, emerging from the curtains of rain with her own umbrella. A man in a dark green uniform lined with gold buttons and braid stood just behind her, his hands behind his back, his cap pulled down over his forehead. The rain dripped from the cap's black brim along his cheeks and chin.

Belle nodded. Still holding the umbrella, she sank into a crouch before her son. A pair of silk-swaddled matrons, maids dragging behind, stared and clucked and turned away.

She put excitement in her voice, bright cheer, no hint of the anguish eating like acid through her heart and her bones. "Are you ready for your grand adventure?"

But Archer was Archer, not so easily misdirected. "Are you sure you can't come with us, Mama?"

"Not right now, sweetheart, but soon, I hope. Maybe even in just a few weeks! We'll see. In the meanwhile, what a wonderful time you'll have with your grandmother and your Aunt Emma and Uncle Thies! When I see you again, you'll be a true cowboy."

"I don't want to be a cowboy." One of the engines blasted its horn; she barely caught his next words beneath it. "I just want to stay here with you and Papa. Can't I stay?"

"Not—" Despite herself the anguish took over, strangling her breath. Belle had to pause to concentrate on the wet air a moment, to reclaim her ridiculously cheerful voice. "Not just yet, but we'll come down to visit you there, both of us. Or at the very least, I will."

Archer looked at her miserably.

"Dear me, I hope *I'm* good enough!" she said, laughing. "Though I know hardly anything about ranches, so I expect you'll have to teach me about the cows and the buckaroos and whatnot."

"They are longhorns," Archer said seriously, "not ordinary cows. That's what Uncle Thies wrote."

"Longhorns. Naturally."

"Ladies," said the stationmaster in green behind Catherine, snapping closed his pocket watch. "I apologize, but the train departs in five minutes. You really must board now if you are going with it."

"Yes, of course," Catherine said, and held out her hand to help Belle rise.

The steam whistle shrilled again. Belle pressed a kiss to her son's smooth cheek, breathing in that last lingering scent of him, precious as frankincense, then straightened. The rain poured and poured.

"Bon voyage. That's what we say when we wish our loved ones a happy journey to wherever they're going."

"Bon voyage," Archer echoed, grave once more. "I love you, Mama."

"And I love you."

Catherine leaned forward, her lips skimming Belle's cheeks, the left, the right. She didn't offer tender phrases of love or farewell or any other sort of platitude when she put her mouth to her daughter's ear; instead she murmured that same familiar phrase that had shaved and whetted Belle's childhood.

"Take what you can, when you can."

Belle bit her lip, nodded. Catherine gripped her daughter's shoulder with one hand. "We'll be fine now. All of us, *all* of us, thanks to you."

And Belle knew it was true, it had to be true, because she had sacrificed her heart's blood to secure it.

"Goodbye," she said. She was glad that her voice didn't fail her again, that Archer didn't throw her another sad, searching look. He only transferred his hand from hers to Catherine's and away he went, her entire world walking away from her, devoured by the rain and this dark aching moment.

On the ride home she found her fingers clenched around a canary satin pillow on the seat beside her. She pressed it to her face and screamed and screamed, and even so the anguish would not leach from her bones.

In the back of her mind, she was half afraid of spooking the horses. But the clip of the carriage never waned.

For over a fortnight, Belle would barely speak to him.

Collis still arrived faithfully at her door, however. He would show up bearing roses, furs, diamonds. She would accept his offerings without a smile, without yielding an inch, only leading him into the dining room, where she would have their meal already waiting.

She'd ordered her chef to prepare the most toothsome dishes he could imagine; nothing could be too extravagant. She burned beeswax candles all around so that the room filled with perfume and honeyed light. She wore the most sultry gowns she owned, paired with all of her sparkling new jewels.

(Let him see her in the diamond drop necklace he'd just given her; let him think about the suggestion of her collarbone beneath that chain of scintillating gems, how the very last pear-shaped stone nestled between her breasts. Let him admire the rainbow flashing of her bracelets and rings as she ate grilled asparagus with her fingers in small, sensuous bites.)

They would dine in silence. And when the meal was finished, she would send him back to his wife.

Sixteen days of that. Fifteen nights. She gained four bracelets, seven rings, a pair of Burmese ruby earbobs so heavy they hurt to wear, two sable wraps and a houseful of flowers.

But Belle waited until the sixteenth evening to tell him what she actually required to allow him back into her bed.

"If our son is to be hidden from her view," she said, "then I refuse to be."

Mr. Huntington watched her from across the table, his plate of apple cobbler nearly scraped clean.

"I don't want to walk behind you any longer," she said. "I will be seen at your side again. Discreetly, if that still matters to you.

We can be distant relations, or old family friends. But I will stay out of the shadows, and she will stay out of my affairs."

His eyebrows lowered into a frown, but after a moment's hesitation, he only nodded. "If those are your terms, Mrs. Worsham."

"They are."

"Very well."

Belle touched her napkin to her lips, laid it upon the table. "Dinner was delicious, but I believe we are done. Shall we retire upstairs, sir?"

Part IV

The Lover

1878-1883

CHAPTER 29

❦

Clara
Manhattan, 1878

Mrs. Nicholas Fish had paneled the ceiling and walls of her ballroom in slabs of deep pink marble imported from the far peaks of Mauritania, exceptionally fine. The floor was also marble, a blush color so crystalline pale it was nearly, but not quite, white. For the occasion of her grand February Frost Ball, she had draped the chamber in miles of sheer golden silk and filled it with scores of candles, flickering in sconces or nestled in chandeliers, tiny pinpricks of illumination that combined to spread a mighty, ambered glow.

As Clara moved through that gleaming pink-and-gold light, she had the impression that she was dancing inside an enormous pearl, or perhaps the center of a rose. Poor Dirck Groesbeck, her partner for the mazurka, was concentrating so fiercely on his steps that his forehead dripped and his cheeks had turned the color of turnips. But that was likely a trick of the light.

It didn't matter. Clara was having a glorious time, a fabulous time, even with left-footed Dirck. She could dance for hours and never even feel the blisters on her heels until the next morning, when her maid would have ready a special footbath of warm water and Epsom salts.

The Huntingtons did not do the summer seasons in Newport or Bar Harbor; Father had no patience for the endless parade of fashionables, and Mother had not the enthusiasm. Clara, however, brimmed with all the longing and hope for excitement that a seventeen-year-old debutante could be expected to endure. Despite what her parents might privately prefer, Clara *would* go out, attend tea dances and salons and balls alongside her peers, at least in the city. To avoid them entirely would spell social ruin, something even Elizabeth was not willing to risk. And whither Clara went, Elizabeth, as her chaperone, had to follow.

Still, Clara knew it was a struggle for her mother. An oblation to the Gods of the Upper Cut. It was no secret that Elizabeth preferred dark rooms and silent evenings, and cold compresses for the headaches brought on by her nerves. So Clara did her best to temper her mother's unhappiness, making a point to keep an eye on her, to ensure that Elizabeth always had adequate food or drink or company on evenings such as this.

She had learned to read the lines on her mother's face as easily as if they were the hands of a clock. She could tell at once when Elizabeth had suffered enough of the social whirl just by the depth of the furrow between her eyebrows.

As Clara completed another turn—wincing as Dirck caught her toes under his—she searched reflexively for her mother, finding her standing by the champagne station with their hostess and another matron, the three of them sipping from their glasses as they gazed out at the dancers.

Unlike Dirck and most of the other people in the room, Mother was not flushed. She was, in fact, so pallid she looked almost transparent.

Another dip, another turn, and the mazurka concluded with breathless laughter and a smattering of gloved applause. Clara curtsied deeply to Dirck's bow, then lifted her fan and flexed her sore toes.

"Shall we go again?" he panted, wiping at his brow.

"Oh, better not," she said, softening the sting with a smile. "You know how people love to whip up gossip over tidbits of nothing. I think I'd better go check on my mother. She's got that frozen expression that says she needs an excuse to flee."

Dirck bowed again (it was more of a nod, really) and offered his arm. At the edge of the floor he released her without another word and moved off into the crowd. He was the scion of an old Dutch family with dwindling prospects. Clara wasn't surprised at all to watch him make his way toward Carrie Astor, holding court at the far side of the room.

She turned back to the champagne table. Knots of guests had gathered before it, mostly black-coated gentlemen fetching refreshments for their ladies. By the time Clara was near enough to find her mother again, Elizabeth was gone, leaving only Mrs. Fish and Mrs. Randolph, the other matron. Clara glanced around, spotting Elizabeth's stiff satin back and crown of curls retreating into an antechamber. She lifted a heavy fold of her skirts and began to follow, but then Mrs. Fish spoke.

"Miss Huntington. Are you enjoying yourself?"

Clara swung obediently about. "Yes, ma'am, thank you. What a marvelous gathering. Such inspired décor."

Clemence Fish gave a queenly nod. "I'm glad." She surveyed Clara up and down, her mouth smiling, her eyes heavy-lidded and bright, as Clara shifted uncomfortably on her feet.

"Congratulations on Ambassador Fish's appointment to Switzerland," Clara said, plucking that little bit of inspiration from the wrinkles of her memory. "Will you be departing soon?"

"Oh, Mr. Fish has already gone over. I don't know that the children and I will be joining him anytime soon. Perhaps late spring. We're barely beyond New Year's and I find travel so tedious, especially over the holidays. And Bern in the wintertime? I think not."

"I understand."

"Do you?" Mrs. Fish's gaze bored straight into Clara's. "But I heard that you very much enjoy traveling. I heard that you and your father and a—a cousin, was it?—are to make a grand tour of Yosemite this summer."

Clara had the uneasy sensation of being a mouse snared in a trap, one she hadn't even realized existed until the entrance had closed behind her.

"Oh, dear," said Clemence Fish smoothly, "am I mistaken? Was it just you and your father? Gracious, how embarrassing! I was only just discussing it with your mother! I could have sworn I heard you were going too. You and Senator Dennis from Maryland, and his wife, and one of your cousins."

"Ah," Clara said, relieved. "Yes, that's right. I—I believe my cousin Mary Alice is invited, along with her husband, Mr. Edward Huntington."

Mrs. Fish tapped her fan against her chin, exchanging a look with her friend. "No, that wasn't the name. Do you recall it, Georgia?"

"I do. It was a Mrs. Worsham. A niece of Mr. Collis Huntington, I was told."

Clara found, to her great mortification, that she could not speak. That her jaw was locked so tightly she found it difficult to even swallow.

Clemence Fish studied her a few seconds longer, then drained the last of her champagne. "Your mother is no doubt looking for you, child. Perhaps you'd best go find her."

Clara managed to nod. As she turned away Mrs. Randolph's coy, soprano voice followed her over the music, over the laughter and down through the light, burning her ears.

"In my experience, Clemence, *nieces* come and go. Wedded bliss, however, is forever."

"Whether we enjoy it or not," agreed Mrs. Fish dryly.

CHAPTER 30

Journal entry of Belle D. Worsham
August 6th, 1878

Disaster. Ruin. What has happened? I cannot fathom it in the least.

I feel as though I have tripped and fallen down a dark, endless well, and I am still falling. I cannot stop it.

But I must. I must.

Arabella
Merced, 1878

"How good it is to be back in California!" Collis said, descending first from their luxurious palace car to the station platform, turning around to offer Belle his hand for the metal steps. She placed her left hand atop his, her right gathering up her rose-patterned skirts. The treads were narrow and steep; she had to place her feet almost sideways upon them to keep her balance.

"Have you been here before, Mrs. Worsham?" inquired the Maryland senator touring with them, a man with a knowing gaze but a relaxed air, who so far on their trip had never failed to look her directly in the eyes, and nowhere else.

"I have not, sir. I fear I'm very little traveled."

"And this is a splendid place to get your start," Collis said. He glanced around them. "Where is Clara?"

"Here, Papa."

"Make certain you don't wander off. Stay with Mrs. Worsham or Mrs. Dennis, if you please. We'll need to board the next stage in order to reach the hotel in time. We can't afford to miss it searching for you."

"I'm eighteen," Clara said, her tone edged with exasperation. "I wouldn't wander off."

Belle tucked her arm through Clara's. "Of course not. In fact, I think you'd better make it your mission to keep your father in your line of sight. He's far more likely to head off into the unknown than the rest of us."

"It is his specialty," Clara said, and the senator laughed.

"These visionary men, Miss Huntington! You've hit the nail square on the head."

Mrs. Dennis, rather short and with a demeanor as equally astute as her husband's, joined them, fanning a hand before her face.

"My word, I thought it might be a bit cooler here. I thought we'd be by the ocean?"

Collis said, "No, madam, we are miles inland. Perhaps you thought so because the train ride from Sacramento was so effortless."

The senator laughed again. "You may cease selling your railway to us, Collis. I'm already convinced."

"Are you? Then I won't press you further, Senator. I will only allow the magnificence of our destination to speak to you."

The train station in this dusty town was hardly bustling. There were two porters wrangling their trunks and cases, a third man in a conductor's uniform walking up. Collis and the senator intercepted him, and the three of them fell into a lively discussion.

Clara slipped her arm from Belle's. "I'm already so parched.

Do you think there's water or lemonade or something inside the station?"

"Maybe," Belle said, although the building looked to be little more than a whitewashed doghouse with a sharply pitched roof. "Don't be gone long."

Clara answered that with a roll of her eyes, striding off.

"I like her," said Mrs. Dennis. "She's forthright."

"She is that."

"And you, Mrs. Worsham? I'm sorry we haven't had much of an opportunity to get to know each other yet. These rail trips can simply exhaust one to the core."

"I agree."

"You have a little boy, I'm told? But he did not accompany you now?"

Belle tensed, then feigned a smile. "No, Archer is in Texas. My sister and her husband have a fine ranch outside of Austin, acres and acres spread along the hills. My mother took him down for an extended visit. He's quite enamored of the cattle, I hear."

"Well, perhaps the next time you venture all the way out to the western coast, he'll come along."

"Yes. Perhaps."

"Oh, and here arrives the rest of our party!" Mrs. Dennis beamed at someone approaching from behind Belle, their footsteps bouncing hollow along the boards. "Mr. Huntington! Mrs. Huntington! How gratifying to see you again."

It was not, Belle reminded her nerves, Mrs. Elizabeth Huntington now standing at her back, a vindictive wife summoned, but instead the spouse of one of Collis's nephews, Edward, whom Belle had yet to meet. A nephew and his wife, joining them from back East for a brief family holiday.

A beloved nephew and a wife, she was assured by Collis, who were worldly enough to understand the nature of relationships and convenience, and tactful enough to keep their opinions to themselves.

Belle pivoted, her bland, pleasant smile—her society smile, as she thought of it—already fixed in place. The wife, round-cheeked and blond, was scanning the depot with an impatient air. Clara emerged from its doorway carrying a glass of water, and Mary Alice Huntington brightened, lifted a hand, waving.

Clara waved in return, more reserved.

"Mrs. Worsham." Collis pressed a brief touch against Belle's upper arm. "Mrs. Worsham, may I present to you Mr. Henry Edwards—Edward—Huntington, the son of my brother, and his wife, Mary Alice, who is the daughter of my wife's sister. Edward, Mary Alice, this is Mrs. Arabella Worsham, a dear friend of mine."

Belle was tired and grimy and didn't bother to untangle most of that; she only lifted her gloved hand. "What a pleasure to meet you at last."

Mary Alice Huntington stood nearer so Belle had extended her arm to her first, but her mind was already focused on the stage-coach ride ahead, on the nap she would take at the hotel, the warm bath she'd find, God willing, because traveling by rail was a dirty, exhausting business, no matter how often Collis told her it wasn't.

Mrs. Huntington said nothing, only completed a brief, limp handshake. Her gaze remained fixed somewhere near Belle's left earlobe.

Belle turned to the husband. "I've heard so much about you both. I—"

The sun was in her eyes. Years from this moment—for the rest of her life, actually—she would remember the hot flare of that California sunshine, deceptively mellow from behind the windows of the train but another beast entirely when standing beneath it unshielded, unprotected.

The shadows falling in black blades all around.

The sky enameled into blue infinity overhead.

She would remember everything about the eternity before Henry Edwards—Edward—Huntington clasped her hand in his, *and* after, when it all turned upside down. In their sunset years, she would remind him of it and he would laugh and tell her that the gods must've been feeling either very merciful toward them or else very irate, to capture them both just then in the unmistakable sorcery of California's late afternoon light.

Enchanted together. Bound together, and then torn apart.

But she had turned due west to face him on that dusty Merced platform and so, yes, the sun was in her eyes; Belle couldn't really see the gentleman standing before her, reaching for the hand she held out to him. Not much of him, anyway, not the details she would eventually come to memorize and agonize over and adore: the pale blue of his gaze, gentler than his uncle's, more spring than summer. His tanned skin, his trim jaw. Light brown hair that would, someday, slip like coarse silk through her fingers.

It would be another half hour yet, sitting across from him during the stifling ride to the hotel, before she allowed herself to notice any of these things. (Even then it was only from under her lashes, Clara's knee knocking uncomfortably against hers as the stagecoach bounced along.)

And, once noticed, Belle tried to forget.

But that was not the will of the gods. *Forgetting* was not to be either of their fates.

"—am delighted," Belle managed to finish, and threw off Edward's hand as if it burned.

"As am I, Mrs. Worsham," he said, his voice deep and soft and somehow reproachful.

Collis flattened his palm against the small of her back.

"Let's not miss the stage," he said, as Belle turned her face aside and ran a hand across her eyes, trying to clear her vision, trying to see clearly again.

The Yosemite Falls Hotel was aptly named, except for, perhaps, the "Falls" part. A long, cedar-planked lodge, it offered single rooms arranged along a corridor, two common washrooms, and a somewhat cramped dining chamber. There was also an outdoors eating area, tables and chairs scattered among the trunks of the giant trees growing all around, and that was where most of the guests chose to take their meals, breakfast at eight, luncheon at noon, and a seven o'clock dinner. There were no menus, and no other dining options.

But there was trout, fried crisp in a cornmeal batter. There were oranges set out in willow baskets, bursting with mist as they were peeled, a sharp citrus scent that would cling to Belle's nail-beds for hours. Hashed potatoes, scrambled eggs. Bowls of hot chili covered in shredded cheese, smoked salmon on chewy bread. And, one memorable night, a dinner of medallions of elk dressed in a savory mushroom sauce, the most delicious dish she had ever tasted.

Most impressive of all, there was the view: the massive, unbelievable precipices towering nearly a half mile above them, steep walls of granite hollowed with gorges, studded with trees and pools and boulders, stepping stones of the gods. Normally, Collis had told her, these mountain cliffs would be the source of the *falls* in the hotel's name, a tiered series of three separate plunges, glorious and wild. But it was August, and the meltwater creek at the top of the range had dried to a trickle.

"Even so," he murmured, his face lifted, staring up at that impossible height. A flock of birds, tiny as pins, were caught in a floating line halfway across. "Even so, how small we are down here, how fragile and mortal."

And Belle had to agree. She was fragile, she was mortal. Her heart was a slight, ridiculous muscle that would *not* rule her will, because she had worked too tirelessly and risen too far to consider a schoolgirl fantasy like love at first sight and think, *Yes, why not, I'll try that now.*

As was their custom when traveling, Belle was the one who slipped between their rooms, stealthy and swift. She did not sleep as deeply as Collis; perhaps she would never outgrow those years spent as Johnny's mule, anticipating the rise of *lilac* along the horizon. Waking just before dawn was as natural to her as taking her next breath. Her eyes would open; she'd weigh the silence surrounding her, listening for the slow, back-and-forth chatter of the earliest birds to begin. She'd find her spectacles—always on the nearest table—put them on and let the darkness come into focus.

It was no great hardship to extend their performance of *dear friends* (or sometimes *old family friends* or even *my dear niece*) by being the one who stole from his bed to return to her assigned room. All that really mattered was that she did so before the chambermaids began to creep along the hotel corridors, toting their sheets and pails and matches to refresh the morning fires.

She couldn't say at first why she awoke this particular morning, this first morning in Yosemite, with a sense of doom looming over her, heavy against her chest. Perhaps it was the novelty of her surroundings, her awareness of those cliffs lurking above them, crumbling and sheer. The fantastical pines and firs, all those branches thick as regular tree trunks suspended right above their heads.

But then she remembered the rest of it: soft blue eyes, a pleasing low voice. A milder, gentler version of Collis who had looked at her in astonishment yesterday afternoon as the light sliced across them both. Looked at her as if he'd never seen a woman sketched in sun and shade before, as if he'd never even imagined such a thing.

And she, surely appearing as dazed and stupid as she felt. *Disaster.*

Belle rolled to her side. She retrieved her glasses, eased from the bed.

Collis remained soft and relaxed, a bear in hibernation.

Her toes met the rug covering the chill of the floor. She crossed to her nightdress and robe laid ready across the chair by the door, donning both without a sound beyond the hiss of silk. She never wore slippers on these secret sojourns; even the ones with low heels could click and clack. Her bare feet were far more trustworthy.

Because the hallway beyond the room was still unfamiliar to her, she paused after closing Collis's door, one hand still on the knob behind her, her knuckles pushed against her back. The oil lamps lining the corridor were unlit; the only illumination came from windows showing squares of indigo glass. She listened carefully but heard no stirrings of life, no maids or snoring guests, not even birds. Or maybe she did hear birds; that was certainly a breeze beyond the lodge walls, puffing against the window panes, and the *teeka-dee-dee-dee* of a chickadee beneath it, perhaps?

Her own door opened soundlessly. She went to the bed and pulled back the covers, mashed her palm into the center of one of the pillows. Then she sat at the edge of the mattress, thinking.

She should try to go back to sleep. She should lie down and rumple those sheets and covers for real, rest her head against the pillow. Collis had some sort of an outing planned for everyone after breakfast, a guided horseback tour to some hidden glen he'd visited years past. She should be rested for it. She should be smiling and dewy and refreshed.

But that sense of smothering doom would not dissipate. She had the thought that a bath might help, even though she'd had one in the lodge's giant tin tub last night. With only two washrooms for thirty guest rooms, it would make sense to take advantage of these empty hours before anyone else was up, and besides, it might help her relax. The hotel had a boiler and modern plumbing, a great surprise. She wouldn't even have to wake anyone for hot water.

Belle stood, pushed her feet into her slippers. She swapped her silk robe for one of a denser paisley satin, longer and high-collared and very modest, belted at the waist. She exited her room, locked the door, and walked down the hallway, past both of the washrooms to the end of the corridor, all the way into the main room and then beyond it, out the rustic double doors fronting the hotel, because that was where her feet took her.

There *was* a breeze, and a whole host of chickadees, actually, celebrating the purple light that bled through the forest to the east. It wasn't exactly lilac, not yet, but the deep and luminous lifting of the sky that sometimes preceded it. The air smelled of damp moss and pine.

Beyond that thick rising of purple, the heart of heaven still glinted silver and black. Belle lifted her face to it. She was too old now to wish upon stars but as she watched, a single star sparked and detached from the firmament—*maybe! oh, maybe soon!*—tracing a fiery path down to earth. She followed its descent nearly all the way to the treetops before it flared again and dissolved into darkness.

Yet her eyes continued to trace that invisible curving line the star had drawn for her, down the trees and their trunks to a lone man standing at the brink of the woods, no more than thirty yards away. Dark like the forest, dark like the night, he was looking back at her, unmoving.

She couldn't quite make out his features, but she didn't need to, did she? She had known him less than twenty-four hours but she already knew the shape of him, the *texture* of him, even from this distance. With no warning at all, that sense of doom swelled up again to overwhelm her. Her soul shivered and her pulse leapt and she thought, *No, no, not here, not now—*

Amid the windsong and the birdsong and the brightening dawn, Collis's nephew lifted a hand to Belle in greeting. He took a single step toward her.

She countered with a step back. She brought her left hand to the lapels of her robe, pulling it tight against her throat as she turned about and retreated into the lodge.

From then on, she avoided Henry Edwards Huntington at every opportunity. On their communal daily outings, she stood as far from him as she could manage. She would not meet those beautiful blue eyes the color of spring. She would not be confined with him inside the same coach. When he would murmur *good morning* or *good evening* to her in his sonorous voice, Belle would only nod in return, making certain she had that false smile always in place, masking the hot dread in her blood, masking her turmoil and her treacherous heart. She devoted her attention to Collis so mercilessly that she realized, caressing his hand one evening at dinner (drawing the sour eye of Mary Alice), that she had over-stepped in public, something she'd never done before.

In the hotel's registry she was listed as Mrs. B. D. Worsham, unremarkable member of the Huntington party. She needed to return to that role.

But by their fifth day, she'd had enough. She begged off an excursion to a bison meadow, pleading a headache.

"Mrs. Worsham, are you certain?" Collis had asked, standing just outside her door.

"Yes. I just need to rest in the dark for a while. I'll be fine by tonight, you'll see. Have a marvelous time. I can't wait for you to tell me about it."

She didn't have a headache, and she couldn't bear to stay in her darkened room, which felt more like a cell, really, with its simple iron bed and wooden shutters that let the daylight leak in, and the chipped ewer and basin that reminded her too much of being poor.

She dressed and wandered outside, forgoing her hat and gloves. Although she'd missed both breakfast and lunch, there were still plenty of those plump oranges set out in their baskets, so she took two and started walking, following the trail that led to the rocky pool formed by the third and final waterfall.

"Like as not it's going to rain, ma'am," the clerk manning the front desk had warned her, without looking up from the ledger sheet he was inking in, one laborious letter at a time. "Might want to hurry."

But the sky seemed only a little threatening, a line of gray clouds darkening to the north, far enough away, she thought, to be worth the risk.

The trail took her thirty minutes or so to cover, graveled and lined with lichen and those incredibly dense trees, junipers, perhaps, some oaks and pinyon pines. They were so tall, so peaceful and widely branched it was easy to believe nothing out here had ever been felled by man. Ferns and bracken rippled green along the forest floor, interspersed with tiny wildflowers and, twice, a family of deer, tearing up grass by the mouthfuls, noting her progress with tranquil eyes.

She didn't encounter another person the entire walk. For all its emptiness, however, the forest wasn't silent. The breeze danced with the leaves above and below, and tiny rustlings along the ground told her there were likely mice or voles or whatever little rodent might make its home here. Insects sang and stopped as she neared, sang again after she'd passed by. Woodpeckers bored loudly into the trunks of the trees, *tat-tat-tat-tat*, and a pair of dark blue jays with black tufted heads screeched at her when she ventured too close to their nest.

By the time she reached the pool—not really a *pool* now, just clear shallows squeezed around massive piles of boulders—she had finished the first orange and was looking forward to the second. She emerged from the forest cover to discover the northern clouds had bubbled ominously lower and closer, devouring nearly the entire sky.

Well. She'd come this far and besides, she wouldn't melt. Belle picked up her skirts and made her way carefully along the field of stones spread before her, finding one that was both dry and not too high, with a nice flat top to sit on. She couldn't climb it while carrying the orange in one hand, so she looked around (still no one), and bit into the orange like an apple, keeping it between her teeth as she hitched her dress up to her knees and clambered to the top of the rock.

Her mouth flooded with the flavor of bitter citrus. She spat out the orange, licking her lips, grimacing. A nuthatch dived low by her head, and then three more, landing on a pine a ways away, peeping and hopping from branch to branch. The breeze ruffled by again, this time with more than a hint of rain behind it.

Just as she pressed her thumb against the broken skin of the orange, wedging her nail beneath the bite mark she'd made, a voice spoke.

"Mrs. Worsham."

Her years of being the hunted, of being the observed, had trained Belle well. She did not flinch or make a sound. She only paused with the orange cupped in her hands, then lifted her head to find Edward Huntington standing atop one of the larger boulders at the edge of the field, his hat in hand.

"What a surprise," Belle said.

He gestured awkwardly with the hat. "I didn't mean to disturb you."

She laughed a little at that. She turned her face back to the wild tumble of granite before her as the forest whispered *ruusssh* with the slippery wind.

"Might I join you? Or did you venture out here for solitude?"

"It's fine," she lied. "Please do."

In his city suit and shoes Mr. Edward Huntington began to leap like a billy goat from rock to rock, graceful and certain, until at last the way was so precarious he couldn't, so he slid down the final boulder and walked to her.

Belle resumed peeling her orange. She refused to blush, she refused to be flustered. Her heart was pounding too quickly again but that was nothing, that was all right. She was not some inexperienced debutante unused to men. She was so used to men, in fact, that she wondered what excuse he would offer to find her here, when everyone was supposed to be off admiring bison.

"I heard you were unwell," he said, not attempting to climb her rock. He smacked the brim of his Panama hat back and forth against his thigh. "I hope you're feeling better."

"I am. And you, sir?"

"I?"

"What is your alibi for escaping the day?"

He smiled, an open and handsome smile, unrestrained, and she thought despairingly that he'd probably never played poker in his life, not even faro; how easily his uncle would see through him.

You can't look at me like that.

Edward said, "I required a hiatus from adventure." He tapped a finger against her boulder. "I'm glad I've found you, actually. I wanted to apologize for the other day. The other morning, I mean."

"Oh?" she said.

"I was having trouble sleeping. I suppose I was rather wound up from the train ride—they can be so wretchedly uncomfortable, can't they? Anyway, I was awake and hoped to catch the sunrise. I've never seen one this far west before. I wasn't expecting to encounter anyone else about. I hope I didn't startle you when I waved."

"Was that you? I hadn't realized."

He tapped the boulder again, twice, very firm. "Do you mind if I . . . ?"

She tossed a scrap of peel down the other side of the stone. "Please do," she said once more, very cool as the clouds churned blackish gray against the top of the mountains hanging over them, where the waterfall would begin.

Belle didn't offer him her hand but he didn't need it, managing to reach her with just a single strong lunge. He sat down beside her, leaving a good foot between them, and resettled his hat on his head.

The orange peel was gone; she split the fruit in two, held out his half. Edward accepted it wordlessly. Together they ate and watched as the water at their feet began to wrinkle, breaking into tiny splashes against the stones. A slow curling mist was starting to form along the base of the woods, ghost tendrils that were there and then not.

He was scented of bergamot and masculine, earthy sweat; the wind took it and wrapped it around her, and Belle found herself holding her breath.

"There's a legend, you know," he said, when the orange was finished. "A native legend about this pool. The Ahwahneechee say it's full of witches."

She sent him a dubious glance.

"The spirits of witches," he clarified. "I suppose when the

pool fills in the springtime, it's quite frothing and deep. Anything might lurk in its depths."

Belle nodded, envisioning it.

"They say there was a woman once who went to draw water from it for her family, but instead of water she pulled up a basket of snakes. I think the pool was forbidden to ordinary people, and the witch spirits were so angry the woman had trespassed that they sent a whirlwind to catch up her home. The wind pulled it and her and her baby down to the bottom of the water."

"How terrible," she said.

"Yes."

"Because she took what wasn't hers."

"Yes," he said again.

The wind kicked up again, chillier than before, and Belle's heart beat *no, no, not now, not here* as she thought about kissing him, dragging her lips across his and down his neck, pressing her body against his. About how no one else would ever know, no one except maybe those vengeful witches, and his skin would burn warm against hers, tasting of citrus and salt.

"We shouldn't be here," she said.

Edward said, holding her eyes, "Only if you believe in witches," as the first rumble of thunder rolled over them, low and endless, falling down into their bones.

A raindrop hit hard between them, spattering the granite. Neither of them moved. Within seconds it was a downpour, and Edward pulled the hat from his head and shoved it onto hers. He took her hand and tugged her down the side of the rock, keeping a firm grip on her fingers as they both sprinted for the woods.

By the time they reached the lodge, the thunder was relentless and the rain was falling in sheets. The trickle of meltwater that had been the creek at the top of the mountain had surged into a rushing cascade, a true waterfall come from nowhere, and a handful of workers and guests had gathered along the dining room windows to watch its platinum descent.

Belle and Edward lingered near the entrance, drenched and dripping. She pushed her hair from her eyes; her simple coiffure had come undone at some point during their mad dash, a jumbled mess down her shoulders. She looked at Edward, also shiny wet, his hair plastered to his fine forehead, his collar wilted.

She backed away. She lifted his sodden hat between them as the rainfall spattered and drummed against the roof.

"We mustn't meet alone again," she said.

"No," he agreed, barely audible, and took the hat. "We must not."

CHAPTER 31

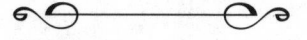

Clara
En route from Merced to Sacramento, 1878

There was a particular magic to trains. Clara had realized that years ago, all the way back to when she climbed aboard one of her father's railroad cars for the first time. She'd been not quite nine then, clinging to her mother's hand on that swarming New York platform, both terrified and thrilled at the prospect of a prolonged journey with both of her parents, of being trapped inside that enormous train like a butterfly in a bottle. It was before the transcontinental railroad had been fully completed; they'd had to go all the way down to Panama and back just to get from New York to California.

Within hours, she was enraptured.

Clara had loved every bit of it, from their brightly plush and bejeweled palace car (like the inside of a genie's bottle from a fable), to the food served in the dining car, to the way the stewards always smiled at her so kindly as they brought her an extra cookie or slice of pie for dessert. She loved watching the land streak by the windows in all different colors, forests and prairie and sometimes the sea in the distance. She loved the depots when they stopped to refuel, every one of them different yet somehow all the same: the same wooden platforms, the same rumpled travelers, the same sense of urgency in the air, everyone thinking and talking about where they were to go next.

But most especially, she loved sleeping on the train at night. It was so easy to drop into her dreams while rocking gently back and forth in her berth, her body thrumming with the *tick-tick, tick-tick* rhythm of the tracks beneath her. Young Clara felt safe and not alone somehow, as if the train itself was her friend, her protector. A magical friend who would send her to sleep in one place and let her awaken in another, like Clara and the train were stationary but the world itself had rotated around them, landing them someplace new every morning.

Even after so many years, that magic had not dimmed.

It was all so much quicker now, of course, so much more convenient. Father's locomotives could whisk them across the country in just a matter of days, a modern marvel. Yet even though the times had changed, the technology had improved and the famed golden spike that linked the West Coast to the East was housed in a museum somewhere, Clara still considered the train her secret friend, her magical protector, where nothing could go wrong. She could still fall asleep at night soothed by the familiar *tick-tick, tick-tick* of the steel wheels skimming the tracks, and awake refreshed and cheerful. The world would still spin around her while she dreamed, and every morning still landed her somewhere wonderful and new.

So she was humming a little under her breath as she strolled through the train that was putting miles between her and the impossible beauty of Yosemite, this miracle of metal and steam flying like an arrow bolt across the countryside, a palpable ode to her father's brilliance. She was making her way to the dining car, hoping for a quick meal before they reached Sacramento, where Mary Alice and Edward would catch a different line and Clara and her group would continue on due east.

It was a short journey from Merced, hours instead of days, and when Clara entered the dining car she found it almost deserted. Just a handful of people occupied the white linen-covered tables, most of them enjoying coffee or spirits as they perused the papers, a few of the gentlemen nursing cigars.

Mrs. Worsham was there, seated alone by a window, bathed in light. She had a bowl of soup in front of her but it looked untouched. Her face was turned to the glass, her hands in her lap. In the blaze of sunlight she was so bright, so fair, that it took Clara a moment to realize that Edward was there too, not at the same table but just behind her, the backs of their chairs nearly touching. He, too, was looking out the window, silent and stiff.

She paused, watching them, feeling as if she had just stumbled into a private conversation, which was silly because they weren't even looking at each other and they certainly weren't conversing. Even so, there was a suggestion of tension between them, of perhaps an argument just concluded, and she hesitated to approach.

Edward noticed her first. He came to his feet, smiled.

"Cousin Clara. The chicken mayonnaise is excellent, if you're in the mood. Forgive me, I must go find Mary Alice. Make certain we're all ready for the next leg."

"Of course," she said, but he had already brushed past her to clip down the aisle, chin lowered, quick hard steps that belied the ready ease of that smile.

Clara turned back to Arabella. She, too, was smiling, her expression relaxed and pleasant and, Clara thought, unbidden, *What a clever actress you are.*

"Do sit," Mrs. Worsham invited, indicating the chair across from hers with an elegant flick of her fingers. Clara did.

"They have mostly hot soup and cold vegetables, a few entrées," her father's mistress said. "I've only tried the soup, tomato and cream. But I heard the chicken mayonnaise is excellent."

"Yes. So Edward just said."

"Did he?" For a second her pleasant façade cracked; she

seemed flummoxed, a hint of pink staining her cheeks, but then she recovered. "Well. There you are."

One of the stewards approached. Clara ordered the chicken and a buttered roll, a glass of Bordeaux.

Tick-tick, tick-tick, whispered the train, as the great American West rushed by in smears of green and gold and brick and blue.

"Are you all right?" Clara asked, since Arabella had fallen back into her silent contemplation of the world beyond the windows.

"Perfectly. And you?"

"Yes. I love being on trains."

"Do you? That makes sense. You are your father's daughter."

"I guess I am." And because she didn't know what else to say, because she still felt that lingering awkwardness that had risen with Edward and departed with Edward and yet was somehow still here, even without Edward, Clara asked, "How is your son? I think I heard you mention he's down in Texas?"

"He is."

For the life of her Clara still could not speak the truth aloud, call Arabella Worsham's boy by his name, call him her brother, even though everyone knew that he was. Even though her mother had shed buckets of tears over it. (Enough so that Clara had, in fact, recently begun to feel a low boiling resentment toward her father, for the ease with which he moved between his two lives.)

Clara was not the naïf she'd once been. She knew that most gentlemen of her father's stature enjoyed the company of women who were not their wives, and at least Mrs. Worsham was smart and charming and attempted to be kind. Clara supposed that she was even loyal in her own way, to stay with Father all this while. But it would surely be a betrayal to call Archer Worsham *brother*; it would be like adding to Elizabeth's bucket of tears. So instead Clara merely smoothed a finger along her bangs and asked, "Is he enjoying his holiday there?"

Arabella's face changed again, a flicker of emotion so bleak and swift Clara might have imagined it.

"I hope so."

The steward arrived with the Bordeaux balanced on a silver salver. He whipped open a napkin for the table with one hand, placed the glass upon it, bowed and moved off. Clara drew the napkin and glass carefully toward her.

"When does he come home?"

Arabella shook her head, smiling again. "I don't know."

"Why, what do you mean? How could you not know?"

The mistress closed her eyes in the brilliant light. "Your mother . . ."

"What of her?" Clara said, bristling.

"Nothing," Miss Arabella said, and turned her face to stare out the window once again. "Nothing at all."

CHAPTER 32

⟋⟍＿＿＿＿＿⟋⟍

Arabella
Manhattan, 1880

DRAMA ANTICIPATED ON THE AUCTION FLOOR
—*New York Art Index Herald*
February 9, 1880

Tomorrow's auction of the Mrs. Benjamin Nathan collection is expected to draw one of the largest crowds of prominent collectors from around the nation. Officials at Leavitt's Clinton Hall Art Rooms have hired extra men to secure the entrances and exits of the rooms containing the 77 works, which include first-rate pieces by such European artists as Stammel, Kronberger, DeHaas, and Bouguereau.

Tickets are required for entry and shall be allotted on a first-come, first-served basis. Serious bidders only shall be seated near the front. Undisciplined persons or those seeking to disrupt the proceedings will be promptly removed from the premises.

She believed it human nature to be attracted to beauty, an instinct as ingrained as fear or hope or lust. The symmetry of a handsome face, the geometric spiral of a seashell. Pastel clouds marking a sunset. Colors that contrasted or complemented each other, combined into pigments, applied to a brush, applied to a canvas. That canvas applied to walls, or at least *some* walls—those of the rich, the cultivated, the aspiring.

Of those three, Belle was at least aspiring.

It was said that the combined value of the artwork amassed in New York's mansions rivaled anything to be found in the old capitals of Europe. It wasn't hard to believe; after all, nearly all of it had been imported straight from Paris or Brandenburg or some desperate, ancient estate that had once been royal, or just about royal. Old Masters paintings that once hung in the bedrooms and throne rooms of kings and emperors now crowded the walls of Mrs. Astor's brownstone, or Mrs. Morgan's, or the Belmonts'. Statues from Versailles or Caesar's Rome now stood guarding their staircases and alcoves.

Something had to fill all of those chilled, hollow spaces, the cavernous ballrooms, the epic entranceways paved with marble, traced in gilt.

Belle would never be invited to admire any of those collections. She would read about them in the society pages; she might, occasionally, come across an especially notable piece that had been lent for display at a gallery or museum.

But she had her own hollow spaces to fill, her own hallways and foyer. She had a very particular emptiness inside of her in the shape of her son, and if acquiring fine art was a way to help ease the suffering caused by that space, if filling her world—what was left of it without the heart of her heart, the sinew connecting her bones, the salt in her tears—with objects of beauty helped her to sleep and breathe and move forward, well, who could blame her?

"Mr. Huntington and Mr. Huntington, ma'am," announced the maid.

Belle turned from her reception room window in shock, followed instantly by dismay. But she only smiled as she walked forward to greet Collis and Edward, her hands outstretched.

"Mr. and Mr. Huntington! I was not expecting you both, but what a pleasant surprise. Mr. Edward Huntington, I don't believe we've seen each other since that time in Yosemite? You're looking well."

And he was: more sun-darkened than she recalled, his hair clipped a little shorter, faint lines around his mouth she didn't remember from before but that only added to a slightly more distinguished whole. He did not smile as Collis moved in front of him to take up her fingers, to press a kiss against them, but neither did he look away. He only watched her with eyes so celestial a blue she wanted to fall into them, she wanted to fly.

So instead Belle angled away, smiling brightly at Collis as he straightened.

"Edward is in town for a few days as we hammer out some business negotiations. I thought attending the auction with us would be a breath of fresh air for him. Clear the cobwebs from his thoughts."

"My thoughts," said Edward, now taking her hand in his, lightly—so lightly!—sending a frisson of electricity through her core, "are barely webbed. But I've never been to an art auction before, and my uncle made it sound invigorating."

"They can be." She crossed to the bell pull; with her back to them both she closed her eyes, opened them, then tugged on the cord.

She turned back around. "Shall we have some refreshment before we go? I've already arranged for tea. Janey? Please tell the kitchen to add another cup to the service."

"Yes, ma'am."

Belle indicated the chairs before the fire, taking a seat across from them. She laced her fingers together in her lap to hide their telltale tremor.

She had not thought of him every day in the year and half since they'd met, so briefly connected, and then parted. Not every day, but something close to it. But for Belle, Edward Huntington existed in a netherworld; she had banished him there, confined him to the mists of her memory and that forest shuddering with rain. To that dawn, with a single falling star.

For a while after her return, she nearly managed to convince herself that the entire experience had been little more than a fever dream, nothing real. Nothing substantial, and certainly nothing she ever wished to repeat.

But two months later he'd sent a letter. Hardly a letter, really, more of a note, short and polite. In a dark and precise hand, Edward had expressed his great pleasure at meeting her, and his hope that they might one day encounter each other again under similarly agreeable circumstances. It was signed by only him, no hint of his sour wife.

She had hunched in her chair as she read it, twice, thrice, taking off her glasses, holding the paper close to her face, trying to tease out words that were not there. Trying to understand what remained unwritten, because why else write her at all? Why else deliberately nudge himself into her thoughts?

Belle had burned that note, envelope and all. Had actually stood over it with the fireplace tongs in her hand until she was certain it was nothing but ash.

But her heart was a traitor. Here he was in her reception room, really *here* in the warm and actual flesh, and the same familiar distress throbbed through her.

No, no, not here, not now.

"I must say, this is a fascinating room, Mrs. Worsham." Edward's gaze roved the walls, the ceiling. "It is . . . sumptuous. You've done it up in the Moorish style?"

Belle gathered herself. The *Moorish style*, as he termed it, had cost her thousands of dollars and two years to complete, but oh— how it had been worth it. The ceiling was decorated in patterns of geometric stars and medallions, the walls hung in coral and gold silk. Carvings of palmettos and flowers lined the wainscoting, and the rugs of muted greens and blues, splashed with topaz, were so thick and new her feet sank with every step.

Taken in at once, the details were almost dizzying, but every inch was beautiful, a perfect tribute to art and order. It was as far from that parlor in Richmond, the ramshackle cabin in Alabama, as Belle could conceive.

She said, "I find the combination of the Spanish and Islamic influences fascinating. Elegance wed to logic."

Janey entered with the tea tray. Collis watched idly as the maid set the service on the table between them. "Mrs. Worsham has exquisite taste. Her perception in matters of art and décor have been of great value to me."

"No doubt," Edward said. "May I commend you on your new home, ma'am."

Belle leaned forward to pour; by now she had mastered the tremble in her hands. "Thank you, but I've had it for almost three years now."

"It's taken this long to make the damned thing habitable," Collis said. "But even so, what a coup. The location is all. She outfoxed both Rockefeller and Vanderbilt for the land around it, you know."

"I did not know."

"Mr. Huntington is exaggerating both my intelligence and my expertise. I was merely lucky."

"Luck," said Collis, "is for the slothful or the simple. And you, Mrs. Worsham, are neither."

He smiled at her warmly, she smiled coyly back, and Edward tapped a foot against the floor. "In that case, ma'am, perhaps I might persuade you to represent me in my negotiations with my uncle here. I find I'm outflanked at every turn."

Belle handed Collis a cup, then his nephew, making very certain her fingers had no contact with his. "Oh, dear. Are you attempting to negotiate with Mr. Huntington?"

"Attempting, yes. Not succeeding."

Belle lifted her own cup, sat back on her indigo settee. "What is the obstacle?"

Collis released a laugh. "My dear, you needn't actually—"

"Location," Edward said over him. "As my uncle mentioned, it is all. He would like me in Kentucky or Tennessee to oversee the construction of the new Chesapeake, Ohio and South Western lines."

"A great honor," Belle said, lowering her lashes, breaking their contact.

"Of course. But far from the home I know. Since our marriage, my—my wife and I, our children, have only lived up north, near family. I don't know how pleased Mary Alice will be with residing anywhere else. She'd prefer us in New York. I suspect her heart is set upon life in the city here."

Here. Edward living *here*, or close enough that she'd see him more and more, by coincidence or by design, with fewer and fewer excuses to avoid him . . .

Absolutely not.

Belle looked up again, found Collis surrounded by the cold winter light flooding in from the window, fringed in gold from the fire. He was watching her as he usually did, with that hard and predatory edge that used to excite her, but now only sent a skitter of warning along her skin.

Be careful, be smart.

She stared down at the surface of her tea, wishing that she'd thought to add more sugar, then set it aside. She lowered her left hand to her side, closed it into a fist and pressed her nails into her skin, letting the pain anchor her.

"I have found that the uprooting of a life, the shedding of expectations and preconceived notions of others, can be a great blessing. I lived through the war, sir. Of course, we all did, but I lived through it in Richmond, a cinder of a town, thousands of souls trapped without recourse. We suffered starvation. Ruin. And perhaps it's only what we deserved, for all the evils surrounding us that we did nothing to stop. That is for God to judge, but I can confess to you with absolute sincerity that I never thought I'd live anywhere else. Not because I did not wish it, but because it seemed impossible to me at the time that I would ever *be* anywhere else. This life I have now, this house, this city, were so far beyond the reach of my imagination back then that I—well, very honestly, I spend my hours now trapped in wonder. In gratitude."

Collis muttered, "Well said, Mrs. Worsham."

Belle smiled at him, a genuine smile now, then turned back to Edward. "If we are too timid to expand our boundaries, we're little more than mice, aren't we? I've never been to either Kentucky or Tennessee, but what a glorious opportunity for you to push against the frontiers of your life, to give your wife and children the chance to do the same."

Edward offered his own narrow smile. "How eloquently I am undone."

"That is one of Mrs. Worsham's best talents," said Collis.

"Yes," agreed Belle. "One of them."

Leavitt's Art Rooms were comprised of a two-story walnut-and-gilt auditorium with a balcony, plus two smaller chambers tucked in the back. The paintings to be auctioned this evening had been on display for a week in advance, to give the public plenty of time to survey the late Mrs. Nathan's treasure trove, to decide which piece might look best in their conservatory, which frame was too old-fashioned, how many hundreds or thousands of dollars might be shouted away in a blink if the bidding grew heated.

The auditorium was almost overflowing with people already, and it was still a half hour before the start. Collis had secured a catalogue and a chair in the third row. From her place at the edge of the balcony Belle could easily pick him out of the crowd, so much larger than any of the men around him, fanning himself with his paddle. There was an empty chair next to his, but that would be reserved for his nephew, not her. It would not do to present themselves as *too* much of a couple in public here in town, in the rarefied realm of Collis's peers—no matter how many furtive smirks Belle was accustomed to receiving.

A woman in a plaid dress and a wasp-like bustle pushed by, the ruffles of her skirt dragging along the floor. A man settled into the green velveteen seat beside Belle, placed his hat upon his knees. Without lifting her eyes, she took in his hands, clean and manicured, the starched edge of his cuffs, the golden links that punctured the linen. The worsted edge of his left sleeve had begun to fray, something a wife might have noticed. It seemed that Mary Alice had not joined Edward on his trip; Belle hadn't screwed up her nerve to ask, back at the house.

"Do you like any of the paintings?" he asked.

She pretended to immerse herself in her own catalogue. "You should be down there by now. Everything will start soon."

"Will it?" he replied, unruffled. "It seems like chaos to me still. But then, I am new to all of this."

She lifted her chin, bit back her impatience. "Mr. Huntington. We had an agreement, I thought."

"Mrs. Worsham, even you must acknowledge that we're hardly alone. We sit here literally surrounded by hundreds of vigilant, upright citizens. Anyway, I just wanted to ask if you were hoping to acquire any of the art. So I'll know when Collis offers his bid. Get a better feel for how it all transpires."

"Bouguereau," she said finally, reluctant. "There are two of his works here, and I'd take either."

"Ah." Edward opened the catalogue, ran his finger down the names of the artists until he found them. "*Crossing the Stream*, and *Mother and Child*. I remember them both—well, I saw them just a few minutes ago, so they're difficult to forget. Both purely radiant, aren't they? And both featuring a lovely mother with her youngster, water and trees and such in the background."

"That's right."

Edward crossed his legs, and it wasn't real, it wasn't true, but she could have sworn she caught the scent of that California forest, pinyon pines and storm. "You have a son, don't you, Mrs. Worsham? Is he still in the schoolroom?"

The same woman in the plaid dress jostled clumsily by again, this time going the opposite direction. She was followed by a gentleman who had crushed his catalogue in his fist, calling, "Tillie! But Tillie!" in a plaintive voice.

Belle hesitated, then said, "Archer lives in Texas with my mother and sister, at my sister's ranch there. I go down when I can."

He turned his head, his expression so calm, his eyes so infinitely patient, that she did that thing she'd sworn to herself she would not do, not with him, not ever: she dropped her guard. It was in her nature, after all, to be attracted to beauty, and what was compassion if not beautiful?

She heard herself say, "Mrs. Elizabeth Huntington finds the idea of my son being nearby . . . difficult."

"Isn't that difficult for *you?*"

"Of course it is," she flashed, and then caught herself. "But this is the bargain struck between us. This is how I placate her, how I keep Archer safe and well. How I keep *all* of us safe and well."

"I'm sorry."

"No, I apologize. My life has nothing to do with yours."

More people pressed by. From the auction floor below, a man bawled out, "Ladies and gentlemen! The ten-minute notice, if you please! This is the *ten-minute* notice!"

Belle squared her shoulders. "You should go now. You won't be allowed on the floor after the bidding begins." She offered her hand, very formal. "I hope your time down south, or wherever you end up, is satisfying to you, Mr. Huntington. Good luck."

Edward accepted her hand in his and for the second time that day, even through her kid gloves, she felt the dreadful spark of their attraction, jolting and hot, from his fingertips all the way up her spine.

"I think you should get him back," he said suddenly, leaning closer, his fingers hard around hers. "Damn the consequences. Bring your son back. Live however you must to do so. Get away from here! Travel with him, see the world with him! Don't live by any rules but your own."

Her lips parted in amazement. Rage rose in her throat, a feral beast that stole her voice and her breath.

Then she laughed, freeing her hand.

"What a romantic notion! What a rosy life you must have! Thank you for your *valued* opinion, Mr. Huntington, but I'm afraid I cannot afford your idealism."

He studied her, tanned and keen-eyed and still calm. "I've made you angry."

"Oh, no. I'd have to care about you a great deal more than I do to be angry. I am merely amused by your naïveté. Excuse me."

She rose from the seat, slapped out her skirts and walked blindly away. She only noticed she'd left her catalogue behind well after the auctioneer had pounded his gavel to close the first sale.

There was drama indeed upon the auction floor that evening, most especially for the two paintings by Monsieur William-Adolphe Bouguereau. A spirited bidding war erupted between two of the wealthiest men in attendance, which concluded with enthusiastic applause at the final price of each painting, by far the most significant sales of the event.

Collis lost one but won the other and in the end, Belle would change the title of *Mother and Child* to *Temptation*, and hang it prominently on her drawing room wall.

CHAPTER 33

Clara
Manhattan, 1882

It was an ordinary evening when she first noticed the change in her mother. Ordinary for them at least, Father gone, Clara and Elizabeth supping alone in the dusky splendor of the dining room, a solitary candelabrum in the center of the table providing the only light. Clara had pinned a fresh gardenia behind her ear before coming down, just a simple bit of pretty, but she regretted it now; the flower's perfumy fragrance clashed with that of the oysters à la russe on her plate, and she was pondering if the gardenia was more at fault or the food when she glanced up and caught the startled, pained expression on her mother's face.

Clara asked, "Are you all right?"

Mother met her eyes, the silver seafood fork clenched between her finger and thumb. "Yes. Yes, dear, I'm fine."

"You've gone quite pale."

"Have I?" Elizabeth replaced the fork to the table, slowly, carefully, as if it might shatter. "I don't think the shellfish agrees with me."

Precisely six months from this night, Clara would linger, unseen, outside her mother's bedroom chamber, listening to Elizabeth describing her symptoms to her physician. How it all began with just a jab through her stomach, short and sharp, as she tried to eat oysters; how in the weeks that followed that jab grew and grew, stabbing through her like a knife, or a hundred knives, a thousand; how the cancer consuming her felt like it was slicing at her insides, severing her organs into messy red bits while miraculously never even bruising her skin.

But that was months away. Tonight Clara only studied her mother a moment longer, mildly concerned, then said, "You know, I was just thinking the dish tasted off. Better safe than sorry. Let's move on to the soup, shall we? I believe we have oxtail tonight."

Mother smiled at her tightly. "Let's," she said, and rang the bell by her bread-and-butter plate for the footman to serve the next course.

CHAPTER 34

Journal entry of Belle D. Worsham
May 5th, 1882

How sharp as blades revelation can be. How bittersweet and heady to seize the reins when no one else wants to let you drive.

Last night I fell asleep alone, because Collis had a business supper uptown, a late one, one that would be foggy with cigar smoke and he knew how much I disliked the smell on him. Besides, he said, the Park Avenue house was closer to it than my own—as if that was all that drew him there. As if Elizabeth would not be waiting up for him as she did every night, I wager, whether he'd creep into their bed or not.

I'd fallen asleep in my own bed of loneliness, and I think that then, not even that many hours ago, I had not realized the depths of my solitude. I'd become so numb to the *apartness* of my life that it felt . . . unremarkable.

Archer and Mother and Emma are gone; my brothers are gone, scattered across states. Even Lizzie's struck out on her own, discovering her possibilities in lands none of us have yet explored. Canada. Alaska. Nova Scotia. I cannot help but think of how well these wild brilliant places will suit her wild soul.

Yet here I am, still a haunt of these New York shadows.

After breakfast I decided to visit a bookstore. Archer's last letter mentioned his growing interest in Shakespeare and Marlowe, in the mechanics of the Globe Theatre and the lives of the Lord Chamberlain's Men. It was possible a resource might be found for him in Austin, whenever Emma or Mama might get down there next, but surely the kingdom of Manhattan would offer a better selection of tomes.

I thought Erick & Cayman's would be the most likely place, and I was browsing there, looking, looking, not finding what I wanted yet in those dustless shelves lined with spines of red and blue and gold. Browsing quiet and alone in the aisles because I didn't need help from the clerks; I just wanted the time to look.

I rounded a corner, stepped around a gentleman reading in a chair, and bumped straight into Clara.

I put out a hand to steady us both, already smiling because I was so glad to see her.

"Gracious—" I began, laughing.

But she knocked my hand from her shoulder. "Stay back," she hissed at me, with such nervous intensity that I instinctively fell away. She tossed a quick look behind her, and it was so odd because I noticed then her hat, dull and plain, far too bulky for her features. I don't know why it struck me with such clarity in that frozen moment, but it did: brown felt the color of dirt, jet-dyed chicken feathers fringing the crown. And just beyond those feathers: Elizabeth Huntington in all her brassy, dumpy glory.

Clara—dear Clara, who for years now has dined with me and joked with me and confided her secrets to me—recoiled now as if I was a snake.

Her mother met my eyes. She walked calmly to Clara's side and hooked her by the elbow. It was possession, that clench of her fingers along the shiny bland silk of Clara's sleeve. Possession absolute.

"You will not subject my daughter to your degenerate presence," she said, as peaceable as if she were merely wishing me a good day.

They left together, arm in arm out the door.

And I was left standing there in the shadows, *apart*, the gentleman in his chair making a huff of complaint beneath his breath at the disturbance as he turned to his next page.

After that, I decided that today would be my last bound by the reign of Elizabeth Stoddard Huntington.

I didn't even wait to feed her husband before my ambush, to ensure he felt content and sated before I said my piece. When Collis arrived this evening, I had him escorted directly to the glamorous magnificence of my reception room. I bade him to sit while I stood before him in a slippery gown of oyster satin, a diamond collar fitted high around my throat.

I was Athena, goddess of wisdom and war. I would not be deterred or denied.

I said, "I will no longer be separated from my son."

(A sentence so close to one I'd uttered years ago, but this one would have an entirely different outcome.)

"Arabella?" He was clearly astonished, his eyebrows rising.

"You're worried your wife will leave you, I know. You're worried about the scandal. But listen to me now, Mr. Huntington. *I* will leave you. I will take Archer to Europe with me. To England and France and anywhere else I want to go. And you will be waiting for us when we return or you will not, but either way I am taking our son and going. I am reclaiming the right to his life, and—excuse me—to hell with your wife's tender sensibilities. I don't give a damn about Elizabeth's feelings. She no longer steers my course."

He pushed out of the chair, scowling, his mouth a flat line.

"It's been *years*," I exclaimed, unsettled by that look; the words began to spill from me like poison from a lanced boil. "Five *years* without him under my roof! Missing his face, missing his voice! Missing everything about his life as he grows up *without* me. Don't you see? My heart beats at half speed without him. My soul is split."

My voice began to crack, so I stopped speaking. Collis reached for my hands, held tight; his fingers felt warm and strong.

"How is yours not?" I whispered up to him, and allowed a single hot tear to slide down my cheek.

He pulled me into his arms, pressed his jaw against my temple. He released a ragged sigh.

"My soul abides in you, sweet demon, if ever I had one. So if yours is troubled, perforce mine is as well."

"I'm taking him," I insisted, still a whisper. "I'm going."

His arms tightened, released. "What am I to say? Beyond . . . please believe that I will be missing you with every stroke of my heart. With every stroke, until you come back to me. I promise you that. I will wait for you, Mrs. Worsham. For you and Archer both."

Arabella
Outside of San Marcos, 1882

Each time they met anew, Belle would fight to shove down the lurking fear that she and her son would look each other in the eyes and see only a stranger looking back. After all, for the past five years they had spent most of their time apart, months and months at a stretch. It would be only natural that such an absence from a young boy's life, such a *maternal* absence, would chip away at their bond, leave them both stranded somewhere between awkward and unknown.

But no. From the second Belle spotted him on the buckboard parked by that Austin depot, grinning and waving at her from beneath a too-big cowboy hat, it was as though a missing piece of her simply slotted into place. Archer was here; she was here; ergo she was whole once more.

Her boy. When he jumped down from the buckboard to sprint across the road to her, she saw her brothers in his lanky grace. She saw the curl of her father's hair beneath his hat, that distinctive cleft in his chin. And when Archer stopped himself short from barreling straight into her (she had backed up a step, bracing herself), falling instead into a bow with the hat whisked over his heart, she finally saw Collis. His studied manners, his ability to read her in a glance and adjust himself in response without missing a beat.

"Mother," Archer said formally, and Belle opened her arms.

"My darling."

He fell hard into her embrace anyway; she laughed and rocked him close. At twelve years old he was already nearly as tall as she, another gift from Collis. *And* he stank, a mixture of adolescent sweat and musk and dirty leather.

Belle had never known a finer scent in her life.

"Grandmother and Aunt Emma are back at the homestead. They said we'd have a feast tonight in your honor. A *feast*! I don't think we've ever had one before. Uncle Thies let me drive the team for a while on the way here and said I did a fine job! I hope he lets me drive them back."

"I can't wait," she said.

The train had arrived late. Something about needing extra coal or water or maybe just the heat warping the tracks. She'd paid attention to every rumor that rippled through the passengers, none of them ever substantiated, but for whatever reason, there was a delay, and it had cost them about six hours. So the sun was setting as her son and brother-in-law captured her bags and rearranged themselves along the buckboard, Belle seated in the front with Mr. Warnken, Archer surrendering the reins to lounge in the back, resting against her valise.

It was a particularly Texas kind of sunset, bold blue and gold clouds streaking above them, a hot apricot flare along the horizon. Pink fire everywhere else. As they turned off the main road, a mockingbird swooped low overhead, looping and returning.

Belle glanced over her shoulder to check on her son. She found him reading a book, squinting because the light was fading, holding it closer and closer to his face as the sky blazed and blushed and eventually dimmed into plum, because Archer would not relinquish a single word until it was full dark.

With Collis's monthly support, the Warnkens were now able to afford not only grain for the cattle, but two hired hands and a cook. Mrs. König had come over from East Prussia thirty years prior and still spoke with an accent so thick Belle sometimes struggled to understand her, but her cooking was sublime. The feast was to consist of pan-roasted beef and potatoes, fried okra, freshly baked bread. Soft, buttery dumplings called spätzle and a salad of sliced apples and walnuts dusted with cinnamon. After days of train travel and frankly mediocre fare, Belle had meant it when she said she couldn't wait.

She could breathe again here. In the little room they always gave her she removed her hat and its long steel pins topped with pearls, undid her hair. She changed out of her stiff traveling suit into a less formal dress of biscuit muslin, simple but still fashion-able, suitable for a family feast.

As she laid out her brushes and combs on the bureau, Belle caught a glimpse of herself in the mirror hung behind it: silvery and dim, because she'd lit only a single oil lamp, a cloud of dark hair and a serious gaze.

In the half-light she looked younger than her thirty-two years; she looked more like that Champagne Girl who'd worked so hard for Johnny, who'd worn paint and lurid silk to keep her family fed. Who had stared at herself in his foxed and tarnished looking glass and thought, *Someday I won't be here any longer. Someday I'll just walk away. I'll be free.*

She brought the lamp closer to her face, throwing gold along the lines and curves of all of her hard-won years. She smiled at her reflection in the mirror, an experiment. She whispered, "I'm happy here. I'm happy again."

And found that it was true.

"How is Miss Lizzie?" Mr. Warnken inquired, slicing the roast.

"Oh, very well, I think." Belle held out her plate when he nod-ded at her, accepting two pink slices, shaking her head at more. "She writes that she's drafting a book about horticulture, and that she's thinking of purchasing a little cabin in Maine."

Mr. Warnken appeared amazed. "Maine! Not exactly Virginia, is it?"

"No. I imagine that was the point."

Emma tapped her fork lightly against the edge of her plate, studying Belle. "You seem different."

"Do I?"

"The apples, please," Mother said to Archer, who passed the bowl with both hands.

Emma said, tilting her head, "You look . . . I don't know. More like yourself?"

"She wasn't herself before?" Archer inquired.

Emma shot him a sideways smile, a smile that hinted at a hundred shared secrets, at all the days and nights of her son's life that Belle had missed.

A pang shot through her chest. It was clear Archer hadn't been *entirely* without a maternal presence.

"Your mother was born a woodland sprite, Archer. Did you know that? Ask her someday about the birds that follow her everywhere."

"Emma," said Catherine, concentrating on buttering her bread. "Let's have a proper dinner conversation, if you please."

Emma smiled down at her plate, her hands moving, working, cutting. Her hair had loosened into tawny curls along her face, softening her cheekbones, her taut jaw. Her knife and fork clattered against the china.

"How are the boys?" Belle asked. "They don't write nearly as much as they used to."

Mother's expression relaxed. "Both are well. John is courting a young lady from Savannah, pretty enough, a bit soft, but time will tell. Richard is considering a small ranch outside of Fort Worth."

"Richard? A rancher?"

"Yes, well, we'll see."

Mr. Warnken said, "I suspect he got a taste of it from all his time spent here."

"A pleasant supposition," said Mother.

Emma lifted her head. "Like all creatures of the fey, Archer, your mother is subject to the whims of the wind and the moon and the stars." Her eyes cut back to Belle's. "When I said she looks more like herself, I mean she looks more now like she did when we were little girls."

"How?" He scooted forward in his chair.

Belle sighed as her sister pretended to consider it. Emma speared a bite of apple with her knife, her elbow propped on the table, turning the fruit slowly back and forth in the light of the lamps. "Wilder, I'd say. More elemental. A wood sprite who leads others down her own mysterious path."

Archer turned to Belle, his eyes wide. "I can see it."

"But all *I* can see is this delicious meal," Belle said. "And all I can hear is your silly aunt spinning fairy tales. And I know you're too old to believe in fairy tales, aren't you, darling?"

"Yes," he said.

No, said his gaze.

Belle returned to her food. "I do so enjoy okra. I wish we could get it up north, but whenever I find it there, it's already spoiled. I don't think the Yankee hothouses have quite mastered it."

"A shame," commented Mother.

"It is."

Emma offered, "I heard okra only grows by the light of the full moon."

Belle looked up. "What?"

"It requires just the most special, magical touch to thrive."

"Emma, really, now—"

"So if you truly want it, you or Archer when you're back up north in New York, you'll have to either summon the full moon to shine for days by the power of your will, or else come back here. Come back to the rest of us. We'll be waiting for you. We'll be—"

Emma bowed her head. She pressed her napkin over her mouth, turning her face away.

Mr. Warnken frowned but it was Mother who reached out. Past the bowl of okra and the platter of roast, she covered Emma's hand with her own.

Mother said, looking at Belle, "We'll *all* be waiting. However long it takes, we'll wait. And our Belle and Archer both will come back."

Emma nodded, her eyes squeezed closed, still covering half her face with her napkin.

Archer wanted to show her something, a special place he'd found, out riding a few weeks ago. Just the two of them, he said, and no more than an hour's ride away. Maybe two hours—all right, three—but it could have been a day's ride as far as Belle was concerned. She was just glad to be in his company, and to have him want to be in hers.

She wore a pair of trousers borrowed from her sister, an oversized cotton shirt tucked in at the waist, a heavy belt. Emma had tied a kerchief around her neck before they'd left, her knuckles bumping hard against Belle's throat, warning her about the dust storms that could whip up without warning.

"Cover your mouth and nose," she'd instructed, scowling. "Keep it tight, but don't suffocate. You won't need it anyway, the sky is clear and Archer knows what he's doing."

Belle even wore a cowboy hat, she had no idea whose. It was slightly too large, but as soon as they were out in the midday sun, she was glad for it. That, and the leather gloves covering her hands.

Archer led the way on one of the paints. Belle followed on a horse that was new since her last visit, a sturdy roan with a coarse gray mane. As they passed the corral a pair of mottled dogs decided to join them, trotting alongside with grins and lolling tongues.

They headed out into the open prairie, following a trail thinner than a whisper. At times she lost sight of it entirely; the spring wildflowers were strewn thick and vivid all around, bluebonnets and scarlet paintbrush, black-eyed Susans and clusters of delicate white rain lilies, already wilting with the heat.

As their little ensemble wound by, a herd of cows lifted their heads, placidly chewing, a lone bull in the distance eyeing them without moving. A hare sprinted from its hiding spot behind a prickly pear, capturing the attention of both dogs. They darted after it, barking madly, but returned nearly at once to lope beside the horses once more.

Belle was getting hungry. They hadn't packed anything but some bread and ham and cheese and a single canteen, all of it carried in Archer's pack. She thought about telling him she wanted to stop for a bit . . . but the day was so warm, the roan's pace so even. Bees were humming in unified splendor among the flowers, and it seemed she was more in danger of drowsing off than anything else.

The trail cut up a low hill, down into a valley, then up a steeper one. She relaxed her grip on the reins and allowed the roan his head, flower-scented air wafting by, the sky an azure bowl cupped above them. She surveyed the hills and grasses and those ridiculously bright flowers and for some reason what she saw was a forest instead. A forest of peaceful tall trees bound in mist, and rain slanting down, and her hand tight in another's, both of them running, laughing, dangerous.

Belle removed her spectacles, rubbed a hand across her eyes. She replaced her glasses and focused on the slim shape of her son ahead of her, his body rocking with the gait of his horse.

Remember this, she thought to herself. *Remember* this *moment, how perfect he is, how wonderful* this *day*.

A mockingbird trilled nearby. There seemed to be so many of them here, sweet gray songsters; when she looked up, trying to spot it, she realized three of them were weaving directly overhead, rushing back and forth.

Archer had turned in his saddle to watch them too, his face half shadowed by his hat.

"Birds do like me," she said. "Your aunt was right about that much."

"Me too," he replied, serious. "I mean, I like you too."

"We're here!" Archer dismounted with a nimble leap, the paint unflinching as the boy's boots hit the grass.

Belle followed, perhaps not quite as gracefully. They had stopped in a grove of pecan trees and black willows, fallen leaves and nuts scattered everywhere, crunching underfoot. Both dogs vanished at once into the underbrush, panting and snuffling. Cicadas trilled a loud, throbbing chorus from branches above.

Archer scooped up a couple of the dark pecans, cracked them apart in his fist. He inspected the results, then tossed them back to the ground.

"Too old," he said, dusting his hands clean. "A feast for the squirrels, maybe. But if we come back right before Thanksgiving we can harvest all we want. Mrs. König puts them in the stuffing."

"Do I hear water?"

"Yes." He grasped the reins of both horses. "This way."

The grove opened up to reveal a flat, glimmering creek studded with stones. Both horses moved willingly toward the water, lowering their heads to drink. The dogs were already there, lapping and lapping.

Archer untied his pack, handed her the canteen first, then the food. They sat together along the bank of the creek to eat, listening to the water smoothing by.

Belle dragged off her hat, placed it on the grass between them and stretched out her legs. "It's beautiful," she said, resting back on her hands. "I can see why you wanted to bring me here."

"It's beautiful," Archer agreed, "but that's not the only reason why we're here."

He pointed to a spot beyond the water. She sat up, squinting.

A wooden sign had been erected beyond a strand of willows, black stenciled lettering against fading whitewash:

305 ACRES PRIME LAND AND WATER RIGHTS
3 WELLS FLOWING
STOCK INCLUDED
CONTACT McMURRY & DUNN, AUSTIN
FOR DETAILS

"Wouldn't it be nice?" Archer asked, turning to her, his face hopeful.

She saw then how much this land had taken hold of him, how much of Texas, of Emma and Thies and this flowery, dusty cowboy life lived in his heart. And she saw that she didn't have to take any of that from him. She could still have him, and he could still have this.

"Yes," Belle agreed slowly. "Yes, I think it would be."

It wasn't London or Paris or Villefranche. But it could be hers and Archer's both.

CHAPTER 35

Mr. Henry E. Huntington, Superintendent
c/o Main Office
Chesapeake, Ohio & South Western Railroad
Memphis, Tennessee

May 29th, 1882

Mr. Huntington,
   It may interest you to know that I've recently come to the conclusion that *a limited amount* of idealism is a commodity I can afford after all. I suppose I'm obliged to thank you for that, and I am a woman who always fulfills her obligations.
   I leave soon for Europe on holiday with my son. Perhaps I shall send you a postcard.

Regards,

Mrs. B. D. Worsham

Arabella
Paris, 1882

Archer was not fond of shopping, a fact that both amused and confounded her. He truly was a mix of the familiar and the unknown, already so smart, so dark-haired and comely with a quick, engaging grin that endeared him to any number of shop girls in both England and France. On their voyage across the Atlantic he'd had a gaggle of misses shadowing him along the steamer, ranging in age from six to fourteen. He'd been so patient with each of them, patient for *days*, spinning tops with the youngest along the decks, sharing tea and cakes with the older girls. Even Janey, the maid, had fallen in his thrall; one evening near the end of the voyage, he developed a slight cough. Janey bundled him in bed and plied him with so much beef tea he joked he wouldn't be able to stand another sip for the rest of his life.

Archer was brilliant like Collis, watchful like her, and overall something even better than either of them: he was kind.

But he did not like to shop, and so Belle learned not to drag her son along with her for her hours and hours of fittings at Worth and beyond. She would leave him at bookshops or museums, at Notre Dame or any of the other smaller, ancient churches gracing the city, where he could study the art and architecture and history at his leisure. And how beautifully he blossomed here! How he filled the lovely chambers of his mind with facts and figures and acute observations. They'd spent dinner after dinner with him talking nonstop about everything he'd learned that day, about saints and artists and scoundrels, Napoleon and Marianne and Charlemagne, about this new turn of phrase or that one, and how he could not wait to plunge back into the city to learn more.

So Archer wasn't with her when Belle was walking down a little *rue* with a name she would not, later on, remember at all. She wouldn't even remember *why* she was there, or where she had been just before it, although she thought it might have been a milliner's shop, or one selling ribbons. If she closed her eyes she could recall bright streamers of satin, rainbow strips draped from wooden dowels hanging above her. Her hand lifted, running her fingers through their colors.

She was walking in the fitful Paris sunshine (after maybe visiting a ribbon shop), watching the ragged clouds blowing and scattering, when she passed a café with a poster in the window of a woman in a scarlet dress, holding aloft a set of antlers in one hand like a torch, like a trophy.

She paused, retraced her steps, murmured *Excusez-moi* to an irritated gentleman in a bowler who had to juke around her.

The poster was an advertisement for a restaurant, it seemed, or a hotel. Or a restaurant in a hotel, and the model didn't even resemble Belle, not really, not much beyond the auburn of her hair and the defiant curve of her lips. But the dress, the antlers . . . the dark background, which almost might have been a forest at midnight . . .

She remembered her dream, the one she'd had in Richmond right before Collis had lodged himself squarely into her life. She remembered with perfect clarity the heat of the hart between her thighs as she'd straddled it. The stony antlers in her hands. The scent of that wide, black river rolling before them. How bold she'd felt, how unafraid, as they'd leapt together toward the unknown.

When she returned to the House of Worth on Rue de la Paix the next day, she described precisely the gown she wanted, and to her surprise (or not; Belle was willing to pay a great deal to get what she wanted), Charles Worth stroked his mustache, eyed her up and down, and said that it wasn't an entirely terrible concept, and that he would see what he could do.

"It's very nice," Archer said politely, when Belle stepped out of their hotel suite's dressing chamber to reveal the final product to him, deep claret velvet draped over an underskirt of brighter crimson, black lace along the bodice and sleeves, pink silk camellias along one shoulder.

"Nice?" she said. "Is that all?"

He fidgeted on the chaise longue, slipped a little down the shiny cushions, pushed himself back up again. "It's fancy?"

Belle laughed, turned a circle in her new gown. Janey hurried behind her to straighten the train, then stood back with her hands pressed over her stomach, pretending not to stare.

"It is," Belle said, crossing to the standing mirror in an alcove, one hand on her hip, "exactly what it should be, a dress of dreams. And it's what I'm going to wear for my portrait session with Monsieur Cabanel. I want to have it remembered."

"All right," said Archer. "With the lace and all, you look rather Spanish, I think. I like it. Wait—"

He leapt to his feet—he seldom moved slowly, this son of hers—disappearing back into the dressing room. He reemerged a few minutes later with one of her fans, rose silk, carved ebony spokes.

"You should add this to the ensemble. It matches the flowers. Well, almost."

She snapped open the fan, admiring the effect in the mirror. "I do believe you're right. What an eye for fashion you have."

"Just color," Archer said, frowning, his hands in his pockets. "We've been drenched in color since we've gotten here, haven't we? I think it's all the visits to the museums that have got me thinking about it. And if you carry the fan, it's even more Spanish. You might be a lady dancing the flamenco."

"I don't think I'll venture that far. But thank you for the fan, and the encouragement. It's good to have an impartial eye about these things."

"I think you're terribly pretty," he said, earnest. "But I don't think I'm impartial."

"That's even better," Belle said, snapping the fan closed again.

It was the habit of the elite to commission their portraits with certain fashionable, celebrated artists; the more celebrated, the more expensive, the better. The end result would be displayed either discreetly or ostentatiously—depending upon the objective of the sitter—in their Manhattan mansions, their châteaux in Newport, their cottages in Bar Harbor, for family and friends and enemies to either admire or gnash their teeth over.

Belle had no ambition for anyone but herself to enjoy her portrait. She had no plans to throw grand cotillions beneath it, or host rarefied dinners with it looming in the background (although, in the years to come, those dinners would happen). In fact, she hadn't planned to have her image painted at all, but after some roundabout idle inquiries, it turned out that famed portraitist Monsieur Alexandre Cabanel happened to have an opening in his schedule that coincided exactly with Mrs. Belle D. Worsham's tour of La Ville Lumière. And yes, much like Monsieur Worth, Monsieur Cabanel was very pleased to accept her American dollars.

So, why not? She was reclaiming her life, wasn't she?

Her first meeting with the monsieur took place in his studio at half past seven in the morning, a time he insisted the clarity of light was best for initial impressions. They shook hands and exchanged pleasantries. Older and gruff, he reminded her vaguely of Collis, but that might have been just his beard and tufts of unruly hair. His assistant, a young woman with a coiffure tied up in an enormous bow, offered Madame Worsham café au lait, which she accepted, and mille-feuille, which she did not. Archer took her share of the iced pastry and retreated to a corner with a book.

Monsieur Cabanel walked a slow circle around Belle, tapping a finger against his mouth as the rattling purr of Paris leaked past the bank of southern windows, and the air grew pungent with the aroma of hot coffee over turpentine. She retreated to change into her new gown. When she stepped back into the light, the great artist, society's favorite painter of portraits, the favorite of Napoleon III himself, scowled at her, then lifted his arms and opened his hands.

"Yes, of course," he said, and she realized the scowl meant that he approved, rather than the opposite. "Of course, of course. *Une beauté américaine.* I know just how we shall proceed."

* * *

On the afternoon of their final day in Paris, Belle sat outside on the patio of Archer's favorite boulangerie, nursing a cup of hot chocolate topped with creamy thick foam. A basket piled with fresh croissants sat in the middle of the table; a scattering of flakes marked a telltale trail across the tablecloth, from the basket straight to her son's plate.

"Who are you writing to?" Archer asked, tearing apart his third croissant with his fingers. A pair of plump banded pigeons fluttered and murmured at his feet.

"To whom are you writing?" she corrected absently.

"*To whom are you writing?*" he echoed, with exaggerated courtesy.

Belle smiled, looked up from the postcard she was addressing. "A nephew of your father's."

"So . . . my cousin?"

"Yes, I suppose so."

What a painful blessing that Archer never questioned the silence emanating from his father's kin; their unspoken rejection was all he'd ever known. How different it was from the messy, noisy Yarringtons, who had adored him from the day he'd been born.

He popped a bite of bread into his mouth, then tossed another down to the birds; they fell upon it enthusiastically. "Why'd you wait until now? We leave in the morning. At this point, we might beat it home."

"Oh, I don't know," she hedged, although she did: because it was a foolish idea, a reckless idea, vain and dangerous, to extend this connection between Edward and her, even with just a scrap of pasteboard mailed across the wide Atlantic. To encourage it— whatever *it* was—in any way. She had argued with herself about it for weeks, had managed to delay any thought of capitulation or denial. But here she was, wasn't she, out here in the Parisian sunlight with an excellent pen of blue ink and a stiff card imprinted with an etching of Napoleon's triumphant arch.

"We've just been so busy," she said. "Time slipped away from me."

Archer pushed forward in his chair, tilted his head to make out her message.

"*Merci*? That's all you're going to say?"

"That's all that's needed," she replied, as the pigeons walked circles beneath the table, hunting and pecking along the paving stones.

"Will I ever meet him? This Mr.—" He pushed forward again, squinting. "Mr. H. E. Huntington?"

"I don't know," she repeated. "Perhaps."

"Well, what are you thanking him for?"

Belle toyed with the pen, rolling it back and forth between her fingers. A cloud drifted over the sun and the shadows softened, blurred into a cool, even pewter. A waitress laughed, very loudly, just behind them as one of the pigeons took offense to the other, flapping its wings and rushing about.

"Because . . . because once, a few years back, he offered me a valuable piece of advice. Advice about living and traveling. I owe him my gratitude for that."

Archer's dark eyebrows raised, imperious; in that moment, he looked every inch his father's son.

"Do you think he'll even remember it, if it was so long ago?"

"Oh yes," she said quietly. "I have no doubt he'll remember."

CHAPTER 36

Clara
Manhattan, 1883

"It's good of you to meet me here," Mary Alice said, never taking her gaze from her own reflection in the millinery shop's looking glass. She fluffed the marigold ribbons of the smart navy chapeau she was trying on, then tilted her head. "Considering."

"Considering what?" Clara asked, standing just behind her and aside, her arms crossed.

"Oh, considering this isn't your part of town. I really am so pressed for time before my train departs, though. I'm sorry we couldn't go somewhere else."

The Brooklyn shop was small and bright, quite charming, really, with a respectable selection of the latest fashions, silk and wool and felt crowned with bursts of short, vivid feathers; densely woven straw with grosgrain ribbons; draped clusters of false flowers or fruit.

Mary Alice turned to the proprietor, an elderly woman with a French accent, hovering nearby. "Is it really supposed to sit this far forward? Half my forehead is covered."

"Yes, madame, this is the style. *Très à la mode*, no?"

"And what," Clara said, "do you believe my part of town to be?"

Mary Alice smiled at her through the mirror, not quite pleasant. "Come, my dear. We're far from the finest fashion houses out here, and if that's not a Madame Pouyanne on your head, I'll eat . . . well, this rather less impressive item I'm wearing now."

"It was a gift," Clara said stiffly. She restrained herself from touching her own hat, gleaming bronze silk, its long, singular pheasant feather that curved to her shoulder. "From Paris. Where I've never been," she added for clarity.

Mary Alice began to untie the ribbons knotted beneath her chin. "Neither have I." She handed the hat back to the Frenchwoman without looking at her, began to move down the row of shelves, perusing the open boxes of ribbons and netting and lace, the wooden display stands topped with frilly bonnets and more daring little hats. "Was it a beau?"

"A bow?" Clara said, confused.

"A suitor." Mary Alice lifted a short-brimmed concoction of raspberry satin and jet sequins, turning it this way and that in her hands. The Frenchwoman sidled close once more. "Who gave you the chapeau, silly."

"Oh. No. It was . . . someone else."

"Not your dear father? He could certainly afford it."

"How are you enjoying living in Memphis?" Clara asked, to change the subject. "Papa tells me Edward is doing well in his new position at the company. He might even make vice president someday."

"My, yes. He's a very hardworking man, my Edward, although I'm not sure overseeing the construction of railroad tracks takes full advantage of his skills. It would be most kind of your papa to elevate him to another position."

There was no mistaking the bitter undertone in Mary Alice's voice.

"Why, what's the matter?" asked Clara.

Mary Alice's eyebrows peaked. "Matter? Nothing."

"You seem . . . unsettled."

"Not in the least. I adore living in the backwaters of Tennessee with my husband and children, swatting off mosquitos day and night, entertaining the boorish locals and their wives. What could be finer? Did you know," she said, turning to confront Clara directly, "that there is not a single decent shop or restaurant within ten miles of us? That we must boil the water before drinking or even bathing in it? The roof of our house leaks, the floors are uneven, and the smell from the Mississippi is like breathing in rubbish."

"Oh . . ."

Mary Alice scowled at the raspberry hat she still held. "I suppose I should count my blessings we've not caught yellow fever yet." She replaced the hat upon the display stand, walked on. The proprietor reached for it at once, lifting it, sequins flashing, resetting it at the proper angle.

"Surely it's not *that* bad," Clara began, trailing after her cousin.

Mary Alice shook her head. "My dear little Clara, who's known nary a day without servants and silk. I think your mother might understand me better. How is she?"

Clara felt her neck and face begin to heat, though she wasn't certain why. "Not well," she admitted. "She doesn't leave her room often anymore."

"Who could blame her? When your father keeps such a better option for entertainment at hand?"

Clara inhaled sharply. "Why are you saying such things?"

"I heard Mrs. Worsham bought a Manhattan mansion worth more than dreams, done up by the most expensive decorators to be found. I heard she outbid Mr. Rockefeller himself for all the plots around it. However do you suppose she earned the funds?"

"Stop this!"

Mary Alice halted in a bar of sunlight, her chignon lit to honey, her head bowed. She pressed her palms together at her waist and steepled her fingers. When she spoke again, her voice was very low.

"I sometimes ponder the twist of fate that offered them you, instead of me. Why did Uncle Collis and Aunt Elizabeth take in you, and not me?"

"Am I to blame for that?"

"No, of course not. You're not to blame for anything, are you, darling? You're just to live your sweet and perfect life, dressed in haute couture, dripping in diamonds."

"I'm not *dripping* in—"

"Why *you*?" Mary Alice repeated, much louder, meeting Clara's eyes at last. Her cheeks were pink, her lips compressed. "I was the oldest. It should have been me."

The Frenchwoman made a garbled sound, looking back and forth at them both, wringing her hands.

"Buy the one with the marigold ribbons," Clara said coolly. "It *is* à la mode, even if *you* can't tell."

She strode to the shop's door, the bell above it sounding a clarion *ting!* as she yanked it open and closed it again.

CHAPTER 37

❦

Arabella
Manhattan, 1883

The fund-raising benefit for the Metropolitan Museum of Art Technical School freely welcomed any soul who could afford the hundred-dollar entrance fee, thirty-five for children. The event took place in the museum itself, so newly completed its brick-red walls still glowed, warm and mellow, beneath the smoky city sun; its gay cream and gray accents were yet unsullied by the smoky city air.

Inside this gracious edifice were tall, open chambers smelling of floor wax overlaid with notes of bleach and fresh paint. Staircases stood framed in half-walls punched through with rows of rosettes, all linked in a line like pretty paper cutouts, and the main entrance opened out to Central Park itself, spread before the museum's guests on this particular evening in all of its May emerald opulence.

Ladies glided from room to room in layers of draped taffeta and cascades of lace, fresh roses or feathery aigrettes in their hair, bustles covered in ruffles. Their gentlemen wore top hats and white silk ties, pocket chains of solid gold and stickpins capped with modest gemstones.

There was nothing modest about the feminine adornment, however. It was not quite two months since Alva Vanderbilt's spectacularly overdone masked ball, when New York's most blue-blooded matrons and their daughters showed off enough jewelry to ransom many, many kings. (The society sheets were, in fact, still writing rapturously about it.) Sapphires and pearls, rubies and opals flashed beneath the museum's gas chandeliers; diamonds twinkled like elven eyes from every corner. No one important would be headed to Newport until at least late June. There was no sense in locking away their brilliant new winter baubles just yet.

For the price of their entrance, guests of the benefit were treated to glasses of lukewarm champagne or punch, a buffet of cold canapés, and a lecture from Colonel Luigi Palma di Cesnola, the museum's director, on his collection of priceless Cypriot antiquities. They could also spend the evening inspecting the museum's assortment of European paintings, and, of course, its famed Roman sarcophagus, said to be never used, but who knew.

The rare exception to the beau monde's stringent rules, it was only at charitable fêtes such as this where Belle might brush sleeves with Manhattan's luminaries, see in public and in person the faces of the men Collis did business with or the women whose homes rivaled her own. Ordinary faces, she thought now, looking at them without looking, expert at the art of the sidelong examination. Ordinary faces, round or thin, youthful or craggy, bewhiskered or clean-shaven. Perhaps she'd been expecting a crowd more god-like, beings from Mount Olympus treading briefly and gloriously upon the earth. The light would bend into coronas around their heads; venomous asps and ivy would spring from their steps.

Yet aside from their fashion and those mounds of diamonds, these Whitneys, these Morgans and Jeromes and Livingstons and Goelets, looked perfectly nondescript to her. She might have passed them on the street a thousand times over and never thought to herself, *There goes an empress of the city, a master of destinies.*

By the handsome rosette stairway, a string quartet offered a muted symphony, four young men in buttercup waistcoats and black tails, sweating in the illumination provided by a cluster of lamps.

Colonel di Cesnola's talk had been heavily attended and lightly applauded. He'd addressed the crowd in an Italian accent Belle found most lyrical; within minutes she was lulled by the heat of the chamber and the rhythm of his sentences into a drowsy inattention. Yet Archer had sat forward in his folding chair the entire hour with his arms crossed and his brows knit, concentrating on every word.

She roused with the applause, joining in as the colonel smiled and bowed from the podium, his cheeks flushed. Afterword, she could not have said if the director had spoken of his excavations or his favorite recipes, but as soon as the applause died away her son rose from his chair with a renewed interest in returning to the back rooms, where ancient Cypriot flasks and waterspouts and glass perfume bottles, rainbowed with time, stood on display.

"Go ahead," Belle said. "I think I might take in some fresh air just outside, but I'll join you in a moment."

He blended into the crowd strolling in their leisurely, godlike way across the floors.

She was standing near the open doors of the entrance, relishing the tepid breeze, when she felt it: fresh heat and presence, the awareness of someone standing just behind her, someone scented of pomade and pinyons and rain.

"Mrs. Worsham," Edward said softly, as a matron in dark silk and spangles floated past.

Belle turned around, her fingers pinched around the stem of her flute.

He was not so conventionally attractive, this man who bedeviled her dreams. He was no prince from a storybook; there was something too amiable, too pleasant about his features to make young and foolish girls swoon. No, not the prince and not even the wily wolf—but the huntsman perhaps, compassionate and flawed.

He smiled at her, and she became distressingly aware of her heart in her chest, beating hard and out of tune with her will.

Not here, not now.

"Mr. Edward Huntington. I had no idea you were in town."

"Not for long. We're visiting only for a few days."

"We?"

"Mary Alice and I. The children."

"Of course," she said, flustered. "Collis didn't mention it."

"Only for a few days," he said again. "In and out, hardly here at all."

Belle brought the champagne to her lips. It tasted like sparkles and nothing, but her mouth was dry so she drank it anyway.

As if he had summoned it, the breeze changed, fragrant with storm. A bank of charcoal-gray clouds brewed above the rough line of trees and buildings to the west.

Another couple pushed by, throwing them vexed glances; she realized they were blocking the way. Belle gathered the train of her skirt, heading back inside. Edward fell in step beside her.

"I received your letter," he said. "And your postcard."

She busied herself with placing her empty flute on a tray, saying nothing, ashamed that she had been weak enough to write either, much less post them.

"I'm glad," he said, and paused, frowning. "Glad that you have your son back."

"Yes."

"Is he here tonight?"

"He is. Archer's a far more dedicated scholar than I. Likely he's pinned Colonel di Cesnola in some corner and is bombarding him with questions."

Edward took a new glass of champagne from a passing server, pressed it into her gloved hand. "I would enjoy meeting him," he said.

It would be a fissure in the mighty Huntington dam, all right, to introduce her son to his cousin here in this public place. A fissure that could lead to a flood, one that she suddenly wasn't certain she was so ready to accept. Edward might be kindhearted, might even be sincere, but the rest of them . . . ?

Safer to change the subject. "Are you a member of the museum, sir, like your uncle?"

"Too rich for my blood, I'm afraid. Perhaps if I lived nearer it would be worth it."

"Of course." She wet her lips, searching for her composure. "And your wife? Did she accompany you?"

"She did, although we missed the lecture. I doubt Mary Alice is much intrigued by the academic aspect of the evening anyway. Her interests are rather more businesslike." He smiled at her puzzled look, opened his palm to the noise and bustle around them. "Her study of the realm to which she aspires."

Cynical words, but he said them still with that easy smile. Belle offered a cautious half-smile in return.

The quartet began a new piece. The air was darkening, the chandeliers brightening, laughter and conversation growing more boisterous as the champagne flowed. In the crush of it all an angular man with a drooping mustache pressed near enough to step on her hem; he stepped back at once, touched a finger to the edge of his hat and gave a terse nod of apology.

"Mrs. Worsham," he muttered.

"Mr. Rockefeller," she answered sweetly, watching him walk away.

Edward only looked at her. She handed him her newly emptied glass, waited until he placed it upon a sideboard before murmuring, "We engaged in some rather competitive negotiations a while back, he and I. A bit of a tussle regarding two vacant parcels by my home."

"I recall my uncle mentioning it." His gaze scanned the crowd; perhaps he was searching for his wife. "If I may ask, Mrs. Worsham, how did you manage to best the fearsome founder of Standard Oil?"

Belle lowered her gaze, spread open the peacock feathers of

her fan. An arc of iridescent eyes, turquoise and ocher and green, looked back at her, fringed and mysterious.

"Come," he said lightly, "am I to know none of your secrets?"

"All right. For the first parcel, I offered the sellers sixty percent of their full price in cash, carrying forward a smaller mortgage for the remainder with a very reputable bank. I added that I would top any other offer they'd received by another ten thousand dollars in cash, no matter how high the other offer might be, as long as they provided evidence of it in writing. I gave them twenty-four hours to respond."

Edward's attention had returned to her entirely. "Less time to consider, less time to negotiate."

"Exactly. Along with the proviso that they not disclose the terms of my bid to anyone else, *anyone*, until the sale was completed. So I could not be outbid."

He began to chortle; she placed a quelling hand upon his arm and drew him to stand beside her against a wall. A painting of the Madonna, pink-robed and serene, hung level to their shoulders; against her gold leaf background, her eyes shone black and bottomless.

"Mind you," Belle whispered, "ten thousand was more than half of the appraised value of that lot. It was an extremely generous offer. A year later, I made a similar bid, with similar terms, on the second parcel, only I increased my cash bonus to fifteen thousand. I wanted the parcels that badly, you see. A residence on either lot so close to mine would have damaged both my tranquility and my view." She brought the fan to her face, batted the tips of the feathers lightly against her lips. "I was told later on— unofficially, you understand—that Mr. Rockefeller found my tactics to be . . . ungentlemanly."

Edward released a bark of laughter. "From John Rockefeller, no less! That is saying something!"

"I fear I bruised his feelings," she admitted, smiling.

"More like his pride, I reckon."

She leaned closer, emboldened. "I've often thought his mustache resembles a weary caterpillar perched along his upper lip."

"Some gentlemen are sadly lacking anyone to guide them in matters of style."

"Alas for them," she laughed.

"Yes," he agreed, unexpectedly serious. His eyes held hers, long brown lashes, pale blue eyes endless with promise and she was unmoored again, she was flying, falling. Spinning and lost like a sparrow struck from the sky. The elite celebrated around them, oblivious, and the back of his hand brushed against hers, glove to glove, the slightest of connections. Belle barely controlled her shiver.

"Alas," he breathed, the huntsman, plain and strong, devoted not to his queen but to what his heart told him was right.

They stood too near. She knew it already, knew she had to retreat from him and that silently smirking Madonna, knew she had to hold her breath against his laugh and the cold rain scent of him. She knew that Edward Huntington was disaster disguised as a friend. She knew that her world could not tilt upon his axis, her soul could not soar alongside his. Not if she wished to thrive in this life.

"Edward," came a woman's voice, cool and carrying.

They did not spring apart, not quite, but there was an instant space between them, a cavity, both of them repelled from its center.

Mary Alice approached, blond and dour. She wore a gown of solid jet, as if she'd planned for a funeral instead of a fête, only a burst of green from the bar pin of cut peridots near her shoulder. She placed her hand upon her husband's arm, exactly where Belle had rested her fingers moments before.

She raked a brief glance across Belle, then looked back at Edward.

"Darling, I've had the good fortune of encountering Mrs. Nicholas Fish upstairs. Mrs. Nicholas *Fish*," she emphasized, as Edward only stared at her blankly. She gave a high, tinkling laugh.

"Oh, my boy, do you ever listen to a word I say over breakfast? Mrs. Fish is a friend of Mrs. Astor—and of my aunt, of course. She has inquired after you and Clara both. If it isn't too much trouble to pry you away from"—another, scathing glance at Belle—"from here, would you kindly escort me back upstairs? I told her I would fetch you forthwith."

"My dear," Edward said, placing his hand over hers. "You remember Mrs. Worsham, I assume?"

Mary Alice's nostrils flared; her mouth made an unpleasant smile. "Naturally."

"What a delight to see you again, Mrs. Huntington." Belle offered her hand. It seemed for a moment that Mary Alice would ignore it entirely, but then she didn't. Belle endured her limp shake.

"Edward, darling, I really must insist you come with me now. I won't have us keeping Mrs. Fish waiting. She's a very important woman."

Belle began to retreat from them both. "You must go. I'm sure the upstairs exhibits are—"

Before she could complete her sentence, a pair of older women sailed by, mauve crêpe de chine and beige corded silk, fat cables of pearls wound around their throats, cinched like belts around their waists. A cloud of perfume preceded them, moved with them, a heavy saturation of vanilla and phlox.

"It is one thing to see the *hetaeras* depicted in art," said the one in flowing mauve, a shade too loud for polite conversation. She gazed rigidly ahead of her as she spoke, fixed on some distant point, acknowledging neither Belle nor the Huntingtons as she passed. "It is another matter entirely to be forced to endure their presence in the flesh."

"Is *that* the peculiar odor I've been detecting?" responded the other smoothly, also staring ahead. "Heavens, I thought the pâté had gone off. I'm afraid the standards of this museum are shockingly lax."

"It is open to all the public, I heard."

"Injudicious."

"Indeed."

And they were gone.

Beneath the pink Madonna, Belle smiled, acerbic. She took in Mary Alice's expression of confused delight, Edward's indignation.

"Shall I spare you the trouble of researching the term, Mrs. Huntington? It means courtesan. Excuse me, I must go find my son."

CHAPTER 38

⟋⟍⟍⟋——————⟍⟋⟋

Clara
Manhattan, 1883

She lavished great care upon her little tree. Early on, Clara had used her allowance to purchase the only book she'd ever found about the proper tending of bonsais from the faraway land of Japan, the peculiarities of watering them (partially submerging them in a basin of cool water for ten minutes was best), how to add fertilizer (very sparingly), or adjust the light (often). The book was in French, so it had taken her a while to work out the translations. She'd even transplanted it once herself, two years ago when the needles browned and it began to die and nothing she tried helped. She'd taken it to a nursery and asked the head gardener for advice on what to do. He'd scratched his head and conceded that he'd never seen a specimen like it before, how very queer it was, wasn't it, so bent and small?

"Try a new pot," he'd finally suggested, and so she had, finding a rectangular one bigger than the glazed container the bonsai had lived in all these years, but not so large her tree might feel lost in it. New soil, fresh fertilizer, and a small decorative rock of quartz, very sparkly, that she placed in one corner.

Clara had yearned for a pet for as long as she could remember. But Mother's constitution was too sensitive for a dog, and cats gave her hives. As a child, Clara had once had three small goldfish, but none of them lived more than a year. It struck her as morbidly funny that her longest relationship with another living being, besides her family, was with a tree.

She was in her room watering it—standing by, minding the clock, while it soaked in the Wedgwood soup tureen she had bought specifically for this purpose—as Mother sat at Clara's writing desk, sorting through the week's stack of invitations.

"Mrs. Vanderbilt again," Mother said, scanning a large, cream-colored card. "A dance at the end of the month, a Thursday. Is she respectable enough, I wonder?"

"Mrs. Astor still barely acknowledges her." Clara dipped her finger in the water, checking the temperature. "I do think that's a point in Mrs. Vanderbilt's favor."

"Hmm. Here's one. Mrs. Paran Stevens is hosting a charity tea. That sounds pleasant enough."

"Eligible young gentlemen do not attend teas, Mother. They attend balls. Dinner parties."

"Is that really our primary criterion?"

Clara sent her a wry look. "Is it not?"

Elizabeth gave a little cough. "Perhaps, my dearest, if you were a tad less particular regarding your qualifications for an admirer . . ."

"I don't think it's particular to want to feel something besides boredom at the prospect of a husband. It seems like I've shaken hands with every possible suitor on the Eastern Seaboard and they're all dull as dishwater. Is it too much to ask for just a *spark* of hope that I might fall in love?"

"Love," said Mother quietly, "does not necessarily lead to a happy marriage."

Clara looked up at her, chagrined. "Of course. I'm sorry. I know."

Mother gazed down at her lap, then up again. "Well. Maybe

you're right about the tea. I'll hunt through these for a ball instead."

The ten minutes were up. Clara returned to the stand holding
the tureen, lifting the bonsai carefully, placing it on the folded
towel she had ready by the window.

"I don't know why we bother with these tedious invitations,
anyway," she said, using one end of the towel to dry the sides of
the pot. "Whatever the event, it's always the same old faces, the
same old conversations. I wish we could do something different.
I wish we could do something *amazing*. We could go to Paris, for
instance. Try society there. Or London—lots of families are doing it, lots of girls, heading off to win a coronet. Supposedly all
you have to do is catch the eye of the Prince of Wales and you're a
guaranteed success, no matter your background." She adjusted the
tree, centering it in a square of sunlight. "Everyone says the only
thing that matters over there is money, and heaven knows we have
plenty of that. When the doctors pronounce you perfectly well, we
should go. What do you think?"

She knew, of course, what her mother would think. Even in
better health, Elizabeth never liked leaving the mansion, much
less the country. Clara had never been to England or the Continent. At this rate, she never would.

But she expected at least a token sigh from her mother at her
daughter's deliberate crassness, a murmur of distaste or regret. Yet
Elizabeth remained silent.

Clara replaced the decorative quartz rock to its corner of the
pot, wiped her fingers on the towel and turned around.

Mother sat slumped in the chair, her head down, her arms lax,
a scattering of bold white cards at her feet. Clara leapt forward so
quickly she slammed into the stand holding the tureen, sending
her reeling and the tureen to the floor, smashed to pieces along the
Afshar rug, water everywhere, and the thought that ran through
her mind then was, *Thank God the tree wasn't in it.*

CHAPTER 39

October 4, 1883

Mrs. John Worsham
4 West 54th Street

Mrs. Worsham,

Please forgive this intrusion, as we have never been introduced. My name is Dorothy Gilbert. I am the nurse of Mrs. Collis Huntington, who is in a grave way. She has bid me to write this note to ask that you pay a call on her at 65 Park Avenue at once, or as soon as may be convenient.

I hope you will honor this request. I beg you, if possible, to accompany the footman who has delivered this note back to Mrs. Huntington's residence in the carriage provided. If it is not possible, I beg you to please hasten here however you may.

Sincerely,
D. Gilbert

Arabella
Manhattan, 1883

A dark and gloomy vestibule opened into a dark and gloomy entrance hall, leading to a dark and gloomy sweep of stairs. The footman Dorothy Gilbert sent to Belle had leapt ahead of her up the steps to open the front door for her, but it was the butler, manifesting with solemn disapproval from the shadows, who accepted her muff and cloak and gloves.

Belle told him her name and said that Mrs. Huntington was expecting her. A pair of maids lingered behind him at the base of the stairs, white drawn faces beneath white frilly caps, gawking at her. The butler acknowledged neither of them; he only inclined his head, saying something about Mrs. Huntington awaiting Mrs. Worsham in the master chamber—but then Clara appeared from nowhere, rushing forward in a mess of bedraggled hair and aquamarine skirts, grabbing both of Belle's hands in her own.

Belle took in her face.

"Oh, my dear," she said softly, and Clara fell into her arms, her forehead pressed to Belle's neck, her body shaking, no sound coming from her but a rattle of harsh, uneven exhalations.

All of the servants, men and women both, folded back into the shadows.

Belle cupped her palm against Clara's nape, her fingers threading the dark curls. "Where is your father?"

Clara drew back, swiping at her cheeks. "At his office. It all started yesterday, I found her—we were simply *talking* and I found her insensible at my desk and—Mother says not to disturb him now, that he needs to work. We knew she was ill, of course we did, we've known for months. But this bout came over her so quickly! I don't understand how he could have even gone in today, I don't know *how*—"

"All right." She took Clara lightly by the upper arms. "Perhaps you'd better send for him."

"But—Mother said—"

"In this instance," Belle said gently, "it might be possible that your mother isn't considering matters with her usual lucidity. I think he'd want to be here with her, don't you?"

"Yes. Yes, you're right."

But Clara only stood there, gazing at her with a hot and pleading desperation. More tears brimmed, streaking down her cheeks, pooling at her chin, but she didn't wipe them away.

Belle gave her a little shake. "*Clara.* Send a man to his office at once. Don't wait. Do it now."

"Yes," she said again, blinking, a sleepwalker coming awake, and strode off.

The butler rematerialized, showing her up the long, curving staircase to the second story, down yet another dark and gloomy hall. He paused at an impressive oak door, knocked twice and eased it open without waiting for a response.

"Mrs. Worsham, ma'am."

Belle didn't catch an audible reply, but the butler stepped back anyway, so she walked through.

More shadows, gaslight burning low from the branches of a glass-globe chandelier. A strong hint of laudanum tinging the air. There was a fire burning in the hearth but it didn't seem to dent the cold.

Belle focused on the poster bed near the fire, its marquetry of purpleheart flowers and leaves, gilded chalices and brass edgings against black lacquer: a design she knew well, since she had selected it herself.

A woman in a starched uniform—Miss Gilbert, Belle assumed—rose from her chair by the bedside, fluffed her apron and came forward. Belle didn't really hear what the woman said to her in her hushed nurse's voice, something about how good it was of Mrs. Worsham to come, how there wasn't much time, how Mrs. Worsham must, for the sake of Mrs. Huntington's flagging energy, keep matters brief.

"I understand," Belle said, and moved like a sleepwalker herself to the chair beside the bed. She lifted her eyes to those of Mrs. Elizabeth Huntington, who stared back at her with a gaze not unlike Clara's, hot and desperate.

"Mrs. Worsham. You came."

"It seemed imperative."

Elizabeth's hands twitched atop the duvet cover, amber satin. Belle had chosen that as well, along with the dust ruffle and the sheets and the heavy, flowery stoneware *jardinière* on the bureau. In fact, nearly everything in here, every bit of the fine décor in her rival's domain was secretly, viciously, Belle's design. It seemed a petty revenge now, to force this fragile woman to dwell in the world Belle had chosen for her, that Collis had paid for and his wife had not resisted. Petty, but at the time the only tool she'd had to express her wrath over losing her son.

The nurse retired to a new chair, farther back in the chamber. She picked up a newspaper on the table at her side and acted as if she was perusing it.

"Do you know what bedrock is, Mrs. Worsham?"

Belle's attention jolted back to Elizabeth. "Pardon me?"

"Bedrock. Do you know it?"

She thought of the coal miners back in Virginia who spent their days trapped beneath the crust of the earth, who'd occasionally show up at the faro parlor to gamble away their pennies, their nailbeds always hemmed with grime. "I do."

"My love for Collis has been the bedrock of our marriage. I am our foundation, our stability. From the moment we first joined hands, I knew it. I would be our bedrock. He would be our magnificent ether. And that is how it turned out, all of these years. I had hoped for children, of course. For some . . . living combination of us both. But I see now where I have failed, you have succeeded."

Belle said nothing. Candlelight stole along the lacquered curves of the bed, elegant lines that caught the thin light and bounced it back, phantom shapes against the dark.

"Your boy is handsome. How . . . very much he resembles his father."

In spite of herself, Belle felt her lip curl. "I'm surprised you know anything of it. He's been gone for so many years at your behest."

Elizabeth smiled. "You resent my interference."

"Wouldn't you?"

"Yes, actually. I imagine I *would* be perturbed if I was so craven as to allow a stranger to steal my son from me."

Belle sucked in a breath. *Craven.*

Mrs. Huntington gestured toward a pitcher of water on the nightstand. Belle steeled herself, rose, filled one of the empty glasses beside it and offered it to her. Elizabeth tipped the glass to her mouth, a tiny swallow, almost nothing, before handing it back.

"Life brims with delicious irony. It's something I've only just noticed, and that itself is an irony too, don't you think, Miss Yarrington? You believe I owe you an apology for your son's absence. I trust you realize that you robbed me first?"

The nurse in her chair kept her chin tucked down and her gaze averted. Licked a finger. Flicked a page of the newspaper.

Belle sat again.

"What," Elizabeth taunted, "no pretty blush of shame? Of false contrition?"

"I am not ashamed of surviving."

"Then how about for taking what was not yours? Have you no shame for that?"

"I never took anything," she said evenly, "that was not freely offered to me first."

Elizabeth turned her head, gave a sad laugh. "*That* I can believe."

A log in the fire crumbled apart, snapping and sparking. The gas chandelier burned above them with its faint feeble glow.

Belle said, "He told me once that he thought you deserved better than him."

"Did he? Well, he was right about that." Elizabeth held her eyes a moment longer, then sighed. "There was a time, you know, when he truly did love me. When I was the only flame combusting his soul. I believe that. I couldn't say now with certainty how long that golden period lasted . . . five years? Ten? He loved me and I loved him and we were united in *every* way that mattered. If he'd asked me to open my veins and let my blood fall waste to the earth, I would've gladly done it for him. Anything . . . anything . . ."

Her voice faded; her eyelids closed. Her hair had thinned since Belle had seen her last on that momentous day in the bookshop, much more gray now than yellow. Her flesh had taken on a waxy, ashen hue that Belle recognized full well.

Her breathing grew uneven. Her chest began to hitch. Belle made a gesture for the nurse, starting to rise, but Elizabeth's eyes snapped open again.

"No," she said, surprisingly strong, although it wasn't clear if she was rejecting the help of the nurse or something else, something close and patient and inevitable, waiting in the shadows.

She lifted her left hand, holding it up until Belle leaned forward to accept it in her own, bemused. Elizabeth's fingers were elegant cold bones. She curled them over Belle's and squeezed until her wedding ring cut into Belle's flesh.

"I want you to know that I gave Collis everything of me, everything within my power. But I could not give him a child of his body. I could not give him . . . a world beyond rules. I realize now I never understood how much he ached for those things. You were the key to them both, Miss Yarrington. You unlocked those doors. I do hate you for it, and I don't mind admitting that. But also, for his sake, I must love you."

"Love," Belle echoed, unable to tear her gaze from the strangeness of it all: Collis's *wife* clutching at her with her specked hand; Collis's *wife* holding on to her as if she were her last firm anchor to this earth. That golden ring, so similar to the one Belle herself wore, but true instead of false.

And in this moment of strangeness and confrontation, of gaslight and the scent of laudanum cloying in the air, she whispered, "What shall I do next?"

Elizabeth sighed again. "Oh, gracious, I don't know. You seem a woman who needs little guidance from someone like me. You are a poisoned thorn. A spider in the rafters, ready to strike."

Despite the chill, Belle felt her cheeks begin to heat. "Am I?"

"You are, I daresay. If it means getting what you want." Elizabeth smiled once more, thin. "Oh, for decades now, I've noticed your face, the same face over and over, no matter the girl. Those soft eyes, your honeyed voice. The tint of your lips, the curve of your chin . . . and him drawn to you like the ocean to the moon. You're not so rare as you think." Elizabeth's bony grip became, somehow, even tighter. Painful. "You *are* poison, but do not harm him, I beg you. Do him no harm."

"No," Belle said. "No, I wouldn't."

"How convincing you are. I see now why everyone puts their faith in you. Swear it to me."

"I swear."

"Swear it to me upon your child's soul. That you'll take care of my husband. That you will protect him. He sinks into despair all on his own, he always has. He is fragile in a way you will never comprehend."

"*Fragile,*" Belle said, with a shake of her head.

"You're young still. Young and beautiful. I can easily imagine how many more men might get caught in your web. Hungry men, ambitious men." She laughed, short and mirthless. "I hear things. I've been paying attention to you for years, even from this very bed. When whispers about you begin to torment my own kin . . . I hear them."

Edward's face flashed before her.

"Swear to me that you will not . . . desert Collis for your own ambitions."

Edward's warm smile, a needle piercing straight through her heart.

"*Arabella,*" Mrs. Huntington said.

Belle bowed her head. "You have my word."

Her hand was released. Elizabeth, in her fervor, had half lifted from her pillows, but now she eased back down, began to cough. The nurse stirred but Elizabeth waved her off.

"So lovely," she rasped, her eyes shining, "and so sincere. I almost believe you." Her hands twitched again, restless, across the duvet. "Perhaps the devil will allow us to shake hands again someday."

Belle flexed her aching fingers. "Perhaps so."

"But I hope not. I hope, with my whole heart, that I never see you *or* Collis again, not ever, ever again. I think that I have earned that small mercy. By God, I have earned it."

She rolled over in the bed, awkwardly, painfully, her back to Belle. Her hair draped ragged across the pillows, a rough spill of silver and brass.

"Go away now, Mrs. Worsham. Go away. I'd rather have the scullery maid beside me right now than you. I'd rather have a whore off the street."

Part V

The Second Wife

1883-1900

CHAPTER 40

❧———❧

Clara
Manhattan, 1883

She was reading by the dim light of the parlor chandelier one afternoon in early December—nothing extraordinary, just the society pages, this dance, that debutante, *the* dress—when Clara looked up and frowned at the window in front of her and realized that she could open the curtains.

It was around two in the afternoon. A bright vertical arrow of sun had pushed past the velvet panels where they met in the middle, where one of the maids had not closed them tightly enough after the morning's dusting.

She could open the curtains.

There was no living reason not to. Not any longer.

Feeling nervous and guilty and somewhat amazed, Clara came to her feet. She crossed the rug with her hands clasped tightly at her waist. She hesitated before the heavy folds of dark bluish gray, a shade that had always reminded her of blueberries, then unclasped her hands.

She grabbed both panels and pushed them apart as wide as her arms would reach, her entire body gilded in pale lemony light. She actually had to shut her eyes and turn her face aside, and then turn around entirely, taking in the wonder of the parlor illumed down the middle with that slice of sunlight, her own shadow stretching dark across the rose-and-red patterned rug. She could not, in all honesty, ever remember seeing it like this before.

There were two other windows. Clara drew back the curtains covering those as well, and when it was done she only stood there, exhilarated and still faintly guilty, as the room flared with color and sunlight glancing off crystal and glass. She felt as if she'd just accidentally discovered a pirate's hidden treasure trove.

She walked to the switch on the wall, turned off the chandelier.

She returned to her chair, picked up the newspaper and went back to reading, in the back of her mind fully aware that she'd just enacted a minor sort of miracle.

CHAPTER 41

Journal entry of Belle D. Worsham
January 25, 1884

Collis is finally sleeping better at night. I'd like to think it's due to the fact that he is spending more time here with Archer and me, in the warm solace of my home. It's required a great deal of patience and coaxing, that delicate game of offering everything and nothing, compassion and iron, to lure him back.

For weeks after her death he made excuses not to come by, not even to see his son.

I understand his remorse, I do, even if I must admit I find it inconvenient. By all accounts, Collis Huntington had never been a faithful husband, but I think that's neither here nor there. I'm hardly the soul to judge him. Nor, alas, am I anyone best suited to remind him that what's done is done.

So I have waited. I have held my peace. I've spent my hours with Archer, studying languages, history, philosophy, so that when his father *did* slip back into our lives, he might not be ashamed of our progress.

And this house. Oh, this house. How I love it here. How I have toiled over it, refined it, made it unconditionally my own. Every single room is designed to perfection, every column, every mural, every inch of trompe l'oeil. I do not blush to admit it.

What a pity it will be to leave it behind. But I cannot move ahead mired in place.

Collis is sleeping better now. So I *will* move ahead.

Arabella
Manhattan, 1884

Another winter in New York, cold and crystalline. Archer delighted in the snow. Belle, far more accustomed to a green Christmas than not, enjoyed it rather less, but she would suffer all the snow angels and snowball fights he wanted because he was here with her, finally here again. She'd enrolled him in the best school she could find, made certain he had everything he could need. At night they would pore over his coursework together, marveling at the collective knowledge of the world.

Elizabeth Huntington lay vanquished beneath a pink granite headstone in the bucolic peace of Woodlawn Cemetery, the snow mounding her grave untouched but for the bouquets of lilies Belle would occasionally, and anonymously, leave her. Superstitious perhaps, or maybe just a thread of residual guilt. Belle would much prefer her former adversary rest in peace than not.

And Collis, dear Collis . . .

Well. He would turn to her when he was ready, body and soul. She was sure of it.

So New York City glimmered on; New York society glimmered on. The rich still held their gala balls, their fund-raisers, their teas. The husbands aboard their steam yachts still sliced languid paths up and down the Hudson, while their wives broke their own trails up and down Fifth Avenue, gathering furs and jewels and the latest fashions.

And, weather permitting, everyone who mattered still completed their Sunday jaunts around Central Park, just like Belle and Collis used to do in their enclosed carriage, hiding together in plain sight.

So when he asked one January afternoon if she would like to go to the park with him in the open landau, not the carriage, she had smiled and said, *Surely*, even though it was chilly enough outside to blow frost.

There were no flowers or green grass in any of the parks up here in the north, not in January. But there were still people. People of all ages and stations, most especially those People Who Mattered, and in the landau with the top down, Mrs. Worsham and the recently bereaved Mr. Huntington would be seen traveling together through the park for the very first time.

Out of the shadows.

It wasn't as cold as she'd feared. Or perhaps it was, and she'd just bundled so thoroughly the frigid air hadn't yet burrowed into her. A warm wool hat, a thick cashmere scarf that covered half her face. Buffalo furs across their laps. The coachman flicked his whip and away they went, off into that long, domesticated wilderness unwinding along the heart of Manhattan.

She touched his hand beneath the furs. He wrapped his fingers around hers and they both gazed directly ahead.

The sun glared; a dark blue heaven curved above, fading into aqua along the skyline. She felt a fine and fragile peace, sitting here beside him as they cantered along.

"Mrs. Worsham," Collis said, still not looking at her. "In the aftermath of the last few months, it happens that I've neglected an unfortunate amount of my business dealings."

"Oh?"

A coach-and-four passed by in the opposite direction, the horses nodding their heads, froth around their bits. The trio of matrons inside it glanced swiftly at Belle and Collis, then even more swiftly away, their faces pale, shocked masks.

Collis turned to her. "I find I'm forced to take an extended trip next month to address some of the most pressing issues. Down to

New Orleans, perhaps Texas. I was wondering if you would care to accompany me? You and Archer both?"

"New Orleans! It sounds wonderfully warm." She laughed lightly, her blood stinging in triumph. "Yes, Mr. Huntington. Of course we would."

"Clara will be coming along too. A few fellows from the company. Oh, and Edward. This all concerns him."

"Yes," Belle said again, without the slightest change of inflection.

Collis ran a finger and thumb along the brim of his hat. "Good." For the first time in a long while, in weeks at least, he slanted her that smile she knew so well, slim and sharp. "I'm glad," he said.

How strange that she hadn't realized how much she'd longed to see his smile again until just this moment, here in the winter-frosted park, beneath the cold new year's sun.

New Orleans *was* warm but also shimmering with rain, a constant drizzle, almost, except for six days of spring glory at the beginning of April, when the clouds cleared and the sidewalks dried and the daffodils and azaleas lining the balconies and streets opened their petals and lifted their heads.

Belle appreciated those days. She appreciated being able to stroll down the busy crooks and avenues of the city with merely a parasol, not an umbrella. Rain or shine, however, the air remained drenched with moisture. Her hair sprang into curls and her skin felt refreshed. Even Collis looked younger, brighter, although he complained about the heaviness of his coats.

"It's new," Clara breathed one morning over breakfast at the hotel, cradling her cup of coffee beneath her nose with both hands, inhaling deep. "It's *new*, and I love it."

"It's old," countered Archer seriously, seated across from her. "The city was founded in—"

"New to *me*," Clara said. "Honestly, Mr. Worsham, you needn't be quite so literal."

"Oh, to *you*, Miss Huntington. Well, then isn't nearly everything?"

It was just the three of them, both Collis and Edward gone to their dire meetings hours earlier, all those Southern Pacific men gone with them, conquering the hemisphere one railroad tie at a time.

Clara set down her cup, tried a bite of her runny eggs over *pain perdu*; it seemed to Belle that the eggs served in this polished, old-fashioned hotel were always slightly undercooked. "Are you not the pot calling the kettle black, Master Archer? Where have you lived besides Texas and New York?"

"And *you*, besides California and New York?"

"My dears," interrupted Belle, signaling the attendant for more coffee; there were times she was keenly aware of how much older she was than them both. "You are equally sage beyond your years. Let us agree that we are all explorers of the wide world."

"I beg your pardon, Mother, but I really don't think—"

"Archer, I believe there's an old bookshop not far from here, stocked with all sorts of dusty, interesting collections, some even from Spain. Four blocks away. So I was told."

He straightened. "Really?"

"And Clara. There are not one but two fine jewelers nearby. I've already made appointments for us at both."

"Miss Arabella," Clara said, and how unusual it was still to hear her say Belle's name, how strangely bittersweet. Her brown eyes were dark and serious. "Do we have time to change?"

With age, it seemed, there did come some wisdom, and Belle was glad enough that her skill at reading others, especially these two, had yet to wane.

Belle found a choker of pearls centered with a sapphire from Ceylon, an emerald-encrusted pin shaped like a trident, a rosy gold ring clustered with diamonds. Onyx and diamond cufflinks for Collis.

Clara decided upon a trio of diamond starbursts for her hair and a pair of earbobs inset with actual scarab beetles, their shells an iridescent blue-green gleam, which Belle privately found macabre but was circumspect enough not to mention.

By the end of their time in New Orleans, they had scoured the finest jewelry shops and modistes the city had to offer, gemstones and gowns, silks and slippers. Archer announced that he'd found an entire set of eighteenth-century Spanish encyclopedias, in addition to three volumes of medieval French poetry and an escritoire he had been assured once belonged to Marat himself.

Edward commented dryly that they would require another entire railcar just to get everything back to New York.

On their last night there it began to rain again, a soft pattering rain that wept along the tall windows of Collis's suite, painting dull trickling patterns along the plaster walls and Jacobean furniture.

"I am tired," he said. His tone was thoughtful, not weary. Belle propped herself up on an elbow to try to better see him in the darkness.

They had discovered early on that the mattress in his room was more comfortable than the one in hers but the chamber itself smelled mustier, so Belle had transferred several vases of roses and freesias from her suite to his by way of their connecting door. Two at first, then five, and now, by their final night, eleven vases surrounded them, the flowers refreshed every other day, and the air was definitely improved.

She *couldn't* see him, not really; only a faint gleam of his eyes and the ghostly outline of his hair and beard.

"It's been a long trip," she said.

"Yes. But I don't mean merely this trip. I am tired of the way I'm living, the manner in which I've been living for years. The hours drained away, my time and attention. This constant pressure of business that weighs upon my chest."

She smiled. "That was only me."

He shifted against the sheets, ran his hand down her arm. "I'm not a young man anymore. I haven't been for decades. I wasn't young even the night we first met."

"Fiddlesticks."

"I feel young with *you*, sweet demon, but that must be your spell over me. I feel it only at your side." He paused. "I would enjoy a change, one for both of us."

"What manner of change?" She kept her gaze on what she could make out of his face, the shape of him almost lost to the night, to the rain.

"A new home. A shared home. A retreat in the wilderness, perhaps, by a lake or a river. Gardens. A single bedroom for us both, a threshold we can cross together at the same time, in daylight."

"Trees," she whispered. "For the birds that will follow."

"Trees," he echoed. "Yes."

Belle nestled against him once more, his warm skin, his bear-like chest. She closed her eyes and ignored her renegade heart, beating *no, no, not him, not now*.

She said, "I should like to choose my own wedding ring, Mr. Huntington, if you please."

Collis laughed quietly, a deep rumble that shook them both. He spread his palm along her shoulder to draw her closer. By morning she would be covered in his scent, not unpleasant but not her own, and would spend a full half hour in the bathtub to smell like herself again.

He said, "Miss Yarrington, I would never be so foolish as to presume otherwise."

Perhaps she did hold him in some enchantment. Minutes after his roundabout proposal, Collis sank completely into slumber, his arm still draped over her shoulder. Yet Belle lay awake the rest of the night, the rain sissing and dripping along the window glass, thinking about Edward. Thinking about her vow to Elizabeth, still bending Belle to her will even from beyond the grave.

* * *

They would wait to announce it. They would return to New York first and then summon Archer and Clara into a single room and inform them together. Belle was considering a summer wedding, June or July, enough time for her mother or even her siblings to arrive. Something small. Something tasteful and exquisite and extremely private, family only. That was all they needed.

She was also considering how best to banish the gloom of her impending home on Park Avenue, that damned lingering ghost of Elizabeth, and of the retreat Collis had said he wanted. How she might accomplish all of those things as quickly as possible because the less time she had to pause, to think, to consider that tiny needle of regret lodged in her chest—a needle shaped and polished by Edward Huntington, whether he knew it or not—the better.

Unfortunately, the journey back was unspooling in slow, sweltering minutes, in hours, in days. They were taking a paddle steamer up the Mississippi to Memphis, Edward's home. Once there, he would remain behind while the rest of them finished the trip north by rail.

The steamboat was flat-bottomed and tall, with a stack of wooden decks outlined in ornate filigree railings, and parlors and cabins swathed in velvet, brass odds and ends, everything glossed liberally in gilt. The enormous paddle wheel churned at the stern, a constant splashing that drowned any other sounds nearby.

Their cabins were located on the second deck, directly above the gambling saloon. The walls thumped with the rhythm of the wheel, the air reeked of tobacco. Muffled male conversation and laughter would seep through the floors at all hours of the night. She hardly slept, but when she did, she was back in Virginia, in Johnny's faro parlor, smiling and starving and gritting her teeth.

So Belle was feeling that needle inside of her with a particular acuteness, trapped on that damned slow boat, compounded by the jangly awareness that she wasn't getting enough rest.

Collis, however, was delighted again. With her, with the steamboat, with the broad muddy wash of the Mississippi River and the money he was betting at the games; win or lose, it hardly mattered.

He enjoyed it best when Belle or Archer was beside him, but she could only abide the saloon for so long. Despite her nightmares, she was many years removed from the Champagne Girl she used to be.

She'd leave with strict instructions for Archer not to wager more than he was given (with Collis staking him, that was a precarious enough line to draw), to not touch the mint juleps, only the lemonade. Then she'd retreat to the relative tranquility of the decks, drowsing in a rocking chair, marinating in the moist warm air.

The second night, full of stars, Edward finally approached.

There was hardly anyone else outside, just her and an elderly couple ten chairs down, all three of them rocking in silence. Occasionally a young cub pilot or mud clerk would dash by, cap askew, sleeves rolled up, but otherwise, after sunset, the river slipped beneath them in rolling peace.

"You cannot contend," Belle said, as Edward drew near, "that we are currently surrounded by hundreds of citizens."

"Surely those two count." He gestured at the other couple, who appeared to have fallen asleep in their chairs.

"Not really."

He stopped, captured in the light from the windows.

"I'll go if you wish it, but I'd rather not. May I sit?"

The needle twisted, but she said, "If you must."

He took the chair next to hers. A moment, long and full of weight, passed between them.

"A fine night," he said.

She did not reply.

Edward sent her a sideways look. "Did you know, Mrs. Worsham, that steamboats such as this usually last no more than five years?"

He sat so close; it was ridiculous to pretend he wasn't there. To ignore his gaze and his hands along the arms of the chair, his serge coat and oxblood-striped tie, his feet perfectly squared.

"All this effort and beauty," he went on, looking away again, "all this ingenious construction and design. Hours and hours of manpower, of dedication and wealth. But the wood rots, or the boilers explode. Or the hulls snag on the hidden cottonwoods and brush littering the water, the sand bars and reefs, and sink."

Belle said, "You seem always so full of facts of disaster, Mr. Huntington."

"Forgive me. I suppose I was merely thinking of the many ways that travel by rail is superior to boat."

"Locomotives have their issues as well, I believe."

"They do. And the passengers have the disadvantage of being contained entirely inside of them, peas confined to a pod. We would never enjoy an open night such as this aboard a train."

"The stars." She took in the sky, the arc of the Milky Way, a fall of silver and dusty blue that vanished behind the trees edging the riverbank.

"The breeze. Soft and muggy and . . ."

"Pungent," she finished for him, and for a hazardous second they shared a secret smile.

Belle ducked her head—*careful! careful!*—resumed her slow rocking in the chair. "I understand that you've taken a position with Collis in New York. That you'll be moving there soon."

"I have."

She pressed her heels against the deck, hard, testing her strength, its resistance. "I'm going to marry him."

"I know." He ran a hand through his hair. "Naturally, I know."

"Good."

"There's nothing more to say."

The needle turned, turned, burrowed deeper into muscle and sinew and bone.

"What else would there be?" she pressed. "Besides congratulations?"

"What, indeed?"

Another mud clerk rushed by, disheveled and surely not older than thirteen, scarcely as old as her son, his boots beating an urgent tattoo along the planks.

The river pulsed and the paddles churned and Belle looked at Edward, his expression drawn and his eyes faded to gray with the night. He looked back at her with all that undisguised longing he'd had since Yosemite, that dangerous, senseless longing carved so clearly on his face and she felt that falling star he'd summoned streaking through her, burning, searing. It would scorch her to cinders if she let it.

"At the end of this trip, Mr. Huntington, you will return home to your wife. To your newly monied wife, thanks to Collis, and your four monied children."

"You must know that I've never—"

She flicked a hand at him. "I don't care."

"—have *never* done anything to jeopardize my marriage—"

"I do not care."

"—and I have never been tempted to. Not once in all these years, so help me, until you."

As she rose to her feet, so did he. The couple down the deck were awake, after all. They turned their heads, curious.

"It's just *you*," Edward said, low, almost helpless. "Only you. I—I respect Mary Alice, I do. She is a fine woman. A fine wife. I love her. I love my family. Yet I cannot deny that I dream of you instead of her."

"How unfortunate for you. Good evening, Mr. Huntington."

He caught her by the elbow, released her at once when she stiffened.

"Arabella—Mrs. Worsham. I beg you—what is this thing between us? I know you feel it too."

How easy it would have been to pull away entirely, to pivot on her heel and leave, as a true lady would. She could ignore the needle in her chest, the stars and the smooth river and everything else . . .

But for the ache in his voice. The pain behind his eyes.

Belle was not a lady. She wasn't even true, as it turned out, not in her heart of hearts. So instead of leaving she only sat down again, surrendering to the sway of the chair.

They were matched in height, matched in age. Matched in, God help her, too many other unspeakable ways.

She had to undo it.

She said quietly, "I was young when my father passed. Perhaps you knew that?" Edward, silent, shook his head. "I don't really remember much of it. Mother nursing him for hours on end. How very thin he was, how skeletal. How ashen. It frightened me to see his bones poking up so sharp beneath his skin like that; sharp as knives, practically. He looked like a stranger to me, like a ghoul, and I didn't want to go close. Even when he tried to smile at me from his deathbed, to reassure me . . . I wouldn't go close."

She paused, staring up at Edward until he recalled his manners and sank back into his own chair.

"Not that Mother was going to let me get near him anyway, or any of us. We were children of the woods then, always covered in mud, half feral—but everyone around, all the trappers and home-steaders, were so terrified of cholera, whispering and gossiping, so I knew what *that* was. I also knew it was a city plague, so why wouldn't we be safe? We had a cabin of our own but lived out-doors mostly, next to this black torrent of water that never stopped running. It was the sound of my early girlhood, that river, and I guess in the back of my childish mind I figured if things got bad enough, why, that river could just carry us all away."

"Mrs. Worsham—" Edward leaned forward with his hands clenched against his chair's arms, but Belle spoke over him.

"Anyway, Papa died and Mama moved us out of the woods to Richmond. Somehow she'd scraped together enough money—she never would say how—to purchase this tumbledown board-ing house in a part of town that might best be called *unsavory*. And, gracious, it was a mess." She chuckled, tipped her head back against the tall top of her chair, the pins from her chignon pressing into her scalp. "Everything falling apart, everything crumbling, the roof, the ceilings, the floors. She set all five of us to work, to make it habitable again. We swept and mopped and chopped and hammered and scrubbed and scrubbed . . . my hands practically burned to bits from all the lye. And do you know what? No matter how hard we worked, no matter how much we *sacrificed*, each and every one of us, it was never enough. Our bellies were never full. Our sleep was never easy. It seemed for a while that John, the youngest, the weakest, might actually starve to death. But we managed to stave it off."

She held her palms before her face, turning them gracefully back and forth—like a dancer telling a story without words, like a ballerina—examining her skin in the spill of the boat's warm lights. "It was only after I went to work for Johnny Worsham that the bloody cracks mapping my hands began to heal, and I stopped leaving stains all over my dresses. But my mother and sisters and brothers . . . well, it was longer for them."

"I'm sorry," Edward said, soft and mournful, as though he meant it. As though he understood.

"Are you, Mr. Huntington? Well, my past is no blame of yours. My future, however—"

"I'd like—"

"Wait, I'm almost done. Consider it my own personal knowledge of disaster, if you will. There was this one particular afternoon, you see, my father's last afternoon, when my mother had gone out. I don't know where she went, probably scavenging for food. Lizzie, my oldest sister, was supposed to be in charge but she wasn't around either, I don't recall why. For a brief stretch of time I was there alone with my father in that reeking cabin, just the two of us, him on the bed, me pressed flat against the wall, trying not to look at him, trying not to *smell* him, groping for the door. He lifted his head from his pillow and gasped my name and do you know what I did then, Mr. Huntington?"

"No," he said gravely.

"I said, *You're not my papa*. Then I fled. Those were my last words to him."

"Oh, Arabella—"

"He died in agony because there was no means to provide otherwise. No money for a physician or medicine. Not even laudanum. It was a ruinous death."

She rose again to her feet; once again, he followed. The couple down the way had already melted off.

"You asked about this *thing* between us? Shall I tell you what it is?" Her tone lowered into silken venom. "It is the return of ruin to my life. It is risk and uncertainty and undoing, and the destruction of all whom I hold dear. And I will *not* be a part of ruin again. Not ever again, by God."

Edward recoiled as if she'd slapped him. His hands dropped to his sides. He closed his eyes and shook his head, turning aside.

"You're right, of course. I beg your pardon."

"You do not have it."

She picked up her skirts and clipped off.

Above them both, the southern stars still glittered. Below them, just feet below, just one thin deck below, Collis and the other gamblers played on and on.

CHAPTER 42

Clara
Manhattan, 1884

It was the first time she had ever visited Mrs. Worsham's magnificent brownstone. It was the first time she'd ever met any of Mrs. Worsham's relatives, besides her son. Arabella Worsham *did* have a mother—Clara would never be able to shake the memory of that ghastly dinner at Delmonico's; how she fell to pieces in the washroom, stabbed and bleeding from all the fresh truths of the night—but Arabella's mother didn't look at all as Clara had expected.

Well, to be honest, she couldn't really say what she'd expected. How should the mother of a mistress look? Beady-eyed, greedy? Cheap, garish jewelry; maybe an assortment of vulgar feathers pinned in her hair? Mrs. Yarrington was smaller than her daughter, gray-haired, her features plain but pleasant. She wore a modish gown of olive green, spare but first-rate, and a single strand of matched pearls, nary a feather to be found. She looked like anyone, Clara thought. Like everyone.

But she did not resemble her daughter. Nor did either of Mrs.

Worsham's sisters, seated opposite from Clara as the minister stood with his back to the reception room windows and chewed through his lecture about love and faith and the obligations of holy matrimony. They were also shorter than Mrs. Worsham, both of them with gold-streaked hair and dark eyes. Before the ceremony they'd shaken Clara's hand and smiled at her warmly, and only then had Clara glimpsed a hint of their sister in their faces.

Apparently there were a pair of brothers and a brother-in-law as well, but none of them had managed to make it in time. Something about working ranches, or cows, or the distance.

Mary Alice and Edward were in attendance, at least. With their stilted greetings and wooden expressions, they seemed ill-at-ease, to put it mildly. But maybe that was just their clenched-jawed, New England propriety bubbling up, chilling their good intentions.

So it was a small group gathered in the splendor of Mrs. Worsham's reception room, the Reverend Beecher still talking, Papa and Miss Arabella standing before him, clasping hands. It was July and it was the morning and the light (glorious sunlight!) seemed to touch and grace everyone in the chamber, binding them all together in a mighty, celestial glow.

Clara had spent weeks fretting about her approval of the match, wondering if it was entirely appropriate. If Mother in heaven would be pleased about it, pleased at last . . . or leastwise, indifferent. Yet now, as Clara basked in the sun, as she breathed in the light, allowing it to fill her up, she decided that Elizabeth *would* be pleased. Because she had, after all, truly loved Papa, all the way to the end.

And if you love someone, even if they don't love you back, all you hope for is their happiness, don't you? Their joy. That look on her father's face as he turned to his bride, touched his fingertips to her alabaster cheek and bent his head for their first married kiss.

CHAPTER 43

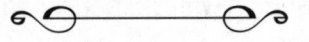

Arabella
Throggs Neck, 1885

Collis P. Huntington Weds
Famed Railroad Magnate and Financier Weds Family
Friend
—*Haut Monde* Social Events, Announcements, and
Reflections
July 14, 1884

Mr. Collis Potter Huntington, well-known multimillionaire railroad builder and recent widower, has taken as his second wife Mrs. Belle Duvall Worsham, an old family friend. The ceremony took place at the W 54 St mansion of the bride at precisely 10 o'clock in the morning, led by the Reverend Henry Ward Beecher, noted in certain circles as an abolitionist and societal reformer. The ceremony was closed to the public. Only a handful of family and friends were in attendance.

The second Mrs. C. P. Huntington, a blue-blooded

descendant of the House of Bourbon itself, moved north from Virginia after the war as a widow, bringing along her infant son. She has won wide praise for her beauty and refinement, as well as for her personal fortune, which was amassed not only by way of her family's holdings and those of her late husband, but also through her own shrewd investments in the real estate markets of Texas and New York.

Sources claim that the families of the newlyweds have been on intimate terms for years, and that the new Mrs. Huntington was, in fact, a dear confidante of her predecessor.

Mr. and Mrs. Huntington will live in both Manhattan and Westchester County, where Mrs. Huntington recently purchased the 100-acre Havemeyer estate known as "Beau Rivage" in Throggs Neck, along the East River, for the tidy sum of $100,000.

In no time at all, the letters began to arrive, each and every one of them from strangers begging for money. She was humbly beseeched to patronize worthy charities, or fund a dying child's medicine, or supply a new steeple for a church, as the old one was in imminent danger of falling and impaling the pastor.

Day after day they were delivered to her dearly lamented brownstone, to the mansion on Park Avenue, to the country estate at Throggs Neck—under renovation for so many months that the exasperated foreman began to leave the mail in piles for Mrs. Huntington, which she would later discover in whichever corner of the house wasn't currently being refinished.

(Mr. John Davison Rockefeller, who had unbent toward her enough to take the brownstone off of Belle's hands, had forwarded packets of letters to her for two months straight before including a note with the final bundle that said, *My Dear Mrs. Huntington, please direct your secretary to arrange weekly collection of your correspondence. Rgrds, JDR*)

And so Belle had found Carrie, Miss Campbell to everyone else, a clever and efficient young woman from Texas who spoke slowly and organized quickly, and who had the invaluable ability to scan a missive and determine nearly at once if the need was genuine, or merely a mountebank fishing for funds.

She also had excellent penmanship and a tolerance for travel. Within a week of hiring her, Belle's only regret was that she hadn't discovered Carrie sooner.

"Capable but not beautiful," Catherine had remarked after meeting her the first time. "Exactly the right fit."

Belle didn't bother to pretend she didn't know what her mother meant.

The Manhattan mansion had been designed and constructed to fit its narrow plot along Park Avenue, tall but with a scarcity of bedrooms. So they had cleared out the old nursery for Carrie, all the way up on the fourth floor but larger than the servants' quarters, and with its own private washroom.

At Beau Rivage, however, there was far more space, rooms enough for Carrie to have a proper one of her own, still with her own washroom but also with a fine view of the rose garden, a ruffled abundance of pink and red from April through September. In the height of summer, the perfume seemed to surround the house entirely, so thick and heady Belle almost felt drunk with it.

Beau Rivage, her beautiful country refuge.

The main house had two fine stories—three if you counted the attic; four with the basement—lined with rows of windows framed in painted blue shutters, cream pillars and a lovely scooped roof with columns and cornices and wooden shingles that ran down the sides of the entire top level in perfect, overlapping dragon scales.

The best part, Belle's favorite part, was the loggia facing the river in the back. Before the contract had been vetted and signed, before even the negotiations were complete, she had ordered a suite of furniture for that loggia, tables and chairs, rugs and plant stands and candle-lanterns. She envisioned years of peaceful sunrises there, sunsets, egrets and mallards and white sails slicing along the water in the distance.

In addition to the rose garden, the previous owner had cut a maze of graveled paths through the lawns and erected a pair of greenhouses with glass panels the gray-blue color of rain. A poultry yard had been established far back against the property line. If the wind was right, sometimes Belle thought she could hear the soft gossiping of the chickens—which, rightly or wrongly, she could not bear to eat. But at least there were plenty of fresh eggs.

For two years, the estate had sat unsold, even after the price had been lowered. Mr. Havemeyer was a sugar baron whose refinery had been lost to a fire. He'd needed the capital; Belle had needed a retreat, and unlike his young wife, he didn't mind acknowledging the second Mrs. Huntington—or at least, her wealth. They had both walked away satisfied.

Eventually, Belle and Collis would add towers to either end of the mansion and another three hundred acres to the whole site, preserving meadows, expanding the gardens, planting more trees, commissioning more fountains and even a separate house right along the shoreline, one just for billiards and bowling.

But on this long, lustrous August evening, two weeks after the final nail had been hammered, the final lunette completed, the bones of the main house stood essentially unchanged.

In the dreamlike beauty of the loggia, the newly formed Huntington family was enjoying sherry and seltzer before dinner, along with Catherine and Edward and Mary Alice and Carrie.

The sun was low, staining the sky with color. Clouds drifted in lines and a gossamer blue haze hugged the ridge of Long Island across the river, everything soft, everything temperate, exactly as Belle had envisioned. A breeze flirted by, tasting of fresh water and honeysuckle, a subtle hint of those roses.

"It's very rural," said Mary Alice, seated in the chair closest to the doors that led back inside the house.

"Do you think so?" Clara, on a bench much closer to the open air, crossed her legs and kicked up a foot, bouncing it. "I don't know. I guess we can't see the neighbors, but I don't miss that."

"Or the noise from the streets," said Catherine.

"Or the lack of stars," said Collis, at the brink of the steps to the lawn. "Look. There's the first one now."

And sure enough, as Belle and Archer stood at the same time to see, a fleck of light shone dim and alone in the center of heaven, gradually joined by a scattering of more, fiery white jewels against faded violet.

"What of you, Miss Campbell?" Mary Alice asked, lifting her glass to the view. "Do you find the place agreeable?"

"Hardly a fair question," Clara shot back. "What else can she say but yes?"

Carrie sat slightly apart from everyone else, Clara's little black spaniel, Titus, on her lap, scratching behind the dog's floppy ears. One of the candle-lanterns burned on the table beside her, faint light glimmering along her ginger curls.

She lowered her eyes and smiled. "That's all right. I don't mind admitting how much I enjoy it here. It's hard to imagine a place more peaceful."

"But so isolating!" Mary Alice persisted. She turned to Collis. "How do you expect to entertain here? Whoever will come?"

"We're here," pointed out her husband.

"Yes, Edward, but we're family. We have no choice."

Archer laughed and Clara kicked her foot a little harder, the hem of her gown flicking ivory chiffon over lace.

Collis was still admiring the vista. "I don't know that we need to entertain. Not as I used to do. I daresay men in need of my good opinion, or my goodwill, won't balk at visiting me here."

Belle leaned a shoulder against the nearest column, half listening, half taking inventory of the scene. Did the arrangement of chairs work? Were the rugs large enough? Did the candles provide enough illumination? Where was Edward looking, was he watching her, how close did he sit to his wife?

"*Men*," Mary Alice drawled with heavy irony, commanding Belle's instant attention. "Forgive me, Uncle, but I wasn't thinking of the sort of business associates you might entertain. I was thinking of Clara."

"Please do not," said Clara sharply.

"You'll never find a husband stuck all the way out here. You need to get into the swing of a genuine season. If not in Manhattan, at least Newport."

Clara's eyes cut, very quickly, to Belle, then away. Belle couldn't tell with certainty in the lowering dusk, but she thought Clara's cheeks might be flushed.

"Newport is a bore, Bar Harbor is a bore, and the constant rounds of dances and teas and charity auctions—"

"Clara," Belle murmured.

"—are bores," she finished, and rose. "Surely it's time to eat."

Titus bounced from Carrie's lap to the floor, ran to Clara. He licked his nose, a swish of pink over jet, and gazed up at her, hopeful.

"Yes," said Belle. "No doubt it's time. Let's go in."

Everyone rose obediently, and the footman on the other side of the glass doors opened them both, stepping back as they filed inside. Yet Belle lingered a moment longer, absorbing the sprawling beauty of her new world before turning to follow.

The dining room danced with light. A chamber that had been quaint and open before was now opulent and open, polished wood, polished marble, polished silver and gold. The windows were framed in satin and the chairs were upholstered in it. Belle's favorite painting, *Temptation*, was hung by the fireplace, surrounded with smaller but equally magnificent works.

Beau Rivage kept a separate staff from the Park Avenue mansion, including a separate chef, a daring young man from Lisbon who cooked almost entirely from imagination, his mind and fingers serving up superbly roasted meats and fruits, seared vegetables topped with bread crumbs or spices, all of it almost impossibly delectable.

Since practically everything else about the place had been transformed, Catherine wondered over her plate of lobster paella, would they keep the name that had come with the estate? After all, the shoreline *was* beautiful.

Collis scratched his cheek. "I hadn't considered it." He raised an eyebrow at Belle. "But perhaps we might prefer something plainer. What do you think, my dear?"

"I wouldn't mind a new name. Something to better reflect that it's ours, all of it, not just the shore."

Collis nodded. "A proper homestead. I agree."

"The Homestead, then," she suggested. "Simple and true."

Collis raised both of his eyebrows this time, and then his glass. "Hear, hear! To the Homestead."

And everyone toasted, even Mary Alice, although the corners of her lips sneered.

The parlor held a mirror-black grand piano imported from Vienna, one Belle had yet to sample much, just a few quick pieces, mostly to test its tune. Clara had turned out to be a much more dedicated musician, devoting an hour each day to play, the notes floating through the air, along the corridors, out the windows as far as the roses.

After dinner she gathered her skirts to sit before it once again, tracing out a melody Belle almost recognized. She lifted her head from her contemplation of her coffee cup, struck at once by the petite figure of her stepdaughter, her deep brown hair, her back straight and her head bent, that expression of frowning concentration, fingers flying.

How many years ago was it that Belle had sat before a piano in just the same way? Not a grand piano, no, only Johnny's upright in the saloon (or the battered old beast Mother had hauled from the boarding house), playing and playing no matter the hour or the weather, her fingers cold or hot, her heart cold or hot, and that purple moiré gown that Johnny had wanted thirty dollars to replace after the raid.

To seventeen-year-old Belle, thirty dollars might as well have been three thousand. It had been a hopeless amount, an impossible amount. An amount beyond despair or reason. But now—oh, now . . .

Clara finished with a flourish. Before anyone could comment or applaud, she began a new piece, Arabeske in C Major by Herr Robert Schumann, that old standby Johnny Worsham had admired so much.

Belle glanced at Collis to see if he'd noticed, but he was deep in conversation with Edward, their heads together before the hearth, and neither of them looked her way.

Later that night, she knocked on Archer's door to say goodnight. He was already abed but reading by the light of the oil lamp on his nightstand. The windows on either side of his bed were open; crickets called from the darkness beyond, a sweeping, creaking ballad.

She bent down, brushed a kiss to the top of his head.

Without looking up at her, he asked, "Mother, why don't you like Mr. Huntington? Mr. Edward Huntington, I mean?"

Belle froze, then smiled. "Goodness, what a question! Who says I don't like him?"

Archer turned a page. "You never look at him."

"Of course I do."

"You don't, though." Now he met her eyes. "But even though you don't look at him, he looks at *you*. Rather queerly too, sometimes."

"Some people are more conventional than others, Archer. I know you know that. It's possible that Mr. Huntington is still coming to terms with the nature of our family."

"Possible. But he never struck me as that type."

"Well! Who can really say what another person thinks?"

"You don't like to touch him, either. I've noticed."

Belle tried to appear amused. "Why on earth would I touch him?"

"You shake his hand but I can tell that you hate it." He shut the book, marking his place with one finger. "Has he done something? Has he offended you?"

"Not in the least," she said firmly.

And then Belle told her first and only barefaced lie to her son, ever, ever, in all their shared years before and to come. The first and only one.

She said, "Mr. Edward Huntington is a fine man, as far as I know. You're imagining this supposed aversion. I have no feelings for him one way or another, except to appreciate him as the nephew and coworker of your father, and cousin to you. And cousin-in-law, of course, to Clara."

Archer lowered his eyes again, a dark sweep of lashes just like hers, just the same, and reopened his book.

"Goodnight, Mama."

"Goodnight, beloved. Don't stay up too late."

He didn't respond, only wet his thumb and flipped another page.

CHAPTER 44

Clara
Manhattan, 1886

There was a boathouse on her father's riverfront estate, but still no boat. Clara assumed it was only a matter of time before he purchased one, if for no other reason than to keep up appearances. Collis Huntington wasn't a fashionable yachtsman like so many of his peers, but then, he didn't have to be, did he? He could buy a sloop or a sailboat or even a rowboat, and no matter what kind of vessel it was, he would pay someone to manage it for him and that would be that. He wouldn't even have to set foot upon it; he could just have the papers write it up that he had. Two men were employed full-time by the offices of the Southern Pacific for just such statements to the press.

People will believe anything they read in newsprint, Papa liked to say.

He never seemed to yearn for the water. Clara couldn't blame him; she herself was prone to seasickness and there were already entertainments aplenty to be found on dry land. All those picnics and dances and late nights at the opera, costume balls and dinner parties and recitals . . .

Not that Papa cared for any of those, either.

And not that it mattered. He'd never fit in as a chaperone, not the way Mother had done. It was not a father's place to guide a young woman through the savage waters of Manhattan's social doings; how could it be? How could a man possibly comprehend the murderous edge of a silent cut direct? How could a man feel the despair of being seated at the pitiable middle of the table at a formal dinner, instead of at the significant end, next to the host? How could a man even fathom the verbal slight of a powerful matron (a Mrs. Mills, for example, or a Mrs. Goelet), who might comment on the brooch at your throat, *diamonds before noon, how refreshing,* with just enough irony that you'd realize she would never acknowledge you again?

It was a mother's job to navigate those shark-infested waters. Yet Clara no longer had a mother, only a stepmother, and frankly that was hardly a help.

Mary Alice wasn't wrong to point out that Clara needed a husband. It seemed that every woman needed a husband, no matter her personal opinion on the subject. Wives were afforded a leniency, a *freedom,* that unmarried women were not and would never be.

It was also true that even at twenty-six, Clara *was* still invited places. She was, after all, an heiress, although there tended to be a poorly muffled debate about the *degree* to which she was one, what with her new stepbrother and those pesky cousins and all. The rough-and-tumble Huntingtons, it was pointed out over and over, were a sprawling sort of family.

Yes, Clara was still invited places, but definitely not to *as many* places as that misty-eyed debutante she used to be had been.

Twenty-six. A spinster now according to every level of society, not merely the elite. And what was more pitiable than a spinster, a powerless creature disdained by all, unwanted, useless except for coordinating flower shows and making up a fourth at whist?

Two weeks after her father's marriage to his paramour, Clara had been at the residence of Mrs. Nicholas Fish—the stately Clemence Fish, her ambassador husband long banished to the Continent—sipping tea and chewing tiny, mealy bites of cucumber sandwiches sliced into rectangles, occasionally alternated with tiny, mealy bites of ones slathered with salmon paste.

The weather was moody and the drawing room smelled of mildew. Mrs. Fish was hosting a meeting for a cause that Clara couldn't even dredge from the murk of her memory, but likely was something to do with orphans or widows or sailors, or all of them together.

Clara did remember wishing she could leave. Not only because she was bored, but because her former friend Patrice was also there across the chamber, laughing a shade too brightly (*just a dirty little baby!*) and showing off her wedding ring to anyone who'd ask.

Monte Carlo, Patrice was tittering. *Marseille, Villefranche, Luxor. The squalor of Egypt is so tedious but my dears such a honeymoon! You would not believe how fabulous.*

Mrs. Fish came to perch beside Clara on the chesterfield, a swish of dark gray satin and a wispy line of black feathers along her bodice, slender tendrils swaying around her neck like eels emerged from an underwater cave. "Miss Huntington, how are you enduring?"

"Oh." Clara turned her shoulder to Patrice, summoned a smile. "Well, thank you."

She looked down at her plate, two salmon sandwiches left, an ooze of pink dripping from the bread. She set it upon the table by her knees.

"It must be so distressing for you," Mrs. Fish said.

"Yes. Yes, it was for a great while. But Mother was very ill for months, of course. She's in the arms of God now."

Mrs. Fish lifted her left eyebrow: stylishly dark, stylishly plucked, a perfect triangular arc over a steely gray gaze. She lowered her voice. "I meant, Miss Huntington, the *marriage*. Your father and that . . . person."

Clara opened her mouth. She searched for the right words, for anything that might slip her back into her proper place in this moment, into whatever sort of role of sympathy or supplication this woman expected from her.

"Oh," was what she said, again.

Mrs. Fish pursed her lips. She looked away and lifted her teacup and almost, but not quite, took a sip before replacing it to the saucer.

"She will never be welcome in this house, I can assure you of that."

"Mrs. Wor— Mrs. Huntington?" Clara asked, her thoughts still three steps behind.

"If that is what we must now call her."

"I . . . I suppose that must be correct. What we must do. Forgive me, I'm not certain what to say."

Mrs. Fish turned to her with an expression of such genuine compassion that, to her horror, Clara felt her eyes begin to sting.

"None of this is a reflection upon you personally, Clara. I do hope you understand that. None of this is about you."

"None of what is?" Clara asked stupidly.

But Mrs. Fish only touched her briefly on the shoulder, then stood and walked away, the feathers along her neckline shivering.

From that day forward, the invitations began to taper off, fewer and fewer every month, an unmistakable signal of Clara Huntington's descent down the social ladder.

CHAPTER 45

Journal entry of Belle D. Huntington
January 3rd, 1887

Last night I had the nightmare again, the one I loathe. The one where I have a little soft rabbit of my own, a sweet small thing nestled in my arms. Something to kiss and love and cherish.

You cannot keep it, Mother tells me, coming close from the dark. Her face is penciled in anguish, stark and stern. *Another mouth to feed, in these times! Of course you cannot keep it.*

I protest that I love it, that it comforts me, but she is unrelenting. She takes the rabbit from my arms and breaks its neck.

Collis shook me awake to tell me that I had been crying in my sleep. As he held me, I mumbled that the nightmare was nothing, that it was gone. Already forgotten.

Arabella
Manhattan, 1887

Carrie placed a stack of opened mail in front of Belle, seated in the library at her writing desk, penning a letter to Emma. It was a bright Monday morning, quiet but for the rumble of the city outside, and Belle was attempting to catch up on her correspondence.

Matters progressing apace. Since Mother has come to stay she has experienced several sick headaches . . .

"Anything of interest?" she asked, but didn't look away from her letter.

Carrie's index finger tapped the top sheet. "The principal and treasurer of the Hampton Normal and Agricultural Institute wish to thank you for your generous donation, and declare themselves at your discretion if you would ever enjoy a tour."

Belle nodded, still writing.

. . . she claims they're nothing serious . . .

"The chairman of the Friends of Hope Hospital expresses his gratitude, as well."

We have brought in physicians . . .

Carrie settled a new page on top of the rest. "And this. From Mr. Ward McAllister."

Clara, curled up to read in the cushioned nook of the bay window, stiffened at once, causing the dog pressed to her side to lift his head and yawn. "Ward McAllister? Mrs. Astor's friend?"

"Indeed, the very one."

"Her minion, more like," offered Archer, lying on his back along the rug with one ankle crossed over his knee. He was still on holiday from school, pent up, ridiculously tall and energetic and teetering on the edge of outright rebellion. He'd been playing ball with Titus earlier, but since the spaniel had retreated to Clara, was tossing the leather orb up to the ceiling, *almost* hitting the fresco of cupids and clouds, *almost* letting it fall to his face before catching it again.

Belle said, "Archer. Use kind words, please."

From his position on the floor, Archer managed an adolescent shrug. "Was I unkind? Everyone knows what a lickspittle he is, even me, and I don't care. The Gatekeeper! The Sacred Holder of the Mighty Chalice of Acceptance!" He rolled to his side and sat up. "Anything he wants of you can't be good."

Belle put down her pen. She frowned at the heavy cream sheet edged in puce, neatly creased in two places to divide the page into exact thirds.

"What does it say?" Clara asked. "What *does* he want?"

Belle read the note and smiled, a thin and knowing smile, one that Johnny Worsham would have instantly recognized.

She tossed the paper back to her desk. "Exactly the same thing everyone else wants. Money."

Mrs. C. P. Huntington,

I beg the pleasure of, and your pardon for, introducing myself by way of this missive. I am Ward McAllister, a Good Friend of several outstanding citizens of our town, including Mrs. J. D. Rockefeller and Mrs. William Astor.

Mrs. Astor has generously volunteered to be the hostess of the upcoming Patriarchs' Ball, this 22 January. She has suggested to me, as the Ball's Director, that you, your husband, and your daughter be included among the guests.

The Patriarchs' Ball is, of course, one the most exciting events of the season, and the guest list is strictly restricted to no more than 350. The price of inclusion this year will be $1,000 (one thousand dollars), payable by bank draft made out to me.

Should you wish to accept this invitation, kindly respond no later than 12 January.

On behalf of Mrs. Astor and myself, I look forward to the great pleasure of meeting you in person there.

Your servant,
W. McAllister

Belle said, "He wants to invite us to the next Patriarchs' Ball." Clara made a small, strangled sound in her throat.

"For the sum of a mere thousand dollars."

Clara swung her feet to the floor, and Titus abandoned her entirely. "That sounds reasonable."

"Oh, yes," mocked Archer. He tossed the ball up into the air. "Perfectly reasonable."

Clara turned on him. "Everyone knows that this is how it's done. Even if one does not speak of it, this is how it's done. Mr. McAllister *is* the gatekeeper. One does not gain admittance into Mrs. Astor's circle without his approval, much less enjoy the privilege of an introduction."

"And an introduction," said Archer, in the same snide tone, "is paramount to one's happiness."

Clara went to the desk, picked up the sheet delicately, as if it might crumble to dust beneath her touch. "It is, *boy*. But I don't expect someone as green as you to understand."

Archer opened his mouth to reply but before he could speak, Belle lifted a hand. "Children. Cease."

Smack! went the ball, caught in Archer's fist.

"I'll put it to your father." Belle leaned back in her chair, clicking her nails against the satinwood arm. "I don't think he'll balk at this."

"Father hates all that social frippery," Archer pointed out.

"He does," she agreed. Clara was walking slowly back to the bay window, lost in the letter, her lips silently shaping the words. "But as much as he hates it, he cherishes us more. I don't think a single night of dinner and dancing is too much of a sacrifice to ask."

Clara looked up at her, haloed in light, big dark eyes, heart-shaped face, the letter clutched in both hands, and Belle was not thinking about helpless little rabbits. She was not.

The Patriarchs' Ball was not held in Mrs. Astor's fine sandstone residence on Fifth Avenue, but rather just down the street at dependable Delmonico's, emptied of its regular customers by midnight, and by half past midnight fully taken over by the crème de la crème. A French supper was offered in the main dining hall; both the Blue and the Red Rooms, in back, served as ballrooms for the dancing that followed.

Workers must have been frantic all day with the decorations. A swarm of workers, Belle thought as she entered the restaurant, a battalion of them to arrange all the palm fronds and evergreen branches along the doorways, to cover the walls in living blankets of asparagus fern woven with violets and roses. Orchid blooms dripped in delicate ropes from the ceiling down every corner, vanishing into false tropical forests. Birds-of-paradise poked their spiky orange heads out from behind potted banana trees and brilliant pink bougainvillea. Belle half expected to see a stuffed jaguar staring back at her from among the leaves.

An orchestra played in the larger Blue Room, the famed Hungarian Band in the Red. In both chambers, the musicians were discreetly separated from the guests by curtains of creeper vines laden with trumpet flowers.

But before the dancing there was the supper, and before the supper there were the introductions. Which, according to Clara, glowing in mandarin silk and pearls, were all that mattered.

True to his word, Mr. McAllister seemed pleased indeed to meet Mr. and Mrs. and Miss Huntington. *At long last,* he exclaimed, smiling beneath his enormously wide mustache, the ends waxed and curled into points. *How delightful that you could come, how very delightful!*

(Collis's check had been deposited days before.)

He shook Collis's hand with enthusiasm, bowed gracefully over Belle's and even more so over Clara's. If any of it was extraordinary, any of it not quite de rigueur, Belle could not tell. No one stared at them—almost no one—and no one turned huffily away. Perhaps it had more to do with the giddy, sticky atmosphere; the lively chatter. Such flattering light and champagne and satin and all the jewels! Jewels wherever she looked, winking and twinkling. Most of the women wore tiaras, or at the very least stacks of diamonds along their necks and wrists, interspersed with gemstones of every hue. One matron had a diamond pendant so large it actually blinded Belle when the lady and she both turned in the wrong direction at the same time. Light from a sconce shot through the stone and split into darts, a painful glinting spray of color straight across her vision.

The Huntington party made their way through the crowd to the table assigned to them, not even as far back in the room as Belle had feared it would be. Before taking their seats, Mr. McAllister again approached, this time with a tall, plump lady on his arm.

Belle knew, of course, who she was. Even if she hadn't glimpsed the famed leader of the beau monde all those years ago back on Park Avenue, ruthlessly climbing the steps to her club, Belle would know, because the other guests fell away from Lina Astor as if she were a queen. They bowed their heads and dropped their voices and absolutely dimmed in the glory of her radiance, enhanced by a gown of gold duchesse satin studded with emeralds and an elaborate diamond-and-ruby diadem that would not, in fact, have looked amiss on Victoria Regina.

Mr. McAllister was saying his words, whatever they were; Belle hardly heard them. She found herself acutely aware of towering Collis on her left, dainty Clara on her right. Collis extended his hand and the grande dame offered a grim smile. Belle followed, and the smile grew more grim. As they exchanged insincere pleasantries, Lina Astor's gaze focused on a point somewhere between Belle's eyes.

Clara, however, also knew how to shine. When it came her turn, she offered her gloved hand and said, "It is a great honor, ma'am" with unfeigned candor.

For the briefest moment, Mrs. Astor seemed to thaw.

"Miss Huntington," she said. "You resemble your mother, I believe."

Belle tensed but Clara only smiled and replied, "Thank you, ma'am. I miss her very much."

"As a good daughter should."

Mrs. Astor offered a regal nod that encompassed the three of them, a queen dismissing her subjects, and moved on.

Everything was going so well! Everything was going so miraculously well! The dinner had been outstanding, and if the other two couples at their table hadn't been precisely overflowing with jubilation to find themselves seated with the notorious Huntingtons, they hadn't been rude. Mr. and Mrs. Belmont, of the banking family. Mr. and Mrs. Perry, of military distinction. Mrs. Perry even mentioned, lifting a bite of *filet de boeuf* to her mouth, that they had a son about Clara's age, a fine young man working his way up through the naval ranks.

Belle had nodded and asked the conventional questions. Yes, the son would be home soon on leave, perhaps as soon as two months. Yes, both parents were looking forward immensely to seeing him again, such a handsome boy, such an eligible boy, not a fault to be found in his bones.

Clara had risked a glance at Belle then, swift and merry. Belle had to drop her gaze to her napkin to hold back her smile.

Collis began a conversation with the banker husband about the panic of '73, and for the next half hour both were so engrossed in their topic that no one had to say anything else, only enjoy the excellent meal.

The supper concluded. The guests began to rise and funnel back into the flowery glory of the ballrooms. At half past one in the morning, the dancing began.

Collis waited until the third dance, a waltz, to hold out his hand to Belle. She accepted with a smile, taking up the jade brocade and silver netting of her skirts, pushing the loop of her fan farther up her wrist.

Clara had been claimed nearly at once by an importer from Boston with a dimple in his cheek; she hadn't returned since.

Oh, the night was lovely. The night was beautiful, and even surrounded by all these social luminaries, Clara glowed like a flame.

"You dance divinely, Miss Lenore," Collis said into her ear, and Belle was startled into a laugh.

"Why, Mr. Huntington, how charming you are. I'd best keep my head around you, or you'll flatter me into smithereens."

"I'm not known to flatter. Only to speak my truth."

Belle lifted her chin, held his eyes as they twirled around and around the floor. "I do love your truth, sir."

His lids lowered; his hand tightened over hers. "How much longer must we stay?"

"Oh, another hour, please! Clara's in her element. Let's let her have her moment. It's been so long since I've seen her this happy."

He looked away, nodded. "You're right. This is for her. And *me*," he added, sweeping her into a quick, flaring loop with a grace that took her back to that night of the raid, on the saloon stairs, as he'd leapt nimbly beside her and followed her into their future.

They retreated to a row of chairs by the punch table, both of them accepting cups from the girl stationed behind the giant crystal bowl. But it was Roman punch, laced with amaretto, so Collis grimaced and set it aside while Belle drank hers, enjoying every sip. She had just finished it when Mr. McAllister strolled up, stroking his mustache and smiling his ingratiating smile. A rosebud fixed to the ceiling above him fell loose just then, bouncing off his shoulder. Ward McAllister only lifted a hand, brushed it belatedly away.

"Mr. and Mrs. Huntington! Well met! I was hoping to find you. It's such a crush, isn't it, such a success! Might I have a word?"

Collis gestured to the empty chair beside his. Mr. McAllister swiped at the cushion with one hand, sat down and straightened his waistcoat.

"I wish to thank you both again for joining us tonight."

"Yes," Collis said.

"It has been our pleasure," added Belle, leaning just enough forward to keep him in sight.

Mr. McAllister tugged at his waistcoat again. "I'm afraid there's been something of a complication regarding your contribution toward the ball. Nothing serious, mind you. Just a small matter of sums."

Belle felt her blood still, her heart still, as Collis said, unflustered, "Sums?"

"Yes, you see, I'm afraid it has been decided that someone of your . . . stature should really make a more significant donation to the event. To the *honor* of the event."

"My stature, sir?"

"Yours, sir, and Mrs. Huntington's." Mr. McAllister leaned around Collis to take in Belle as well, his forehead wrinkled, his mustache upright. "It has been decided that the sum of nine thousand dollars would be more equitable for the evening."

Collis only stared at him, taller, wider, infinitely more alarming.

"You need only pay eight now, of course," added Mrs. Astor's man, earnest. "As the one thousand you've already contributed will be applied to the total."

"Allow me to understand you perfectly well, Mr. McAllister," Collis said, as the orchestra played and Clara glided by in the arms of some new captivated fellow, her head tilted back, her arms a graceful arc over his. "You desire that I pay you—"

"Please, sir! Not *me*. The organizing committee for the ball!"

"—*you* another eight thousand dollars for the *honor* of being here tonight. The honor of this invitation, of speaking to your cronies and offering them my advice. My *business* advice, which, I must inform you, is not a cheap commodity on any market."

"I can assure you that this decision was made by the entire committee, all the Patriarchs themselves, sir. It is not personal."

"I have bested many of these *Patriarchs* in business so many times I cannot count. It seems to me that the matter is entirely personal."

"Mr. Huntington—"

Belle interrupted. "Is this decision of your committee absolutely final, Mr. McAllister?"

"Yes, madam! Yes, I'm afraid it is."

"A pity." Belle came to her feet; both men followed. She looked at Collis. "I've been thinking that Clara might do well in Europe. She has the flair for it, and the backbone."

Collis offered his arm. Belle placed her hand upon his sleeve, and Ward McAllister stepped in front of them both, his affable air vanished.

"Mr. Huntington! We require this payment! Should you not remit it, I *will* go to the press, sir. I will lay bare the truth of your refusal."

"Will you? I wish you the joy of that."

"I am sincere!"

"As are we," said Belle. "We are a family forged in fire, sir. Do you imagine the opinion of the press holds sway over us? Good evening. Do give my best to your patroness. It was a lovely meal."

"But—"

"And the best of luck to *you* in explaining to your confidantes how this very significant, very *influential* fish slipped clean away." She turned to Collis. "In fact, Mr. Huntington, perhaps we might speak to your colleagues at the papers first thing? To better explain the details of the night?"

"An excellent suggestion, Mrs. Huntington. You are, as always, a beacon of clarity. Goodbye, Mr. McAllister. I thank you for laying bare the nature of our dealings. No doubt more than a few members of the public will be interested to read about society's foibles in the tabloids these next few days."

They walked away.

It was more than an hour after that before Belle was able to feel the ends of her fingers again, her blood seeping back to her extremities in a cold, unpleasant tingle.

CHAPTER 46

Catherine
Manhattan, 1887

She did not wish to be a woman suffused with satisfaction at the notion of revenge. She didn't wish to live with resentment in her heart, even resentment thinned by the passage of time. And she absolutely did not wish to be the sort of woman who looked at her own daughter, her own marvel of fair flesh and blood, and feel these bittersweet emotions rise up through her, salty and conflicted and strong as the tide.

Life burned too short, yes. Too short, too hungry, too brutal. But where there was love there was joy, and surely those moments of joy, however brief, burned brightly enough to balance out all the rest.

So here Catherine was, trapped like a mote in a bubble in one of those special moments: Arabella, alight as an avenging angel in a spear of sunlight that pierced Clara Huntington's bedroom window, directing three maids on the packing of her stepdaughter's belongings for their upcoming trip overseas. Clara, smaller, more

mortal, always standing just aside, sometimes murmuring sugges-
tions, more often simply nodding at Belle's decisions.

From Catherine's vantage in her chair by the door (well out
of that unrelenting light), the room was a colorful chaos of open
trunks and dress baskets and cases, delicate leaves of tissue paper lifted, shaken out, folded atop every jacket, every gown, every
chemise and petticoat and lace waist. Sachets of winter savory and
pennyroyal spiced the air, made all the stronger by the sun's heat.

Catherine felt both distant and drowsy as she watched it all, a
sensation that was beginning to sweep over her more and more as
the days passed.

"The azure corded silk," Clara suggested, as Belle stood with
her hands on her hips, her gaze sharp. "The one with the saffron
wrap."

"Yes, good," Arabella said, and nodded to one of the maids,
who vanished into Clara's closet, reemerging with the garments.

"And the green ocher satin."

"No. It's going to be summer, not autumn. Nothing from more
than a year past."

"The . . . coral tulle?"

"Yes. Excellent."

Sleep tugged at her; Catherine's eyelids began to drift closed.
In the haze of her narrowed vision Arabella became even more
commanding, even more brilliant. Sunlight glossed the cherry
dusk of her hair and caressed the curve of her shoulders, her neck
and cheeks. Behind her spectacles, her eyes still shone that rare
violet gray.

From Richard's side, Catherine mused, her thoughts wandering.
Such a blessing from Richard.

Belle had wanted her mother to come with them on the journey, this trip that would be the grand launching of Miss Clara
Huntington overseas. She'd made promises of splendor, England,
France, Westminster Abbey, the Arc de Triomphe de l'Étoile,
all of them just places in books, words Catherine had once read,

dreams she'd once had. How beautiful it would have been to find them all real.

But her bones sang the truth: Catherine would not sail overseas to witness these splendors of men, not even in the luxury her daughter could now provide. She would remain behind in the undeniable splendor of New York, slower than she used to be, more moored to the earth. Her marrow growing heavier and heavier.

I'll stay and look after Archer, Catherine had told her daughter. *He shouldn't miss so much school. I'll stay here with him.*

"I hope it's all right," Clara fretted as the last trunk was closed, carted off by the footmen for the passage to Cherbourg. "I hope I've not forgotten anything. I don't know."

Arabella had settled into a wing chair, her back to the window. "We're headed to Paris first thing, straight to the House of Worth. Everything we just packed up now is detritus, there to fill the trunks on the way over." She sat forward, still aglow. "I shall unleash Monsieur Worth upon you, and you shall subsequently conquer entire realms. With your face, his fashion, and your father's fortune, gentlemen will be falling over themselves to kiss your hand."

Clara looked shocked; even half-asleep, Catherine had to smile. "Gracious! We don't mention our fortune!"

"Not here, perhaps. Over there, it is a very different world. A much more *honest* world. You will adore it."

"Do you think so?"

Arabella tipped her head back against the chair, crossed her ankles. She lowered her lashes and offered a very civilized smile, sidelong and knowing. "I do. I cannot *wait* to see you get the better of them all. It's going to be so amusing."

Revenge, Catherine thought, understanding completely. Revenge for every petty slight, for every snub and blatant injustice.

Because Arabella was Catherine's own revenge upon all the dire days that had come before, all the days when she and her children had been invisible, disposable, scrambling to survive.

The satisfaction of her accomplishment flooded through her, bittersweet and strong.

CHAPTER 47

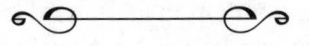

Arabella
London, 1887

LONDON WELCOMES A FRESH BATCH OF AMERICAN DAUGHTERS
WITH THEIR AMERICAN DOLLARS
—*The Advertent Eye*; Observing Social Stirrings since
1872
Now Twice Weekly!
July 12, 1887

The Summer Season continues to spin along at full tilt, with lovely young ladies to be found hither and yon. Sighted at Brown's Hotel was the radiant Miss Clara P. Huntington, daughter of California railroad baron Collis P. Huntington, he of the Many Millions, also in residence. In between buying sprees at the city's finest art galleries and jewelers—will there be any paintings left for our doughty old manor houses, we wonder, or tiaras for milady's head?—Mr. and Mrs. and Miss Huntington are being shepherded around town by famed

social godmother Lady Mandeville, formerly Miss Consuelo Yznaga of New York.

If Miss Huntington, a brunette of delicate demeanor, is a trifle *older* than the usual American heiresses paraded beneath the noses of the *ton*, it may
also be noted that she has already captured certain
hungry hearts with her attractive smile and charming
manners, the latter said to be quite the opposite of
rough Poppa's. Truly, money is not wasted on a refined
education for these New World Roses.

But beware, gentlemen in pursuit! It's rumored the
protective Mum and Pop will not settle for just *any* distinguished pauper. Noblemen only need apply, thank
you very much!

It was an open secret that, in England at least, certain social favors
could be purchased. Not purchased in the way that Ward McAllister had attempted, with flagrant and clumsy greed, but discreetly,
tactfully. Even kindly. An opportunity for grace by way of a check,
or a diamond ring or two, or three. Perhaps some stocks or bonds.
It appeared that the only thing the British aristocracy lacked more
than fresh funds were old funds: the American fortunes that had
been wedded to English noblemen a generation past could easily
be siphoned to nothing within decades. More wives than Lady
Mandeville found themselves in the awkward position of being
forced to act as social chaperones to young American women they
had never before met.

If an exchange of goods was required for such an invaluable
service, who could complain? Not the heiresses, finding themselves ushered, saucer-eyed, into Sandringham's royal drawing
rooms; nor the titled duchesses and countesses and baronesses
who'd found that English living (or, more precisely, their English
husbands) was far more financially draining than they ever anticipated.

Lady Mandeville, the future Duchess of Manchester, had

been a debutante never quite good enough for Knickerbocker New York. It hardly mattered that her family was wealthy, that her mother was descended from reputable New England stock. Her father's people were from Cuba, and that was enough to keep doors closed. Relocating to England seemed a cool and reasonable choice; marrying the heir to a dukedom seemed a cool and reasonable choice. Everything about Consuelo Mandeville, Belle thought, seemed cool and reasonable. Exactly what Clara required.

At their first meeting—tea at the hotel, Limoges china, strawberries and scones and clotted cream—Lady Mandeville had looked Clara up and down, directed her to stand, to walk across the chamber, to turn in a circle.

Like a circus poodle, Clara had said tartly, and when Consuelo only smiled, Belle knew she was the right fit.

Lady Mandeville did not flinch at shaking Belle's hand. She did not flinch at accepting Collis's fat check. She was, she assured them, fully capable of ushering Clara into some of the finest salons in the kingdom. There might even be, she murmured from over the rim of her teacup, an opportunity to meet the Prince of Wales himself, although she could make no promises on that front.

"He's a rather special friend of mine," she said in her cool and reasonable voice.

And Belle had smiled back at her just as coolly, because she understood exactly the special sort of friend the prince was to the someday-duchess.

London was etched in soot. The air smelled either of burning coal or the Thames, choked with flotsam and refuse. London was also sparkling, filled with Consuelo's urbane, aristocratic friends, their balls and garden parties, their stylish horseback parades along Rotten Row.

At least she's properly outfitted, Consuelo had said, after taking inventory of Clara's wardrobe, fifty-four new gowns, tea gowns and opera gowns and ball gowns; morning and afternoon and dinner dresses; over twenty thousand dollars vanished into the pockets of Monsieur Charles Worth. *Now let's get her some attention.*

And Consuelo had done so. Clara now had noblemen of all ranks and ilk fawning over her, inviting her to the races, or for luncheons aboard their yachts. Riding through Hyde Park, no matter how early in the morning, would inevitably conclude with a gentleman or two *accidentally* coming across them and offering to keep them company.

Belle did her best to keep her humor about it all. She did her best to appreciate this magnificent momentum she had planned and realized. She didn't think of Edward, or if she did, not very often. Not often at all, in fact.

Only by streams, for instance, did his smile resurface in her memory.

Only when standing before certain paintings offered for sale, landscapes especially, did she remember him inspecting her collection at the Homestead, hands clasped behind his back, carefully taking in every detail of the art she loved enough to hang in her home.

Only when it rained—and damned London did have more than its share of rain—did she think about the forest in Yosemite, when he had sat beside her atop that boulder and eaten half her orange, and everything between them had felt alive and dreadful and wonderful and just beginning.

Elizabeth had said, *Swear it to me upon your child's soul, Mrs. Worsham.*

Archer had said, *You never look at him.*

Belle would catch herself repeating, aloud or just in her thoughts, *Don't think on it. Do not think it, do not feel it, do not.*

And then, *I will not be a part of ruin again.*

But they were only words, only memories. They stiffened her spine but did nothing for her heart, pierced by a needle still, one lodged there by a man she could not have, who she would never have, who lived far away, in a life far from her own, and that was for the best. The best for everyone.

* * *

Lady Mandeville, with her understated frankness, offered her opinion of each of Clara's suitors.

Of a baron with a florid face: *Do you enjoy fishing? It's all he does.*

Of a copper-haired lord: *Fourth son of an earl. You'd be lucky to get a clerical appointment on a minor estate.*

Of a hook-nosed viscount: *Dedicated strictly to his horses and his mama, in that order.*

Of a grandson of a duke: *He'll get the manor one day all right, and every penny of your dowry will be devoured by it.*

But they were persistent, these impoverished British peers; it proved hard to shake off the worst of them. The viscount in particular was especially difficult to evade. He began to stalk Belle and Clara every morning on their rides through Hyde Park, insisting on offering protection from the shadows and the trees.

"Highwaymen, you know," he said mysteriously one day, his gelding cantering alongside them. "One can't be too careful."

"Really," Belle couldn't help but retort. "But I thought they were driven from the park decades ago. I have it on the greatest authority, in fact."

"Tosh! Who told you such a falsehood, madam? I'll call him out!"

"His Royal Highness," Belle lied, and that was the end of the viscount.

They *would* meet the prince, though, just over a month into their visit. A celebrated revival of Sullivan's cantata *On Shore and Sea* was taking place at the Royal Albert Hall, and Consuelo had secured them all seats in the Mandeville family box, located only eight down from the Royal Box, both on the Grand Tier inside the massive domed hall. When the crown prince arrived just moments before the lights dimmed, his Danish princess on his arm, all of polite society lifted their theater binoculars and turned to look, then turned politely away again.

The rest of London's masses, seated below them or else far above, stirred and buzzed and did not look away.

Lady Mandeville, however, never once turned her head. She only waved her ostrich-and-lace fan before her, slowly, slowly, her eyes fixed on the arena below them, on the sparkling people taking their seats. When she lifted her chin, the diamond strands woven through her hair flashed, white and blue and green.

Clara leaned toward Consuelo. She lifted her fan to cover her mouth and said quietly, "He's more handsome than I thought he'd be."

Consuelo cut her eyes to her, surrendering the smallest smile. "He is, isn't he?"

At the intermission Lady Mandeville stood, whipped her fan closed.

"Come with me," she commanded. "And remember to curtsy as I showed you."

The curved hallway was thronged with people, so many people, so much satin and brocade and beading and glass pearls, women chattering, men shaking hands. In the midst of a particularly impenetrable crush, Clara reached out and found Belle's arm, holding fast as they made their way after Consuelo. And so when they reached the royal box they stood linked like school chums; Belle was only able to gently disengage them when Consuelo swung about, Prince Albert suddenly and magically beside her, the crown princess just behind him.

"Your Royal Highnesses," Lady Mandeville said. "May I present my new friends, Mrs. Collis Huntington and her daughter, Miss Clara, both from New York."

The prince was not, in fact, handsome. Belle heard that he'd used to be; during his trip to New York in 1860, prim and virginal debutantes were said to fall swooning right at his feet. Even the Richmond papers carried stories of it, all the silly young girls throwing themselves at him. Back then Albert had been sleek and fair and so very unwed. Belle supposed those Knickerbocker daughters had imagined anything was possible.

But the man who took her hand now, who smiled at her and

greeted her by name was portly at best, with bulging, watery eyes and a gaze that kept returning to Consuelo, no matter whom he addressed. Belle retreated to allow Clara to the fore and the prince looked a little more closely at her, rising like a swan from her curtsy . . . but by then Belle's attention had shifted to the Princess of Wales.

She remained two steps behind her husband, drowning in ropes of pearls, collars of pearls, heaps of pearls, her hair piled in tall, tight curls shaped to support the diamond tiara hugging them, more pearls the size of quail eggs dangling from the points.

Her face was white as chalk. As her husband took Clara's hand in his own, her mouth twisted, very briefly, into an expression that Belle could only call anguished.

Belle dropped her eyes. Since her marriage to Collis she had come so far. She had voyaged across the Atlantic, had sailed into drawing rooms and restaurants and odd corners of fashionable society she'd never thought would allow her in. And yet here was the ghost of Elizabeth again, still tormenting her. Here was Collis's dead wife, standing in front of her in the form of this other betrayed woman, this royal, bereft woman, with her false smile and clenched hands.

Belle feigned humility. She would not meet the princess's eyes again, not even when they were introduced.

Back in the Mandeville box, Clara was glowing, Consuelo was smugly satisfied, and the lights dimmed once, came back up, to announce the end of the intermission.

Clara sat forward in her chair, her lorgnette held to her face. "Who is that gentleman?"

Both Belle and Consuelo unfolded their opera glasses to see.

A trim, mustachioed blond man sat in the red-curtained box almost exactly opposite theirs, his own glasses in hand, obviously watching them. He took note of their attention, lowered the glasses and smiled. The young woman seated next to him tilted toward him, saying something into his ear, but he did not look away.

"Bold, for an Englishman," Belle noted.

Consuelo lifted her fan. "He's not English. Bavarian." She returned her gaze to the stage below, the chorus walking in, taking their places. "Prince Franz von Hatzfeldt-Wildenburg. His uncle is the German ambassador here. His family is known for their castle on the Rhine and their merry-go-round of expensive divorces. *He* is known for his gambling debts." Her lips tightened; she looked at Belle and gave the barest shake of her head. "Do not think it."

Belle didn't think it. But Clara, who looked swiftly down and away from the Bavarian prince, her shoulders bowed, a flush rising up her throat, apparently did.

She'd rejected viscounts and earls and barons, but this fellow, this chancy fellow, warranted a blush?

Belle thought, suddenly tired, *Thank God it's almost time to go home.*

CHAPTER 48

Catherine
Throggs Neck, 1888

Bit by bit, her blue-sky days were waning.

By the beginning of June, Catherine couldn't help but rise before the sun. In an unexpected reversal of the lethargy that had
dragged at her all the year before, she never seemed to sleep much
of late, yet was seldom tired. When she found herself opening her
eyes to early morning darkness, it was no bother to get up and
dress herself, despite the arthritis riddling her joints. To make her
way through the slumbering mansion alone, creeping along the
chilled, unlit parlors and corridors and out to the back lawn over-
looking the river.

A scattering of mature trees, she didn't know what kind, grew
here and there along the grounds, some clustered in groves, some
standing by themselves, guarding the flower beds and the view.
There was never anyone else around, only an occasional rabbit, or
one of the cats from the barn. Sometimes a heron, watchful at the
water's edge.

In those gray hollow hours before dawn, the East River would give rise to a curling mist, almost a fog, that skated along its dark surface, concealing whatever swam or sank or drifted, lost, beneath it.

A teakwood bench had been stationed by one of the lonely trees, and Catherine liked to sit there wrapped in a blanket, watching the mist coil. Watching the sky transform.

She used to worry so much about the changes in her life (to be fair, they tended to be frequent *and* drastic). How she would survive them, how she'd manage to drag her children along, keeping all of their heads above water, and then *their* children too. Everybody swimming.

But in the end, Catherine Yarrington was all alone, shed of her children and grandchildren and her sleep. Shed even of anticipation for what the day would bring. She appreciated *these* moments, her world pared down to the simplest of sensations. Her heartbeat; the water whispering secrets. The tree branches shivering with the strengthening breeze, pushed by the sun from the other side of the world.

Often with the fog she found herself thinking about that other river, the one from her days as a bride and young mother. How she used to worry about that as well: the silvery, smoky mist that crept up to the cabin door and beckoned her babies to come out, to come play and be vanished. Lizzie liked to frighten the little ones with her stories of ghosts twisting in the vapor, but the truth was worse, because that Alabama river had stolen lives before, generations of settlers. So maybe some of those ghost stories were true.

Catherine wondered if Arabella realized that she had built her nest in a place so like the foggy edge of her childhood. If she had done it deliberately, or it was only a manifestation of a memory half-recovered, a memory that might even give her comfort. She thought sometimes about asking her, but then—if Belle *didn't* remember—Catherine didn't want to make her daughter doubt her dreams.

After all, they'd turned out to be such splendid dreams.

On this particular morning Catherine sat on her bench and felt a lightness in her bones she'd not experienced in some while. To the west was black velvet, no stars; to the east a slow burning line of maroon defining the horizon. The river mist rose in defiance of the coming day, still curling, still creeping, pearly gray not yet tinged with dawn.

When her husband emerged from it, Catherine felt no surprise at all. He smiled at her and his hair stirred and his perfect face was so unchanged, so exactly as he'd been when she'd first seen him—nothing but hired help fixing the cider press in her father's barn, covered in dirt and oil, an Adonis composed of such divine proportions of muscle and flesh that she actually forgot to breathe.

She felt it happen again, the rush of her breath leaving her chest, the delirious suspension of her heart and lungs, because he was here, he was here, and she had never stopped loving him, no matter what had come next, no matter how hard she'd tried to stop.

Richard held out his hands. Catherine accepted them, standing, letting the blanket fall away from her shoulders. She joined him, her bones still so weightless, in the smooth beyond of the river.

CHAPTER 49

Journal entry of Belle D. Huntington
February 1st, 1889

It's been eight months since she passed, and sometimes it still feels as though I can't breathe. That I'm smothered in cotton batting, that I'm drowning in an ocean of black glass. I can't take a deep breath. I can't feel my legs or my arms. I can't reach out and embrace my mother as I used to do, press my forehead to her shoulder. I can't smell her perfume, that scent she wore that always reminded me of fields of lavender, like the ones in France, purple stems swaying under the sun. I can't talk to her, I can't find her, I don't know where she went, how a life can *be* there and then suddenly *not*—

She was my wisdom, my guide. She kept me safe, as safe as she could. She kept me alive.

I visit her grave at Woodlawn and I feel just as empty there as I do when I stand before Elizabeth's, a woman I didn't even like. I thought perhaps I'd feel *something*, some connection, reading the epitaph chiseled along her headstone.

BELOVED WIFE, BELOVED MOTHER.

But they're only words. No hint of who she really was, how she faltered and how she loved, how she carved her own path through the brambles and came out on the other side of the thicket with all of her children in tow.

Mother taught me to cut my way through as ruthlessly as she did and never mind the thorns, because when the thorns scratch and we bleed, we learn from it. We heal stronger. She taught me to welcome the summer days as well as those of frost, because waking up to either meant I was still alive, and as long as I was alive, I could force my fate into a better place.

Nothing in this mortal world is certain, except that I miss her.

Arabella
Manhattan, 1889

The crooks and corners of the Park Avenue mansion were haunted by phantoms: reflections of people long dead, antique statues and busts, paintings from Europe or the New World crowded along the walls. An alabaster Eleanor of Aquitaine stood cradling a toddler in the conservatory. A bearded and glowering bronze of Aristotle, and another of Socrates, rested heavily by the library doors. Everywhere Belle turned there was art, there was grandeur, and there was a darkness she could not lift, not even when she replaced the drapery in every single room—*every* room—with French silk instead of musty velvet, with gold and white and cream instead of brown and blue.

Still the phantoms rose, reaching for her with their pale stone arms, watching her from pale painted eyes. The rooms of the house were crammed with Belle's collections, with Collis's, and with the memory of Elizabeth, whose slippered feet had crossed these floors well before Belle's own. Whose hands had gripped the railings and the bell pulls just as Belle's did; whose voice and will first summoned the servants from their hidden realm behind the walls—

Elizabeth lingered everywhere here, this place where she had lived and died. Even her funeral service had been held here, right here inside the home where Belle had been forbidden to set foot for so many years. Newspapers had devoted somber columns to descriptions of the day, the mansion crammed to the gills with churchgoers and relatives, the black-coated business associates of Collis's, a scattering of social elite filling in the edges.

The papers took careful note of the Reverend Eaton's eulogy overflowing with praise for Mrs. Collis Potter Huntington, a celebration of her kindness, her generosity of spirit, her forgiving soul.

Elizabeth, it had been reported, was a woman who would gladly give a chilled stranger her own gloves; who had looked upon none with harsh judgment; who had never met a child she did not cherish as her own.

Indeed.

Sometimes when Belle walked the halls she imagined movement from the corner of her eye, subtle and never there when she turned, unless it was the swelling curve of one of her new curtains touched by a draft, or a cloud passing silently over the sun.

Sometimes it was more. The sensation of a hand pressing lightly atop her shoulder. A sigh of breath, scented of sorrow, just behind Belle's ear.

It was never a real phantom, of course. It was never Elizabeth, but the constant *impression* of her that haunted Belle, mistress of her rival's former domain.

Collis didn't seem to notice her efforts to banish the dark—or if he did, at the very least, he didn't mind. He left matters of décor, of the elegance of ornamentation, entirely up to Belle, even to the point that he raised no protest when she began (slowly at first, then with increasing frequency) to exchange Elizabeth's choices for her own. Plain oak tables and chairs became intricately carved rosewood or cherry; old-fashioned rugs of worn birds and vines were rolled up and swapped for plush modern masterpieces straight from importers uptown. Dull paisley wallpaper was stripped away, replaced with salmon silk patterned with silver fleurs-de-lis, or pale lemon with hand-painted sprays of blue poppies. What walls she couldn't refurbish with paintings or paper she covered with Boucher tapestries instead, scenes of exuberant life: maidens dancing in the woods, flowers blooming, gods cavorting.

And still, and still . . .

This would never be entirely her own home, not like her gem on West Fifty-Fourth, not like the *cuivre doré* retreat she had created at Throggs Neck.

Already she'd sacrificed much to placate the whims of the previous Mrs. Huntington, for no reason beyond the fact that Elizabeth had worn Collis's wedding ring first. Precious years from Archer's life, the precious potential of Edward. Belle's own ambitions, burning and insistent yet tempered by this secondary space she occupied, or perhaps even tertiary, scandalous courtesan turned scandalous wife.

She would not be forced to endure this Park Avenue house as well, echoing from floor to ceiling with the late Mrs. Huntington.

She would not abide this sacrifice any longer.

"I am surprised at this sudden abandonment of your preparations for our trip," Collis said, seated beside her in their grand black carriage as they rolled along Fifth Avenue. He slanted her an inquisitive look from beneath heavy lids. "You always devote such care to the packing, especially for our longer journeys."

Belle adjusted the furs covering them both. "We don't depart for Mexico for another two days. I have great faith in the household to carry on without me for an hour or so. The staff won't mutiny and the walls won't tumble down. Besides, Clara was happy to take over."

"Good practice for her," he grunted, looking away again. "For her own household, someday."

"Yes," Belle said, even though lately and privately she had begun to think that Clara's *someday* might never arrive.

It made little sense to her. Her stepdaughter was pretty and clever and very, *very* rich, which should have been enough to snare half of blue-blooded Manhattan. Yet she dismissed every admirer who chanced her way, calling them *dull* or *ordinary* or—most damning of all—*desperate.* Belle wasn't certain if she should attempt to tame Clara's contempt or merely stand back and admire her ferocity.

"Will you tell me yet where we're going?" Collis asked.

"Not yet. But I think . . . yes, we're nearly there."

The carriage slowed, stopped. Belle peered out the window, then opened the door without waiting for the footman to do it, descending and turning at once to offer her hand to Collis. His fingers closed over hers; he followed more slowly.

A wifely gesture, to guide him with her own hand, but also one more and more of necessity these days. He wasn't as certain on his feet as he used to be; gout had settled in his right knee and his eyesight was dimming. On his second step along the pavement he stumbled, just barely, but Belle was there to press up against him and keep them both steady.

She escorted him onto the large, barren lot of dirt and scruffy dead grass, remnants of the last snow still clinging to its edges. The carriage lurched back into the flow of traffic; the coachman would circle the block until she signaled for him again.

Collis released her hand, tipped back his hat. "Be my eyes, demon. Tell me what I'm seeing."

It was a corner parcel, slightly raised above street level. Someone had taken the trouble of scraping and squaring the top of it, but that was all. Surrounded as it was by towering mansions, the lot resembled a missing tooth in a gleaming smile.

"Fifth Avenue," Belle said, lifting a hand before them, her words curling silver with frost, "and Fifty-Seventh. To your right is the charming château of Mr. Cornelius Vanderbilt. To your left, the palace of Mr. W. C. Whitney. Across the way we have the venerable Mr. Floyd Jones. And here, my love, right here where we stand, will be our palace to come."

Collis removed his hat entirely, turned a gradual circle through the shorn weeds, squinting at the streets, the cold-frosted mansions, the bitter blue sky.

"Our future," she said. "Three stories, or four. Granite and marble and brick. Rooftops rimmed in carved stone. Libraries and terraces and elevators. Room after room designed to astound, to amaze. A place to declare to one and all that *we* are here." She interlaced her fingers through his as hansom horses snorted and jingled and men and women in heavy coats walked past, throwing them inquisitive stares. "The parcel just came on the market yesterday. I know we're leaving soon, but I am ready to act, if you are."

It was a testament to them both, she would think in their final years together, to the enduring kinship of their souls, that in this bold moment Collis didn't hesitate, that he asked no questions of her and implied no doubt. He didn't even ask the price, but instead only looked back at her and nodded, his expression thoughtful but sure.

"Of course," he said, and that was all.

Mexico was dry and dusty and scorching with heat, prickly cactus plants of all kinds sprouting from unexpected places, a haze of mauve mountains always in the distance.

Mexico was also lush and welcoming, with tropical forests and strands of sugary white beaches and water so painfully turquoise it looked almost unreal. If Belle had seen such a sea in a painting she would have thought the artist either mad or inspired by a dream.

In Mexico City they stayed in a pale cream stucco hotel with white scrollwork and heavy black timbers. Floors of echoing ceramic. The very center of the property protected an enclosed garden open to the sky, a serene space overflowing with fountains and vines and ladybugs, and dainty tables for taking meals. The rooms shone with crystal chandeliers and stained-glass windows. The ceilings towered so high it was almost impossible to make out the patterns of poppies in the pressed tin tiles.

While Collis was off negotiating plans to expand the Southern Pacific Railroad—the *ever* expanding Southern Pacific Railroad— Belle and Archer and Clara and Carrie spread out, split apart, following their interests or just their instincts. Belle was happy to visit the Plaza de la Constitución, with its heavy air of antiquity and thick stone edifices, and vendors selling everything from roasted corn to men's shirts embroidered with flowers.

Archer vanished almost immediately in the smaller alleyways of the city, always in search of books, of knowledge, of any scrap of history he didn't already possess. His Spanish was excellent, far better than Belle's or anyone else's, and if he didn't duck away quickly enough in the mornings, he found himself roped into acting as their translator for the rest of the day.

Carrie and Clara enjoyed the outdoor markets, the stunning jasper and abalone jewelry pressed upon them wherever they went, or the cathedrals, those vast and ornamental spaces fragrant with incense and guttering votives. Belle preferred smaller places, more intimate venues. A tiny shop off the edge of a plaza selling nothing but opals, for example, or another selling nothing but thread. One bright afternoon she came across a cocoa house that served steaming hot drinks so spicy it brought tears to her eyes, but so delicious she could not help but order a second cup. She purchased bricks of the chocolate to take home with her: chili-flavored, honey-flavored, or sprinkled with tiny sugared buds of mint.

The shop also offered stacks of tattered books for its patrons to peruse as they gossiped and enjoyed their drinks. Belle found herself absorbed in a slender, leather-bound volume of poetry, *El polvo de las almas perdidas*, which was so achingly wonderful she offered to purchase it before she left.

"No, no," replied the teenaged boy behind the counter, expertly pouring out a cup of greenish froth from his kettle, his hands bound in cloth. He looked up for a second, a flash of hazel eyes, before returning to his task. "*Por favor, señora, tómalo.* Take it. This is God's wish. It is yours."

She left an amount three times the cost of her chocolate bricks and drinks anyway, wishing him health and happiness before she left.

* * *

And Mexico was an old place, an ancient place. The one destination they all journeyed to together, Collis included, was the terraces and pyramids of Monte Albán, that lost, long-ago city slowly being devoured by nature.

Collis agreed to the carriage ride up the hills to the ruins, but he would not attempt the crumbling steps of any of the platforms or pyramids, and nothing Belle said would sway him. So it was up to her and Archer and Clara to begin the arduous climb up the tallest pyramid. Carrie stayed behind with Collis, fanning herself in the shade of a spindly tree at the base.

It took just over a half hour. They paused frequently for water, carried by Archer in a flask, but there would be a picnic luncheon awaiting them below, and everyone was eager to reach the top.

The world spread before them, green valleys that folded up into mountains, a feverishly blue sky that stretched into a wavering mirage at the edge of the earth.

Belle eased down to sit on the edge of the final step, adjusted her hat and planted her feet. She thought about all the people who had climbed these steps before her, who had built this tower of stone and this citadel of gods, living and thriving in the miracle of their vision until one day they hadn't, and all had been abandoned to ruins.

"Revelation," Archer said, coming to sit beside her. He unbuttoned his collar, sat back on his hands and blew out a breath. She looked at him, waiting.

"This *place*," he went on. "This entire *country*. I feel . . . unpeeled. Like an onion without its skin, soft and exposed."

She smiled, though it was clear he was quite serious. "An onion?"

"Or an oyster! One shucked from its shell. I can *see* now, and *feel*. All this raw beauty, Mother. Such powerful beauty. It almost hurts."

"Ah," she said now, because beauty and pain entwined was something Belle understood very well.

He turned to her. "We're so impermanent. It's hard to grasp, isn't it, until faced with a view such as this."

"But we've always been impermanent." She bumped her knee against his. "There's no getting around it. Understanding that just means you treasure your hours all the more. Nothing in this mortal world is certain. Nothing is forever."

"Not even love? Family?"

"Maybe that." She scraped the heel of one boot against the grit of the stone, grit a hundred years old, two thousand. She thought about her new tattered book from the chocolate shop, poems about the drifting dust of souls. She thought of her mother, always undaunted, and her father, a silhouette in her memory, barely a smudge, and of how she had forsaken him in the end.

"Yes," she said to her son. "Love and family. If anything endures, it must be that."

"And art."

"Hmm. Art . . ."

"Which is why we collect so much of it?"

Belle laughed. "But of course."

Their hotel in Oaxaca was smaller than the one in Mexico City but just as lovely, and with very nearly the same layout, the guest suites all fronting an inner garden, this one containing a single tall fountain carved from banded onyx, five levels of scalloped dishes catching the water bubbling from the top. Lily pads floated in the bottom basin; butterflies and bees gathered along their edges to sip water before winging off again.

It was the high heat of the afternoon. Collis was in a meeting; Clara and Carrie were napping and Archer had hared off to who knew where. Belle wasn't tired enough to nap, so instead she wandered into the sanctuary of the garden, thinking about *la merienda*, that pleasant little meal served midday, just when the thought of dinner seemed impossibly far off.

She found an attendant and placed her order, then claimed a

table near the fountain. The garden was quiet, nearly empty but for her and a hummingbird with a bright blue head and a bejeweled body, darting from flower to flower before soaring off.

The lily pads were gathering their usual collection of insects, drowsy winged creatures. A ladybug had either fallen off the edge of the basin or one of the pads and was struggling to swim, a slow drowning, a bright red shell and translucent wings that were no match for the inevitable end.

Belle rose, leaned over and scooped it up in her hand, letting the water flow between her fingers. She placed the ladybug on the nearest pad. It wandered in a circle for a bit, trailing wet silver, before gathering itself and flying off, a zigzag ascent up to the sky.

The water was cool as the air was not, and now she was thinking of a swimming bath, like the ones they sometimes had in the more modern hotels, ladies in the morning and gentlemen in the later hours, and how nice that would be right now, to be out of her corset and floating on her back like the perfect green leaf of a water lily.

Distracted by this delicious thought, when she turned back to her table it took a few seconds to realize that Clara was also in the garden, seated in a chair partially hidden behind a potted palm. Belle could see only her profile; she was reading something, a letter perhaps, utterly absorbed.

Belle hesitated, then approached. She paused at the edge of Clara's table and still her stepdaughter didn't look up from the sheet of paper in her hands.

Belle tried a cough. Clara started and crushed the letter to her chest.

"I apologize. I only came over to offer some tea and pan dulce." Clara's cheeks were reddening; Belle pretended not to notice, only lifting a hand to her table, the service already being set out by the attendant. "I believe they have that pineapple sweet you're so fond of. If you're interested?"

Clara swallowed, smiled. "Thank you."

She folded up the letter and tucked it into her reticule.

"News from home?" Belle inquired mildly, finding her seat again, pouring the tea.

"Yes. Yes, actually. My friend Julie Sherwood writes to tell me that she's thinking of a trip to Europe this summer, a sort of re-sort tour of Spain. Perhaps also Aix-les-Bains and London. She's invited me to join her."

"Spain!" exclaimed a new voice. Archer yanked back a chair, collapsed into it and tossed his hat on the table. At five inches over six feet, he'd finally stopped growing, but most chairs were too small for him, and his arms and legs always spilled over. "A terrific idea. When shall we go?"

"*I* will be going in June," Clara said, moving his hat to the empty seat between them. "With a friend. She's only interested in the more popular resorts. You'd be bored to death stuck with us."

Archer grabbed a sweet roll without waiting for a plate, tore off a bite. When he noticed Belle's expression, he sat up straighter, dashed the sugar from his lips. "Sorry, Mother. I missed breakfast. Anyway, Clara, you're right, it sounds awful. Why go all the way to glorious Spain if you're only going to see the very same people you see at home, doing the very same things?"

"I imagine there will be *some* new people there," Clara said.

CHAPTER 50

Clara
Barcelona, 1889

How strange it was to keep such a secret from her family. How difficult.

Clara was not what many people would call transparent; she had her mysteries, she had her moments of ugly emotions and petty thoughts and wildly brilliant reveries, but she was not used to hiding her life to *this* degree from her father, or even her stepmother or brother.

But she knew what would happen if she told them the truth, any of them. She wasn't a child any longer but she was, like almost every woman she knew, dependent upon someone else's largesse to sponsor her life. She could not vote and she could not take a single step along the streets of Manhattan without a chaperone at her heels. She could not secure a job without the expectation of scandal, and she could not hope to shake hands with Caroline Astor again.

But she could escape.

And so escape was what she did. She fled the stifling confines of New York for Spain, *glorious Spain*, as Archer had called it, and he wasn't wrong. Spain! That dry Mediterranean heat, those orange groves and olive groves and wineries set back amid undulating, ambered hills. Spain, with its complicated history and complicated mixture of languages and races and divine grandeur, as if God had decided to make the most perfect place, just enough rain, just enough ocean, just enough cathedrals and windmills and gothic architecture . . . and then let everyone in snobbish, bustling American high society forget all about it.

She and Julie had arrived in Barcelona in mid-June and within the week, Francis was also there. They had coordinated his arrival, of course. Julie was a willing participant in their little deception— *As long as you don't tell your father,* she'd warned—and was happy enough to slip away to the other side of the coffeehouse or the sidewalk café, as Clara and Francis sat in the open and talked and talked and talked.

He was seven years older than she. Golden-haired, gray-eyed. He was the only son (convenient for the title) but had a younger sister named Antonia he found delightful, he claimed, if sometimes perplexing.

Why do you ladies care so deeply about holding soirées, for example? he'd asked Clara, his mouth not quite smiling.

Because we find out who we are through them, she'd replied. *Who shows up, who does not. Then we know the perimeters of our world.*

His first letter to her had arrived at her house a year and a half ago, mixed in with the clutter of all the rest of the December mail. She was lucky she'd been the first one down the stairs that chilly morning, had decided to pause in the hallway before breakfast to see if there was anything of interest in the early delivery, stacked on the salver by the front door.

And oh, there it was, that brief, formal missive addressed to her from Prince Franz Edmund Joseph Gabriel Vitus von Hatzfeldt zu Wildenburg, begging her pardon at his presumption, two short paragraphs expressing his admiration of her, even though they had not been introduced, only seated in an auditorium far across from each other. How he had noticed her; how he hoped he had not offended her with his impudent smile; how he was profoundly sorry to intrude into her life today but merely wished that hers was one of bounty and grace, as a lady of her beauty and excellent reputation only deserved.

Well!

Clara knew all about flagrant flattery. Even so, she wrote back, equally brief, equally flowery, perhaps the *slightest* sarcastic edge to her tone, just to let him know she understood his game and didn't mind it in the least. Why should she, when her life was, as he'd hoped, so full of bounty and grace?

And that was how it began, the series of letters over the next eighteen months that had led her to Spain. Perhaps it had not been the *absolute* beginning of their lives entwined, their names entwined, their souls entwined, because that must include that instant in the Royal Albert Hall in London, when Francis had looked at her from his box and she had raised her lorgnette to look back, the lenses magnifying his thin, elegant face, and she'd felt her heart skip, expand, transcend.

What will your father think, Francis had asked her, taking up her hands in the shadow of the Catedral de Sevilla one hot afternoon in July. He was Catholic, first in line to the noble title that meant he could (in theory; not reality) lead his people, or at the very least not betray them by abandoning their shared faith. He could not marry outside of his church.

I don't care, she'd said. *I'll do whatever you want, be whatever you want.*

I care, though, mein Liebling. *I am a gentleman. I cannot wed you without Papa's blessing.*

Then, Clara had said, determined, *I'll make him bless us.*

CHAPTER 51

From: Clara Huntington
c/o Brown's Hotel
London, United Kingdom

To: Collis P. Huntington
65 Park Ave.
NYC, New York
United States

August 3, 1889

Dearest Papa,

I hope you can forgive me this letter. I hope you'll be happy for me, actually. I hope, I hope.

I have fallen in love at long last. His name is Franz Hatzfeldt zu Wildenburg, although he prefers to go by "Francis." He is a Bavarian prince. He wants me to become his wife.

Please do not think I have been meeting with him all this while behind your back! I have not. I would not. The fact is, until a few weeks ago, I had only ever glimpsed Francis in person from a distance, at a concert in London two years past. Arabella might recall it. But we began a private correspondence between us not long after which transcended *every manner* of ordinary conversation. Through our letters we came to know each other to a degree I can't imagine could occur by way of stuffy soirées or overcrowded ballrooms.

He is a *prince*, Papa! So kindhearted! So solicitous of me, so wary of you! And so traditional. He says that even though we are in love, he will not continue our association until he has been granted your permission to do so, face to face.

Forgive me for not informing you of any of this sooner. I do realize that Francis has a less than sterling reputation among the top set. I didn't want you to attempt to dissuade me from him before I even had a chance to shake his hand.

And honestly, when has *reputation* mattered much to any of us? I know you are far more interested in the quality of a gentleman's character, Papa, than the quality of his reputation. I pray you will give him the opportunity to prove he is a good man. A worthy one.

Please, will you come to England? You and Arabella and Archer, and Mary Alice and Edward too? We haven't announced anything to anyone, only our hopes and only those to you, but we were thinking to have the ceremony in the Brompton Oratory, here in London, by the end of October. It's a gorgeous chapel, full of art and history. I thought you might appreciate that.

Please come. Please meet him and love him as your own son, and wish us both joy, and tell me that you're glad I have found a safe haven for my heart.

Your devoted daughter,
Clara

Arabella
London, 1889

Prince Franz hovered just behind the spinster heiress he had wooed in secret, with swooning words scrawled across hidden missives, with clandestine travels across Spain and France, all the way to England. He hovered and smiled and once went as far as to place his hand possessively upon Clara's shoulder before almost immediately realizing his mistake. As Collis looked coldly on, Franz dropped his arm.

The staid British newspapers described the prince as *charming* and *somewhat slouched in the shoulders*. The more salacious tabloids went as far as *leering* and *insolvent*.

As the clocks struck four in their private parlor in Brown's Hotel—the exact same parlor Belle had sat in two years before with Consuelo Mandeville, as a matter of fact; she who had warned *do not think it*—Belle was forced to think it. To offer her hand to this *charmingly* accented nobleman when Clara introduced them, to squeeze her fingers around his and accept his handshake without revealing her distaste for him and his accent and his pale, flat eyes, which reminded her of day-old fish at the market.

Belle looked at Clara, at this unflinching girl who had grown into an unflinching woman, and felt a crumbling inside her she could only liken to a sandcastle dissolving with the tide. Clara was alight. Clara was in love. Clara already knew what the press said and what high society thought, what the pauper prince's own lifestyle must have revealed, and none of it mattered to her.

Nothing they could say would matter to her, beyond *Yes, of course, God bless you both.*

Archer grabbed the prince's hand in both of his and gave it a quick, forceful shake. If Belle hadn't already been studying Franz so closely, she might have missed the fleeting grimace that crossed his face.

She smiled approvingly at her son, then looked at Collis, still cold. Mary Alice and Edward took their turns, both polite but unsmiling as the prince exclaimed how honored he was, how thrilled to make everyone's acquaintances at long last. His ambassador uncle looked on, grinning like the cat with all the cream.

"I'm so happy," Clara enthused, more beautiful than Belle had ever seen her, her brown hair gleaming, her lips petal red. "I'm so happy you're here!"

Belle leaned down to press her cheek against hers. She breathed in the scent of her stepdaughter's rapture, her giddy elation, and had to hold her breath against it.

"We'll always come when you need us," she murmured, pulling away again. "You must know that."

A pair of footmen entered with the tea service. So much tea in her life, Belle would later reflect, rivers of tea, oceans of tea, and perhaps she should not have adhered quite so strictly to Collis's rule of abstinence. In this moment, especially, she could have used a stiff glass of whiskey.

But they had tea.

And perhaps it was the civilizing presence of Clara in the room, or her air of elation, shining and sincere, that none of them wanted to puncture. Everyone in the parlor drank their four o'clock tea and broke apart their scones like polite, worldly-wise people, like people who were not eyeing each other sideways from their tufted settees while weighing potentially broken hearts against potentially promised fortunes.

Prince Franz beamed down at Clara, seated beside him on a love seat. Clara lifted her face and beamed back as the room flooded with the late summer light.

"The prince desires to meet with me privately. With *us*," Collis clarified, perusing the note delivered to their suite the next morning during breakfast.

Belle set aside her fork and knife and gazed at her husband, patient.

Collis sighed, tossed the note within her reach. "Ingratiating, but insistent."

She picked it up, unfolded the message penned across a single sheet of the Brown's Hotel stationery.

*. . . if it would please you, good sir. A matter of utmost importance . . .
your earliest convenience . . . Miss Clara need not be informed . . .*

She tapped the note against the damask tablecloth. "He doesn't
mention anything about his solicitor being there, or even the ambassador. But surely it's regarding the terms of Clara's dowry."

"I agree."

"He reminds me not a little of Johnny Worsham."

Collis pushed back his skullcap, rubbing his forehead. He
seemed weary suddenly, weary and lined, every bit of his almost
seventy years.

"Yes, my demon," he said. "I'm afraid he does me, as well."

The prince was smiling as he entered the private parlor that
afternoon. He wore a lounge suit of gray serge that somehow rendered his eyes even duller, a black necktie striped in liver, a silver
stud centered just below the knot. He carried a large, flat folder
with him that he kept tucked under one arm as he shook their
hands.

The dowry settlement, Belle thought again, sitting by the fireplace, contemplating that folder. The American millions almost
within his reach. What else could it be?

Prince Franz was plainly surprised to find Edward there too,
although he tried to mask it. He lifted his eyebrows but held out
his hand with just as much aplomb.

"Mr. Edward Huntington, sir. I was not expecting the pleasure
of your company for this conversation."

Collis took the wing chair nearest Belle's. "My nephew is my
righthand man in all matters of business. Anything you have to say
to my wife and me may be said to him."

"As you wish." The prince only stood there, still smiling, before
Belle relented, lifted her hand and gestured toward the love seat.

"And Miss Clara?" Franz sat, placing the folder on the chenille
cushion beside him. "If I may inquire where she is right now?"

"At the Burlington Arcade," Belle said, "with her cousin, no doubt contemplating a great many additions to her trousseau."

"Excellent. These matters before us would be better kept from her ears."

"What matters?" Collis asked.

The prince flattened his left hand upon the folder. "I hope you will forgive me. A man in my position—of my stature, if you will—is required to take certain precautions when choosing a bride. Certain standards must be met, you see."

"Your *stature* of being a man without assets, do you mean?" Edward said, sardonic.

The prince smiled. "Such American frankness! No doubt I will become used to it in time. But no, good sir. The stature of my blood. Of my title. The House of Hatzfeldt is ancient and honorable. Our lineage goes back many centuries."

"As does the lineage of every soul upon this earth," snapped Collis. "What is your point?"

Franz inclined his head; the pomade in his hair gleamed. "It is expected that my wife will be of absolute purity. Her family, as well."

Belle felt her patience beginning to fray. "If this is regarding the fact of Clara's adoption—"

"Please, madam! Clara informed me weeks ago about her parentage. It is no shame of hers. I take no offense that she is the offspring of a common grocer, God rest his soul. I said the concern was with her purity, not her heritage."

Collis's face went red; he rose to his feet. "Are you implying that my daughter—"

The prince finally had the sense to become alarmed, shrinking back against the love seat. "No! No, sir, indeed I am not! Clara is a flower of virtue, I know that!" He cleared his throat, stroked a hand down his tie. "*Clara* is without flaw."

Belle felt something inside her, some watchful, half-forgotten thing, come awake.

Collis resumed his seat. Edward, who hadn't moved during the entire exchange, was watching Belle, alert.

Franz touched the folder again with the tips of his fingers, lightly, almost as if it burned. "It is the habit of my family to investigate all who wed into the line. This is a routine precaution, I must tell you. Clara has not been singled out for it. My own mother underwent an inquiry so thorough it took over a year to complete. This one, however, took only seven months."

"Seven months?" Edward slung an arm around the back of his chair. "You *have* been optimistic."

The prince flicked open the top leaf of the folder; Belle felt a chill as cold and brittle as a January wind begin to creep along her flesh.

She turned her face away from it, from this god-awful man with his sly smile and his perfectly oiled hair.

"Mrs. Huntington. You were once the wife of a man named John Archer Worsham, were you not?"

"She doesn't have to answer that," Edward said swiftly. He looked at her. "You don't have to say anything to him. None of this is compulsory and it's a damned outrage that this fellow is presenting it like it is."

"My dear?" said Collis quietly.

Belle sat back in her chair. She crossed her ankles and held the prince's flat fish eyes. She twisted her wedding band around her finger and allowed herself a faint smile.

"I was."

"This same Mr. Worsham who ran an illegal saloon in Richmond, Virginia?"

"That's right." She lifted a shoulder. "It was the war. It turned out the entire Confederacy was illegal. Who knew?"

Franz lifted the top sheet of paper, turned it over and laid it facedown upon the seat. "I will dismiss the question of how many wives this Mr. Worsham actually had. There appears to be some confusion on that matter. There was you, there was a woman named Annette, and another named Mary, I believe. Perhaps all of you were even Mrs. Worsham at the same time. But again, the matter is clouded. Who can say who was married when? Your disastrous war meant a great many official records, church records, were lost. But this saloon of his, this house of his, you were employed there?"

Belle cocked her head, holding her smile.

"So?" Edward said.

Franz said, "It was a house of prostitution, was it not?"

This time it was Edward who leapt to his feet. "You filthy liar. You damned blackguard! How dare you?"

The prince ignored him, keeping his eyes on Belle. Collis slanted her a look, then stood. The prince instantly joined him.

Collis took the folder from him without opening it. "You'll want to think very carefully about your next words, young man."

Prince Franz shook his head. "This is what my investigators found. Those are the documents provided to me. Are my facts incorrect?"

"What are your terms?" Belle asked.

Franz ran his fingers down his tie again. "I think you will find that we Europeans are somewhat more . . . relaxed about arrangements such as yours. Clara is a delightful girl. I am very fond of her. I think even my family would be willing to overlook the past, for her sake. But, of course, I would like to be able to provide her with the life she deserves. Mansions, jewels. She's expressed interest in a yacht as well, if you can believe it."

"I cannot," Belle said.

"Such lovely things are, unfortunately, beyond my reach at the moment. But I think they are not beyond yours, sir, as her loving father."

Edward, pale with two spots of color high in his cheeks, said through clenched teeth, "You are a goddamned thief."

Franz shrugged. "A prince, merely. The one your Clara adores."

Collis smacked the edge of the folder against his palm. "These stay with me, as well as any other copies."

"Of course."

"And you will say nothing about this to Clara or anyone else. Neither you nor your henchmen."

"Hench—? Ah, I understand."

"Do you?" Collis loomed a step closer to the prince, as menacing as Belle had ever seen him, his lips curled, his eyes burning, towering and ferocious. "I hope you do. Because I assure you that if I discover that even the smallest detail of this so-called investigation is mentioned to *anyone*, for *any* reason, I will bury you in lawsuits so thoroughly you will spend the remainder of your days in hiding from me and my attorneys. I will personally ensure that you are driven to your grave without a cent. Every newspaperman I own will write about your lunacy, and your only legacy will be the public snickering at the mention of your name. So I'll ask you again, *sir. Do* you understand?"

Prince Franz opened his mouth, closed it again. He nodded.

"Your word on it."

"Of course," Franz said once more, backing away. At the doorway he paused and turned, then offered them a bow in that courtly, old-fashioned way men here sometimes did, with one hand over his heart.

He did not try to hide his satisfied smile.

CHAPTER 52

Arabella
Richmond, 1865

The massive fires set by the retreating Confederate soldiers were finally smothered, most of them, but the air still stank of burnt tobacco and gunpowder and, more distressingly, charred meat.

Sometimes the skies still shone blue. Sometimes the moon reappeared, clean and distant, a pristine river pearl shining on high. Sometimes there was food besides fatback and rice. Lizzie showed up one day with a large red apple covered in caramel; she refused to say where she'd gotten it, but none of them cared all that much. They'd split it six ways, each of the Yarringtons devouring a mouthwatering slice, seeds and all.

Sometimes Belle thought there was hope that her world would finally brighten, that her thoughts would brighten, like the skies. That they could go back to what they had before . . . not *just* like before, no, but better than *this*, what they had now, which was nearly nothing.

Only ash. Only ruins. One apple for six starving people.

She was fifteen when she walked through Johnny Worsham's

door for the first time, taller than most girls her age, slender with hunger, her gaze myopic—*dreamy*, the other Fancies would label it, *our Miss Lenore is always dreaming*—willing to work for her meals.

Mother had told her to go. Mother had contacted Mr. Worsham and described her unusually beautiful daughter, the clarity of her complexion, her strong back. Everyone knew that Johnny was practically the only man left in town with the means to pay his employees, real Yankee money he extracted nightly from the pockets of the Yankee invaders.

In the saloon's dressing chamber Johnny instructed her to walk away from him in a straight line, to turn in a circle (much like the future Duchess of Manchester would one day instruct Belle's future stepdaughter, under very different circumstances). He tilted his head and ran his finger along his handsome lips and said that it was fine that she knew how to play the piano, but half the girls here also could, and what else could she do?

"Carry things," she replied, because right behind Johnny was the hallway that led to the faro parlor, and she could see the girls with their trays. "Serve things."

"And?" he said.

"I don't tire easily. I'm good at telling stories. I know the rules of faro, and I don't mind smoke or liquor or rough laughter."

"What else," he asked, "don't you mind?"

Forty minutes later he sent someone to find her a dress from the storeroom, willow-green taffeta, slightly too large but nothing that couldn't be taken in, especially with a belt. Johnny informed her the cost of the dress would be deducted from her wages, but since it was previously worn, it shouldn't prove too dear.

She changed in a daze, one of the girls not yet out on the floor silently helping with her corset, dabbing rouge on Belle's lips, repinning her hair. Belle stared at herself in that foxed looking glass on the wall and realized that she didn't look all that different from who she'd been when she'd woken that morning. And that felt . . . wrong, somehow.

Wrong, because, dear God, she was different. She was sore and sticky and everything was different.

At the brink of that hallway that led to the rest of the house, Belle found herself paralyzed. She could not lift a foot. She could not force herself into that next step.

The other girl had disappeared; Johnny was at her elbow. He studied her face, ran the back of his knuckles along her cheek.

"Tears won't do," he said.

"I . . ." she began, hardly above a whisper.

Johnny leaned closer, his mouth by her ear. "Poverty is a hard hill to climb, girl."

I am not that poor, she wanted to say, but she was. She was.

His voice was so soft, so reasonable. "It's barely a song, Belle. Barely a short, simple song in your life, easily sung and soon forgotten. Yet you'll gain so much for just singing it. One night at a time. And none of your family need go hungry again."

"But—my mother," she pleaded, turning to face him, to drown in those brilliant green eyes.

Johnny smiled. "Your mother knows full well the nature of my business. She told me you're a clever thing, so be clever now. Be smart."

Still she stared at him, unable to move.

"I can't. I don't know what to do."

"Sure you do, *ma belle.* Sure you do. Leave off your spectacles"—he lifted them gently from her face, tucked them into her hand—"and just go in there and smile. The rest will happen all on its own."

CHAPTER 53

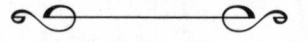

Arabella
London, 1889

ANOTHER AMERICAN HEIRESS FINALLY SNARED?
—*The Advertent Eye*; Observing Social Stirrings since
1872
Once a Week, Guaranteed!
August 28, 1889

The rumors are flying fast and thick regarding Miss Clara P. Huntington, 29, and Prince Franz von Hatzfeldt zu Wildenburg, 36, who met only a few months past in Spain. Miss Huntington and her doting Mum and Pop are once again settling in for a lengthy stay at fashionable Brown's Hotel, along with Mr. Huntington's adopted son Archer Huntington and various other family members. If the entire clan of the famed railroad tycoon has shown up in force, can an official announcement be far off?

Count Paul von Hatzfeldt, Esteemed Ambassador,

refused any comment On the Record. Yet we think his wide smile and jovial air significant clues regarding the nature of certain upcoming events.

"The prince is a man of great stature and fine reputation," is all that he would say. "And Miss Huntington is a young lady of reputedly excellent taste."

We at *The Eye* blush to mention that she is also a young lady of immense, dare we say *kingly*, fortune. Perhaps the prince's "fine reputation" might indeed benefit from Miss Huntington's "excellent taste," although Poppa Huntington's opinion on the matter has yet to be revealed.

More to follow! As we discover the scoop, Dear Reader, so shall you!

Edward would no longer meet her eyes.

That was fine. That was better than fine; that was preferable. Belle's past, those years and years that had led up to today, struck her as simultaneously indefensible and unavoidable. She hadn't chosen the path she'd walked then, but of course, she *had*, she'd done what she'd done and ultimately her family hadn't joined the legions of the wrecked and starving.

So what was there to apologize for? As she had once murmured to a dying woman upon her elegantly gleaming deathbed, Belle was not ashamed, because who could feel shame for reaching for a better life?

It was what everyone, *everyone*, did.

But Edward would not look at her. It enraged her; it worried her. She felt the weight of his loss, which was laughable since they'd always worked so hard to avoid each other. They lived away from each other, they worked away from each other, they had practically no interaction, except when they had no choice but to interact. Even then, they circled each other like two magnets with their poles aligned, forced together yet repelled apart.

Belle did *not* close her eyes at night and see Edward's face behind her lids, his expression of shock and betrayal as the prince had played his hand.

She did *not* lose sleep over it.

She drowned herself in diamond necklaces and topaz rings and amethyst earrings, in medieval tapestries and marble mantelpieces and antique, hand-carved engravings for the spectacular new palace she and Collis were slowly constructing on Fifty-Seventh Street, so large it would hold everything they already owned and more. In a tiny Piccadilly art gallery so undistinguished she passed it twice, she came across a small, luminous painting, yellowed with age, of a smiling girl playing a lute. It was a Vermeer, a bargain at only four hundred dollars, and she bought it at once. Perhaps she'd make it a wedding gift to Clara.

She busied herself with her stepdaughter, stepping carefully into her bubble of euphoria, helping to shop for dresses and nightdresses and pink satin dancing shoes, for ropes of rubies and sapphires to adorn her hair, for rings and bracelets and pearl chokers fit for a princess.

She tried only once to test the depths of Clara's devotion to her oily prince.

At Regent's Park one afternoon they strolled along a lake bobbing with ducks and swans and brightly colored rowboats. A pair of islands rose from the water, vibrant green trees and brush, a decoration of sandpipers walking delicately along their banks.

"Papa is unhappy," Clara said, as they passed a group of children splashing along the shore, their clothes spattered with mud. "Isn't he?"

"Yes," Belle admitted.

"But why? Is it the settlement? He's being so generous. I don't know why he would do so unless he approved of Francis."

"He is . . . concerned for you. At the haste of it all. We both are, actually."

"It doesn't seem hasty to me at all. We've been getting to know each other for well over a year—"

"Through *letters*," Belle said. "It's not quite the same thing as seeing someone in person, is it?"

"I *did* see him in person before this. I did, at the cantata. You were there. And even though we never spoke, I just—I just knew."

With great effort, Belle managed not to sigh. "Knew what?"

"Knew that he was the reason I've been waiting all these years, why none of my other suitors were ever quite right. Knew that Francis was the only man I could ever possibly wed."

She noticed Belle's expression and turned away again, exasperated.

"Give me no credit, then! Fine. I don't suppose you even believe in love at first sight. Not you, who has never loved."

Belle stopped walking. "Never loved? Is that what you think?"

"Oh, I know you love Archer and even me, in your own way. Maybe your brothers and sisters too. But you told me yourself long ago that you and Papa have an arrangement. A compatibility. That's not love."

"I *do* love your father. He's very dear to me."

"*True* love," Clara said, soft and fervent as the afternoon light soaked into the green grass and threw copper across the surface of the lake, and the swans cut around the boaters in smooth, gliding lines. "Certain and quick and instant love. Like your heart has been plucked from your chest, your bones dissolved, your soul laid upon his, and then everything knitted together again, one being from two."

Belle stared at her. A brass band began to play from somewhere out of view, a cheerful military march. The muddy children thundered past, shrieking.

Clara said, "You told me once you wanted me to get the better of New York society, to show them who I could be. And this is me doing that! A princess! This is *me*, following my heart. Becoming who I am meant to be." She shook her head. "I suppose you'll never understand."

"Is that truly how you feel? About this prince, I mean?"

"It is."

"I'll . . . speak to your father. Perhaps I might persuade him to unbend a bit."

Clara swung back to her, delighted. "Will you?"

"Yes. But you're right, you know, I'm coldhearted—"

"I never said—"

"So don't expect miracles. Even so." Now Belle did sigh, soul deep. "I'll see what I can do."

The ceremony was long and rather solemn, with just a handful of people in attendance. Certainly it was nothing close to what might be called a sparkling social gathering, although some American newspapers would later report that it was. They'd write that the Huntington–von Hatzfeldt wedding had been *the* event of the season; that the Brompton Oratory had been crammed with lords and ladies in silk and hereditary jewels dating back centuries; that the women's hats were wide as platters, stacked with the plumage of rare birds.

But the truth was, the bride's side of the chapel held just Belle and Collis and Archer, plus Edward and Mary Alice and Carrie. The groom's side was slightly more robust, with the prince's parents and sister in attendance, as well as his uncle and numerous aristocratic cousins.

Clara spoke in a murmur throughout, svelte and regal in buttercream satin and a veil of Brussels lace so long it fell like a waterfall down her shoulders and back, ending just past the hem of her gown. It had been pinned to her hair with the diamond-encrusted stars she'd found in New Orleans. When the prince lifted the front of her veil for their first kiss, the stars twinkled and flashed in the oratory's dusty, golden light.

Belle and Edward continued on in their uncomfortable, magnets-repelled dance, even as the Huntington party packed up and finally departed England. Even aboard the excellent RMS *Teutonic*—so new the carved woodwork and wall paneling were still scented of the trees they used to be—steaming slowly across the Atlantic to take them all home. Belle wondered if this was the way it was going to be from now on, for the rest of her life. She would not look at him and he would not look at her, and Archer would probably still notice but there was nothing she could do about that, was there? She could only just carry on. She was good at carrying on.

The very thought of it filled her with a despair so dark she hardly knew herself. Her life was so beautiful. She had surrounded herself with every object of beauty she could find and that Collis could afford. It was ridiculous to feel so unhappy, to sink into this barren, bleak darkness as she did every night, only to drag herself up again with false smiles and cheer in the mornings.

Belle *did* love her husband; she had not lied to Clara about that. Just not with the terrible, irrational burn she felt for his nephew.

Her heart plucked from her chest. Her bones dissolved.

They were able to maintain this charade for three days, four nights aboard the steamship. But that fourth night Mary Alice had retired to her stateroom just after dinner with a headache, and Collis had taken Archer up to the smoke room, and Carrie wanted to visit the ship's library, where Belle had already spent half the day.

It was November now, absurdly cold, but even so she retreated to the sun deck, where she sat in a wooden recliner wrapped in furs and watched the stars tilt overhead, the moon guiding them, frozen as she was, bitter as she was. Every now and again other first-class passengers would walk by, but not often, because it was late and everything warm and worthy in the world was captured inside the steamship, not wallowing in self-exile without.

Edward came to her in silence, his hands shoved deep into the pockets of his coat, his scarf wrapped tight around his neck, and sat in the recliner next to hers.

Belle gazed straight ahead; these were their rules.

"Do not list for me," she said, "the many ways this ship might eventually sink."

"I only hoped we could talk. As friends."

"Is that what we are?"

"It is what we must be."

She laughed, small and wretched. "Very well. Are you expecting me to defend myself? Are you expecting some sort of groveling plea for forgiveness because my past offends your modesty? My life is my own. I won't apologize for a second of it."

"Nor should you. I'm the one who must beg for forgiveness."

Her breath smoked in front of her face, a dull silvery puff that lifted and dispersed.

"When the prince said what he did, I was surprised." Edward hunched deeper into his chair. "I was—jolted. That's all."

Silver smoke, nothing. Silver, nothing

"Frankly, I was in awe of you," he said. "I *am* in awe of you. By God, I still am."

Now she looked at him, the lines around his mouth deeply creased, his brow furrowed. His eyes were tearing with the salty Atlantic wind, liquid stars caught in his lashes. She looked at him and felt that terrible familiar sinking sensation, fiery and doomed, as though she herself had become that falling star that had once drawn her eye down to him through a purple Yosemite dawn. As though she herself was dissolving into darkness before him, and there was nothing to be done about it.

He said, "You told me once, long ago, the circumstances that led you to that place. To that man, that Worsham fellow. But I can imagine . . . forgive me! I can imagine even more terrible things. Unthinkable things."

She laughed again, scornful: to freeze him in place, to make him leave, to disguise her pain. "Can you?"

But Edward would not leave.

"By the time I was old enough to enlist, the war was over. But the entire while, all those years, my family enjoyed almost every comfort we always had. We never suffered blockades or cannon fire. We were never anywhere near the battlegrounds. There were restrictions on cotton, I recall. On iron and meat, of course, but

we always ate. We were always housed and clothed. My uncle—
your husband—ensured that none of us went without."

She nodded, silent, her gloved fingers clamped together in
her lap.

Edward said quietly, "I am tortured at the thought of your distress. Of what you endured."

"My *distress*." Belle couldn't help her hard smile. "Do not think
on it."

"I'm sorry. I'm lost. I no longer know what to say, what to offer
you."

"Nothing. Obviously, Mr. Huntington, there is nothing you
can offer me."

"I wanted you to know that nothing has changed for me. Nor
will it, ever. My feelings for you will never change. This anguish
inside I feel for you, this damned constant anguish. It might be
our curse, but—I wanted you to know."

"All right."

At last he rose from the chair, bowed his head and began to
walk away.

"I feel the same," Belle whispered.

He paused, turned back to her. She raised her chin, held his
eyes.

"Just the same." She exhaled a smoky breath. "Now, go. Please."
And he did.

One day the new mansion was finished. It had consumed years
of the lives of New York's most skilled laborers and buckets of
money, railcars of money, millions on just the structure alone,
stately and almost bank-like when viewed from the street, with
its five imposing stories of gray granite and iron and brick. But
indoors, it was a resplendent wonder.

She'd spared no expense on her eighteenth-century French
dream, and it showed. There was nowhere to look without being
dazzled, from the imported Corinthian columns to the intricate,
masterful murals adorning the walls and every ceiling. She'd cho-

sen mythical themes of gods and muses and monsters, themes celebrating science, poetry, even the days of the week. Repeating in small, elegant patterns were gilt-and-navy monograms of Collis's initials and her own, so stylized they appeared to be little more than abstract contributions to the magnificent whole, until studied with a careful eye.

Their palace had a swimming bath and two elevators, and a marble bathtub with an ingenious feature that could scent the air with a mist of Belle's favorite perfume. A stairway comprised of Mexican onyx curved from the bottom floor all the way to the top beneath a skylight, lit to translucent fire in the sun. Libraries, salons, drawing rooms. A main hall so vast and open that the echoes of footfalls could sound like gunshots.

Nothing was accidental, nothing was forgotten. And since Mr. and Mrs. Collis Huntington were not inclined to entertain high society, and vice versa, there were no rooms meant for the public. Not a ballroom, not a gallery. Every single chamber was just for them or their family or the people who served them.

Belle moved through these rooms, the magnificent odes to the best of *anything* that money could supply her, and knew how fortunate she was. When Archer would come visit from his far-flung travels, telling her about Spain or Portugal, about a cave he'd found in France painted with ancient bulls and horses, or the rare books he'd purchased for the library he was planning, for the museum he would someday open, she tasted her good fortune on her tongue like sugar. Like a slice of sweet red apple covered in caramel, delicious.

When more years passed and Collis mentioned his soul longed for a retreat a shade more *rustic*, even more so than the Homestead (which honestly was no longer rustic in the least, not under her firm hand), Belle found him Camp Pine Knot, deep in the Adirondacks, a compound of log-and-stone cabins right by the sapphire gleam of Raquette Lake. It swiftly became his favorite place. Collis, now nearing his eightieth year, told her that being there reminded him of his days exploring the mountains and woods as a younger man, a man who'd not yet earned his fortune, who'd only slept in the open beneath the promise of the Milky Way and dreamed of grander days.

They had agreed, once upon a time beneath a tulip tree, that there was solace in greenery, and that was what Collis now relished, and Belle too. So she didn't mind relinquishing more and more of her hours to Pine Knot, to slow strolls through the cedars and hemlocks and firs, and intimate gatherings of their beloveds, their friends. When Archer showed up one wintry day with Helen, the daughter of one of Collis's sisters, a diamond ring on her finger, Belle had privately fretted, *First cousins, couldn't they explore more*, and her husband had responded, *It will be fine*, and it was for a while, until it wasn't. Thankfully, the pair would divorce.

When Clara and her prince arrived for Christmas celebrations one year, Belle smothered them in the splendor of her Manhattan home (Franz's eyes never stopped bulging), before whisking everyone away to the Camp, to that far simpler place that smelled of vanilla-barked trees and snow and wet earth, and there were twelve servants instead of thirty.

Clara and Archer. Helen and the prince. Collis presiding at the other end of the dinner table, white-haired and bearded, still important, still immense. Belle lifted her glass to her husband and everyone followed, and she thought her heart could hardly be more filled, her world hardly more complete.

The worth of her life, she would later reflect, would be measured in these moments. She was not the blood mother of Clara. Collis was not the acknowledged father of Archer. Yet as a foursome they persevered, loving, existing, bound by Belle's and Collis's steadfast, determined devotion.

And Elizabeth, their fifth. Elizabeth, the first wife. Who had done what she could, and prevented what she could. These days, Belle found she could hardly fault her for any of it. Or herself.

Who could feel shame for reaching for a better life?

* * *

On a steamy August morning in the first year of a brilliant new century, Collis developed a cough. At first Belle thought little of it; he was older, she was older. Coughs and pains and limps came and went with the privilege of age. Even he dismissed it.

"I'm hale as a horse. Once the weather clears, I'll be up and about again."

But the weather did not clear, and the cough did not improve. The humid steam turned into rain, all the forest around them shrouded in fog, filled with memories, all the ghosts Lizzie had once warned Belle about, crowding near.

She ignored the vapor pressing against the windowpanes and stretched out beside him on their bed, their bodies aligned. She stroked the hair from his damp forehead and mentioned summoning a physician, as a precaution only.

No, Collis had insisted. Obviously a doctor would not be required.

But they were not the people they'd been decades ago. They were not so invincible as they'd been at their beginning, and on his last night Collis opened his eyes to tell her so, in the murky shadows of the room, only a single candle lit, Renaissance masterpieces on the birch walls. Because Belle had decorated it, after all.

"Will you forgive me?" he asked, his voice a terrible rasp.

"For what?" she tried, smiling. "For charging forth to be my knight in shining armor?"

"For our truth. Our history. I . . . I should have been a better man."

"You're speaking to me, you know. No one else is here. You needn't explain anything. We're only as good as God shapes us. I have no complaints."

"Arabella," he gasped. "My beautiful demon. I want you to know that you saved me. I can't even say from what, except . . . an uneventful life."

"Mr. Huntington, your life has been the very definition of *eventful*. It was so, long before I came into view."

"A life without depth," he whispered, "or gratitude. Without perspective."

She pulled off her spectacles, rubbed them on her skirts.

"Ah." His lips curved. "There's that girl I fell in love with. The girl with the miles-away gaze, seeing everything."

"Oh, Collis," she said, and bit the inside of her cheek to stop the tremble in her voice. "I see nothing, and you well know it."

"You saw me. Saved me."

She moved closer, took up both of his hands in her own. "You saved *me*. My entire world. Without you, my family would have perished. *I* would have perished, and Archer—our amazing Archer—would have never been. Come *back* now. Come *back* to me." She drew in a breath. "Collis, please. I don't want you to go."

He freed his left hand to cup his palm to her cheek, lightly, carefully, his skin pale as parchment, his wedding ring cold.

"You're strong. Never afraid. You'll . . . go on."

His arm fell back to the coverlet. He tipped his chin to the ceiling, struggling for air. The cords of his neck strained, the feather pillow dimpling into fat folds. She watched anxiously as he managed a slow exhale, thin and rattling, his lips blue, his eyes brilliant.

"How I envy you," he said, as the rain pattered down.

Part VI

The Widow

1900

CHAPTER 54

Journal entry of Belle D. Huntington
August 16, 1900

The world is tilted now, askew. A brilliance that existed before is gone. A life is gone. A soul is gone.

How can the earth still be turning without him? How can there be a sunrise? It feels as if the very stars should darken and plummet from the sky.

Arabella
Manhattan, 1900

There would be libraries and museums named after him, schools named after him. Hotels and hospitals, awards and scholarships, streets and ships and parks.

A mountain in California.

A city in Texas, and another in West Virginia.

But for right now, for today, there was the mausoleum Collis had commissioned after Elizabeth's death, a marble and granite temple atop a gentle knoll in Woodlawn Cemetery, two flights of gracious gray steps leading up to the entrance, framed in trees and grass.

Belle got through the interment heavily veiled. If her eyes were red and puffy, no one could see it. If her lips were stretched into a thin, pained line, no one could see that, either. Her vanity remained intact, if not her heart.

Across the nation, Collis's employees ceased their work. For the span of three hours, no trains ran, no nails were hammered, no reports were filed. America's mightiest railroad and shipbuilding companies fell silent in honor of their founder. Ships paused mid-journey to float in place. Railway traffic on more than ten thousand miles of track slowed and halted and waited, smokestacks puffing.

Edward had been on a business trip down in Texas when Collis died, performing his duties as First Vice President of the Southern Pacific, inspecting the lines. He'd received Belle's short, brutal cable—CP Passed Stop Funeral August 17 Stop Will You Be Here Query—and had rushed back to New York so quickly that the papers would not stop writing about it, about how his private train was breaking records for speed, taking full advantage of its right-of-way and its magnificent, modern engines that chewed through coal in red-hot minutes.

Even so, it had taken days. By the time Edward had arrived at the mansion, he'd been pale and bleary-eyed himself, his hair neatly combed but his suit unpressed.

They'd held the funeral service inside the Manhattan home. The main hall blazed with sunlight, beams of white gold that angled down from the skylight and set all the onyx and marble and priceless paintings aglow. Edward had sat in the back with his wife as the minister spoke, far from Belle and Archer up by the coffin.

(Princess Hatzfeldt and her husband resided in England, and had no hope of arriving in time.)

Edward had kept his hands clasped and his head bowed. He accepted the condolences of his fellow mourners with barely a nod.

At Woodlawn he'd climbed the granite steps beside Belle, Mary Alice on his other side. They'd all watched without speaking as the silver-chased coffin was carried inside.

Belle looked at him only once from behind her black lace veil, at that face she had tried so hard and for so long never to see, never to mourn, and found that she didn't have to force her eyes away anymore; her gaze slid past him all on its own.

She couldn't bear to see him now. She couldn't bear his stricken eyes and his wan complexion. Even standing here beside him made her sick with guilt. She couldn't bear to even think of him, because every inch of her body grieved for Collis.

Collis.

She had been his Miss Lenore, his willing demon. And she found now, on this hot and miserable day, sucking at the stifling air trapped behind her lace, light-headed, maybe halfway to a faint—she found that Collis Huntington had been her very earth. Her foundation. The invaluable support for every step she had taken since the moment her seventeen-year-old self accepted his cameo bracelet and imagined placing her lips on his. And now he was gone, and she didn't know how she was going to take another step again. How she would ever feel her feet upon the solid earth again.

She could not stop crying. She stood still and stiff and did it without sound, without a hitch to her breath. But the tears would not stop.

She was climbing down those wide mausoleum steps, one hand holding the veil just high enough so that she could see where she was going, when she realized Edward had lingered behind at the crypt but Mary Alice hadn't.

They reached the funeral carriages below, waiting in a long solemn line. Belle went to Archer and Helen, pressed her hand against her son's arm.

"I'll be right there. Give me a moment."

Archer hesitated, nodded, and by then Helen was already urging him inside their private coach, second from the lead.

Belle straightened her veil. She turned and looked back up at Collis's impressive Grecian vault, its austere and final lines, Edward stationed like a sentry by the entrance. But she couldn't stand to watch the figures moving inside of it, the cemetery men doing their business, so she turned away again.

"We're leaving," Mary Alice said quietly, right at her elbow.

Belle lifted her head. "Right now? There's the supper prepared back at—"

"The children and I. My children. His. We're leaving America. We're going to England to live. I've found a nice estate for us there, not too far from Clara, or London. I'm sure we'll be content."

"Oh," Belle said, baffled.

Mary Alice gave a smothered laugh. "Well, I know they're not *children* anymore, are they? But they *are* his, and mine. Not yours." Her tone hardened. "I won't leave them to you."

"I don't know what—"

"Of course you do," Mary Alice cut in. "You know exactly what I mean. Do you imagine, Mrs. *Worsham*, that I have been blind all these years? Ever since Yosemite, my God, ever since then, I have sweated and worried and realized that I hold him by hardly a thread. He has been mine by hardly a thread. Just a mere certificate of marriage, a piece of paper signed in front of God and our community, long before we had the misfortune to encounter *you*. I am taking my family halfway across the world to escape you. I will tell you very frankly that I don't understand your sorcery. You're not *that* handsome. But we won't be coming back."

And after everything she'd endured that day—every soul-draining minute of Collis's funeral, the plodding horse-drawn procession to the cemetery, the tears and the guilt that had solidified somehow into a pit of nausea at the bottom of her stomach—the corners of her vision finally began to collapse. Darkness closed in.

Do not faint, do not faint. Do not be weak.

She said, helpless, "Edward is resigning?"

"Don't be ridiculous," Mary Alice hissed. "Edward wouldn't abandon his position if his life depended upon it. He's staying here. By *you*. I am salvaging what I can from my marriage. I am taking what I can. Don't *think* to try to steal my children from me like you did with Aunt Elizabeth. Or one blessed penny of my allowance."

"I wouldn't—"

"*Really*," she sneered, lifting her skirts in both hands. "Excellent. I am glad we understand each other."

Mary Alice stalked off to the third mourning carriage, the jet horses bending their heads in the summer heat, their ebony plumes bobbing.

For the funeral supper Belle sat at the foot of the formal dining room table, with Archer newly installed at the head. She said little and fortunately was asked little, preferring instead to allow the sounds of the room to wash over her, quiet conversations, heavy silver clacking against bone china. She toyed with her knives and forks and took small bites of the menu she had so scrupulously planned for her late husband's friends and colleagues, those titans of industry sharing a meal with her at last.

Croquettes de Chapon, the black-rimmed card beside each place setting read, in Carrie's polished hand. *Pâté de Gibier aux Truffes. Galantine de Poularde aux Pistaches Macédoine. Meringue Bavaroise.*

But when a footman bent to serve her baked ham and apples in orange sauce, Belle stopped pretending to eat. She sighed, looked away from her plate.

Edward was staring at her from his place down the table, that stark open stare, that stark open longing he never seemed able or willing to disguise. Mary Alice, a specter at his side, was slicing furiously at her meat.

For the first time that day, in hours, in eternity, Belle held his gaze. She shook her head, only barely and only once, before dropping her eyes back to her meal, to the fragrant ham dressed in sauce that she could not bring herself to consume.

Time rolled onward. Somehow she did manage to trudge through those early, flattened days after Collis's death, when the stars didn't fall and the sun still rose and the ground didn't crumble away beneath her feet. She used the millions he had left her— so many millions—not just for the acquisition of art and pearls and real estate holdings, but also to fund the charities they'd both supported, the causes they'd believed in, lifting up lives as she could.

Collis had understood hardship in the same bone-searing way Belle did, because for too many years it had defined them both. *You never forget it, do you?* he'd said to her once. *That feeling of hunger. Of desperation, not just for food or shelter, but for opportunity. The opportunity to climb out of such a life. Let us ensure that as many good people as possible are given that chance.*

So, Belle was trying. She'd already understood that her precious collections were not really her own, but were meant to be shared with everyone. She was the shepherdess, she would be the guide, and after her own death, she would leave her son what he wanted but the rest to museums, so that anyone who cared would have a way to admire all the beauty she had found in the world.

The months grew more bearable. Edward had chased his wife to England and returned alone. He remained with the Southern Pacific and at the edge of Belle's orbit, held back, perhaps, by a lingering sense of loyalty to Mary Alice, or Collis. Or maybe it was just because Belle had not invited him closer.

She began to adjust to the burden of her aloneness, to feel pleasure in the hours again. She devoted herself to traveling and learning, to her estates, to the many people whose livelihoods depended upon her. She devoted herself to living a life unbound, as her heart always told her she should.

One summer day, two years after Collis's death, when a young woman showed up in Belle's greenhouse and passed along a straightforward blackmail demand from a greedy pressman, Belle was able to meet it with serenity. She even gave the young woman a gift, a fragrant pot of violets, before sending her away.

Lucy Clarence left with a bit less spring in her step than she'd had when first approaching the greenhouse for her interview. Through the glass walls Belle had observed the Town Topics employee marching into her domain, and now observed her marching out of it, her long skirts kicking, her hair drooping, her shirtwaist clinging to her back and shoulders in damp dark patches.

Well, a little heat wouldn't hurt a girl like that, Belle thought. Not much would. Experience, maybe. Compassion, if she ever had cause to embrace it.

When she was certain the young Miss Clarence was entirely gone, Belle returned her watering can to its proper shelf, snapped her fingers for the dog to follow. Titus IV lumbered obediently upright, panting. At the entrance Belle paused, went back. She found the brass wheel connected by pulley and chain to the row of roof vents, where that solitary bee was trapped, spun it until the panes opened. Within seconds, the bee found fresh air, spiraling away to freedom.

The evening descended, lustrous as ever. Belle sat inside her loggia and admired the mother-of-pearl sky, the river, strong and certain and alive with commerce, much like the James River of her youth. A pair of fleet yellow birds, grosbeaks perhaps, flitted into view before vanishing beyond a lacework line of trees.

She asked her butler for a glass of cold white wine and pen and paper. The wine arrived first, chilled and tart, and then her desk set from her study.

She inched closer to the table before her, bent her head and began to write as the dog settled at her feet. The cameo bracelet around her wrist gleamed in the softened light.

Edward,

Although I have tried, I cannot convince myself that souls split apart should remain always apart. Nor can I believe that the ordinary rules of society should be applied to the extraordinary, whether words or thoughts or actions.

Please come to me. Whenever you are ready, please come.

Yours,
Belle

EPILOGUE

∽⊝————⊝∾

MRS. COLLIS P. HUNTINGTON WEDS NEPHEW
—special cable to *Town Topics*
Manhattan, New York
July 17, 1913

After many years of rumors of an impending engagement (always answered with steadfast denials), it has been confirmed that the wealthy widow of famed railway baron Collis Potter Huntington, Mrs. Arabella Duvall Huntington, has indeed wed the nephew of her late husband, Mr. Henry Edwards Huntington. The ceremony took place yesterday in Paris.

It may be recalled that Mr. H. E. Huntington was sued for divorce by his first wife, Mary Alice Huntington, in 1906 on grounds of desertion. Since that time, he has been seen in the company of his aunt nearly nonstop. H. E. Huntington, formerly of the Southern Pacific Company, also inherited millions from his uncle. But as the founder of the electric railways in and around Los Angeles, he is prosperous in his own right, and has built a tremendous Beaux-Arts mansion on the idyllic grounds of the old Shorb Ranch near Pasadena, California. The parcel is five hundred acres large, and a place some claim was purchased by H. E. H. with the wooing of his aunt forefront in his mind.

Mrs. Huntington is known to have offered her invaluable advice regarding the planning and construction of the new residence and its gardens, as well as on matters of décor and rare objects of art for the home.

The newlywed couple, both of an age (it may be delicately stated) when one typically dreams of endings rather than beginnings, plan to divide their time between California and New York.

Cheers to them.

AUTHOR'S NOTE

About a zillion years ago I went to the Huntington Library, Art Museum, and Botanical Gardens (www.huntington.org) in San Marino, California, for the first time. I was a college student, dead broke, no car, so I'd taken the bus to get there (if you've ever traveled across the labyrinth of Los Angeles by bus, you know what an exercise in surrealism and fatigue this is). I'd heard about this fantastical place, this marvelous, gorgeous, astounding place that housed priceless paintings and tomes and objets d'art inside Beaux-Arts mansions, all amid acres of lush, themed gardens featuring flora from around the world.

None of it disappointed. I wandered around enthralled, came back again and again. I brought my friends and family there, showed them my favorite garden walks, my favorite paintings, my favorite quiet nooks often overlooked by the other patrons. Once I even saw a ghost in one of the gleaming halls, no kidding. (I was with a friend and she saw it too, so there.)

It was not the ghost of Arabella, but a man, smiling at me. Even so, something like that sticks with you, stays shivery down in your bones.

Arabella likewise has stuck with me over the years. It took

a while for me to recover enough from the gilded splendor of The Huntington to contemplate the couple behind it, Belle and Henry Edwards Huntington. Belle, the scandalous second wife of Edward: his aunt, his contemporary, his equal in wealth and ingenuity. Belle, the unabashed mistress of Edward's uncle; the unabashed woman who didn't care that high society never liked her, who accepted their shunning of her with grit and grace and went on to live her fabulous life exactly as she wished.

My hero.

Belle worked very, very hard to shroud her origins. She lied freely and frequently about her age, about where she had been born and even her first (maybe!) husband, Johnny Worsham. (An image I found of her 1908 passport application showed she'd coolly knocked eight years off her real age and then signed the document, under oath, with aplomb.)

What isn't in doubt is that she became the mistress of Collis when she was either in her late teens or early twenties, and that she rose from obscurity and poverty in Richmond, Virginia, to suddenly have a lovely home in Manhattan, not far from Collis's Park Avenue mansion (as did her family). From then on, she only soared higher.

She became a great philanthropist in her lifetime, giving freely to a variety of causes. Devoted abolitionists, both she and Collis gave important sums to the Hampton Normal and Agricultural Institute and the Tuskegee Normal and Industrial Institute. Among his and her many other public gifts and interests: the Huntington Free Library and Reading Room in Westchester, New York; the Hispanic Society of America; the American Geographical Society; the Harvard Medical School; and the Collis P. Huntington Fund of the General Memorial Hospital for the Treatment of Cancer and Allied Diseases (now the Memorial Sloan Kettering Cancer Center).

But Belle was still Belle: it's said her personal collection of jewelry was so impressive that after her death it became the genesis of the Harry Winston juggernaut. Not only that, several of the sumptuously decorated rooms from her houses are now in museums, along with significant pieces from her jaw-dropping collection of art.

Colonel Mann's *Fads and Fancies of Representative Americans at the Beginning of the Twentieth Century* book was real. What was also real was the fact that Belle paid an outrageous sum to purchase a copy, or maybe two, when it was widely considered to be sentimental pap. (Although I haven't been able to get my sticky fingers on a copy myself, alas.) She wasn't Mann's only target; the colonel was known for gathering dirt on the elite and threatening to publish it unless "loaned" vast sums of money from his victims. At one point his schemes backfired; he was sued for blackmail. Belle, warned that she was about to be subpoenaed to testify in his trial, promptly fled the country, reportedly mere hours ahead of the process server due to show up at her door.

She avoided that public relations fiasco, but it didn't stop Mann from returning to her in later years to demand more "loans." He even attempted to pry money from Archer and Edward.

Belle remained pragmatic enough to ensure that control of her past stayed firmly in her own hands.

When discussing ideas regarding who to write about after Madeleine Astor (*The Second Mrs. Astor*), a few shiny names of the Gilded Age elite were mentioned, but I kept returning to Belle. She wasn't one of the Four Hundred; she wasn't anyone the Four Hundred would ever admit into their parlors, but she was, at one point, the wealthiest woman in Gilded Age America, with a beautifully mysterious backstory besides. I'm so grateful to my wonderful editor Wendy McCurdy, and everyone at Kensington Publishing, for recognizing the potential of this tale. I owe Wendy an especially huge thank you for her keen insights and guidance throughout the process.

I would also like to thank Annelise Robey and Andrea Cirillo, and everyone at the Jane Rotrosen Agency, for sticking with me and believing in me. And Alex, for translations!

There wasn't much unfiltered public information about Belle

to be found beyond a scattering of period newspaper articles and census records (a fact that I have no doubt would have delighted her), but the *New York Times* archives, were, as always, invaluable. However, there is a crucial nonfiction resource about Belle and Edward and Collis and Archer too: *The Art of Wealth: The Huntingtons in the Gilded Age* by Shelley M. Bennett. If you care to dive more deeply into any of their lives, I cannot recommend her book highly enough. It's meticulously researched, beautifully detailed and illustrated, and it broke my heart a bit to have to take my highlighter to it, but I just couldn't keep all the facts straight otherwise.

And thanks, finally, to Sean, always so patient, always so brilliant and great with the dogs. I don't even mind that they love you more than me.

It's been a long road, but I'm glad to be here with you, beloved Reader. Thank you for traveling along with me. None of this happens without you.

—SA

For more enthralling historical fiction from
the *New York Times* bestselling Shana Abé, don't miss . . .

THE SECOND MRS. ASTOR

A mesmerizing novel of historical fiction from *New York Times*
bestselling author Shana Abé. *The Second Mrs. Astor* tells the sweeping
real-life *Titanic* love story of Madeleine Force, who became the
teenaged bride of one of the world's richest men, and triumphed over
tragedy and heartache.

*"I won't begin with our ending, which everyone in the world knows anyway.
Our beginning, however, belonged only to us. . . ."*

Madeleine Talmage Force is just seventeen when she attracts the attention
of John Jacob "Jack" Astor. Madeleine is beautiful, intelligent, and solidly
upper-class, but the Astors are in a league apart. Jack's mother was *the*
Mrs. Astor, American royalty and New York's most formidable socialite.
Jack is dashing and industrious—a hero of the Spanish-American War,
an inventor, and a canny businessman. Despite their twenty-nine-year
age difference, and the scandal of Jack's recent divorce, Madeleine falls
headlong into love—and becomes the press's favorite target.

On their extended honeymoon in Egypt, the newlyweds finally find a
measure of peace from photographers and journalists.

Madeleine feels truly alive for the first time—and is happily pregnant. The
couple plans to return home in the spring of 1912, aboard an opulent new
ocean liner. When the ship hits an iceberg close to midnight on April 14th,
there is no immediate panic. The swift, state-of-the-art RMS *Titanic* seems
unsinkable. As Jack helps Madeleine into a lifeboat, he assures her that
he'll see her soon in New York . . .

Four months later, at the Astors' Fifth Avenue mansion, a widowed
Madeleine gives birth to their son. In the wake of the disaster, the press has
elevated her to the status of virtuous, tragic heroine. But Madeleine's most
important decision still lies ahead: whether to accept the role assigned to
her, or carve out her own remarkable path . . .

Available from Kensington Publishing Corp. wherever books are sold.

Visit our website at
KensingtonBooks.com
to sign up for our newsletters, read
more from your favorite authors, see
books by series, view reading group
guides, and more!

BOOK  **CLUB**

BETWEEN THE CHAPTERS

Become a Part of Our
Between the Chapters Book Club
Community and Join the Conversation

Betweenthechapters.net